THE CZAR'S SPY

The Mystery of a Silent Love

WILLIAM LE QUEUX

1st WORLD
LIBRARY
Literary Society

The Czar's Spy

William Le Queux

© 1st World Library – Literary Society, 2004
PO Box 2211
Fairfield, IA 52556
www.1stworldlibrary.org
First Edition

LCCN: 2005906627

Softcover ISBN: 1-4218-1612-1
Hardcover ISBN: 1-4218-1512-5
eBook ISBN: 1-4218-1712-8

Purchase *"The Czar's Spy"*
as a traditional bound book at:
www.1stWorldLibrary.org/purchase.asp?ISBN=1-4218-1612-1

1st World Library Literary Society is a nonprofit organization dedicated to promoting literacy by:

- Creating a free internet library accessible from any computer worldwide.
- Hosting writing competitions and offering book publishing scholarships.

Readers interested in supporting literacy through sponsorship, donations or membership please contact:
literacy@1stworldlibrary.org
Check us out at: www.1stworldlibrary.ORG
and start downloading free ebooks today.

The Czar's Spy
contributed by Tim, Ed & Rodney
in support of
1st World Library Literary Society

CONTENTS

CHAPTER I

HIS BRITANNIC MAJESTY'S SERVICE

"There was a mysterious affair last night, signore."

"Oh!" I exclaimed. "Anything that interests us?"

"Yes, signore," replied the tall, thin Italian Consular-clerk, speaking with a strong accent. "An English steam yacht ran aground on the Meloria about ten miles out, and was discovered by a fishing-boat who brought the news to harbor. The Admiral sent out two torpedo-boats, which managed after a lot of difficulty to bring in the yacht safely, but the Captain of the Port has a suspicion that the crew were trying to make away with the vessel."

"To lose her, you mean?"

The faithful Francesco, whose English had mostly been acquired from sea-faring men, and was not the choicest vocabulary, nodded, and, true Tuscan that he was, placed his finger upon his closed lips, indicative of silence.

"Sounds curious," I remarked. "Since the Consul went away on leave things seem to have been humming - two stabbing affrays, eight drunken seamen locked up, a mutiny on a tramp steamer, and now a yacht being cast away - a fairly decent list! And yet some stay-at-home people complain that British consuls are only paid to be ornamental! They should spend a week here, at Leghorn, and they'd soon alter their opinion."

"Yes, they would, signore," responded the thin-faced old fellow with a grin, as he twisted his fierce gray mustache. Francesco Carducci was a well-known character in Leghorn; interpreter to the Consulate, and keeper of a sailor's home, an honest, good-hearted, easy-going fellow, who for twenty years had occupied the same position under half a dozen different Consuls. At that moment, however, there came from the outer office a long-drawn moan.

"Hulloa, what's that?" I enquired, startled.

"Only a mad stoker off the *Oleander*, signore. The captain has brought him for you to see. They want to send him back to his friends at Newcastle."

"Oh! a case of madness!" I exclaimed. "Better get Doctor Ridolfi to see him. I'm not an expert on mental diseases."

My old friend Frank Hutcheson, His Britannic Majesty's Vice-Consul at the port of Leghorn, was away on leave in England, his duties being relegated to young Bertram Cavendish, the pro-Consul. The latter, however, had gone down with a bad touch of malaria which he had picked up in the deadly Maremma, and I, as the only other Englishman in Leghorn, had been asked by the Consul-General in Florence to act as pro-Consul until Hutcheson's return.

It was in mid-July, and the weather was blazing in the glaring sun-blanched Mediterranean town. If you know Leghorn, you probably know the Consulate with its black and yellow escutcheon outside, a large, handsome suite of huge, airy offices facing the cathedral, and overlooking the principal piazza, which is as big as Trafalgar Square, and much more picturesque. The legend painted upon the door, "Office hours, 10 to 3," and the green persiennes closed against the scorching sun give one the idea of an easy appointment, but such is certainly not the case, for a Consul's life at a port of discharge must necessarily be a very active one, and his duties never-ending.

Carducci had left me to the correspondence for half an hour or so, and I confess I was in no mood to write replies in that stifling heat, therefore I sat at the Consul's big table, smoking a cigarette and stretched lazily in my friend's chair, resolving to escape to the cool of England as soon as he returned in the following week. Italy is all very well for nine months in the year, but Leghorn is no place for the Englishman in mid-July. My thoughts were wandering toward the English lakes, and a bit of grouse-shooting with my uncle up in Scotland, when the faithful Francesco re-entered, saying -

"I've sent the captain and his madman away till this afternoon, signore. But there is an English signore waiting to see you."

"Who is he?"

"I don't know him. He will give no name, but wants to see the Signor Console."

"All right, show him in," I said lazily, and a few moments later a tall, smartly-dressed, middle-aged Englishman, in a navy serge yachting suit, entered, and bowing, enquired whether I was the British Consul.

When he had seated himself I explained my position, whereupon he said -

"I couldn't make much out of your clerk. He speaks so brokenly, and I don't know a word of Italian. But perhaps I ought to first introduce myself. My name is Philip Hornby," and he handed me a card bearing the name with the addresses "Woodcroft Park, Somerset - Brook's." Then he added: "I am cruising on board my yacht, the *Lola*, and last night we unfortunately went aground on the Meloria. I have a new captain whom I engaged a few months ago, and he seems an arrant fool. Very fortunately for us a fishing-boat saw our plight and gave the alarm at port. The Admiral sent out two torpedo-boats and a tug, and after about three hours they managed to get us off."

"And you are now in harbor?"

"Yes. But the reason I've called is to ask you to do me a favor and write me a letter of thanks in Italian to the Admiral, and one to the Captain of the Port - polite letters that I can copy and send to them. You know the kind of thing."

"Certainly," I replied, the more interested in him on account of the curious suspicion that the port authorities seemed to entertain. He was evidently a gentleman, and after I had been with him ten minutes I scouted the idea that he had endeavored to cast away the *Lola*.

I took down a couple of sheets of paper and scribbled the drafts of two letters couched in the most elegant phraseology, as is customary when addressing Italian officialdom.

"Fortunately, I left my wife in England, or she would have been terribly frightened," he remarked presently. "There was a nasty wind blowing all night, and the fool of a captain seemed to add to our peril by every order he gave."

"You are alone, then?"

"I have a friend with me," was the answer.

"And how many of the crew are there?"

"Sixteen, all told."

"English, I suppose?"

"Not all. I find French and Italians are more sober than English, and better behaved in port."

I examined him critically as he sat facing me, and the mere fact of his desire to send thanks to the authorities convinced me that he was a well-bred gentleman. He was about forty-five, with a merry round, good-natured face, red with the southern sun, blue eyes, and a short fair beard. His countenance was essentially that of a man devoted to open-air sport, for it was slightly furrowed and weather-beaten as a true yachtsman's should be. His speech was refined and cultivated, and as we chatted he gave me the impression that as an enthusiastic lover of the sea, he had cruised the Mediterranean many times from Gibraltar up to Smyrna. He had, however, never before put into Leghorn.

After we had arranged that his captain should come to me in the afternoon and make a formal report of the accident, we went out together across the white sunny piazza to Nasi's, the well-known pastry-cook's, where it is the habit of the Livornese to take their ante-luncheon vermouth.

The more I saw of Hornby, the more I liked him. He was chatty and witty, and treated his accident as a huge joke.

"We shall be here quite a week, I suppose," he said as we were taking our vermouth. "We're on our way down to the Greek Islands, as my friend Chater wants to see them. The engineer says there's something strained that we must get mended. But, by the way," he added, "why don't you dine with us on board to-night? Do. We can give you a few English things that may be a change to you."

This invitation I gladly accepted for two reasons. One was because the suspicions of the Captain of the Port had aroused my curiosity, and the other was because I had, honestly speaking, taken a great fancy to Hornby.

The captain of the *Lola*, a short, thickset Scotsman from Dundee, with a barely healed cicatrice across his left cheek, called at the Consulate at two o'clock and made his report, which appeared to me to be a very lame one. He struck me as being unworthy his certificate, for he was evidently entirely out of his bearings when the accident occurred. The owner and his friend Chater were in their berths asleep, when suddenly he discovered that the vessel was making no headway. They had, in fact, run upon the dangerous shoal without being aware of it. A strong sea was running with a stiff breeze, and although his seamanship was poor, he was capable enough to recognize at once that they were in a very perilous position.

"Very fortunate it wasn't more serious, sir," he added, after telling me his story, which I wrote at his dictation for the ultimate benefit of the Board of Trade.

"Didn't you send up signals of distress?" I Inquired.

"No, sir - never thought of it."

"And yet you knew that you might be lost?" I remarked with recurring suspicion.

The canny Scot, whose name was Mackintosh, hesitated a few moments, then answered -

"Well, sir, you see the fishing-boat had sighted us, and we saw her turning back to port to fetch help."

His excuse was a neat one. Probably it was his neglect to make signals of distress that had aroused the suspicions of the Captain of the Port. From first to last the story of the master of the *Lola* was, I considered, a very unsatisfactory one.

"How long have you been in Mr. Hornby's service?" I inquired.

"Six months, sir," was the man's reply. "Before he engaged me, I was with the Wilsons, of Hull, running up the Baltic."

"As master?"

"I've held my master's certificate these fifteen years, sir. I was with the Bibbys before the Wilsons, and before that with the General Steam. I did eight years in the Mediterranean with them, when I was chief mate."

"And you've never been into Leghorn before?"

"Never, sir."

I dismissed the captain with a distinct impression that he had not told me the whole truth. That cicatrice did not improve his personal appearance. He had left his certificates on board, he said, but if I wished he would bring them to me on the morrow.

Was it possible that an attempt had actually been made to cast away the yacht, and that it had been frustrated by the master of the felucca, who had sighted the vessel aground? There certainly seemed some mystery surrounding the circumstances, and my interest in the yacht and its owner deepened each hour. How, I wondered, had the captain received that very ugly wound across the cheek? I was half-inclined to inquire of him, but on reflection decided that it was best to betray no undue curiosity.

That evening when the fiery sun was sinking in its crimson glory, bathing the glassy sea with its blood-red light and causing the islands of Gorgona and Capraja to loom forth a deep purple against the distant horizon, I took a cab along the old sea-road to the port where, within the inner harbor, I found the *Lola*, one of the most magnificent private vessels I had ever seen. Her dimensions surprised me. She was painted dead white, with shining brass everywhere. At the stern hung limply the British flag, while at the masthead the ensign of the Royal Yacht Squadron. The yellow funnel emitted no smoke, and as she lay calmly in the sunset a crowd of dock-loungers and crimps leaned upon the parapet discussing her merits and wondering who could be the rich Englishman who could afford to travel in a small liner of his own - for her size surprised even those Italian dock-hands, used as they were to seeing every kind of craft enter the busy port.

On stepping on deck Hornby, who like myself wore a clean suit of white linen as the most sensible dinner-garb in a hot climate, came forward to greet me, and took me along to the stern where, lying in a long wicker deck-chair beneath the awning, was a tall, dark-eyed, clean-shaven man of about forty, also dressed in cool white linen. His keen face gave one the impression that he was a barrister.

"My friend, Hylton Chater - Mr. Gordon Gregg," he said, introducing us, and then when, as we shook hands, the clean-shaven man exclaimed, smiling pleasantly -

"Glad to make your acquaintance, Mr. Gregg. You are not a stranger by any means to Hornby or myself. Indeed, we've got a couple of your books on board. But I had no idea you lived out here."

"At Ardenza," I said. "Three miles along the sea-shore. To-morrow I hope you'll both come and dine with me."

"Delighted, I'm sure," declared Hornby. "To eat ashore is quite a treat when one has been boxed up on board for some time. So we'll accept, won't we, Hylton?"

"Certainly," replied the other; and then we began chatting about the peril of the previous night, Hornby telling me how he had copied the two letters of thanks in Italian and sent them to their respective addresses.

"Phil blasphemed like a Levant skipper when he copied those Italian words!" laughed Chater. "He had made three copies of each letter before he could get all the lingo in accordance with your copy."

"I've been the whole afternoon at them - confound them!" declared the owner of the *Lola* with a laugh. "But, of course, I didn't want to make a lot of errors in spelling. These Italians are so very punctilious."

"Well, you certainly did the right thing to thank the Admiral," I said. "It's very unusual for him to send out torpedo-boats to help a vessel in distress. That is generally left to the harbor tug."

"Yes, I feel that it was most kind of him. That's why I took all the trouble to write. I don't understand a word of Italian, neither does Chater."

"But you have Italians on board?" I remarked. "The two sailors who rowed me out are Genoese, from their accent."

Hornby and Chater exchanged glances - glances of distinct uneasiness, I thought.

Then the owner of the *Lola* said -

"Yes, they are useful for making arrangements and buying things in Italian ports. We have a Spaniard, a Greek, and a Syrian, all of whom act as interpreters in different places."

"And make a handsome thing in the way of secret commissions, I suppose?" I laughed.

"Of course. But to cruise in comfort one must pay and be pleasant," declared the man with the fair beard. "In Greece and the Levant they are more rapacious than in Naples, and the Customs officers always want squaring, otherwise they are for ever rummaging and discovering mares' nests."

"Did you have any trouble here?" I inquired.

"They didn't visit us," he said with a smile, and at the same time he rubbed his thumb and finger together, the action of feeling paper money.

This increased my surprise, for I happened to know that the Leghorn Customs officers were not at all given to the acceptance of bribes. They were too well watched by their superiors. If the yacht had really escaped a search, then it was a most unusual thing. Besides, what motive could Hornby have in eluding the Customs visit? They would, of course, seal up his wines and liquors, but even if they did, they would leave him out sufficient for the consumption of himself and his friends.

No. Philip Hornby had some strong motive in paying a heavy bribe to avoid the visit of the *dogana*. If he really had paid, he must have paid very heavily; of that I was convinced.

Was it possible that some mystery was hidden on board that splendidly appointed craft?

Presently the gong sounded, and we went below into the elegantly fitted saloon, where was spread a table that sparkled with cut glass and shone with silver. Around the center fresh flowers had been trailed by some artistic hand, while on the buffet at the end the necks of wine bottles peered out from the ice pails. Both carpet and upholstery were in pale blue, while everywhere it was apparent that none but an extremely wealthy man could afford such a magnificent craft.

Hornby took the head of the table, and we sat on either side of him, chatting merrily while we ate one of the choicest and best cooked dinners it has ever been my lot to taste. Chater and I drank wine of a brand which only a millionaire could keep in his cellar, while our host, apparently a most abstemious man, took only a glass of iced Cinciano water.

The two smart stewards served in a manner which showed them to be well trained to their duties, and as the evening light filtering through the pale blue silk curtains over the open portholes slowly faded, we gossiped on as men will gossip over an unusually good dinner.

From his remarks I discerned that , contrary to my first

impression, Hylton Chater was an experienced yachtsman. He owned a craft called the *Alicia*, and was a member of the Cork Yacht Club. He lived in London, he told me, but gave me no information as to his profession. It might be the law, as I had surmised.

"You've seen our ass of a captain, Mr. Gregg?" he remarked presently. "What do you think of him?"

"Well," I said rather hesitatingly, "to tell the truth, I don't think very much of his seamanship - nor will the Board of Trade when his report reaches them."

"Ah!" exclaimed Hornby, "I was a fool to engage him. From the very first I mistrusted him, only my wife somehow took a fancy to the fellow, and, as you know, if you want peace you must always please the women. In this case, however, her choice almost cost me the vessel, and perhaps our lives into the bargain."

"You knew nothing of him previously?"

"Nothing."

"And he engaged the crew?" I asked.

"Of course."

"Are they all fresh hands?"

"All except the cook and the two stewards."

I was silent. I did not like Mackintosh. Indeed, I entertained a distinct suspicion of both master and crew.

"The captain seems to have had a nasty cut across the cheek," I remarked, whereupon my two companions again exchanged quick, apprehensive glances.

"He fell down the other day," explained Chater, with a rather sickly smile, I thought. "His face caught the edge of an iron stair in the engine-room, and caused a nasty gash."

I smiled within myself, for I knew too well that the ugly wound in the captain's face had never been inflicted by falling on the edge of a stair. But I remained silent, being content that they should endeavor to mislead me.

After dessert had been served we rose, and in the summer twilight, when all the ports were opened, Hornby took me over the vessel. Everywhere was abundant luxury - a veritable floating palace. To each of the cabins of the owner and his guests a bathroom was attached with sea-water or fresh water as desired, while the ladies' saloon, the boudoir, the library, and the smoking-room were furnished richly with exquisite taste. As he was conducting me from his own cabin to the boudoir we passed a door that had been blown open by the wind, and which he hastened to close, not, however, before I had time to glance within. To my surprise I discovered that it was an armory crammed with rifles, revolvers and ammunition.

It had not been intended that I should see that interior, and the reason why the Customs officers had been bribed was now apparent.

I passed on without remark, making believe that I had not discerned anything unusual, and we entered the boudoir, Chater having gone back to the saloon to obtain cigars.

The dainty little chamber was upholstered in carnation-pink silk with furniture of inlaid rosewood, and bore everywhere the trace of having been arranged by a woman's hand, although no lady passenger was on board.

Just as we had entered, and I was admiring the dainty nest of luxury, Chater shouted to his host asking for the keys of the cigar cupboard, and Hornby, excusing himself, turned back along the gangway to hand them to his friend, thus leaving me alone for a few moments.

I stood glancing around, and as I did so my eyes fell upon a quantity of photographs, framed and unframed, that were scattered about - evidently portraits of Hornby's friends. Upon a small side table, however, stood a heavy oxidized silver frame, but empty, while lying on the floor beneath a couch was the photograph it had contained, which had apparently been taken hastily out, torn first in half and then in half again, and cast away.

Curiosity prompted me to stoop, pick up the four pieces and place them together, when I found them to form the cabinet portrait of a sweet-looking and extremely pretty English girl of eighteen or nineteen, with a bright, smiling expression, and wearing a fresh morning blouse of white pique. Her hair was dressed low and fastened with a bow of black ribbon, while the brooch at her throat was in the form of a heart edged with pearls. Whether it was her sweet expression, or whether the curious look in her eyes had attracted my attention and riveted the face upon my memory, I know not. Perhaps it was the mystery of why it should have been so hastily torn from its frame and destroyed that held my attention.

It seemed as though it had been torn up surreptitiously by someone who had been sitting on that couch, and who had had no opportunity of casting the fragments away through the port-hole into the water.

I looked at the back of the torn photograph, and saw that it had been taken by a well-known and fashionable firm in New Bond Street.

About the expression of that pictured face was something which I cannot describe - a curious look in the eyes which was at the same time both attractive and mysterious. In that brief moment the girl's features were indelibly impressed upon my memory.

Next second, however, hearing Hornby's returning footsteps, I flung the fragments hastily beneath the couch where I had discovered them.

Why, I wondered, had the picture been destroyed - and by whom?

The face of the empty frame had been purposely turned towards the panelling, therefore when he entered he did not notice that the picture had been destroyed; but after a brief pause, explaining that that cosy little place was his wife's particular nook, he conducted me on through the ladies' saloon and afterwards on deck, where we flung ourselves into the long chairs, took our coffee and certosina, that liqueur essentially Tuscan, and smoked on as the moon rose and the lights of the harbor began to twinkle in the steely night.

As I sat talking, my thoughts ran back to that torn photograph. To me it seemed as though some previous visitor that day had sat upon the couch, destroyed the picture, and cast it where I had found it. But for what reason? Who was the merry-faced girl whose picture had aroused such jealousy or revenge?

I purposely led the conversation to Hornby's family, and learned from him that he had no children.

"You'll get the repairs to your engines done at Orlando's, I suppose?" I remarked, naming the great shipbuilding firm of Leghorn.

"Yes. I've already given the order. They are contracted to be finished by next Thursday, and then we shall be off to Zante and Chio."

For what reason, I wondered, recollecting that formidable armory on board. Already I had seen quite sufficient to convince me that the *Lola*, although outwardly a pleasure yacht, was built of steel, armored in its most vulnerable parts, and capable of resisting a very sharp fire.

The hours passed, and beneath the brilliant moon we smoked long into the night, for after the blazing sunshine of that Tuscan town the cool sea-wind at night is very refreshing. From where we sat we commanded a view of the whole of the sea-front of Leghorn and Ardenza, with its bright open-air cafe-concerts and restaurants in full swing - all the life and gayety of that popular watering-place.

Presently, when Hornby had risen to call a steward and left me alone with Hylton Chater, the latter whispered to me in confidence -

"If you find my friend Hornby a little bit strange in his manner, Mr. Gregg, you must take no notice. To tell the truth, he is a man who has become suddenly wealthy beyond the wildest dreams of avarice, and I fear it has had an effect upon his brain. He does very queer things at times."

I looked at my companion in surprise. He was either telling the truth, or else he was endeavoring to allay my suspicions by an extremely clever ruse. Now I had already decided that Philip Hornby was no eccentric, but a particularly level-headed and practical man. Therefore I instantly arrived at the conclusion that the clean-shaven fellow who looked so much like a London barrister had some distinct and ulterior purpose in arousing within my mind suspicion of his host's sanity.

It was past midnight when, having bade the strange pair adieu, I was put ashore by the two sailors who had rowed me out and drove home along the sea-front, puzzled and perplexed.

Next morning, on my arrival at the Consulate, old Francesco, who had entered only a moment before, met me with blanched face, gasping -

"There have been thieves here in the night, signore! The Signor Console's safe has been opened!"

"The safe!" I cried, dashing into Hutcheson's private room,

and finding to my dismay the big safe, wherein the seals, ciphers and other confidential documents were kept, standing open, and the contents in disorder, as though a hasty search had been made among them.

Was it possible that the thieves had been after the Admiralty and Foreign Office ciphers, copies of which the Chancelleries of certain European Powers were ever endeavoring to obtain? I smiled within myself when I realized how bitterly disappointed the burglars must have been, for a British Consul when he goes on leave to England always takes his ciphers with him, and deposits them at the Foreign Office for safekeeping. Hutcheson had, of course, taken his, according to the regulations.

Curiously enough, however, the door of the Consulate and the safe had been opened with the keys which my friend had left in my charge. Indeed, the small bunch still remained in the safe door.

In an instant the recollection flashed across my mind that I had felt the keys in my pocket while at dinner on board the *Lola*. Had I lost them on my homeward drive, or had my pocket been picked?

Carducci, with an Italian's volubility, commenced to hurl imprecations upon the heads of the unknown sons of dogs who dared to tamper with his master's safe, and while we were engaged in putting the scattered papers in order the door-bell rang, and the clerk went to attend to the caller.

In a few moments he returned, saying -

"The English yacht left suddenly last night, signore, and the Captain of the Port has sent to inquire whether you know to what port she is bound."

"Left!" I gasped in amazement "Why, I thought her engines were disabled!"

A quarter of an hour later I was sitting in the private office of the shrewd, gray-haired functionary who had sent this messenger to me.

"Do you know, Signor Commendatore," he said, "some mystery surrounds that vessel. She is not the *Lola*, for yesterday we telegraphed to Lloyd's, in London, and this morning I received a reply that no such yacht appears on their register, and that the name is unknown. The police have also telegraphed to your English police inquiring about the owner, Signor Hornby, with a like result. There is no such place as Woodcroft Park, in Somerset, and no member of Brook's Club of the name of Hornby."

I sat staring at the official, too amazed to utter a word. Certainly they had not allowed the grass to grow beneath their feet.

"Unfortunately the telegraphic replies from England are only to hand this morning," he went on, "because just before two o'clock this morning the harbor police, whom I specially ordered to watch the vessel, saw a boat come to the wharf containing a man and woman. The pair were put ashore, and walked away into the town, the woman seeming to walk with considerable difficulty. The boat returned, and an hour after, to the complete surprise of the two detectives, steam was suddenly got up and the yacht turned and went straight out to sea."

"Leaving the man and the woman?"

"Leaving them, of course. They are probably still in the town. The police are now searching for traces of them."

"But could not you have detained the vessel?" I suggested.

"Of course, had I but known I could have forbidden her departure. But as her owner had presented himself at the Consulate, and was recognized as a respectable person, I felt that I could not interfere without some tangible information - and that, alas! has come too late. The vessel is a swift one, and has already seven hours start of us. I've asked the Admiral to send out a couple of torpedo-boats after her, but, unfortunately, this is impossible, as the flotilla is sailing in an hour to attend the naval review at Spezia."

I told him how the Consul's safe had been opened during the night, and he sat listening with wide-open eyes.

"You dined with them last night," he said at last. "They may have surreptitiously stolen your keys."

"They may," was my answer. "Probably they did. But with what motive?"

The Captain of the Port elevated his shoulders, exhibited his palms, and declared -

"The whole affair from beginning to end is a complete and profound mystery."

CHAPTER II

WHY THE SAFE WAS OPENED

That day was an active one in Questura, or police office, of Leghorn.

Detectives called, examined the safe, and sagely declared it to be burglar-proof, had not the thieves possessed the key. The Foreign Office knew that, for they supply all the safes to the Consulates abroad, in order that the precious ciphers shall be kept from the prying eyes of foreign spies. The Questore, or chief of police, was of opinion that it was the ciphers of which the thieves had been in search, and was much relieved to hear that they were in safekeeping far away in Downing Street.

His conjecture was the same as my own, namely, that the reason of Hornby's call upon me was to ascertain the situation of the Consulate and the whereabouts of the safe, which, by the way, stood in a corner of the Consul's private room. Captain Mackintosh, too, had taken his bearings, and probably while I sat at dinner on board the *Lola* my keys had been stolen and passed on to the scarred Scotsman, who had promptly gone ashore and ransacked the place while I had remained with his master smoking and unsuspicious.

But what was the motive? Why had they ransacked all those confidential papers?

My own idea was that they were not in search of the ciphers at all, but either wanted some blank form or other, or else they desired to make use of the Consular seal. The latter, however, still remained on the floor near the safe, as though it had rolled out and been left unheeded. As far as Francesco and I could ascertain, nothing whatever had been taken. Therefore, we re-arranged the papers, re-locked the safe and resolved not to telegraph to Hutcheson and unduly disturb him, as in a few days he would return from England, and there would be time enough then to explain the remarkable story.

One fact, however, we established. The detective on duty at the railway station distinctly recollected a thin middle-aged man, accompanied by a lady in deep black, passing the barrier and entering the train which left at three o'clock for Colle Salvetti to join the Rome express. They were foreigners, therefore he did not take the same notice of them as though they had been Italians. Inquiries at the booking-office showed, however, that no passengers had booked direct to Rome by the train in question. To Grossetto, Cecina, Campiglia, and the other places in the Maremma, passengers had taken tickets, but not one had been booked to any of the great towns. Therefore it was apparent that the mysterious pair who had come ashore just prior to the sailing of the yacht had merely taken tickets for a false destination, and had re-booked at Colle Salvetti, the junction with that long main line which connects Genoa with Rome.

The police were puzzled. The two fishermen who sighted the *Lola* and first gave the alarm of her danger, declared that when they drew alongside and proffered assistance the captain threatened to shoot the first man who came aboard.

"They were English!" remarked the sturdy, brown-faced toilers of the sea, grinning knowingly. "And the English, when they drink their cognac, know not what they do."

"Did you get any reward for returning to harbor and reporting?" I asked.

"Reward!" echoed one of the men, the elder of the pair. "Not a soldo! The English only cursed us for interfering. That is why we believed that they were trying to make away with the vessel."

The description of the *Lola*, its owner, his guest, and the captain were circulated by the police to all the Mediterranean ports, with a request that the yacht should be detained. Yet if the vessel were really one of mystery, as it seemed to be, its owner would no doubt go across to some quiet anchorage on the Algerian coast out of the track of the vessels, and calmly proceed to repaint, rename and disguise his craft so that it would not be recognized in Marseilles, Naples, Smyrna, or any of the ports where private yachts habitually call. Thus, from the very first, it seemed to me that Hornby and his friends had very cleverly tricked me for some mysterious purpose, and afterwards ingeniously evaded their watchers and got clean away.

Had the Italian Admiral been able to send a torpedo-boat or two after the fugitives they would no doubt soon have been overhauled, yet circumstances had prevented this and the *Lola* had consequently escaped.

For purposes of their own the police kept the affair out of the papers, and when Frank Hutcheson stepped out of the sleeping-car from Paris on to the platform at Pisa a few nights afterwards, I related to him the extraordinary story.

"The scoundrels wanted these, that's evident," he responded, holding up the small, strong, leather hand-bag he was carrying, and which contained his jealously-guarded ciphers. "By Jove!" he laughed, "how disappointed they must have been!"

"It may be so," I said, as we entered the midnight train for Leghorn. "But my own theory is that they were searching for some paper or other that you possess."

"What can my papers concern them?" exclaimed the jovial,

round-faced Consul, a man whose courtesy is known to every skipper trading up and down the Mediterranean, and who is perhaps one of the most cultured and popular men in the British Consular Service. "I don't keep bank notes in that safe, you know. We fellows in the Service don't roll in gold as our public at home appears to think."

"No. But you may have something in there which might be of value to them. You're often the keeper of valuable documents belonging to Englishmen abroad, you know."

"Certainly. But there's nothing in there just now except, perhaps, the registers of births, marriages and deaths of British subjects, and the papers concerning a Board of Trade inquiry. No, my dear Gordon, depend upon it that the yacht running ashore was all a blind. They did it so as to be able to get the run of the Consulate, secure the ciphers, and sail merrily away with them. It seems to me, however, that they gave you a jolly good dinner and got nothing in return."

"They might very easily have carried me off too," I declared.

"Perhaps it would have been better if they had. You'd at least have had the satisfaction of knowing what their little game really was!"

"But the man and the woman who left the yacht an hour before she sailed, and who slipped away into the country somewhere! I wonder who they were? Hornby distinctly told me that he and Chater were alone, and yet there was evidently a lady and a gentleman on board. I guessed there was a woman there, from the way the boudoir and ladies' saloon were arranged, and certainly no man's hand decorated a dinner table as that was decorated."

"Yes. That's decidedly funny," remarked the Consul thoughtfully. "They went to Colle Salvetti, you say? They changed there, of course. Expresses call there, one going north and the other south, within a quarter of an hour after the train arrives from Leghorn. They showed a lot of ingenuity, otherwise they'd have gone direct to Pisa."

"Ingenuity! I should think so! The whole affair was most cleverly planned. Hornby would have deceived even you, my dear old chap. He had the air of the perfect gentleman, and a glance over the yacht convinced me that he was a wealthy man traveling for pleasure."

"You said something about an armory."

"Yes, there were Maxims stowed away in one of the cabins. They aroused my suspicions."

"They would not have aroused mine," replied my friend. "Yachts carry arms for protection in many cases, especially if they are going to cruise along uncivilized coasts where they must land for water or provisions."

I told him of the torn photograph, which caused him some deep reflection.

"I wonder why the picture had been torn up. Had there been a row on board - a quarrel or something?"

"It had been destroyed surreptitiously, I think."

"Pity you didn't pocket the fragments. We could perhaps have discovered from the photographer the identity of the original."

"Ah!" I sighed regretfully. "I never thought of that. I recollect the name of the firm, however."

"I shall have to report to London the whole occurrence, as British subjects are under suspicion," Hutcheson said. "We'll see whether Scotland Yard knows anything about Hornby or Chater. Most probably they do. Not long ago a description of men on board a yacht was circulated from London as being a pair of well-known burglars who were cruising about in a vessel crammed with booty which they dared not get rid of. They are, however, not the same as our friends on the *Lola*, for both men wanted were arrested in New Orleans about eight months ago, without their yacht, for they confessed that they had deliberately sunk it on one of the islands in the South Pacific."

"Then these fellows might be another pair of London burglars!" I exclaimed eagerly, as the startling theory occurred to me.

"They might be. But, of course, we can't form any opinion until we hear what Scotland Yard has to say. I'll write a full report in the morning if you will give me minute descriptions of the men, as well as of the captain, Mackintosh."

Next morning I handed over my charge of the Consulate to Frank, and then assisted him to go through the papers in the safe which had been examined by the thieves.

"The ruffians seem to have thoroughly overhauled everything," remarked the Consul in dismay when he saw the disordered state of his papers. "They seem to have read every one deliberately."

"Which shows that had they been in search for the cipher-books they would only have looked for them alone," I remarked decisively. "What on earth could interest them in all these dry, unimportant shipping reports and things?"

"Goodness only knows," replied my friend. Then, calling Cavendish, a tall, fair young man, who had now recovered from his touch of fever and had returned to the Consulate, he commenced to check the number of those adhesive stamps, rather larger than ordinary postage-stamps, used in the Consular service for the registration of fees received by the Foreign Office. The values were from sixpence to one pound, and they were kept in a portfolio.

After a long calculation the Consul suddenly raised his face to me and said -

"Then six ten shilling ones have been taken!"

"Why? There must be some motive!"

"They are of no use to anyone except to Consuls," he explained. "Perhaps they were wanted to affix to some false certificate. See," he added, opening the portfolio, "there were six stamps here, and all are gone."

"But they would have to be obliterated by the Consular stamp," remarked Cavendish.

"Ah! of course," exclaimed Hutcheson, taking out the brass seal from the safe and examining it minutely. "By Jove!" he cried a second later, "it's been used! They've stamped some document with it. Look! They've used the wrong ink-pad! Can't you see that there's violet upon it, while we always use the black pad!"

I took it in my hand, and there, sure enough, I saw traces of violet ink upon it - the ink of the pad for the date-stamp upon the Consul's table.

"Then some document has been stamped and sealed!" I gasped.

"Yes. And my signature forged to it, no doubt. They've fabricated some certificate or other which, bearing the stamp, seal and signature of the Consulate, will be accepted as a legal document. I wonder what it is?"

"Ah!" I said. "I wonder!" And the three of us looked at each other in sheer bewilderment.

"The reason the papers are all upset is because they were evidently in search of some blank form or other, which they hoped to find," remarked my friend. "As you say, the whole affair was most carefully and ingeniously planned."

We crossed the great sunlit piazza together and entered the Questura, that sun-blanched old palace with its long cool loggia where the sentry paces day and night. The Chief of Police, whom we saw, had no further information. The mysterious yacht had not put in at any Italian port. From him, however, we learned the name of the detective who had seen the two strangers leave Leghorn by the early morning train, and an hour afterwards the police-officer, a black-eyed man short of stature, but of an intelligent type, sat in the Consulate replying to our questions.

"As far as I could make out, signore," he said, "the man was an Englishman, wearing a soft black felt hat and a suit of dark blue serge. He had hair just turning gray, a small dark mustache and rather high cheek-bones. In his hand he carried a small bag of tan leather of that square English shape. He seemed in no hurry, for he was calmly smoking a cigarette as he went across to the ticket office."

"And his companion?" asked the Consul.

"She was in black. Rather tall and slim. Her hair was fair, I noticed, but she wore a black veil which concealed her features."

"Was she young or old?"

"Young - from her figure," replied the police agent. "As she passed me her eyes met mine, and I thought I saw a strange fixed kind of glare in them - the look of a woman filled with some unspeakable horror."

Next day the town of Leghorn awoke to find itself gay with bunting, the Italian and English flags flying side by side everywhere, and the Consular standard flapping over the Consulate in the piazza. In the night the British Mediterranean fleet, cruising down from Malta, had come into the roadstead, and at the signal from the flagship had maneuvered and dropped anchor, forming a long line of gigantic battleships, swift cruisers, torpedo-boat destroyers, torpedo-boats, despatch-boats, and other craft extending for several miles along the coast.

In the bright morning sunlight the sight was both picturesque and imposing, for from every vessel flags were flying, and ever and anon the great battleship of the Admiral made signals which were repeated by all the other vessels, each in turn. Lying still on those calm blue waters was a force which one day might cause nations to totter, the overwhelming force which upheld Britain's right in that oft-disputed sea.

A couple of thousand British sailors were ashore on leave, their white caps conspicuous in the streets everywhere as they walked orderly in threes and fours to inspect the town. In the square outside the Consulate a squad from the flagship were setting up a temporary band-stand, where the ship's band was to play when evening fell, while Hutcheson, perspiring in his uniform, drove with the Admiral to make the calls of courtesy upon the authorities which international etiquette demanded.

Myself, I had taken a boat out to the *Bulwark*, the great battleship flying the Admiral's flag, and was sitting on deck with my old friend Captain Jack Durnford, of the Royal Marines. Each year when the fleet put into Leghorn we were inseparable, for in long years past, at Portsmouth, we had been close friends, and now he was able to pay me annual visits at my Italian home.

He was on duty that morning, therefore could not get ashore till after luncheon.

"I'll dine with you, of course, to-night, old chap," he said. "And you must tell me all the news. We're in here for six days, and I was half a mind to run home. Two of our chaps got leave from the Admiral and left at three this morning for

London - four days in the train and two in town! Gone to see their sweethearts, I suppose."

The British naval officer in the Mediterranean delights to dash across Europe for a day at home if he can get leave and funds will allow. It is generally reckoned that such a trip costs about two pounds an hour while in London. And yet when a man is away from his *fiancee* or wife for three whole years, his anxiety to get back, even for a brief day, is easily understood. The youngsters, however, go for mere caprice - whenever they can obtain leave. This is not often, for the Admiral has very fixed views upon the matter.

"Your time's soon up, isn't it?" I remarked, as I lolled back in the easy deck-chair, and gazed away at the white port and its background of purple Apennines.

The dark, good-looking fellow in his smart summer uniform leaned over the bulwark, and said, with a slight sigh, I thought -

"Yes. This is my last trip to Leghorn, I think. I go back in November, and I really shan't be sorry. Three years is a long time to be away from home. You go next week, you say? Lucky devil to be your own master! I only wish I were. Year after year on this deck grows confoundedly wearisome, I can tell you, my dear fellow."

Durnford was a man who had written much on naval affairs, and was accepted as an expert on several branches of the service. The Admiralty do not encourage officers to write, but in Durnford's case it was recognized that of naval topics he possessed a knowledge that was of use, and, therefore, he was allowed to write books and to contribute critical articles to the service magazines. He had studied the relative strengths of foreign navies, and by keeping his eyes always open he had, on many occasions, been able to give valuable information to our naval *attaches* at the Embassies. More than once, however, his trenchant criticism of the action of the naval lords had brought upon his head rebukes from head-quarters; nevertheless, so universally was his talent as a naval expert recognized, that to write had never been forbidden him as it had been to certain others.

"How's Hutcheson?" he asked a moment later, turning and facing me.

"Fit as a fiddle. Just back from his month's leave at home. His wife is still up in Scotland, however. She can't stand Leghorn in summer."

"No wonder. It's a perfect furnace when the weather begins to stoke up."

"I go as soon as you've sailed. I only stayed because I promised to act for Frank," I said. "And, by Jove! a funny thing occurred while I was in charge - a real first-class mystery."

"A mystery - tell me," he exclaimed, suddenly interested.

"Well, a yacht - a pirate yacht, I believe it was - called here."

"A pirate! What do you mean?"

"Well, she was English. Listen, and I'll tell you the whole affair. It'll be something fresh to tell at mess, for I know how you chaps get played out of conversation."

"By Jove, yes! Things slump when we get no mail. But go on - I'm listening," he added, as an orderly came up, saluted, and handed him a paper.

"Well," I said, "let's cross to the other side. I don't want the sentry to overhear."

"As you like - but why such mystery?" he asked as we walked together to the other side of the spick-and-span quarter-deck of the gigantic battleship.

"You'll understand when I tell you the story." And then, standing together beneath the awning, I related to my friend the whole of the curious circumstances, just as I have recorded them in the foregoing pages.

"Confoundedly funny!" he remarked with his dark eyes fixed upon mine. "A mystery, by Jove, it is! What name did the yacht bear?"

"The *Lola*."

"What!" he gasped, suddenly turning pale. "The *Lola*? Are you quite sure it was the *Lola* - L-O-L-A?"

"Absolutely certain," I replied. "But why do you ask? Do you happen to know anything about the craft?"

"Me!" he stammered, and I could see that he had involuntarily betrayed the truth, yet for some reason he wished to conceal his knowledge from me. "Me! How should I know anything about such a craft? They were thieves on board evidently - perhaps pirates, as you say."

"But the name *Lola* is familiar to you, Jack! I'm sure it is, by your manner."

He paused a moment, and I could see what a strenuous effort he was making to avoid betraying knowledge.

"It's - well - " he said hesitatingly, with a rather sickly smile. "It's a girl's name - a girl I once knew. The name brings back to me certain memories."

"Pleasant ones - I hope."

"No. Bitter ones - very bitter ones," he said in a hard tone, striding across the deck and back again, and I saw in his eyes a strange look, half of anger, half of deep regret.

WILLIAM LE QUEUX

Was he telling the truth, I wondered? Some tragic romance or other concerning a woman had, I knew, overshadowed his life in the years before we had become acquainted. But the real facts he had never revealed to me. He had never before referred to the bitterness of the past, although I knew full well that his heart was in secret filled by some overwhelming sorrow.

Outwardly he was as merry as the other fellows who officered that huge floating fortress; on board he was a typical smart marine, and on shore he danced and played tennis and flirted just as vigorously as did the others. But a heavy heart beat beneath his uniform.

When he returned to where I stood I saw that his face had changed: it had become drawn and haggard. He bore the appearance of a man who had been struck a blow that had staggered him, crushing out all life and hope.

"What's the matter, Jack?" I asked. "Come! Tell me - what ails you?"

"Nothing, my dear old chap," he answered hoarsely. "Really nothing - only a touch of the blues just for a moment," he added, trying hard to smile. "It'll pass."

"What I've just told you about that yacht has upset you. You can't deny it"

He started. His mouth was, I saw, hard set. He knew something concerning that mysterious craft, but would not tell me.

The sound of a bugle came from the further end of the ship, and immediately men were scampering along the deck beneath as some order or other was being obeyed with that precision that characterizes the "handy man."

"Why are you silent?" I asked slowly, my eyes fixed upon my friend the officer. "I have told you what I know, and I want to discover the motive of the visit of those men, and the reason they opened Hutcheson's safe."

"How can I tell you?" he asked in a strained, unnatural voice.

"I believe you know something concerning them. Come, tell me the truth."

"I admit that I have certain grave suspicions," he said at last, standing astride with his hands behind his back, his sword trailing on the white deck. "You say that the yacht was called the *Lola* - painted gray with a black funnel."

"No, dead white, with a yellow funnel."

"Ah! Of course," he remarked, as though to himself. "They would repaint and alter her appearance. But the dining saloon. Was there a long carved oak buffet with a big, heavy cornice with three gilt dolphins in the center - and were there not dolphins in gilt on the backs of the chairs - an armorial device?"

"Yes," I cried. "You are right. I remember them! You've surely been on board her!"

"And there is a ladies' saloon and a small boudoir in pink beyond, while the smoking-room is entirely of marble for the heat?"

"Exactly - the same yacht, no doubt! But what do you know of her?"

"The captain, who gave his name to you as Mackintosh, is an undersized American of a rather low-down type?"

"I took him for a Scotsman."

"Because he put on a Scotch accent," he laughed. "He's a man who can speak a dozen languages brokenly, and pass for an Italian, a German, a Frenchman, as he wishes."

"And the - the man who gave his name as Philip Hornby?"

Durnford's mouth closed with a snap. He drew a long breath, his eyes grew fierce, and he bit his lip.

"Ah! I see he is not exactly your friend," I said meaningly.

"You are right, Gordon - he is not my friend," was his slow, meaning response.

"Then why not be outspoken and tell me all you know concerning him? Frank Hutcheson is anxious to clear up the mystery because they've tampered with the Consular seals and things. Besides, it would be put down to his credit if he solved the affair."

"Well, to tell you the truth, I'm mystified myself. I can't yet discern their motive."

"But at any rate you know the men," I argued. "You can at least tell us who they really are."

He shook his head, still disinclined, for some hidden reason, to reveal the truth to me.

"You saw no woman on board?" he asked suddenly, looking straight into my eyes.

"No. Hornby told me that he and Chater were alone."

"And yet an hour after you left a man and a woman came ashore and disappeared! Ah! If we only had a description of that woman it would reveal much to us."

"She was young and dark-haired, so the detective says. She had a curious fixed look in her eyes which attracted him, but she wore a thick motor veil, so that he could not clearly discern her features."

"And her companion?"

"Middle-aged, prematurely gray, with a small dark mustache."

Jack Durnford sighed and stroked his chin.

"Ah! Just as I thought," he exclaimed. "And they were actually here, in this port, a week ago! What a bitter irony of fate!"

"I don't understand you," I said. "You are so mysterious, and yet you will tell me nothing!"

"The police, fools that they are, have allowed them to escape, and they will never be caught now. Ah! you don't know them as I do! They are the cleverest pair in all Europe. And they have the audacity to call their craft the *Lola* - the *Lola*, of all names!"

"But as you know who and what the fellows are, you ought, I think, in common justice to Hutcheson, to tell us something," I complained. "If they are adventurers, they ought to be traced."

"What can I do - a prisoner here on board?" he argued bitterly. "How can I act?"

"Leave it all to me. I'm free to travel after them, and find out the truth if only you will tell me what you know concerning them," I said eagerly.

"Gordon, let me be frank and open with you, my dear old fellow. I would tell you everything - everything - if I dared. But I cannot - you understand!" And his final words seemed to choke him.

I stood before him, open-mouthed in astonishment.

"You really mean - well, that you are in fear of them - eh?" I whispered.

He nodded slowly in the affirmative, adding: "To tell you the truth would be to bring upon myself a swift, relentless vengeance that would overwhelm and crush me. Ah! my dear fellow, you do not know - you cannot dream - what brought those desperate men into this port. I can guess - I can guess only too well - but I can only tell you that if you ever do discover the terrible truth - which I fear is unlikely - you will solve one of the strangest and most remarkable mysteries of modern times."

"What does the mystery concern?" I asked, in breathless eagerness.

"It concerns a woman."

CHAPTER III

THE HOUSE "OVER THE WATER"

The Mediterranean Squadron, that magnificent display of naval force that is the guarantee of peace in Europe, after a week of gay festivities in Leghorn, had sailed for Gaeta, while I, glad to escape from the glaring heat, found myself back once more in dear old London.

One passes one's time in the south well enough in winter, but after a year even the most ardent lover of Italy longs to return to his own people, be it ever for so brief a space. Exile for a whole year in any continental town is exile indeed; therefore, although I lived in Italy for choice, I, like so many other Englishmen, always managed to spend a month or two in summer in our temperate if much maligned climate.

London, the same dear, dusty old London, only perhaps more dear and more dusty than ever, was my native city; hence I always spent a few weeks in it, even though all the world might be absent in the country, or at the seaside.

I had idled away a pleasant month up in Buxton, and from there had gone north to the Lakes, and it was one hot evening in mid-August that I found myself again in London, crossing St. James's Square from the Sports Club, where I had dined, walking towards Pall Mall. Darkness had just fallen, and there was that stifling oppression in the air that fore-tokened a thunderstorm. The club was not gay with life and merriment as it is in the season, for everyone was away, many of the rooms were closed for re-decoration, and most of the furniture swathed in linen.

I was on my way to pay a visit to a lady who lived up at Hampstead, a friend of my late mother's, and had just turned into Pall Mall, when a voice at my elbow suddenly exclaimed in Italian -

"Ah, signore! - why, actually, my padrone!"

And looking round, I saw a thin-faced man of about thirty, dressed in neat but rather shabby black, whom I instantly recognized as a man who had been my servant in Leghorn for two years, after which he had left to better himself.

"Why, Olinto!" I exclaimed, surprised, as I halted. "You - in London - eh? Well, and how are you getting on?"

"Most excellently, signore," he answered in broken English, smiling. "But it is so pleasant for me to see my generous padrone again. What fortune it is that I should pass here at this very moment!"

"Where are you working?" I inquired.

"At the Restaurant Milano, in Oxford Street - only a small place, but we gain discreetly, so I must not complain. I live over in Lambeth, and am on my way home."

"I heard you married after you left me. Is that true?"

"Yes, signore. I married Armida, who was in your service when I first entered it. You remember her? Ah, well!" he added, sighing. "Poor thing! I regret to say she is very ill indeed. She cannot stand your English climate. The doctor says she will die if she remains here. Yet what can I do? If we go back to Italy we shall only starve." And I saw that he was in deep distress, and that mention of his ailing wife had aroused within him bitter thoughts.

Olinto Santini walked back at my side in the direction of Trafalgar Square, answering the questions I put to him. He had been a good, hard-working servant, and I was glad to see him again. When he left me he had gone as steward on one of the Anchor Line boats between Naples and New York, and that was the last I had heard of him until I found him there in London, a waiter at a second-rate restaurant.

When I tried to slip some silver into his hand he refused to take it, and with a merry laugh said -

"I wonder if you would be offended, signore, if I told you of something for which I had been longing and longing?"

"Not at all."

"Well, the signore smokes our Tuscan cigars. I wonder if by chance you have one? We cannot get them in London, you know."

I felt in my pocket, laughing, and discovered that I had a couple of those long thin penny cigars which I always smoke in Italy, and which are so dear to the Tuscan palate. These I handed him, and he took them with delight as the greatest delicacy I could have offered him. Poor fellow! As an exiled Italian he clung to every little trifle that reminded him of his own beloved country.

When we halted before the National Gallery prior to parting I made some further inquiries regarding Armida, the black-eyed, good-looking housemaid whom he had married.

"Ah, signore!" he responded in a voice choked with emotion, dropping into Italian. "It is the one great sorrow of my life. I work hard from early morning until late at night, but what is the use when I see my poor wife gradually fading away before my very eyes? The doctor says that she cannot possibly live through the next winter. Ah! how delighted the poor girl would be if she could see the padrone once again!"

I felt sorry for him. Armida had been a good servant, and had served me well for nearly three years. Old Rosina, my housekeeper, had often regretted that she had been compelled to leave to attend to her aged mother. The latter, he told me, had died, and afterwards he had married her. There is more romance and tragedy in the lives of the poor Italians in London than London ever suspects. We are too apt to regard the Italian as a bloodthirsty person given to the unlawful use of the knife, whereas, as a whole, the Italian colony in London is a hard-working, thrifty, and law-abiding one, very different, indeed, to those colonies of aliens from Northern Europe, who are so continually bringing filth, disease, and immorality into the East End, and are a useless incubus in an already over-populated city.

He spoke so wistfully that his wife might see me once more that, having nothing very particular to do that evening, and feeling a deep sympathy for the poor fellow in his trouble, I resolved to accompany him to his house and see whether I could not, in some slight manner, render him a little help.

He thanked me profusely when I consented to go with him.

"Ah, signor padrone!" he said gratefully, "she will be so delighted. It is so very good of you."

We hailed a hansom and drove across Westminster Bridge to the address he gave - a gloomy back street off the York Road, one of those narrow, grimy thoroughfares into which the sun never shines. Ah, how often do the poor Italians, those children of the sun, pine and die when shut up in our dismal, sordid streets! Dirt and squalor do not affect them; it is the damp and cold and lack of sunshine that so very soon proves fatal.

A low-looking, evil-faced fellow opened the door to us and

growled acquaintance with Olinto, who, striking a match, ascended the worn, carpetless stairs before me, apologizing for passing before me, and saying in Italian -

"We live at the top, signore, because it is cheaper and the air is better."

"Quite right," I said. "Quite right. Go on." And I thought I heard my cab driving away.

It was a gloomy, forbidding, unlighted place into which I would certainly have hesitated to enter had not my companion been my trusted servant. I instinctively disliked the look of the fellow who had opened the door. He was one of those hulking loafers of the peculiarly Lambeth type. Yet the alien poor, I recollected, cannot choose where they shall reside.

Contrary to my expectations, the sitting-room we entered on the top floor was quite comfortably furnished, clean and respectable, even though traces of poverty were apparent. A cheap lamp was burning upon the table, but the apartment was unoccupied.

Olinto, in surprise, passed into the adjoining room, returning a moment later, exclaiming -

"Armida must have gone out to get something. Or perhaps she is with the people, a compositor and his wife, who live on the floor below. They are very good to her. I'll go and find her. Accommodate yourself with a chair, signore." And he drew the best chair forward for me, and dusted it with his handkerchief.

I allowed him to go and fetch her, rather surprised that she should be well enough to get about after all he had told me concerning her illness. Yet consumption does not keep people in bed until its final stages.

As I stood there, gazing round the room, I could not well distinguish its furthermost corners, for the lamp bore a shade of green paste-board, which threw a zone of light upon the table, and left the remainder of the room in darkness. When, however, my eyes grew accustomed to the dim light, I discerned that the place was dusty and somewhat disordered. The sofa was, I saw, a folding iron bedstead with greasy old cushions, while the carpet was threadbare and full of holes. When I drew the old rep curtains to look out of the window, I found that the shutters were closed, which I thought unusual for a room so high up as that was.

Olinto returned in a few moments, saying that his wife had evidently gone to do some shopping in the Lower-Marsh, for it is the habit of the denizens of that locality to go "marketing" in the evening among the costermongers' stalls that line so many of the thoroughfares. Perishable commodities, the overplus of the markets and shops, are cheaper at night than in the morning.

"I hope you are not pressed for time, signore?" he said apologetically. "But, of course, the poor girl does not know the surprise awaiting her. She will surely not be long."

"Then I'll wait," I said, and flung myself back into the chair he had brought forward for me.

"I have nothing to offer you, signer padrone," he said, with a laugh. "I did not expect a visitor, you know."

"No, no, Olinto. I've only just had dinner. But tell me how you have fared since you left me."

"Ah!" he laughed bitterly. "I had many ups and downs before I found myself here in London. The sea did not suit me - neither did the work. They put me in the emigrants' quarters, and consequently I could gain nothing. The other stewards were Neapolitans, therefore, because I was a Tuscan, they relegated me to the worst post. Ah, signore, you don't know what it is to serve those emigrants! I made two trips, then returned and married Armida. I called on you, but Tito said you were in London. At first I got work at a cafe in Viareggio, but when the season ended, and I was thrown out of employment, I managed to work my way from Genoa to London. My first place was scullion in a restaurant in Tottenham Court Road, and then I became waiter in the beer-hall at the Monico, and managed to save sufficient to send Armida the money to join me here. Afterwards I went to the Milano, and I hope to get into one of the big hotels very soon - or perhaps the grill-room at the Carlton. I have a friend who is there, and they make lots of money - four or five pounds every week in tips, they say."

"I'll see what I can do for you," I said. "I know several hotel-managers who might have a vacancy."

"Ah, signore!" he cried, filled with gratification. "If you only would! A word from you would secure me a good position. I can work, that you know - and I do work. I will work - for her sake."

"I have promised you," I said briefly.

"And how can I sufficiently thank you?" he cried, standing before me, while in his eyes I thought I detected a strange wild look, such as I had never seen there before.

"You served me well, Olinto," I replied, "and when I discover real sterling honesty I endeavor to appreciate it. There is, alas! Very little of it in this world."

"Yes," he said in a hoarse voice, his manner suddenly changing. "You have to-night shown me, signore, that you are my friend, and I will, in return, show you that I am yours." And suddenly grasping both my hands, he pulled me from the chair in which I was sitting, at the same time asking in a low intense whisper: "Do you always carry a revolver here in England, as you do in Italy?"

"Yes," I answered in surprise at his action and his

question. "Why?"

"Because there is danger here," he answered in the same low earnest tone. "Get your weapon ready. You may want it."

"I don't understand," I said, feeling my handy Colt in my back pocket to make sure it was there.

"Forget what I have said - all - all that I have told you to-night, sir," he said. "I have not explained the whole truth. You are in peril - in deadly peril!"

"How?" I exclaimed breathlessly, surprised at his extraordinary change of manner and his evident apprehension lest something should befall me.

"Wait, and you shall see," he whispered. "But first tell me, signore, that you will forgive me for the part I have played in this dastardly affair. I, like yourself, fell innocently into the hands of your enemies."

"My enemies! Who are they?"

"They are unknown, and for the present must remain so. But if you doubt your peril, watch - " and taking the rusty fire-tongs from the grate he carefully placed them on end in front of the deep old armchair in which I had sat, and then allowed them to fall against the edge of the seat, springing quickly back as he did so.

In an instant a bright blue flash shot through the place, and the irons fell aside, fused and twisted out of all recognition.

I stood aghast, utterly unable for the moment to sufficiently realize how narrowly I had escaped death.

"Look! See here, behind!" cried the Italian, directing my attention to the back legs of the chair, where, on bending with the lamp, I saw, to my surprise, that two wires were connected, and ran along the floor and out of the window, while concealed beneath the ragged carpet, in front of the chair, was a thin plate of steel, whereon my feet had rested.

Those who had so ingeniously enticed me to that gloomy house of death had connected up the overhead electric light main with that innocent-looking chair, and from some unseen point had been able to switch on a current of sufficient voltage to kill fifty men.

I stood stock-still, not daring to move lest I might come into contact with some hidden wire, the slightest touch of which must bring instant death upon me.

"Your enemies prepared this terrible trap for you," declared the man who was once my trusted servant. "When I entered into the affair I was not aware that it was to be fatal. They gave me no inkling of their dastardly intention. But there is no time to admit of explanations now, signore," he added breathlessly, in a low desperate voice. "Say that you will not prejudge me," he pleaded earnestly.

"I will not prejudge you until I've heard your explanation," I said. "I certainly owe my life to you to-night."

"Then quick! Fly from this house this instant. If you are stopped, then use your revolver. Don't hesitate. In a moment they will be here upon you."

"But who are they, Olinto? You must tell me," I cried in desperation.

"*Dio!* Go! Go!" he cried, pushing me violently towards the door. "Fly, or we shall both die - both of us! Run downstairs. I must make feint of dashing after you."

I turned, and seeing his desperate eagerness, precipitately fled, while he ran down behind me, uttering fierce imprecations in Italian, as though I had escaped him.

A man in the narrow dark passage attempted to trip me up as I ran, but I fired point blank at him, and gaining the door unlocked it, and an instant later found myself out in the street.

It was the narrowest escape from death that I had ever had in all my life - surely the strangest and most remarkable adventure. What, I wondered, did it mean?

Next morning I searched up and down Oxford Street for the Restaurant Milano, but could not find it. I asked shopkeepers, postmen, and policemen; I examined the London Directory at the bar of the Oxford Music Hall, and made every inquiry possible. But all was to no purpose. No one knew of such a place. There were restaurants in plenty in Oxford Street, from the Frascati down to the humble coffeeshop, but nobody had ever heard of the "Milano."

Even Olinto had played me false!

I was filled with chagrin, for I had trusted him as honest, upright, and industrious; and was puzzled to know the reason he had deceived me, and why he had enticed me to the very brink of the grave.

He had told me that he himself had fallen into the trap laid by my enemies, and yet he had steadfastly refused to tell me who they were! The whole thing was utterly inexplicable.

I drove over to Lambeth and wandered through the maze of mean streets off the York Road, yet for the life of me I could not decide into which house I had been taken. There were a dozen which seemed to me that they might be the identical house from which I had so narrowly escaped with my life.

Gradually it became impressed upon me that my ex-servant had somehow gained knowledge that I was in London, that he had watched my exit from the club, and that all his pitiful story regarding Armida was false. He was the envoy of my unknown enemies, who had so ingeniously and so relentlessly plotted my destruction.

That I had enemies I knew quite well. The man who believes he has not is an arrant fool. There is no man breathing who has not an enemy, from the pauper in the workhouse to the king in his automobile. But the unseen enemy is always the more dangerous; hence my deep apprehensive reflections that day as I walked those sordid back streets "over the water," as the Cockney refers to the district between those two main arteries of traffic, the Waterloo and Westminster Bridge Roads.

My unknown enemies had secured the services of Olinto in their dastardly plot to kill me. With what motive?

I wondered as I crossed Waterloo Bridge to the Strand, whether Olinto Santini would again approach me and make the promised explanation. I had given my word not to prejudge him until he revealed to me the truth. Yet I could not, in the circumstances, repose entire confidence in him.

When one's enemies are unknown, the feeling of apprehension is always much greater, for in the imagination danger lurks in every corner, and every action of a friend covers the ruse of a suspected enemy.

That day I did my business in the city with a distrust of everyone, not knowing whether I was not followed or whether those who sought my life were not plotting some other equally ingenious move whereby I might go innocently to my death. I endeavored to discover Olinto by every possible means during those stifling days that followed. The heat of London was, to me, more oppressive than the fiery sunshine of the old-world Tuscany, and everyone who could be out of town had left for the country or the sea.

The only trace I found of the Italian was that he was registered at the office of the International Society of Hotel Servants, in Shaftesbury Avenue, as being employed at Gatti's Adelaide Gallery, but on inquiry there I found he had left more than a year before, and none of his fellow-waiters knew his whereabouts.

Thus being defeated in every inquiry, and my business at last concluded in London, I went up to Dumfries on a duty visit which I paid annually to my uncle, Sir George Little. Having known Dumfries since my earliest boyhood, and having spent some years of my youth there, I had many friends in the vicinity, for Sir George and my aunt were very popular in the county and moved in the best set.

Each time I returned from abroad I was always a welcome guest at Greenlaw, as their place outside the city of Burns was called, and this occasion proved no exception, for the country houses of Dumfries are always gay in August in prospect of the shooting.

"Some new people have taken Rannoch Castle. Rather nice they seem," remarked my aunt as we were sitting together at luncheon the day after my arrival. "Their name is Leithcourt, and they've asked me to drive you over there to tennis this afternoon."

"I'm not much of a player, you know, aunt. In Italy we don't believe in athletics. But if it's out of politeness, of course, I'll go."

"Very well," she said. "Then I'll order the victoria for three."

"There are several nice girls there, Gordon," remarked my uncle mischievously. "You have a good time, so don't think you are going to be bored."

"No fear of that," was my answer. And at three o'clock Sir George, his wife, and myself set out for that fine old historic castle that stands high on the Bognie, overlooking the Cairn waters beyond Dunscore, one of the strongholds of the Black Douglas in those turbulent days of long ago, and now a splendid old residence with a big shoot which was sometimes let for the season at a very high rent by its aristocratic if somewhat impecunious owner.

We could see its great round towers, standing grim and gray on the hillside commanding the whole of the valley, long before we approached it, and when we drove into the grounds we found a gay party in summer toilettes assembled on the ancient bowling-green, now transformed into a modern tennis-lawn.

Mrs. Leithcourt and her husband, a tall, thin, gray-headed, well-dressed man, both came forward to greet us, and after a few introductions I joined a set at tennis. They were a merry crowd. The Leithcourts were entertaining a large house-party, and their hospitality was on a scale quite in keeping with the fine old place they rented.

Tea was served on the lawn by the footmen, and afterwards, being tired of the game, I found myself strolling with Muriel Leithcourt, a bright, dark-eyed girl with tightly-bound hair, and wearing a cotton blouse and flannel tennis skirt.

I was apologizing for my terribly bad play, explaining that I had no practice out in Italy, whereupon she said -

"I know Italy slightly. I was in Florence and Naples with mother last season."

And then we began to discuss pictures and sculptures and the sights of Italy generally. I discerned from her remarks that she had traveled widely; indeed, she told me that both her father and mother were never happier than when moving from place to place in search of variety and distraction. We had entered the huge paneled hall of the Castle, and had passed up the quaint old stone staircase to the long banqueting hall with its paneled oak ceiling, which in these modern days had been transformed into a bright, pleasant drawing-room, from the windows of which was presented a marvelous view over the lovely Nithsdale and across to the heather-clad hills beyond.

It was pleasant lounging there in the cool old room after the hot sunshine outside, and as I gazed around the place I noted how much more luxurious and tasteful it now was to what it had been in the days when I had visited its owner several years before.

"We are awfully glad to be up here," my pretty companion was saying. "We had such a busy season in London." And then she went on to describe the Court ball, and two or three of the most notable functions about which I had read in my English paper beside the Mediterranean.

She attracted me on account of her bright vivacity, quick wit and keen sense of humor, therefore I sat listening to her pleasant chatter. Exiled as I was in a foreign land, I seldom spoke English save with Hutcheson, the Consul, and even then we generally spoke Italian if there were others present, in order that our companions should understand. Therefore her gossip interested me, and as the golden sunset flooded the handsome old room I sat listening to her, inwardly admiring her innate grace and handsome countenance.

I had no idea who or what her father was - whether a wealthy manufacturer, like so many who take expensive shoots and give big entertainments in order to edge their way into Society by its back door, or whether he was a gentleman of means and of good family. I rather guessed the latter, from his gentlemanly bearing and polished manner. His appearance, tall and erect, was that of a retired officer, and his clean-cut face was one of marked distinction.

I was telling my pretty companion something of my own life, how, because I loved Italy so well, I lived in Tuscany in preference to living in England, and how each year I came home for a month or two to visit my relations and to keep in touch with things.

Suddenly she said -

"I was once in Leghorn for a few hours. We were yachting in the Mediterranean. I love the sea - and yachting is such awfully good fun, if you only get decent weather."

The mention of yachting brought back to my mind the visit of the *Lola* and its mysterious sequel.

"Your father has a yacht, then?" I remarked, with as little concern as I could.

"Yes. The *Iris*. My uncle is cruising on her up the Norwegian Fiords. For us it is a change to be here, because we are so often afloat. We went across to New York in her last year and had a most delightful time - except for one bad squall which made us all a little bit nervous. But Moyes is such an excellent captain that I never fear. The crew are all North Sea fishermen - father will engage nobody else. I don't blame him."

"So you must have made many long voyages, and seen many odd corners of the world, Miss Leithcourt?" I remarked, my interest in her increasing, for she seemed so extremely intelligent and well-informed.

"Oh, yes. We've been to Mexico, and to Panama, besides Morocco, Egypt, and the West Coast of Africa."

"And you've actually landed at Leghorn!" I remarked.

"Yes, but we didn't stay there more than an hour - to send a telegram, I think it was. Father said there was nothing to see there. He and I went ashore, and I must say I was rather disappointed."

"You are quite right. The town itself is ugly and uninteresting. But the outskirts - San Jacopo, Ardenza and Antigniano are all delightful. It was unfortunate that you did not see them. Was it long ago when you put in there?"

"Not very long. I really don't recollect the exact date," was her reply. "We were on our way home from Alexandria."

"Have you ever, in any of the ports you've been, seen a yacht called the *Lola*?" I asked eagerly, for it occurred to me that perhaps she might be able to give me information.

"The *Lola*!" she gasped, and instantly her face changed. A flush overspread her cheeks, succeeded next moment by a death-like pallor. "The *Lola*!" she repeated in a strange, hoarse voice, at the same time endeavoring strenuously not to exhibit any apprehension. "No. I have never heard of any such a vessel. Is she a steam-yacht? Who's her owner?"

I regarded her in amazement and suspicion, for I saw that mention of the name had aroused within her some serious misgiving. That look in her dark eyes as they fixed themselves upon me was one of distinct and unspeakable terror.

What could she possibly know concerning the mysterious craft?

"I don't know the owner's name," I said, still affecting not to have noticed her alarm and apprehension. "The vessel ran aground at the Meloria, a dangerous shoal outside Leghorn, and through the stupidity of her captain was very nearly lost."

"Yes?" she gasped, in a half-whisper, bending to me eagerly, unable to sufficiently conceal the terrible anxiety consuming her. "And you - did you go aboard her?"

"Yes," was the only word I uttered.

A silence fell between us, and as my eyes fixed themselves upon her, I saw that from her handsome mobile countenance all the light and life had suddenly gone out, and I knew that she was in secret possession of the key to that remarkable enigma that so puzzled me.

Of a sudden the door opened, and a voice cried gayly -

"Why, I've been looking everywhere for you, Muriel. Why are you hidden here? Aren't you coming?"

We both turned, and as she did so a low cry of blank dismay involuntarily escaped her.

Next instant I sprang to my feet. The reason of her cry was apparent, for there, in the full light of the golden sunset streaming through the long open windows, stood a broad-shouldered, fair-bearded man in tennis flannels and a Panama hat - the fugitive I knew as Philip Hornby!

I faced him, speechless.

CHAPTER IV

IN WHICH THE MYSTERY INCREASES

Neither of us spoke. Equally surprised at the unexpected encounter, we stood facing each other dumbfounded.

Hornby started quickly as soon as his eyes fell upon me, and his face became blanched to the lips, while Muriel Leithcourt, quick to notice the sudden change in him, rose and introduced us in as calm a voice as she could command.

"I don't think you are acquainted," she said to me with a smile. "This is Mr. Martin Woodroffe - Mr. Gordon Gregg."

I bowed to him in sudden resolve to remain silent in pretense that I doubted whether the man before me was actually my host of the *Lola*. I intended to act as though I was not sufficiently convinced to openly express my doubt. Therefore we bowed, exchanging greetings as strangers, while, carefully watching, I saw how greatly the minds of both were relieved. They shot meaning glances at each other, and then, as though reassured that I was mystified and uncertain, the man who called himself Woodroffe explained to my companion -

"I've been over to Newton Stewart with Fred all day, and only got back a quarter of an hour ago. Aren't you playing any more to-day?"

"I think not," was her reply. "We've been out there the whole afternoon, and I'm rather tired. But they're still on the lawn. You can surely get a game with someone."

"If you don't play, I shan't. I returned to keep the promise I made this morning," he laughed, standing before the big open fireplace, holding his tennis racquet behind his back.

I examined his countenance, and was more than ever convinced that he was actually the man who gave me the name of Hornby and the false address in Somerset. The pair seemed to be on familiar terms, and I wondered whether they were engaged. In any case, the man seemed quite at home there.

As he chatted with the daughter of the house, he cast a quick, covert glance at me, and then darted a meaning look at her - a look of renewed confidence, as though he felt that he had successfully averted any suspicions I might have held.

We talked of the prospects of the grouse and the salmon, and from his remarks he seemed to be as keen at sport as he had once made out himself to be at yachting.

"My friend Leithcourt is awfully fortunate in getting such a splendid old place as this. On every hand I hear glowing accounts of the number of birds. The place has been well preserved in the past, and there's plenty of good cover."

"Yes," I said. "Gilrae, the owner, is a keen sportsman, and before he became so hard up he spent a lot of money on the estate, which, I believe, has always been considered one of the very best in the southwest. There's salmon, they say, down in the Glen yonder - but I've never tried for any."

"Certainly there is. I've seen several. I hope to try one of these days. The Glen is deep and shady - an ideal place for fish. The only disappointment here, as far as I can make out, is the very few head of black-game."

"Yes, but every year they are getting rarer and rarer in this part of Scotland. A really fine black-cock is quite an event nowadays," I said.

While we were talking, or rather while I was carefully watching the rapid working of his mind, Leithcourt himself entered and joined us. He had been playing tennis, and had come in to rest and cool.

Host and guest were evidently on the most intimate terms. Leithcourt addressed him as "Martin," and began to relate a quarrel which his head-gamekeeper had had that day with one of the small farmers on the estate regarding the killing of some rabbits. And while they were talking Muriel suggested that we should stroll down to the tennis-courts again, an invitation which, much as I regretted leaving the two men, I was bound to accept.

It seemed as though she wished purposely to take me away from that man's presence, fearing that by remaining there longer my suspicions might become confirmed. She was acting in conjunction with the man whom I had known as Hornby.

There were still a good many people watching the game, for it was pleasant in those old-world gardens in the sunset hour. The dried-up moat was now transformed into a garden filled with rhododendrons and bright azaleas, while the high ancient beech-hedges, the quaint old sundial with its motto: "Each time ye shadowe turneth ys one daye nearer unto dethe," and the old stone balustrades gray with lichen, all spoke mutely of those glorious days when the fierce horsemen of the Lairds of Rannoch were feared across the Border, and when many a prisoner of the Black Douglas had pined and died in those narrow stone chambers in the grim north tower that still stood high above.

Among the party strolling and lounging there prior to departure were quite a number of people I knew, people who had shooting-boxes in the vicinity and were my uncle's friends. In Scotland there is always a hearty hospitality among the sporting folk, and the laws of caste are far less rigorous than they are in England.

I was standing chatting with two ladies who were about to take leave of their hostess, when Leithcourt returned, but alone. Hornby had not accompanied him. Was it because he feared to again meet me?

In order to ascertain something regarding the man who had so mysteriously fled from Leghorn, I managed by the exercise of a little diplomacy to sit on the lawn with a young married woman named Tennant, wife of a cavalry captain, who was one of the house-party. After a little time I succeeded in turning the conversation to her fellow guests, and more particularly to the man I knew as Hornby.

"Oh! Mr. Woodroffe is most amusing," declared the bright little woman. "He's always playing some practical joke or other. After dinner he is usually the life and soul of our party."

"Yes," I said, "I like what little I have seen of him. He's a very good fellow, I should say. I've heard that he's engaged to Muriel," I hazarded. "Is that true?"

"Of course. They've been engaged nearly a year, but he's been abroad until quite lately. He is rather close about his own affairs, and never talks about his travels and adventures, although one day Mr. Leithcourt declared that his hairbreadth escapes would make a most exciting book if ever written."

"Leithcourt and he are evidently most intimate friends."

"Oh, quite inseparable!" she laughed. "And the other man who is always with them is that short, stout, red-faced old fellow standing over there with the lady in pale blue, Sir Ughtred Gardner. Mr. Woodroffe has nicknamed him 'Sir Putrid.'" And we both laughed. "Of course, don't say I said so," she whispered. "They don't call him that to his face, but it's so easy to make a mistake in his name when he's not within hearing. We women don't care for him, so the nickname just fits."

And she gossiped on, telling me much that I desired to know regarding the new tenant of Rannoch and his friends, and more especially of that man who had first introduced himself to me in the Consulate at Leghorn.

Half an hour later my uncle's carriage was announced, and I left with the distinct impression that there was some deep mystery surrounding the Leithcourts. What it was, however, I could not, for the life of me, make out. Perhaps it was Philip Leithcourt's intimate relation with the man who had so cleverly deceived me that incited my curiosity concerning him; perhaps it was that mysterious intuition, that curious presage of evil that sometimes comes to a man as warning of impending peril. Whatever the reason, I had become filled with grave apprehensions. The mystery grew deeper day by day, and was inexplicable.

During the week that followed I sought to learn all I could regarding the new people at the castle.

"They are taken up everywhere," declared my aunt when I questioned her. "Of course, we knew very little of them, except that they had a shoot up near Fort William two years ago, and that they have a town house in Green Street. They are evidently rather smart folks. Don't you think so?"

"Judging from their house-party, yes," I responded. "They are about as gay a crowd as one could find north of Carlisle just at present."

"Exactly. There are some well-known people among them, too," said my aunt. "I've asked them over to-morrow afternoon, and they've accepted."

"Excellent!" I exclaimed, for I wanted an opportunity for another chat with the dark-eyed girl who was engaged to the man whose alias was Hornby. I particularly desired to ascertain the reason of her fear when I had mentioned the *Lola*, and whether she possessed any knowledge of Hylton Chater.

The opportunity came to me in due course, for next afternoon the Rannoch party drove over in two large brakes, and with other people from the neighborhood and a band from Dumfries, my aunt's grounds presented a gay and animated scene. There was the usual tennis and croquet, while some of the men enjoyed a little putting on the excellent course my uncle, a golf enthusiast, had recently laid down.

As I expected, Woodroffe did not accompany the party. Mrs. Leithcourt, a slightly fussy little woman, apologized for his absence, explaining that he had been recalled to London suddenly a few days before, but was returning to Rannoch again at the end of the week.

"We couldn't afford to lose him," she declared to my aunt. "He is so awfully humorous - his droll sayings and antics keep us in a perfect roar each night at dinner. He's such a perfect mimic."

I turned away and strolled with Muriel, pleading an excuse to show her my uncle's beautiful grounds, not a whit less picturesque than those of the castle, and perhaps rather better kept.

"I only heard yesterday of your engagement, Miss Leithcourt," I remarked presently when we were alone. "Allow me to offer my best congratulations. When you introduced me to Mr. Woodroffe the other day I had no idea that he was to be your husband."

She glanced at me quickly, and I saw in her dark eyes a look of suspicion. Then she flushed slightly, and laughing uneasily said, in a blank, hard voice -

"It's very good of you, Mr. Gregg, to wish me all sorts of such pleasant things."

"And when is the happy event to take place?"

"The date is not exactly fixed - early next year, I believe," and I thought she sighed.

"And you will probably spend a good deal of time yachting?" I suggested, my eyes fixed upon her in order to watch the result of my pointed remark. But she controlled herself perfectly.

"I love the sea," she responded briefly, and her eyes were set straight before her.

"Mr. Woodroffe has gone up to town, your mother says."

"Yes. He received a wire, and had to leave immediately. It was an awful bore, for we had arranged to go for a picnic to Dundrennan Abbey yesterday."

"But he'll be back here again, won't he?"

"I really don't know. It seems quite uncertain. I had a letter this morning which said he might have to go over to Hamburg on business, instead of coming up to us again."

There was disappointment in her voice, and yet at the same time I could not fail to recognize how the man to whom she was engaged had fled from Scotland because of my presence.

How I longed to ask her point-blank what she really knew of the yachtsman who was shrouded in so much mystery. Yet by betraying any undue anxiety I should certainly negative all my efforts to solve the puzzling enigma, therefore I was compelled to remain content with asking ingeniously disguised questions and drawing my own conclusions from her answers.

As we passed along those graveled walks it somehow became vividly impressed upon me that her marriage was being forced upon her by her parents. Her manner was that of one who was concealing some strange and terrible secret which she feared might be revealed. There was a distant look of unutterable terror in those dark eyes as though she existed in some constant and ever-present dread. Of course she told me nothing of her own feelings or affections, yet I recognized in both her words and her bearing a curious apathy - a want of the real enthusiasm of affection. Woodroffe, much her senior, was her father's friend, and it therefore seemed to me more than likely that Leithcourt was pressing a matrimonial alliance upon his daughter for some ulterior motive. In the mad hurry for place, power, and wealth, men relentlessly sell their daughters in the matrimonial market, and ambitious mothers scheme and intrigue for their own aggrandizement at sacrifice of their daughter's happiness more often than the public ever dream. Tragedy is, alas! written upon the face of many a bride whose portrait appears in the fashion-papers and whose toilette is so faithfully chronicled in the paragraph beneath. Indeed, the girl in Society who is allowed her own free choice in the matter of a husband is, alas! nowadays the exception, for parents who want to "get on" up the social scale have found that pretty daughters are a marketable commodity, and many a man has been placed "on his legs," both financially and socially, by his son-in-law. Hence the marriage of convenience is fast becoming common, while in the same ratio the divorce petitions are unfortunately on the increase.

I read tragedy in the dark luminous eyes of Muriel Leithcourt. I knew that her young heart was over-burdened by some secret sorrow or guilty knowledge that she would reveal to me if she dared. Her own words told me that she was perplexed; that she longed to confide and seek advice of someone, yet by reason of some hidden and untoward circumstance her lips were sealed.

I tried to question her further regarding Woodroffe, of what profession he followed and of his past.

But she evidently suspected me, for I had unfortunately mentioned the *Lola*.

She wanted to speak to me in confidence, and yet she would reveal to me nothing - absolutely nothing.

Martin Woodroffe did not rejoin the house-party at Rannoch.

Although I remained the guest of my uncle much longer than I intended, indeed right through the shooting season, in order to watch the Leithcourts, yet as far as we could judge they were extremely well-bred people and very hospitable.

We exchanged a good many visits and dinners, and while my uncle several times invited Leithcourt and his friends to his shoot with *al fresco* luncheon, which the ladies joined, the tenant of Rannoch always invited us back in return.

Thus I gained many opportunities of talking with Muriel, and of watching her closely. I had the reputation of being a confirmed bachelor, and on account of that it seemed that she was in no way averse to my companionship. She could handle a rook-rifle as well as any woman, and was really a very fair shot. Therefore we often found ourselves alone tramping across the wide open moorland, or along those delightful glens of the Nithsdale, glorious in the autumn tints of their luxurious foliage.

Her father, on the other hand, seemed to view me with considerable suspicion, and I could easily discern that I was only asked to Rannoch because it was impossible to invite my uncle without including myself.

Leithcourt, who perhaps thought I was courting his daughter, was ever endeavoring to avoid me, and would never allow me to walk with him alone. Why? I wondered. Did he fear me? Had Woodroffe told him of our strange encounter in Leghorn?

His pronounced antipathy towards me caused me to watch him surreptitiously, and more closely than perhaps I should otherwise have done. He was a man of gloomy mood, and often he would leave his guests and take walks alone, musing and brooding. On several occasions I followed him in secret, and found to my surprise that although he made long detours in various directions, yet he always arrived at the same spot at the same hour - five o'clock.

The place where he halted was on the edge of a dark wood on the brow of a hill about three miles from Rannoch - a good place to get woodpigeon, as they came to roost. It was fully two miles across the hills from the high road to Moniaive, and from the break the gray wall where he was in the habit of sitting to rest and smoke, there stretched the beautiful panorama of Loch Urr and the heatherclad hills beyond.

Leithcourt never went direct to the place, but always so timed his walks that he arrived just at five, and remained there smoking cigarettes until half-past, as though awaiting the arrival of some person he expected. Once or twice his guests suggested shooting pigeons at sundown, but he always had some excuse for opposing the proposal, and thus the party, unsuspecting the reason, were kept away from that particular lonely spot.

In my youth I had sat many a quiet hour there in the darkening gloom and shot many a pigeon, therefore I knew the wood well, and was able to watch the tenant of Rannoch from points where he least suspected the presence of another.

Once, when I was alone with Muriel, I mentioned her father's capacity for walking alone, whereupon she said -

"Oh, yes, he was always fond of walking. He used to take me with him when we first came here, but he always went so far that I refused to go any more."

She never once mentioned Woodroffe. I allowed her plenty of opportunity for doing so, chaffing her about her forthcoming marriage in order that she might again refer to him. But never did his name pass her lips. I understood that he had gone abroad - that was all.

Often when alone I reflected upon my curious adventure on that night when I met Olinto, and of my narrow escape from the hands of my unknown enemies. I wondered if that ingenious and dastardly attempt upon my life had really any connection with that strange incident at Leghorn. As day succeeded day, my mind became filled by increasing suspicion. Mystery surrounded me on every hand.

Indeed, by one curious fact alone it was increased a hundredfold.

Late one afternoon, when I had been out shooting all day with the Rannoch party, I drove back to the castle in the Perth-cart with three other men, and found the ladies assembled in the great hall with tea ready. A welcome log-fire was blazing in the huge old grate, for in October it is chilly and damp in Scotland and a fire is pleasant at evening.

Muriel was seated upon the high padded fender - like those one has at clubs - which always formed a cosy spot for the ladies, especially after dinner. When I entered, she rose quickly and handed me my cup, exclaiming as she looked at me -

"Oh, Mr. Gregg! what a state you are in!"

"Yes, I was after snipe, and slipped into a bog," I laughed. "But it was early this morning, and the mud has dried."

"Come with me, and I'll get you a brush," she urged. And I followed her through the long corridors and upstairs to a small sitting-room which was her own little sanctum, where she worked and read - a cosy little place with two queer old windows in the colossal wall, and a floor of polished oak, and great black beams above. When the owner had occupied the house that room had been disused, but it had, I found, been now completely transformed, and was a most tasteful little nest of luxury with its bright chintzes, its Turkey rugs and its cheerful fire on the old stone hearth.

She laughed when I expressed admiration of her little den, and said -

"I believe it was the armory in the old days. But it makes quite a comfy little boudoir. I can lock myself in and be quite quiet when the party are too noisy," she added merrily.

But as my eyes wandered around they suddenly fell upon an object which caused me to start with profound wonder - a cabinet photograph in a frame of crimson leather.

The picture was that of a young girl - a duplicate of the portrait I had found torn across and flung aside on board the *Lola*!

The merry eyes laughed out at me as I stood staring at it in sheer bewilderment.

"What a pretty girl!" I exclaimed quickly, concealing my surprise. "Who is she?"

My companion was silent a moment, her dark eyes meeting mine with a strange look of inquiry.

"Yes," she laughed, "everyone admires her. She was a schoolfellow of mine - Elma Heath."

"Heath!" I echoed. "Where was she at school with you?"

"At Chichester."

"Long ago?"

"A little over two years."

"She's very beautiful!" I declared, taking up the photograph and discovering that it bore the name of the same well-known photographer in New Bond Street as that I had found on the carpet of the *Lola* in the Mediterranean.

"Yes. She's really prettier than her photograph. It hardly does her justice."

"And where is she now?"

"Why are you so very inquisitive, Mr. Gregg?" laughed the handsome girl. "Have you actually fallen in love with her from her picture?"

"I'm hardly given to that kind of thing, Miss Leithcourt," I answered with mock severity. "I don't think even my worst enemy could call me a flirt, could she?"

"No. I will give you your due," she declared. "You never do flirt. That is why I like you."

"Thanks for your candor, Miss Leithcourt," I said.

"Only," she added, "you seem smitten with Elma's charms."

"I think she's extremely pretty," I remarked, with the photograph still in my hand. "Do you ever see her now?"

"Never," she replied. "Since the day I left school we have never met. She was several years younger than myself, and I heard that a week after I left Chichester her people came and took her away. Where she is now I have no idea. Her people lived somewhere in Durham. Her father was a doctor."

Her reply disappointed me. Yet I had, at least, retained knowledge of the name of the original of the picture, and from the photographer I might perhaps discover her address, for to me it seemed that she was somehow intimately connected with those mysterious yachtsmen.

What Muriel told me concerning her, I did not doubt for a single instant. Yet it was certainly more than a coincidence that a copy of the picture which had created such a deep impression upon me should be preserved in her own little boudoir as a souvenir of a devoted school-friend.

"Then you have heard absolutely nothing as to her present position or whereabouts - whether she is married, for instance?"

"Ah!" she cried mischievously. "You betray yourself by your own words. You have fallen in love with her, I really believe, Mr. Gregg. If she knew, she'd be most gratified - or at least, she ought to be."

At which I smiled, preferring that she should adopt that theory in preference to any other.

She spoke frankly, as a pure honest girl would speak. She was not jealous, but she nevertheless resented - as women do resent such things - that I should fall in love with a friend's photograph.

There was a mystery surrounding that torn picture; of that I was absolutely certain. The remembrance of that memorable evening when I had dined on board the *Lola* arose vividly before me. Why had the girl's portrait been so ruthlessly destroyed and the frame turned with its face to the wall? There was some reason - some distinct and serious motive in it. Had Muriel told me the truth, I wondered, or was she merely seeking to shield the suspected man who was her lover?

Hour by hour the mystery surrounding the Leithcourts became more inscrutable, more intensely absorbing. I had searched a copy of the London Directory at the Station Hotel at Carlisle, and found that no house in Green Street was registered as occupied by the tenant of Rannoch; and, further, when I came to examine the list of guests at the castle, I found that they were really persons unknown in society. They were merely of that class of witty, well-dressed parasites who always cling on to the wealthy and make believe that they are smart and of the *grande monde*. Rannoch was an expensive place to keep up, with all that big retinue of servants and gamekeepers, and with those nightly dinners cooked by a French *chef*, yet Leithcourt seemed to possess a long pocket and smiled upon those parasites, officers of doubtful commission and younger sprigs of the pseudo-aristocracy who surrounded him, while his wife, keen-eyed and of superb bearing, was punctilious concerning all points of etiquette, and at the same time indefatigable that her mixed set of guests should enjoy a really good time.

But I was not the only person who could not make them out. My uncle was the first to open my eyes regarding the true character of certain of the men staying at Rannoch.

"I think, Gordon, that one or two of those fellows with Leithcourt are rank outsiders," he said confidentially to me one night after we had had a hard day's shooting, and were playing a hundred up at billiards before retiring. "One man, who arrived yesterday, I know too well. He was struck off the list at Boodle's three years ago for card-sharping - that thin-faced, fair-mustached man named Cadby. I suppose Leithcourt doesn't know it, or he wouldn't have him up here among respectable folk." And my uncle, chewing the end of his cigar, sniffed angrily, seeming half inclined to give his friend a gentle hint that the name Cadby was placed beyond the pale of good society.

"Better not say anything about it," I urged. "It's Leithcourt's own affair, uncle - not ours."

"Yes, but if a man sets up a position in the country he mustn't be allowed to ask us to meet such fellows. It's coming it a little too thick, Gordon. We men can stand the women of the party, but the men - well, I tell you candidly, I shan't accept his invites to shoot again."

"No, no, uncle," I protested. "Probably it's owing to ignorance. You'll be able, a little later on, to give him valuable tips. He's a good fellow, and only wants experience in Scotland to get along all right."

"Yes. But I don't like it, my boy, I don't like it! It isn't playing a fair game," declared the rigid old gentleman, coloring resentfully. "I'm not going to return the invitation and ask that sharper, Cadby, to my house - and I tell you that plainly."

Next day I shot with the Carmichaels of Crossburn, and about four o'clock, after a good day, took leave of the party in the Black Glen, and started off alone to walk home, a distance of about six miles. It was already growing dusk, and would be quite dark, I knew, before I reached my uncle's house. My most direct way was to follow the river for about two miles and then strike straight across the large dense wood, and afterwards over a wide moor full of treacherous bogs and pitfalls for the unwary.

My gun over my shoulder, I had walked on for about three-quarters of an hour, and had nearly traversed the wood, at that hour so dark that I had considerable difficulty in finding my way, when - of a sudden - I fancied I distinguished voices.

I halted. Yes. Men were talking in low tones of confidence, and in that calm stillness of evening they appeared nearer to me than they actually were.

I listened, trying to distinguish the words uttered, but could make out nothing. They were moving slowly together, in close vicinity to myself, for their feet stirred the dry leaves, and I could hear the boughs cracking as they forced their way through them.

Of a sudden, while standing there not daring to breathe lest I should betray my presence, a strange sound fell upon my eager ears.

Next moment I realized that I was at that place where Leithcourt so persistently kept his disappointed tryst, having approached it from within the wood.

The sound alarmed me, and yet it was neither an explosion of fire-arms nor a startling cry for help.

One word reached me in the darkness - one single word of bitter and withering reproach.

Heedless of the risk I ran and the peril to which I exposed myself, I dashed forward with a resolve to penetrate the mystery, until I came to the gap in the rough stone wall where Leithcourt's habit was to halt each day at sundown.

There, in the falling darkness, the sight that met my eyes at the spot held me rigid, appalled, stupefied.

In that instant I realized the truth - a truth that was surely the strangest ever revealed to any man.

CHAPTER V

CONTAINS CERTAIN CONFIDENCES

As I dashed forward to the gap in the boundary wall of the wood, I nearly stumbled over a form lying across the narrow path.

So dark was it beneath the trees that at first I could not plainly make out what it was until I bent and my hands touched the garments of a woman. Her hat had fallen off, for I felt it beneath my feet, while the cloak was a thick woolen one.

Was she dead, I wondered? That cry - that single word of reproach - sounded in my ears, and it seemed plain that she had been struck down ruthlessly after an exchange of angry words.

I felt in my pocket for my vestas, but unfortunately my box was empty. Yet just at that moment my strained ears caught a sound - the sound of someone moving stealthily among the fallen leaves. Seizing my gun, I demanded who was there.

There was, however, no response. The instant I spoke the movement ceased.

As far as I could judge, the person in concealment was within the wood about ten yards from me, separated by an impenetrable thicket. As, however, I stood out against the sky, my silhouette was, I knew, a well-defined mark for anyone with fire-arms.

It seemed evident that a tragedy had occurred, and that the victim at my feet was a woman. But whom?

Of a sudden, while I stood hesitating, blaming myself for being without matches, I heard the movement repeated. Someone was quickly receding - escaping from the spot. I listened again. The sound was not of the rustling of leaves or the crackling of dried sticks, but the low thuds of a man's feet racing over softer ground. He had scaled the rough stone dyke and was out in the turnip-field adjacent.

I sprang through the gap, straining my eyes into the gloom, and as I did so could just distinguish a dark figure receding quickly beneath the wall of the wood.

In an instant I dashed after it. But the agility of whoever the fugitive was, man or woman, was marvelous. I considered myself a fairly good runner, but racing across those rough turnips and heavy, newly-plowed land in the darkness and carrying my gun soon caused me to pant and blow. Yet the figure I was pursuing was so fleet of foot and so nimble in climbing the high rough walls that from the very first I was outrun.

Down the steep hill to the Scarwater I followed the fugitive, crossing the old footbridge near Penpont, and then up a wild winding glen towards the Cairnsmore of Deugh. For a couple of miles or more I was close behind, until, at a turn in the dark wooded glen where it branched in two directions, I lost all trace of the person who flew from me. Whoever it was they had very cleverly gone into hiding in the undergrowth of one or other of the two glens - which I could not decide.

I stood out of breath, the perspiration pouring from me, undecided how to act.

Was it Leithcourt himself whom I had surprised?

That idea somehow became impressed upon me and I suddenly resolved to go boldly across to Rannoch and ascertain for myself. Therefore, with the excuse that I was belated on my walk home, I turned back down the glen, and half an hour afterward entered the great well-lighted hall of the castle where the guests, ready dressed, were assembling prior to dinner.

I was welcomed warmly, as I was always by the men of the party, who seeing my muddy plight at once offered me a glass of the sportsman's drink in Scotland, and while I was adding soda to it Leithcourt himself joined his guests, ready dressed in his dinner jacket, having just descended from his room.

"Hulloa, Gregg!" he exclaimed heartily, holding out his hand. "Had a long day of it, evidently. Good sport with Carmichael - eh?"

"Very fair," I said. "I remained longer with him than I ought to have done, and have got belated on my way home, so looked in for a refresher."

"Quite right," he laughed merrily. "You're always welcome, you know. I'd have been annoyed if I knew you had passed without coming in."

And Muriel, a pretty figure in a low-cut gown of turquoise chiffon, standing behind her father, smiled secretly at me. I smiled at her in return, but it was a strange smile, I fear, for with the knowledge of that additional mystery within me - the mystery of the woman lying unconscious or perhaps dead, up in the wood - held me stupefied.

I had suspected Leithcourt because of his constant trysts at that spot, but I had at least proved that my suspicions were entirely without foundation. He could not have got home and dressed in the time, for I had taken the nearest route to the castle while the fugitive would be compelled to make a wide detour.

I only remained a few minutes , then went forth into the

darkness again, utterly undecided how to act. My first impulse was to return to the woman's aid, for she might not be dead after all.

And yet when I recollected that hoarse cry that rang out in the darkness, I knew too well that she had been struck fatally. It was this latter conviction that prevented me from turning back to the wood. You will perhaps blame me, but the fact is I feared that if I went there suspicion might fall upon me, now that the real culprit had so ingeniously escaped.

If the victim were dead, what aid could I render? A knife had, I believed, been used, for my foot caught against it when I had started off after the fugitive. The only doubt in my own mind was whether the unfortunate woman was actually dead, for if she were not then my disinclination to return to the scene of the tragedy was culpable.

Whether or not I acted rightly in remaining away from the place, I leave it to you to judge in the light of the amazing truth which afterwards transpired.

I decided to walk straight back to my uncle's, and dinner was over before I had had my tub and dressed. I therefore ate my meal alone, Davis, the grave old butler, serving me with that stateliness which always amused me. I usually chatted with him when others were not present, but that night I remained silent, my mind full of that strange and startling affair of which I alone held secret knowledge.

Next day the body would surely be found; then the whole countryside would be filled with horror and surprise. Was it possible that Leithcourt, that calm, well-groomed, distinguished-looking man, held any knowledge of the ghastly truth? No. His manner as he stood in the hall chatting gayly with me was surely not that of a man with a guilty secret. I became firmly convinced that although the tragedy affected him very closely, and that it had occurred at the spot which he had each day visited for some mysterious purpose, yet up to the present he was in ignorance of what had transpired.

But who was the woman? Was she young or old?

A thousand times I regretted bitterly that I had no matches with me so that I might examine her features.

One sudden thought that struck me as I sat there at table caused me to lay down my fork and pause in breathless bewilderment. Was the victim that sweet-faced young girl whose photograph had been so ruthlessly cast from its frame and destroyed? The theory was a weird one, but was it the truth?

I longed for the coming of the dawn when the Rannoch keepers would most certainly discover her. Then at least I should know the truth, for I might go and see the body out of curiosity without arousing any suspicion.

I tried to play my usual game of billiards with my uncle, but my hand was so unsteady that the old gentleman began to chaff me.

"It's the gun, I suppose," I remarked. "I've been carrying it all day, and am tired out. I walked all the way home from Crossburn."

"The Carmichaels are very thick with the Leithcourts, I hear," my uncle remarked. "Strange they didn't ask Leithcourt to their shoot."

"They did, but he'd got another engagement - over at Kenmure Castle, I think."

I retired to my room that night full of fevered apprehension. Had I acted rightly in not returning to that lonely spot on the brow of the hill? Had I done as a man should do in keeping the tragic secret to myself?

I opened my window and gazed away across the dark Nithsdale, where, in the distant gloom, the black line of wood loomed up against the stormy sky. The stars were no longer shining and the rain clouds had gathered. I stood with my face turned to the dark indistinct spot that held the secret, lost in wonderment.

At last I closed the window and turned in, but no sleep came to my eyes, so full was my mind of the startling events of those past few months and of that gruesome discovery I had made.

Had the fugitive actually recognized me? Probably my voice when I had called out had betrayed me. Hour after hour I lay puzzling, trying to arrive at some solution of that intricate problem which now presented itself. Muriel could tell me what I wished to know. Of that I was certain. Yet she dared not speak. Some inexpressible terror held her dumb - she was affianced to the man Martin Woodroffe.

Again I rose, lit the gas, and tried to read a novel. But I could not concentrate my thoughts, which were ever wandering to that strange mystery of the wood. At six I shaved, descended, and went out with the dogs for a short walk; but on returning I heard of nothing unusual, and was compelled to remain inactive until near mid-day.

I was crossing the stable-yard where I had gone to order the carriage for my aunt, when an English groom, suddenly emerging from the harness-room, touched his cap, saying -

"Have you 'eard, sir, of the awful affair up yonder?"

"Of what?" I asked quickly.

"Well, sir, there seems to have been a murder last night up in Rannoch Wood," said the man quickly. "Holden, the gardener, has just come back from that village and says that Mr. Leithcourt's under-gamekeeper as he was going home at five this morning came upon a dead body."

"A dead body!" I exclaimed, feigning great surprise.

"Yes, sir - a youngish man. He'd been stabbed to the heart."

"A man!"

"Yes, sir - so Holden says."

"Call Holden. I'd like to know all he's heard," I said. And presently, when the gardener emerged from the grape-house, I sought of him all the particulars he had gathered.

"I don't know very much, sir," was the man's reply. "I went into the inn for a glass of beer at eleven, as I always do, and heard them talking about it. A young man was murdered last night up in Rannoch Wood. The gamekeeper thought at first there'd been a fight among poachers, but from the dead man's clothes they say he isn't a poacher at all, but a stranger in this district."

"The body was that of a man, then?" I asked, trying to conceal my utter bewilderment.

"Yes - about thirty, they say. The police have taken him to the mortuary at Dumfries, and the detectives are up there now looking at the spot, they say."

A man! And yet the body I found was that of a woman - that I could swear.

After lunch I took the dog-cart and drove alone into Dumfries.

When I inquired of the police-constable on duty at the town mortuary to be allowed to view the body of the murdered man, he regarded me, I thought, with considerable suspicion. My request was an unusual one. Nevertheless, he took me up a narrow alley, unlocked a door, and I found myself in the cold, gloomy chamber of death. From a small dingy window above the light fell upon an object lying upon a large slab of gray stone and covered with a soiled sheet.

The sight was ghastly and gruesome; the body lay there awaiting the official inquiry into the cause of death. The silence of the tomb was unbroken, save for the heavy tread of the policeman, who having removed his helmet in the presence of the dead, lifted the end of the sheet, revealing to me a white, hard-set face, with closed eyes and dropped jaw.

I started back as my eyes fell upon the dead countenance. I was entirely unprepared for such a revelation. The truth staggered me.

The victim was the man who had acted as my friend - the Italian waiter, Olinto.

I advanced and peered into the thin inanimate features, scarce able to realize the actual fact. But my eyes had not deceived me. Though death distorts the facial expression of every man, I had no difficulty in identifying him.

"You recognize him, sir?" remarked the officer. "Who is he? Our people are very anxious to know, for up to the present moment they haven't succeeded in establishing his identity."

I bit my lips. I had been an arrant fool to betray myself before that man. Yet having done so, I saw that any attempt to conceal my knowledge must of necessity reflect upon me.

"I will see your inspector," I answered with as much calmness as I could muster. "Where has the poor fellow been wounded?"

"Through the heart," responded the constable, as turning the sheet further down he showed me the small knife wound which had penetrated the victim's jacket and vest full in the chest.

"This is the weapon," he added, taking from a shelf close by a long, thin poignard with an ivory handle, which he handed to me.

In an instant I recognized what it was, and how deadly. It was an old Florentine *misericordia*, a long thin, triangular blade, a quarter of an inch wide at its greatest width, tapering to a needle-point, with a hilt of yellow ivory, the most deadly and fatal of all the daggers and poignards of the Middle Ages. The blade being sharp on three angles produced a wound that caused internal hemorrhage and which never healed - hence the name given to it by the Florentines.

It was still blood-stained, but as I took the deadly thing in my hand I saw that its blade was beautifully damascened, a most elegant specimen of a medieval arm. Yet surely none but an Italian would use such a weapon, or would aim so truly as to penetrate the heart.

And yet the person struck down was a woman, and not a man!

A wound from a *misericordia* always proves fatal, because the shape of the blade cuts the flesh into little flaps which, on withdrawing the knife, close up and prevent the blood from issuing forth. At the same time, however, no power can make them heal again. A blow from such a weapon is as surely fatal as the poisoned poignard of the Borgia or the Medici.

I handed the stiletto back to the man without comment. My resolve was to say as little as possible, for I had no desire to figure publicly at the inquiry, and consequently negative all my own efforts to solve the mystery of the Leithcourts and of Martin Woodroffe.

I returned to where the figure was lying so ghastly and motionless, and looked again for the last time upon the dead face of the man who had served me so well, and yet who had enticed me so nearly to my death. In the latter incident there was a deep mystery. He had relented at the last moment, just in time to save me from my secret enemies.

Could it be that my enemies were his? Had he fallen a victim by the same hand that had attempted so ingeniously to kill me?

Why had Leithcourt gone so regularly up to Rannoch Wood? Was it in order to meet the man who was to be entrapped and killed? What was Olinto Santini doing so far from London, if he had not come expressly to meet someone in secret?

As I glanced down at the cold, inanimate countenance upon which mystery was written, I became seized by regret. He had been a faithful and honest servant, and even though he had enticed me to that fatal house in Lambeth, yet I recollected his words, how he had done so under compulsion. I remembered, too, how he had implored me not to prejudge him before I became aware of the full facts.

With my own hand I re-covered the face with the sheet, and inwardly resolved to avenge the dastardly crime.

I regretted that I was compelled to reveal the dead man's name to the police, yet I saw that to make some statement was now inevitable, and therefore I accompanied the constable to the inspector's office some distance across the town.

Having been introduced to the big, fair-haired man in a rough tweed suit, who was apparently directing the inquiries into the affair, he took me eagerly into a small back room and began to question me. I was, however, wary not to commit myself to anything further than the identification of the body.

"The fact is," I said confidentially, "you must omit me from the witnesses at the inquest."

"Why?" asked the detective suspiciously.

"Because if it were known that I have identified him, all chance of getting at the truth will at once vanish," I answered. "I have come here to tell you in strictest confidence who the poor fellow really is."

"Then you know something of the affair?" he said, with a strong Highland accent.

"I know nothing," I declared. "Nothing except his name."

"H'm. And you say he's a foreigner - an Italian - eh?"

"He was in my service in Leghorn for several years, and on leaving me he came to London and obtained an engagement as waiter in a restaurant. His father lived in Leghorn; he was doorkeeper at the Prefecture."

"But why was he here, in Scotland?"

"How can I tell?"

"You know something of the affair. I mean that you suspect somebody, or you would have no objection to giving evidence at the inquiry."

"I have no suspicions. To me the affair is just as much of an enigma as to you," I hastened at once to explain. "My only fear is that if the assassin knew that I had identified him he would take care not to betray himself."

"You therefore think he will betray himself?"

"I hope so."

"By the fact that the man was attacked with an Italian stiletto, it would seem that his assailant was a fellow-countryman," suggested the detective.

"The evidence certainly points to that," I replied.

"You don't happen to be aware of anyone - any foreigner, I mean - who was, or might be his enemy?"

I responded in the negative.

"Ah," he went on, "these foreigners are always fighting among themselves and using knives. I did ten years' service in Edinburgh and made lots of arrests for stabbing affrays. Italians, like Greeks, are a dangerous lot when their blood is up." Then he added: "Personally, it seems to me that the murdered man was enticed from London to that spot and coolly done away with - from some motive of revenge, most probably."

"Most probably," I said. "A vendetta, perhaps. I live in Italy, and therefore know the Italians well," I added.

I had given him my card, and told him with whom I was staying.

"Where were you yesterday, sir?" he inquired presently.

"I was shooting - on the other side of the Nithsdale," I answered, and then went on to explain my movements, without, however, mentioning my visit to Rannoch.

"And although you know the murdered man so intimately, you have no suspicion of anyone in this district who was acquainted with him?"

"I know no one who knew him. When he left my service he had never been in England."

"You say he was engaged in service in London?"

"Yes, at a restaurant in Oxford Street, I believe. I met him accidentally in Pall Mall one evening, and he told me so."

"You don't know the name of the restaurant?"

"He did tell me, but unfortunately I have forgotten."

The detective drew a deep breath of regret.

"Someone who waited for him on the edge of that wood

stepped out and killed him - that's evident," he said.

"Without a doubt."

"And my belief is that it was an Italian. There were two foreigners who slept at a common lodging-house two nights ago and went on tramp towards Glasgow. We have telegraphed after them, and hope we shall find them. Scotsmen or Englishmen never use a knife of that pattern."

With his latter remark I entirely coincided. In my own mind that was the strongest argument in favor of Leithcourt's innocence. That the tenant of Rannoch had kept that secret tryst in daily patience I knew from my own observations, yet to me it scarcely seemed feasible that he would use a weapon so peculiarly Italian and yet so terribly deadly.

And then when I reflected further, recollecting that the body I had discovered was that of a woman and not a man, I stood staggered and bewildered by the utterly inexplicable enigma.

I promised the burly detective that in exchange for his secrecy regarding my statement that I would assist him in every manner possible in the solution of the problem.

"The real name of the murdered man must be at all costs withheld," I urged. "It must not appear in the papers, for I feel confident that only by the pretense that he is unknown can we arrive at the truth. If his name is given at the inquiry, then the assassin will certainly know that I have identified him."

"And what then?"

"Well," I said with some hesitation, "while I am believed to be in ignorance we shall have opportunity for obtaining the truth."

"Then you do really suspect?" he said, again looking at me with those cold, blue eyes.

"I know not whom to suspect," I declared. "It is a mystery why the man who was once my faithful servant should be enticed to that wood and stabbed to the heart."

"There is no one in the vicinity who knew him?"

"Not to my knowledge."

"We might obtain his address in London through his father in Leghorn," suggested the officer.

"I will write to-day if you so desire," I said readily. "Indeed, I will get my friend the British Consul to go round and see the old man and telegraph the address if he obtains it."

"Capital!" he declared. "If you will do us this favor we shall be greatly indebted to you. It is fortunate that we have established the victim's identity - otherwise we might be entirely in the dark. A murdered foreigner is always more or less of a mystery."

Therefore, then and there, I took a sheet of paper and wrote to my old friend Hutcheson at Leghorn, asking him to make immediate inquiry of Olinto's father as to his son's address in London.

I said nothing to the police of that strange adventure of mine over in Lambeth, or of how the man now dead had saved my life. That his enemies were my own he had most distinctly told me, therefore I felt some apprehension that I myself was not safe. Yet in my hip pocket I always carried my revolver - just as I did in Italy - and I rather prided myself on my ability to shoot straight.

We sat for a long time discussing the strange affair. In order to betray no eagerness to get away, I offered the big Highlander a cigar from my case, and we smoked together. The inquiry would be held on the morrow, he told me, but as far as the public was concerned the body would remain as that of some person "unknown."

"And you had better not come to my uncle's house, or send anyone," I said. "If you desire to see me, send me a line and I will meet you here in Dumfries. It will be safer."

The officer looked at me with those keen eyes of his, and said:

"Really, Mr. Gregg, I can't quite make you out, I confess. You seem to be apprehensive of your own safety. Why?"

"Italians are a very curious people," I responded quickly. "Their vendetta extends widely sometimes."

"Then you have reason to believe that the enemy of this poor fellow Santini may be your enemy also?"

"One never knows whom one offends when living in Italy," I laughed, as lightly as I could, endeavoring to allay his suspicion. "He may have fallen beneath the assassin's knife by giving quite a small and possibly innocent offense to somebody. Italian methods are not English, you know."

"By Jove, sir, and I'm jolly glad they're not!" he said. "I shouldn't think a police officer's life is a very safe one among all those secret murder societies I've read about."

"Ah! what you read about them is often very much exaggerated," I assured him. "It is the vendetta which is such a stain upon the character of the modern Italian; and depend upon it this affair in Rannoch Wood is the outcome of some revenge or other - probably over a love affair."

"But you will assist us, sir?" he urged. "You know the Italian language, which will be of great advantage; besides, the victim was your servant."

"Be discreet," I said. "And in return I will do my very utmost to assist you in hunting down the assassin."

And thus we made our compact. Half-an-hour after I was driving in the dog-cart through the pouring rain up the hill out of gray old Dumfries to my uncle's house.

As I descended from the cart and gave it over to a groom, old Davis, the butler, came forward, saying in a low voice:

"There's Miss Leithcourt waiting to see you, Mr. Gordon. She's in the morning-room, and been there an hour. She asked me not to tell anyone else she's here, sir."

"Then my aunt has not seen her?" I exclaimed, scenting mystery in this unexpected visit.

"No, sir. She wishes to see you alone, sir."

I walked across the big hall and along the corridor to the room the old man had indicated.

And as I opened the door and Muriel Leithcourt in plain black rose to meet me, I plainly saw from her white, haggard countenance that something had happened - that she had been forced by circumstances to come to me in strictest confidence.

Was she, I wondered, about to reveal to me the truth?

CHAPTER VI

THE GATHERING OF THE CLOUDS

"Mr. Gregg," exclaimed the girl with agitation, as she put forth her black-gloved hand, "I - I suppose you know - you've heard all about the discovery to-day up at the wood? I need not tell you anything about it"

"Yes, Miss Leithcourt, I only wish you would tell me about it," I said gravely, inviting her to a chair and seating myself. "I've heard some extraordinary story about a man being found dead, but I've been in Dumfries nearly all day. Who is the man?"

"Ah! that we don't know," she replied, pale-faced and anxious. Her attitude was as though she wished to confide in me and yet still hesitated to do so.

"You've been waiting for me quite a long time, Davis tells me. I regret that you should have done this. If you had left word that you wished to see me, I would have come over to you at once."

"No. I wanted to see you alone - that's the reason I am here. They must not know at home that I've been over here, so I purposely asked the man not to announce me to your aunt."

"You want to see me privately," I said in a low, earnest voice. "Why? Is there any service I can render you?"

"Yes. A very great one," she responded with quick eagerness, "I - well - the fact is, I have summoned courage to come to you and beg of you to help me. I am in great distress - and I have not a single friend whom I can trust - in whom I can confide."

"I shall esteem it the highest honor if you will trust me," I said in deep earnestness. "I can only assure you that I will remain loyal to your interests and to yourself."

"Ah! I believe you will, Mr. Gregg!" she declared with enthusiasm, her large, dark eyes turned upon me - the eyes of a woman in sheer and bitter despair. Her face was perfect, one of the most handsome I had ever gazed upon. The more I saw of her the greater was the fascination she held over me.

A silence fell between us as she sat with her gloved hands lying idly in her lap. Her lips moved nervously, but no sound came from them, so agitated was she, so eager to tell me something; and yet at the same time reluctant to take me into her confidence.

"Well?" I asked at last in a low voice. "I am quite ready to render you any service, if you will only command me."

"Ah! But I fear what I require will strike you as so unusual - you will hesitate to act when I explain what service I require of you," she said doubtfully.

"I cannot tell you until I hear your wishes," I said, smiling, and yet puzzled at her attitude.

"It concerns the terrible discovery made up in Rannoch Wood," she said in a hoarse, nervous voice at last. "That unknown man was murdered - stabbed to the heart."

"Well?"

"Well," she said, scarcely above a whisper, "I have suspicions."

"Of the murdered man's identity?"

"No. Of the assassin."

I glanced at her sharply and saw the intense look in her dark, wide-open eyes.

"You believe you know who dealt the blow?"

"I have a suspicion - that is all. Only I want you to help me, if you will."

"Most certainly," I responded. "But if you believe you know the assassin you probably know something of the victim?"

"Only that he looked like a foreigner."

"Then you have seen him?" I exclaimed, much surprised.

My remark caused her to hold her breath for an instant. Then she answered, rather lamely, it seemed to me:

"I saw him when the keepers brought the body to the castle."

Now, according to the account I had heard, the police had conveyed the dead man direct from the wood into Dumfries. Was it possible, therefore, that she had seen Olinto before he met with his sudden end?

I feared to press her for an explanation at that moment, but, nevertheless, the admission that she had seen him struck me as a very peculiar fact.

"You judge him to be a foreigner?" I remarked as casually as I could.

"From his features and complexion I guessed him to be Italian," she responded quickly, at which I pretended to express surprise. "I saw him after the keepers had found him."

"Besides," she went on, "the stiletto was evidently an Italian one, which would almost make it appear that a foreigner was the assassin."

"Is that your own suspicion?"

"No."

"Why?"

She hesitated a moment, then in a low, eager voice she said:

"Because I have already seen that three-edged knife in another person's possession."

"That's pretty strong evidence," I declared. "The person in question will have to prove that he was not in Rannoch Wood last evening at nightfall."

"How do you know it was done at nightfall?" she asked quickly with some surprise, half-rising from her chair.

"I merely surmised that it was," I responded, inwardly blaming myself for my ill-timed admission.

"Ah!" she said with a slight sigh, "there is more mystery in this affair than we have yet discovered, Mr. Gregg. What, I wonder, brought the unfortunate young man up into our wood?"

"An appointment, without a doubt. But with whom?"

She shook her head, saying:

"My father often goes to that spot to shoot pigeon in the evening. He told us so at luncheon to-day. How fortunate he was not there last night, or he might be suspected."

"Yes," I said. "It is a very fortunate circumstance, for it cannot be a pleasant experience to be under suspicion of being an assassin. He was at home last night, was he?" I added casually.

"Of course. Don't you recollect that when you called he chatted with you? I did some typewriting for him in the study, and we were together all the afternoon - or at least till nearly five o'clock, when we went out into the hall to tea."

"Then what is your theory regarding the affair?" I inquired, rather puzzled why she should so decisively prove an alibi for her father.

"It seems certain that the poor fellow went to the wood by appointment, and was killed. But have you been up to the spot since the finding of the body?"

"No. Have you?"

"Yes. The affair interested me, and as soon as I recognized the old Italian knife in the hand of the keeper, I went up there and looked about. I am glad I did so, for I found something which seems to have escaped the notice of the detectives."

"And what's that?" I asked eagerly.

"Why, about three yards from the pool of blood where the unfortunate foreigner was found is another small pool of blood where the grass and ferns around are all crushed down as though there had been a struggle there."

"There may have been a struggle at that spot, and the man may have staggered some distance before he fell dead."

"Not if he had been struck in the heart, as they say. He would fall, would he not?" she suggested. "No. The police seem very dense, and this plain fact has not yet occurred to them. Their theory is the same as what you suggest, but my own is something quite different, Mr. Gregg. I believe that a second person also fell a victim," she added in a low, distinct tone.

I gazed at her open-mouthed. Did she, I wondered, know the actual truth? Was she aware that the woman who had fallen there had disappeared?

"A second person!" I echoed, as though in surprise. "Then do you believe that a double murder was committed?"

"I draw my conclusion from the fact that the young man, on being struck in the heart, could not have gone such a distance as that which separates the one mark from the other."

"But he might have been slightly wounded - on the hand, or in the face - at first, and then at the spot where he was found struck fatally," I suggested.

She shook her head dubiously, but made no reply to my argument. Her confidence in her own surmises made it quite apparent that by some unknown means she was aware of the second victim. Indeed, a few moments later she said to me:

"It is for this reason, Mr. Gregg, that I have sought you in confidence. Nobody must know that I have come here to you, or they would suspect; and if suspicion fell upon me it would bring upon me a fate worse than death. Remember, therefore, that my future is entirely in your hands."

"I don't quite understand," I said, rising and standing before her in the fading twilight, while the rain drove upon the old diamond window panes. "But I can only assure you that whatever confidence you repose in me, I shall never abuse, Miss Leithcourt."

"I know, I know!" she said quickly. "I trust you in this matter implicitly. I have come to you for many reasons, chief of them being that if a second victim has fallen beneath the hand of the assassin, it is, I know, a woman."

"A woman! Whom?"

"At present I cannot tell you. I must first establish the true facts. If this woman were really stricken down, then her body lies concealed somewhere in the vicinity. We must find it and bring home the crime to the guilty one."

"But if we succeed in finding it, could we place our hand upon the assassin?" I asked, looking straight at her.

"If we find it, the crime would then tell its own tale - it would convict the person in whose hand I have seen that fatal weapon," was her clear, bold answer.

"Then you wish me to assist you in this search, Miss Leithcourt?" I said, wondering if her suspicions rested upon that mysterious yachtsman, Philip Hornby, the man to whom she was engaged.

"Yes, I would beg of you to do your utmost in secret to endeavor to discover the body of the second victim. It is a woman - of that I am certain. Find her, and we shall then be able to bring the crime home to the assassin."

"But my search may bring suspicion upon me," I remarked. "It will be difficult to examine the whole wood without arousing the curiosity of somebody - the keeper or the police."

"I have already thought of that," she said. "I will pretend to-morrow to lose this watch-bracelet in the wood," and she held up her slim wrist to show me the little enameled watch set in her bracelet. "Then you and I will search for it diligently, and the police will never suspect the real reason of our investigation. To-morrow I shall write to you telling you about my loss, and you will come over to Rannoch and offer to help me."

I was silent for a moment.

"Is Mr. Woodroffe back at the castle? I heard he was to return to-day."

"No. I had a letter from him from Bordeaux a week ago. He is still on the Continent. I believe, indeed, he has gone to Russia, where he sometimes has business."

"I asked you the question, Miss Muriel, because I thought if Mr. Woodroffe were here, he might object to our searching in company," I explained, smiling.

Her cheeks flushed slightly, as though confused at my reference to her engagement, and she said mischievously:

"I don't see why he should object in the least. If you are good enough to assist me to search for my bracelet, he surely ought to be much obliged to you."

It was on the tip of my tongue to explain to that dark-eyed, handsome girl the circumstances in which I had met her lover on the sunny Mediterranean shore, yet prudence forbade me to refer to the matter, and I at once gladly accepted her invitation to investigate the curious disappearance of the body of poor Olinto's fellow-victim.

What secret knowledge could be possessed by that smart, handsome girl before me? That her suspicions were in the right direction I felt confident, yet if the dead woman had been removed and hidden by the assassin it must have been after the discovery made by me. The fellow must have actually dared to return to the spot and carry off the victim. Yet if he had actually done that, why did he allow the corpse of the Italian to remain and await discovery? He might perhaps have been disturbed and compelled to make good his escape.

"If the woman was really removed the assassin must surely have had some assistance," I pointed out. "He could not have carried the body very far unaided."

She agreed with me, but expressed a belief that the double crime had been committed alone and unaided.

"Have you any idea as to the motive?" I asked her, eager to hear her reply.

"Well," she answered hesitatingly, "if the woman has fallen a victim, the motive will become plain; but if not, then the matter must remain a complete mystery."

"You tell me, Miss Muriel, that you suspect the truth, and yet you deny all knowledge of the murdered man!" I exclaimed in a tone of slight reproach.

"Until we have cleared up the mystery of the woman I can say nothing," was her answer. "I can only tell you, Mr. Gregg, that if what I suspect is true, then the affair will be found to be one of the strangest, most startling and most ingenious plots ever devised by one man against the life of another."

"Then a man is the assassin, you think?" I exclaimed quickly.

"I believe so. But even of that I am not at all sure. We must first find the woman."

She seemed so positive that a woman had also fallen beneath that deadly *misericordia* that I fell to wondering whether she, like myself, had discovered the body, and was therefore certain that a second crime had been committed. But I did not seek to question her further, lest her own suspicions might become aroused. My own policy was to remain silent and to wait. The woman sitting before me was herself a mystery.

Then, when the rain had abated, I told Davis to send her trap a little way up the high-road, so that my aunt and uncle should not see her departing; and after helping her on with her loose driving-coat, we left by one of the servants' entrances, and I saw her into her high dog-cart and stood bareheaded in the muddy high-road as she drove away into the gloom.

* * * * *

Rannoch Wood was already in its gold-brown glory of

autumn, and as I stood with Muriel Leithcourt on the edge of it, near the spot where Olinto Santini had fallen, the morning sun was shining in a cloudless sky.

True to her promise, she had sent me a note by one of the grooms asking me to help search for her bracelet, and I had driven over at once to Rannoch and found her alone awaiting me. The shooting party had gone over to a distant part of the estate, therefore we were able to stroll together up the hill and commence our investigations without let or hindrance. She was sensibly dressed in a short tweed skirt, high shooting-boots and a tam-o'-shanter hat, while I also had on an old shooting-suit and carried a thick serviceable stick with which I could prod likely spots.

On arrival at the wood I asked her opinion which was the most likely corner, but she replied:

"I know so little of this place, Mr. Gregg. You have known it for years, while this is only my first season here."

"Very well," I answered. "Let us place ourselves in the position of the murderer, who probably knew the wood and wished to conceal a body in the vicinity without risk of conveying it far. On this, the left side, the wood has been thinned out for nearly half a mile, and therefore affords but little cover, while here, to the right, it slopes down gently to the valley and is very thick and partly impenetrable. There can therefore have been no two courses open to him. He would look for a likely place to the right. Let us start here, and first take a small circle, examining every bush carefully. The body may have easily been pushed in beneath a thicket and well escape observation."

And so together, after taking our bearings, we started off, working our way into the thick undergrowth, beating with our sticks, and making minute examination of every bush or heap of dead leaves. In parts, the great spreading trees shut out the light, rendering our investigations very difficult; but we kept on, my companion advancing with an eagerness which showed that the fact of the woman's body being there was no mere surmise.

All through the morning we walked on, our hands badly torn by brambles. Even Muriel's thick gloves did not wholly protect her, and once when she received a nasty scratch across the cheek, she stopped and laughingly exclaimed:

"Now what untruth must I invent to account for that?"

My own coat was badly torn, and more than once I was compelled to scramble through almost impassable thickets; yet we found no trace of any previous intruder, and having completed our circle were compelled to admit that the gruesome evidence of the second crime did not exist at that spot.

More than once I felt half inclined to tell her how I had actually discovered the body of the woman, yet on reflection I foresaw that in such circumstances silence was best. If I desired to solve the strange complicated enigma which had thus culminated in a double crime, it would be necessary for me to keep my own counsel and remain patient and watchful.

When Hutcheson replied from Leghorn, and when I discovered where Olinto was employed, I might perhaps follow up the clues from that end. I might find his wife Armida and learn something of importance from her. So I was hopeful, and by reason of that hope remained silent.

Muriel was untiring in her activity. Hither and thither she went, beating down the high bracken and tangles of weeds, poking with her stick into every hole and corner, and going further and further into the wood in the certainty that the body was therein concealed.

For my own part, however, I was not too sanguine of success. The portion of the wood which we had already exhausted seemed to be the most likely point. To carry the body far would require assistance, and in my own mind I believed the crime to have been the work of one person. There was no path in the wood in that direction, but soon we came to a deep wooded ravine of the existence of which I was in ignorance. It was a kind of small glen through which a rivulet flowed, but the banks were covered with a thick impenetrable undergrowth out of which sprang many fine old trees, a place that had apparently existed for centuries undisturbed, for here and there a giant trunk that had decayed and fallen lay across the bank, or had rolled into the rocky bed far below.

"This is a most likely place," declared my dainty little companion as we approached it. "Anything could easily be concealed in that high bracken down there. Let us search the whole glen from end to end," she cried with enthusiasm.

Acting upon her suggestion and without thought of luncheon, we made a descent of the steep bank until we reached the rocky bed of the stream, and then by springing from stone to stone - sometimes slipping into the water, be it said - we commenced to beat the bracken and carefully examine every bush. Progress was not swift. Once the girl, lithe and athletic as she was, slipped off a mossy stone into a hole where the water was up to her knees. But she only laughed gayly at the accident, and wringing out her wet skirt, said:

"It doesn't matter in the least, if we only find what we're in search of."

And then, undaunted, she went on, springing from stone to stone and steadying herself with her stick. If we could only discover the body of the dead woman, then the rest would be clear, she declared. She would openly denounce the assassin.

As we went on I revolved within my mind all the curious circumstances in connection with the amazing affair, and recollected my old friend Jack Durnford's words when we stood upon the quarter-deck of the *Bulwark* and I had related to him the visit of the mysterious yacht. I too had left one effort untried, and I blamed myself for overlooking it. I had not sought of that Bond Street photographer the name and address of the original of the photograph that had been mutilated and destroyed - that girl with the magnificent eyes that had so attracted me.

The afternoon passed, and yet we were not successful. I was faint with hunger and thirst, yet my companion did not once complain. Her energy was marvelous - and yet was she not hunting down a criminal? was she not determined to obtain such evidence as would enable her to speak the truth fearlessly, and with confidence that it would have the effect of convicting the guilty one?

Slowly we toiled on up the picturesque little glen for nearly a mile and a half. Its beauties were extraordinary, and the silence was unbroken save for the musical ripple of the water over the stones. Hidden there in the center of that great wood, no one had visited it perhaps for years, not even the keepers, for no path led there, and by reason of the tangle of briars and bush it was utterly ungetatable. Indeed, it had ruined our clothes to search there, and as we went on with so many windings and turns we became utterly out of our bearings. We knew ourselves to be in the center of the wood, but that was all.

The sun had set, and the sky above showed the crimson of the distant afterglow, warning us that it was time we began to think of how to make our exit. We were passing around a sharp bend in the glen where the boulders were so thickly moss-grown that our feet fell noiselessly, when I thought I heard a voice, and raising my hand we both halted suddenly.

"Someone is there," I whispered quickly. "Behind that rock." She nodded in the affirmative, for she, too, had heard the voice.

We listened, but the sound was not repeated. That someone was on the other side of the rock I knew, for in a tree in the vicinity a thrush was hopping from twig to twig, sounding its alarm-cry and objecting to being disturbed.

Therefore we crept silently forward together to ascertain who were the intruders. The only manner, however, in which to get a view beyond the huge rock that, having fallen across the stream centuries ago, had diverted its channel, was to clamber up its mossy sides to the summit. This we did eagerly and breathlessly, without betraying our presence by the utterance of a single word.

To reach the side of the boulder we were compelled to walk through the shallow water, but Muriel, quite undaunted, sprang lithely along at my side, and with one accord we swarmed up the steep rock, gripping its slippery face with our hands and laying ourselves flat as we came to its summit.

Then together we peered over, just, however, in time to see two dark figures of men disappearing into the thicket on the opposite side of the glen.

"Who are they, I wonder?" I asked. "Do you recognize them?"

"No. They are entire strangers to me," was her answer. "But they seem fairly well dressed. Perhaps two sportsmen from some shooting-party in the neighborhood. They've lost their way most probably."

"But I don't think they carried guns," I said. "One of them had something over his shoulder?"

"Wasn't it a gun? I thought it was."

"No, he wasn't carrying it like he'd carry a gun. It was short - and seemed more like a spade."

"A spade!" she gasped quickly in a low voice. "A spade! Are you certain of that?"

"No, not at all certain. We only had an instantaneous glance of them. We were unfortunately too late to see them face to face."

"The back of one of the men, the tall fellow in the brown suit, was broad and square - the back of someone who is familiar to me, only for the moment I can't recollect whose it resembles." She only spoke in a whisper, fearing lest we should be discovered.

I longed to scramble down and rush after the intruders, only the belief that one of them carried a spade and the other an iron bar struck me as curious, while at the same moment my eye caught sight of a portion of the ground below us at the base of the rock which had evidently been recently disturbed.

"It is a spade the man is carrying!" I cried excitedly. "Look down there! They've just been burying something!"

Her quick eyes followed the direction I indicated, and she answered:

"I really believe they have concealed something!"

Then when we had allowed the men to get beyond hearing, we both slipped down to the other side of the boulder and there discovered many signs that the earth had been hurriedly excavated and only just replaced.

Quicker than it takes to describe the exciting incident which followed, we broke down the branch of a tree and with it commenced moving the freshly disturbed earth, which was still soft and easily removed.

Muriel found a dead branch in the vicinity, and both of us set to work with a will, eager to ascertain what was hidden there. That something had certainly been concealed was, to us, quite evident, but what it really was we could not surmise. The hole they had dug did not seem large enough to admit a human body, yet leaves had been carefully strewn over the place which, if approached from any other point than the high-up one whence we had seen it, would arouse no suspicion that the ground had ever been interfered with.

Digging with a piece of wood was hard and laborious work and it was a long time before we removed sufficient earth to make a hole of any size. But Muriel exerted all her energy, and both of us worked on in dogged silence full of wonder and anticipation. With a spade we should have soon been able to investigate, but the earth having apparently been stamped down hard prior to the last covering being put upon it, our progress was very slow and difficult.

At last, a quarter of an hour or so after we had commenced, Muriel, standing in the hole and having dug her stake deeply into the ground, suddenly cried:

"Look! Look, Mr. Gregg! Why - whatever is that?"

I bent forward as she indicated, and my eyes met an object so unexpected that I was held dumb and motionless.

By what we had succeeded in discovering, the mystery was increased rather than diminished.

I gave vent to an ejaculation of complete bewilderment, and looked blankly into my companion's face.

The amazing enigma was surely complete!

CHAPTER VII

CONTAINS A SURPRISE

The first object brought to light, about two feet beneath the surface, was a piece of dark gray woolen stuff which, when the mold was removed, proved to be part of a woman's skirt.

With frantic eagerness I got into the hole we had made and removed the soil with my hands, until I suddenly touched something hard.

A body lay there, doubled up and crushed into the well-like hole the men had dug.

Together we pulled it out, when, to my surprise, on wiping away the dirt from the hard waxen features, I recognized it as the body of Armida, the woman who had been my servant in Leghorn and who had afterwards married Olinto. Both had been assassinated!

When Muriel gazed upon the dead woman's face she gave vent to an expression of surprise. The body was evidently not that of the person she had expected to find.

"Who is she, I wonder?" my companion ejaculated. "Not a lady, evidently, by her dress and hands."

"Evidently not," was my response, for I still deemed it best to keep my own counsel. I recollected the story Olinto had told me about his wife; of her illness and her longing to return to Italy. Yet the dead woman's countenance must have been healthy enough in life, although her hands were rough and hard, showing that she had been doing manual labor.

Armida had been a particularly good housemaid, a black-haired, black-eyed Tuscan, quick, cleanly, and full of a keen sense of humor. It was a great shock to me to find her lying there dead. The breast of her dress was stained with dried blood, which, on examination, I found had issued from a deep and fatal wound beneath the ear where she had been struck an unerring blow that had severed the artery.

"Those men - those men who buried her! I wonder who they were?" my companion exclaimed in a hushed voice. "We must follow them and ascertain. They are certainly the murderers who have returned in secret and concealed the evidence of this second crime."

"Yes," I said. "Let us go after them. They must not escape us."

Then, leaving the exhumed body beneath a tree, I caught Muriel by the waist and waded across the deep channel worn by the stream at that point, after which we both ascended the steep bank where the pair had disappeared in the darkness of the wood.

I blamed myself a thousand times for not following them, yet my suspicions had not been aroused until after they had disappeared. The back of the man in a snuff-colored suit was, she felt confident, familiar to her. She repeated what she had already told me, yet she could not remember where she had seen a similar figure before.

We went on through the gloomy forest, for the light had faded and evening was now creeping on. From time to time we halted and listened. But there was a dead silence, broken only by the shrill cry of a night bird and the low rustling of the leaves in the autumn wind. The men knew their way, it seemed, even though the wood was trackless. Yet they had nearly twenty minutes start of us, and in that time they might be already out in the open country. Would they succeed in evading us? Yet even if they did, I could describe the dress of one of them, while that of his companion was, as far as I made out, dark blue, of a somewhat nautical cut. He wore also a flat cap, with a peak.

We went on, striking straight for the open moorland which we knew bounded the woods in that direction, and before the light had entirely faded we found ourselves out amongst the heather with the distant hills looming dark against the horizon. But we saw no sign of the men who had so secretly concealed the body of their victim.

"I will take you back to the castle, Miss Leithcourt," I said. "And then I'll drive on into Dumfries and see the police. These men must be arrested."

"Yes, do," she urged. "I will get into the house by the stable-yard, for they must not see me in this terrible plight."

It was rough walking, therefore at my invitation she took my arm, and as she did so I felt that she was shivering.

"You are very wet," I remarked. "I hope you won't take cold."

"Oh! I'm used to getting wet. I drive and cycle a lot, you know, and very often get drenched," was her reply. Then after a pause she said: "We must discover who that woman was. She seems, from her complexion and her hair, to be a foreigner, like the man."

"Yes, I think so," was my reply. "I will tell the police all that we have found out, and they will go there presently and recover the body."

"If they can only find those two men, then we should know the truth," she declared. "One of them - the one in brown - was unusually broad-shouldered, and seemed to walk with a slight stoop."

"You expected to discover another woman, did you not, Miss Leithcourt?" I asked presently, as we walked across the moor.

"Yes," she answered. "I expected to find an entirely different person."

"And if you had found her it would have proved the guilt of someone with whom you are acquainted?"

She nodded in the affirmative.

"Then what we have found this evening does not convey to you the identity of the assassins?"

"No, unfortunately it does not. We must for the present leave the matter in the hands of the police."

"But if the identity of the dead woman is established?" I asked.

"It might furnish me with a clue," she exclaimed quickly. "Yes, try and discover who she is."

"Who was the woman you expected to find?"

"A friend - a very dear friend."

"Will you not tell me her name?" I inquired.

"No, it would be unfair to her," she responded decisively, an answer which to me was particularly tantalizing.

On we plodded in silence, our thoughts too full for words. Was it not strange that the mysterious yachtsman should be her lover, and stranger still that on recognizing me he should have escaped, not only from Scotland, but away to the Continent?

Was not that, in itself, evidence of guilt and fear?

It was quite dark when I took leave of my bright little companion, who, tired out and yet uncomplaining, pressed my
hand and wished me good fortune in my investigations.

"I shall await you to-morrow afternoon. Call and tell me
everything, won't you?"

I promised, and then she disappeared into the great stable-yard
behind the castle, while I went on down the dark road and
then struck across the open fields to my uncle's house.

At half-past nine that night I pulled up the dog-cart before the
chief police-station in Dumfries, and alighting at once sought
the big fair Highlander, Mackenzie, with whom I had had the
consultation on the previous day.

When we were seated in his room beneath the hissing gas-jet, I
related my adventure and the result of my investigation.

"What?" he cried, jumping up. "You've unearthed another
body - a woman's?"

"I have. And what is more, I can identify her," I replied. "Her
name is Armida, and she was wife of the murdered man Olinto
Santini."

"Then both husband and wife were killed?"

"Without a doubt - a double tragedy."

"But the two men who concealed the body! Will you describe
them?"

I did so, and he wrote at my dictation, afterwards remarking -

"We must find them." And calling in one of his sub-
inspectors, he gave him instructions for the immediate

circulation of the description to all the police-stations in the county, saying the two men were wanted on a charge of willful murder.

When the official had gone out again and we were alone, Mackenzie turned to me and asked -

"What induced you to search the wood? Why did you suspect a second crime?"

His question nonplused me for the moment.

"Well, you see, I had identified the young man Olinto, and knowing him to be married and devoted to his wife, I suspected that she had accompanied him here. It was entirely a vague surmise. I wondered whether, if the poor fellow had fallen a victim to his enemies, she had not also been struck down."

His lips were pressed together in distinct dissatisfaction. I knew my explanation to be a very lame one, but at all hazards I could not import Muriel's name into the affair. I had given her my promise, and I intended to keep it.

"Then the body is still in the glen, where you left it?"

"Yes. If you wish, I will take you to the spot. I can drive you and your assistant up there."

"Certainly. Let us go," he exclaimed, rising at once and ringing his bell.

"Get three good lanterns and some matches, and put them in this gentleman's trap outside," he said to the constable who answered his summons. "And tell Gilbert Campbell that I want him to go with me up to Rannoch Wood."

"Yes, sir," answered the man; and the door again closed.

"It's a pity - a thousand pities, Mr. Gregg, that you didn't stop those two men who buried the body."

"They were already across the stream, and disappearing into the thicket before I mounted the rock," I explained. "Besides, at the moment I had no suspicion of what they'd been doing. I believed them to be stragglers from a neighboring shooting-party who had lost their way."

"Ah, most unfortunate!" he said. "I hope they don't escape us. If they're foreigners, they are not likely to get away. But if they're English or Scots, then I fear there's but little chance of us coming up with them. Yesterday at the inquest the identity of the murdered man was strictly preserved, and the inquiry was adjourned for a fortnight."

"Of course my name was not mentioned?" I said.

"Of course not," was the detective's reply. Then he asked: "When do you expect to get a telegram from your friend, the Consul at Leghorn? I am anxious for that, in order that we may commence inquiries in London."

"The day after to-morrow, I hope. He will certainly reply at once, providing the dead man's father can still be found."

And at that moment a tall, thin man, who proved to be Detective Campbell, entered, and five minutes later we were all three driving over the uneven cobbles of Dumfries and out in the darkness towards Rannoch.

It was cloudy and starless, with a chill mist hanging over the valley; but my uncle's cob was a swift one, and we soon began to ascend the hill up past the castle, and then, turning to the left, drove along a steep, rough by-road which led to the south of the wood and out across the moor. When we reached the latter we all descended, and I led the horse, for owing to the many treacherous bogs it was unsafe to drive further. So, with Mackenzie and Campbell carrying lanterns, we walked on carefully, skirting the wood for nearly a mile until we came to the rough wall over which I had clambered with Muriel.

I recognized the spot, and having tied up the cob we all three plunged into the pitch-darkness of the wood, keeping straight on in the direction of the glen, and halting every now and then to listen for the rippling of the stream.

At last, after some difficulty, we discovered it, and searching along the bank with our three powerful lights, I presently detected the huge moss-grown boulder whereon I had stood when the pair of fugitives had disappeared.

"Look!" I cried. "There's the spot!" And quickly we clambered down the steep bank, lowering ourselves by the branches of the trees until we came to the water into which I waded, being followed closely by my two companions.

On gaining the opposite side I clambered up to the base of the boulder and lowered my lantern to reveal to them the gruesome evidence of the second crime, but the next instant I cried -

"Why! It's gone!"

"Gone!" gasped the two men.

"Yes. It was here. Look! this is the hole where they buried it! But they evidently returned, and finding it exhumed, they've retaken possession of it and carried it away!"

The two detectives gazed down to where I indicated, and then looked at each other without exchanging a word.

As we stood there dumbfounded at the disappearance of the body, the Highlander's quick glance caught something, and stooping he picked it up and examined the little object by the aid of his lantern.

Within his palm I saw lying a tiny little gold cross, about an inch long, enameled in red, while in the center was a circular miniature of a kneeling saint, an elegant and beautifully executed little trinket which might have adorned a lady's bracelet.

"This is a pretty little thing!" remarked the detective. "It may possibly lead us to something. But, Mr. Gregg," he added, turning to me, "are you quite certain you left the body here?"

"Certain?" I echoed. "Why, look at the hole I made. You don't think I have any interest in leading you here on a fool's errand, do you?"

"Not at all," he said apologetically. "Only the whole affair seems so very inconceivable - I mean that the men, having once got rid of the evidence of their crime, would hardly return to the spot and re-obtain possession of it."

"Unless they watched me exhume it, and feared the consequences if it fell into your hands," I suggested.

"Of course they might have watched you from behind the trees, and when you had gone they came and carried it away somewhere else," he remarked dubiously; "but even if they did, it must be in this wood. They would never risk carrying a body very far, and here is surely the best place of concealment in the whole country."

"The only thing remaining is to search the wood at daylight," I suggested. "If the two men came back here during my absence they may still be on the watch in the vicinity."

"Most probably they are. We must take every precaution," he said decisively. And then, with our lanterns lowered, we made an examination of the vicinity, without, however, discovering anything else to furnish us with a clew. While I had been absent the body of the unfortunate Armida had disappeared - a fact which, knowing all that I did, was doubly mysterious.

The pair had, without doubt, watched Muriel and myself, and as soon as we had gone they had returned and carried off the ghastly remains of the poor woman who had been so foully done to death.

But who were the men - the fellow with the broad shoulders whom Muriel recognized, and the slim seafarer in his pilot-coat and peaked cap? The enigma each hour became more and more inscrutable.

At dawn Mackenzie, with four of his men, made a thorough examination of the wood, but although they continued until dusk they discovered nothing, neither was anything heard of the mysterious seafarer and his companion in brown tweeds.

I called on Muriel as arranged, and explained how the body had so suddenly disappeared, whereupon she stared at me pale-faced, saying -

"The assassins must have watched us! They are aware, then, that we have knowledge of their crime?"

"Of course," I said.

"Ah!" she cried hoarsely. "Then we are both in deadly peril - peril of our own lives! These people will hesitate at nothing. Both you and I are marked down by them, without a doubt. We must both be wary not to fall into any trap they may lay for us."

Her very words seemed an admission that she was aware of the identity of the conspirators, and yet she would give me no clue to them.

We went out and up the drive together to the kennels, where her father, a tall, imposing figure in his shooting-kit, was giving orders to the keepers.

"Hulloa, Gregg!" he cried merrily, extending his hand. "You'll make one of a party to Glenlea to-morrow, won't you? Paton and Phillips are coming. Ten sharp here, and the ladies are coming out to lunch with us."

"Thanks," I said, accepting with pleasure, for by so doing I saw that I might be afforded an opportunity of being near Muriel. The fact that the assassins were aware of our knowledge seemed to have caused her the greatest apprehension lest evil should befall us. Then, as we turned away to go back to the house, Leithcourt said to me -

"You know all about the discovery up at the wood the other day! Horrible affair - a young foreigner found murdered."

"Yes. I've heard about it," I responded.

"And the police are worse than useless," he declared with disgust. "They haven't discovered who the fellow is yet. Why, if it had happened anywhere else but in Scotland, they'd have arrested the assassin before this."

"He's an entire stranger, I hear," I remarked. And then added: "You often go up to the wood of an evening after pigeons. It's fortunate you were not there that evening, eh?"

He glanced at me quickly with his brows slightly contracted, as though he did not exactly comprehend me. In an instant I saw that my remark had caused him quick apprehension.

"Yes," he answered with a sickly smile which he intended should convey to me utter unconcern. "They might have suspected me."

"It certainly is a disagreeable affair to happen on one's property." I said, still watching him narrowly. And then Muriel at his side managed with her feminine ingenuity to divert the conversation into a different channel.

Next day I accompanied the party over to Glenlea, about five miles distant, and at noon at a spot previously arranged, we found the ladies awaiting us with luncheon spread under the trees. As soon as we approached Muriel came forward quickly, handing me a telegram, saying that it had been sent over by one of my uncle's grooms at the moment they were leaving the castle.

I tore it open eagerly, and read its contents. Then, turning to my companions, said in as quiet a voice as I could command -

"I must go up to London to-night," whereat the men, one and all, expressed hope that I should soon return. Leithcourt's party were a friendly set, and at heart I was sorry to leave Scotland. Yet the telegram made it imperative, for it was from Frank Hutcheson in Leghorn, and read -

"Made inquiries. Olinto Santini married your servant Armida at Italian Consulate-General in London about a year ago. They live 64B, Albany Road, Camberwell: he is employed waiter Ferrari's Restaurant, Westbourne Grove. - British Consulate, Leghorn"

The lunch was a merry one, as shooting luncheons usually are, and while we ate the keepers packed our morning bag - a considerable one - into the Perth-cart in waiting. Then, when we could wander away alone together, I explained to Muriel that the reason of my sudden journey to London was in order to continue my investigations regarding the mysterious affair.

This puzzled her, for I had not, of course, revealed to her that I had identified Olinto. Yet I managed to make such excuses and promises to return that I think allayed all her suspicions, and that night, after calling upon the detective Mackenzie, I took the sleeping-car express to Euston.

The restaurant which Hutcheson had indicated was, I found, situated about half-way up Westbourne Grove, nearly opposite Whiteley's, a small place where confectionery and sweets were displayed in the window, together with long-necked flasks of Italian chianti, chump-chops, small joints and tomatoes. It was soon after nine o'clock when I entered the long shop with its rows of marble-topped tables and greasy lounges of red plush. An unhealthy-looking lad was sweeping out the place with wet saw-dust, and a big, dark-bearded, flabby-faced man in shirt-sleeves stood behind the small counter polishing some forks.

"I wish to see Signor Ferrari," I said, addressing him.

"There is no Ferrari, he is dead," responded the man in broken English. "My name is Odinzoff. I bought the place from madame."

"You are Russian, I presume?"

"Polish, m'sieur - from Varsovie."

I had seen from the first moment we had met that he was no Italian. He was too bulky, and his face too broad and flat.

"I have come to inquire after a waiter you have in your service, an Italian named Santini. He was my servant for some years, and I naturally take an interest in him."

"Santini?" he repeated. "Oh I you mean Olinto? He is not here yet. He comes at ten o'clock."

This reply surprised me. I had expected the restaurant-keeper to express regret at his disappearance, yet he spoke as though he had been at work as usual on the previous day.

"May I have a liqueur brandy?" I asked, seeing that I would be compelled to take something. "Perhaps you will have one with me?"

"Ach no! But a kuemmel - yes, I will have a kuemmel!" And he filled our glasses, and tossed off his own at a single gulp, smacking his lips after it, for the average Russian dearly loves his national decoction of caraway seeds.

WILLIAM LE QUEUX

"You find Olinto a good servant, I suppose?" I said, for want of something else to say.

"Excellent. The Italians are the best waiters in the world. I am Russian, but dare not employ a Russian waiter. These English would not come to my shop if I did."

I looked around, and it struck me that the trade of the place mainly consisted in chops and steaks for chance customers at mid-day, and tea and cake for those swarms of women who each afternoon buzz around that long line of windows of the "world's provider." I could see that his was a cheap trade, as revealed by the printed notice stuck upon one of the long fly-blown mirrors: "Ices *4d* and *6d*."

"How long has Olinto been with you?" I inquired.

"About a year - perhaps a little more. I trust him implicitly, and I leave him in charge when I go away for holidays. He does not get along very well with the cook - who is Milanese. These Italians from different provinces always quarrel," he added, laughing. "If you live in Italy you know that, no doubt."

I laughed in chorus, and then glancing at my watch, said: "I'll wait for him, if he will be here at ten. I'd much like to see him again."

The Russian was by no means nonplused, but merely remarked -

"He is late sometimes, but not often. He lives on the other side of London - over at Camberwell." His confidence that the waiter would return struck me as extremely curious; nevertheless I possessed myself in patience, strolled up and down the restaurant, and then stood watching the traffic in the Grove outside.

The man Odinzoff seemed a quick, hard-working fellow with a

keen eye to business, for he fell to polishing the top of the marble tables with a pail and brush, at the same time directing the work of the pallid-looking youth. Suddenly a side door opened, and the cook put his head in to speak with his master in French. He was a typical Italian, about forty, with dark mustaches turned upwards, and an easy-going, careless manner. Seeing me, however, and believing me to be a customer, he turned and closed the door quickly. In that instant I noticed the high broadness of his shoulders, and his back struck me as strangely similar to that of the man in brown whom we had seen disappearing in Rannoch Wood.

The suspicion held me breathless.

Was this Russian endeavoring to deceive me when he declared that Olinto would arrive in a few minutes? It seemed curious, for the man now dead must, I reflected, have been away at least four days. Surely his absence from work had caused the proprietor considerable inconvenience?

"That was your cook, wasn't it? The Milanese who is quarrelsome?" I laughed, when the side door had closed.

"Yes, m'sieur. But Emilio is a very good workman - and very honest, even though I had constantly to complain that he uses too much oil in his cooking. These English do not like the oil."

I stood in the doorway again watching the busy throng passing outside towards Royal Oak. Ten o'clock struck from a neighboring church, and I still waited, knowing only too well that I waited in vain for a man whose body had already been committed to the grave outside that far-away old Scotch town. But I waited in order to ascertain the motive of the bearded Russian in leading me to believe that the young fellow would really return.

Presently Odinzoff went outside, carrying with him two boards upon which the menu of the "Eight-penny Luncheon! This

Day!" was written in scrawly characters, and proceeded to affix them to the shop-front.

This was my opportunity, and quick as thought I moved towards where the unhealthy youth was at work, and whispered:

"I'll give you half-a-sovereign if you'll answer my questions truthfully. Now, tell me, was the cook, the man I've just seen, here yesterday?"

"Yes, sir."

"Was he here the day before?"

"No, sir. He's been away ill for four days."

"And your master?"

"He's been away too, sir."

I had no time to put any further question, for the Russian re-entered at that moment, and the youth busied himself rubbing the front of the counter in pretense that I had not spoken to him. Indeed, I had some difficulty in slipping the promised coin into his hand at a moment when his master was not looking.

Then I paced up and down the restaurant, waiting patiently and wondering whether the absence of Emilio had any connection with the tragedy up in Rannoch Wood.

While I stood there a rather thin, respectably-dressed man entered, and seating himself upon one of the plush lounges at the further end, removed his bowler hat and ordered from the proprietor a chop and a pot of tea. Then, taking a newspaper from his pocket, he settled himself to read, apparently oblivious to his surroundings.

And yet as I watched I saw that over the top of his paper he was carefully taking in the general appearance of the place, and his eyes were keenly following the Russian's movements. The latter shouted - in French - the order for the chop through the speaking-tube to the man Emilio, and then returning to his customer he spread out a napkin and placed a small cruet, with knife, fork, and bread before him. But the customer seemed immersed in his paper, and never looked up until after the Russian's back was turned. Then so deep was his interest in the place, and so keen those dark eyes of his, that the truth suddenly dawned upon me. Mackenzie had telegraphed to Scotland Yard, and the customer sitting there was a detective who had come to investigate. I had advanced to the counter to chat again with the proprietor, when a quick step behind me caused me to turn.

Before me stood the slim figure of a man in a straw hat and rather seedy black jacket.

"*Dio Signor Padrone!*" he cried.

I staggered as though I had received a blow.

Olinto Santini in the flesh, smiling and well, stood there before me!

CHAPTER VIII

LIFE'S COUNTER-CLAIM

No words of mine can express my absolute and abject amazement when I faced the man, whom I had seen lying cold and dead upon that gray stone slab in the mortuary at Dumfries.

My eye caught the customer who, on the entry of Olinto, had dropped his paper and sat staring at him in wonderment. The detective had evidently been furnished with a photograph of the dead man, and now, like myself, discovered him alive and living.

"Signor Padrone!" cried the man whose appearance was so absolutely bewildering. "How did you find me here? I admit that I deceived you when I told you I worked at the Milano," he went on rapidly in Italian. "But it was under compulsion - my actions that night were not my own - but those of others."

"Yes, I understand," I said. "But come out into the street. I don't wish to speak before these people. Your padrone knows Italian, no doubt."

"Ah! only a very little," he answered, smiling. "Have no fear of him."

"But there is Emilio, the cook?"

"Then you have met him!" he exclaimed quickly, with a strange look of apprehension. "He is an undesirable person, signore."

"So I gather," I answered. "But I desire to speak to you outside - not here." And then turning with a smile to the Pole, I apologized for taking away his servant for a few minutes. "Recollect, I am his old master, I added."

"Of course, m'sieur," answered the Pole, bowing politely. "Speak with him where and how long you will. He is entirely at your service."

And when we were outside in Westbourne Grove, Olinto walking by my side in wonderment, I asked suddenly:

"Tell me. Have you ever been in Scotland - at Dumfries?"

"Never, signore, in my life. Why?"

"Answer me another question," I said quickly. "You married Armida at the Italian Consulate. Where is she now - where is she this morning?"

He turned pale, and I saw a complete change in his countenance.

"Ah, signore!" he responded, "I only wish I could tell."

"It is untrue that she is an invalid," I went on, "or that you live in Lambeth. Your address is in Albany Road, Camberwell. You can't deny these facts."

"I do not deny them, Signor Commendatore. But how did you learn this?"

"The authorities in Italy know everything," I answered. "Like that of all your countrymen, your record is written down at the Commune."

"It is a clean one, at any rate, signore," he declared with some slight warmth. "I have a permesso to carry a revolver, which is in itself sufficient proof that I am a man of spotless character."

"I cast no reflection whatever upon you, Olinto," I answered. "I have merely inquired after your wife, and you do not give me a direct reply."

We had walked to the Royal Oak, and stood talking on the curb outside.

"I give you no reply, because I can't," he said in Italian. "Armida - my poor Armida - has left home."

"Why did you tell me such a tale of distress regarding her?"

"As I have already explained, signore, I was not then master of my own actions. I was ruled by others. But I saved your life at risk of my own. Some day, when it is safe, I will reveal to you everything."

"Let us allow the past to remain," I said. "Where is your wife now?"

He hesitated a moment, looking straight into my face.

"Well, Signor Commendatore, to tell the truth, she has disappeared."

"Disappeared!" I echoed. "And have you not made any report to the police?"

"No."

"Why not?"

"For reasons known only to myself I did not wish the police to pry into my private affairs."

"I know. Because you were once convicted at Lucca of using a knife - eh? I recollect quite well that affair - a love affair, was it not?"

"Yes, Signor Commendatore. But I was a youth then - a mere boy."

"Then tell me the circumstances In which Armida has disappeared," I urged, for I saw quite plainly that his sudden meeting with me had upset him, and that he was trying to hold back from me some story which he was bursting to tell.

"Well, signore," he said at last in a low tone of confidence, "I don't like to trouble you with my private affairs after those untruths I told you when we last met."

"Go on," I said. "Tell me the truth."

After the exciting incidents of our last meeting, I was half inclined to doubt him.

"The truth is, Signor Commendatore, that my wife has mysteriously disappeared. Last Saturday, at eleven o'clock, she was talking over the garden wall with a neighbor and was then dressed to go out. She apparently went out, but from that moment no one has seen or heard of her."

It was on the tip of my tongue to tell him the ghastly truth, yet so strange was the circumstance that his own double, even to the mole upon his face, should be lying dead and buried in Scotland that I hesitated to relate what I knew.

"She spoke English, I suppose?"

"She could make herself understood very well," he said with a sigh, and I saw a heavy, thoughtful look upon his brow. That he was really devoted to her, I knew. With the Italian of whatever station in life, love is all-consuming - it is either perfect love or genuine hatred. The Tuscan character is one of two extremes.

I glanced across the road, and saw that the detective who had ordered his chop and coffee had stopped to light his pipe and was watching us.

"Have you any idea where your wife is, or what has induced her to go away from home? Perhaps you had some words!"

"Words, signore!" he echoed. "Why, we were the happiest pair in all London. No unkind word ever passed between us. There seems absolutely no reason whatever why she should go away without wishing me a word of farewell."

"But why haven't you told the police?"

"For reasons that I have already stated. I prefer to make inquiries for myself."

"And in what have your inquiries resulted?"

"Nothing - absolutely nothing," he said gravely.

"You do not suspect any plot? I recollect that night in Lambeth you told me that you had enemies?"

"Ah! so I have, signore - and so have you!" he exclaimed hoarsely. "Yes, my poor Armida may have been entrapped by them."

"And if entrapped, what then?"

"Then they would kill her with as little compunction as they would a fly," he said. "Ah! you do not know the callousness of those people. I only hope and pray that she may have escaped and is in hiding somewhere, and will arrive unexpectedly and give me a startling surprise. She delights in startling me," he added with a laugh.

Poor fellow, I thought, she would never again be able to startle him. She had actually fallen a victim just as he dreaded.

"Then you think she must have been called away from home by some urgent message?" I suggested.

"By the manner in which she left things, it seemed as though she went away hurriedly. There were five sovereigns in a drawer that we had saved for the rent, and she took them with her."

I paused again, hesitating whether to tell him the terrible truth. I recollected that the body had disappeared, therefore what proof had I of my allegation that she had been murdered?

"Tell me, Olinto," I said as we moved forward again in the direction of Paddington Station, "have you any knowledge of a man named Leithcourt?"

He started suddenly and looked at me.

"I have heard of him," he answered very lamely.

"And of his daughter - Muriel?"

"And also of her. But I am not acquainted with them - nor, to tell the truth, do I wish to be."

"Why?"

"Because they are enemies of mine - bitter enemies."

His declaration was strange, for it threw some light upon the tragedy in Rannoch Wood.

"And of your wife also?"

"I do not know that," he responded. "My enemies are my wife's also, I suppose."

"You have not told me the secret of that dastardly attempt upon me when we last met," I said in a low voice. "Why not tell me the truth? I surely ought to know who my enemies really are, so as to be warned against any future plot."

"You shall know some day, signore. I dare not tell you now."

"You said that before," I exclaimed with dissatisfaction. "If you are faithful to me, you ought at least to tell me the reason they wished to kill me in secret."

"Because they fear you," was his answer.

"Why should they fear me?"

But he shrugged his shoulders, and made a gesture with his hands indicative of utter ignorance.

"I ask you one question. Answer yes or no. Is the man Leith-court my enemy?"

The young Italian paused, and then answered:

"He is not your friend. I am quite well aware of that."

"And his daughter? She is engaged, I hear."

"I think so."

"Where did you first meet Leithcourt?"

"I have known him several years. When we first met he was poor."

"Suddenly became rich - eh?"

"Bought a fine house in the country; lives mostly at the Carlton when he and his wife and daughter are in London - although I believe they now have a house somewhere in the

West End - and he often makes long cruises on his steam-yacht."

"And how did he make his money?"

Again Olinto elevated his shoulders, without replying.

If he would only betray to me the reason he had been induced to entice me to that house, I might then be able to form some conclusion regarding the tenants of Rannoch and their friends.

Who was the man who, having represented the man now before me, had been struck dead by an unerring hand? Was it possible that Armida had been called by telegram to meet her husband, and recognizing the fraud perpetrated upon her threatened to disclose it and, for that reason, shared the same fate as the masquerader?

This was the first theory that occurred to me; one which I believed to be the correct one. The motive was a mystery, yet the facts seemed to me plain enough.

As the young Italian had refused to give any satisfactory explanation, I resolved within myself to wait until the unfor-tunate woman's body was recovered before revealing to him the ghastly truth. Without doubt he had some reason in withholding from me the true facts, either because he feared that I might become unduly alarmed, or else he himself had been deeply implicated in the plot. Of the two suggestions, I was inclined to believe in the latter.

He walked with me as far as the end of Bishop's Road, endeavoring with all the Italian's exquisite diplomacy to obtain from me what I knew concerning the Leithcourts. But I told him nothing, nor did I reveal that I had only that morning returned from Scotland. Then at last we parted, and he retraced his steps to the little restaurant in Westbourne Grove, while I entered a hansom and drove to the well-known photographer's in New Bond Street, whose name had been upon the torn photograph of the young girl in the white pique blouse and her hair fastened with a bow of black ribbon, the picture that I had found on board the *Lola* on that memorable night in the Mediterranean, and a duplicate of which I had seen in Muriel's cosy little room up at Rannoch.

I recollected that she had told me the name of the original was Elma Heath, and that she had been a schoolfellow of hers at Chichester. Therefore I inquired of the photographer's lady-clerk whether she could supply me with a print of the negative.

For a considerable time she searched in her books for the name, and at last discovered it. Then she said:

"I regret, sir, that we can't give you a print, for the customer purchased the negative at the time."

"Ah, I'm very sorry for that," I said. "To what address did you send it?"

"The customer who ordered it was apparently a foreigner," she said, at the same time turning round the ledger so that I could read. And I saw that the entry was: "Heath - Miss Elma - 3 dozen cabinets and negative. Address: Baron Xavier Oberg, Vosnesenski Prospect 48, St. Petersburg, Russia."

"Did this gentleman come with the young lady when her portrait was taken?" I inquired.

"I can't tell, sir," she replied. "I've only been here a year, and you see the date - over two years ago."

"The photographer would know, perhaps?"

"He's a new man, sir. He only came a month ago. In fact, the business changed hands a year ago, and none of the previous employees have remained."

"Ah! that's unfortunate , " I said, greatly disappointed; and having copied the address to which the negative and prints had been sent, I thanked her and left.

Who, I wondered, was this Baron Oberg, and what relation was he to Elma Heath?

The picture of the girl in the white blouse somehow exercised a strange attraction for me.

Have you never experienced the fascination of a photograph, inexplicable and yet forcible - a kind of magnetism from which you cannot release yourself? Perhaps it was the curious fact that some person had taken it from its frame on board the *Lola* and destroyed it that first aroused my interest; or it might have been the discovery of it in Muriel's room at Rannoch. Anyhow, it had for me an absorbing interest, for I often wondered whether the unknown girl who had secretly gone ashore from the yacht when I had left it was not Elma Heath herself.

Who was this Baron Oberg? The name was German undoubtedly, yet he lived in the Russian capital. From London to Petersburg is a far cry, yet I resolved that if it were necessary I would travel there and investigate.

At the German Embassy, in Carlton House Terrace, I found my friend Captain Nieberding, the second secretary, of whom I inquired whether the name of Baron Oberg was known, but having referred to a number of German books in his Excellency's library, he returned and told me that the name did not appear in the lists of the German nobility.

"He may be Russian - Polish most probably," added the captain, a tall, fair fellow in gold spectacles, whom I had known when he was third secretary of Embassy at Rome. His opinion was that it was not a German name, for there was a little place called Oberg, he said, on the railway between Lodz and Lowicz.

Then, after luncheon, I went to Albany Road, one of those dreary, old-fashioned streets that were pleasant back in the early Victorian days when Camberwell was a suburb and Walworth Common was still an open waste. I found the house where Olinto lived - a small, smoke-blackened, semi-detached place standing back in a tiny strip of weedy garden, with a wooden veranda before the first floor windows. The house, according to the woman who kept a general shop at the corner, was occupied by two families. The "Eye-talians," as she termed them, lived above, while the Gibbonses rented the ground floor.

"Oh, yes, sir. The foreigners are respectable enough. Always pays me ready money for everythink, except the milk. That they pays for weekly."

"I understand that the wife has disappeared. What have you heard about that?"

"They do say, sir, that they 'ad some words together the other day, and that the woman's took herself off in a tantrum. Only you can't believe all you 'ear, you know."

"Did they often quarrel?"

"Not to my knowledge, sir. They were really very quiet, respectable persons for foreigners."

I repassed the house of the dead woman, and then regaining the busy Camberwell Road I took an omnibus back to the Hotel Cecil in the Strand where I had put up, tired and disappointed.

Next day I ran down to Chichester, and after some difficulty found the Cheverton College for Ladies, a big old-fashioned house about half-a-mile out of the town on the Drayton Road. The seminary was evidently a first-class one, for when I entered I noticed how well everything was kept.

To the principal, an elderly lady of a somewhat severe aspect, I said:

"I regret, madam, to trouble you, but I am in search of information you can supply. It is with regard to a certain Elma Heath whom you had as pupil here, and who left, I believe, about two years ago. Her parents lived in Durham."

"I remember her perfectly," was the woman's response as she sat behind the big desk, having apparently at first expected that I had a daughter to put to school.

"Well," I said, "there has been some little friction in the family, and I am making inquiries on behalf of another branch of it - an aunt who desires to ascertain the girl's whereabouts."

"Ah, I regret, sir, that I cannot tell you that. The Baron, her uncle, came here one day and took her away suddenly - abroad, I think."

"Had she no school-friend to whom she would probably write?"

"There was a girl named Leithcourt - Muriel Leithcourt - who was her friend, but who has also left."

"And no one else?" I asked. "Girls often write to each other after leaving school, until they get married, and then the correspondence usually ceases."

The principal was silent and reflective.

"Well," she said at last, "there was another pupil who was also on friendly terms with Elma - a girl named Lydia Moreton. She may have written to her. If you really desire to know, sir, I dare say I could find her address. She left us about nine months after Elma."

"I should esteem it a great favor if you would give me that

young lady's address," I said, whereupon she unlocked a drawer in her writing-table and took therefrom a thick, leather-bound book which she consulted for a few minutes, at last exclaiming:

"Yes, here it is - 'Lydia Moreton, daughter of Sir Hamilton Moreton, K.C.M.G., Whiston Grange, Doncaster.'" And she scribbled it in pencil upon an envelope, and handing it to me, said:

"Elma Heath was, I fear, somewhat neglected by her parents. She remained here for five years, and had no holidays like the other girls. Her uncle, the Baron, came to see her several times, but on each occasion after he had left I found her crying in secret. He was mean and unkind to her. Now that I recollect, I remember that Lydia had said she had received a letter from her, therefore she might be able to give you some information."

And with that I took my leave, thanking her, and returned to London.

Could Lydia Moreton furnish any information? If so, I might find this girl whose photograph had aroused the irate jealousy of the mysterious unknown.

The ten o'clock Edinburgh express from King's Cross next morning took me up to Doncaster, and hiring a musty old fly at the station, I drove three miles out of the town on the Rotherham Road, finding Whiston Grange to be a fine old Elizabethan mansion in the center of a great park, with tall old twisted chimneys, and beautifully-kept gardens.

When I descended at the door and rang, the footman was not aware whether Miss Lydia was in. He looked at me somewhat suspiciously, I thought, until I gave my card and impressed upon him meaningly that I had come from London purposely to see his young mistress upon a very important matter.

"Tell her," I said, "that I wish to see her regarding her friend, Miss Elma Heath."

"Miss Elma 'Eath," repeated the man. "Very well, sir. Will you walk this way?"

And then I followed him across the big old oak-paneled hall, filled with trophies of the chase and arms of the civil wars, into a small paneled room on the left, the deep-set window with its diamond panes giving out upon the old bowling-green and the flower-garden beyond.

Presently the door opened, and a tall dark-haired girl in white entered with an enquiring expression upon her face as she halted and bowed to me.

"Miss Lydia Moreton, I believe?" I commenced, and as she replied in the affirmative I went on: "I have first to apologize for coming to you, but Miss Sotheby, the principal of the school at Chichester, referred me to you for information as to the present whereabouts of Miss Elma Heath, who, I believe, was one of your most intimate friends at school." And I added a lie, saying: "I am trying, on behalf of an aunt of hers, to discover her."

"Well," responded the girl, "I have had only one or two letters. She's in her uncle's hands, I believe, and he won't let her write, poor girl. She dreaded leaving us."

"Why?"

"Ah! she would never say. She had some deep-rooted terror of her uncle, Baron Oberg, who lived in St. Petersburg, and who came over at long intervals to see her. But possibly you know the whole story?"

"I know nothing," I cried eagerly. "You will be furthering her interests, as well as doing me a great personal favor, if you will tell me what you know."

"It is very little," she answered, leaning back against the edge of the table and regarding me seriously. "Poor Elma! Her people treated her very badly indeed. They sent her no money, and allowed her no holidays, and yet she was the sweetest-tempered and most patient girl in the whole school."

"Well - and the story regarding her?"

"It was supposed that her people at Durham did not exist," she explained. "Elma had evidently lived a greater part of her life abroad, for she could speak French and Italian better than the professor himself, and therefore always won the prizes. The class revolted, and then she did not compete any more. Yet she never told us of where she had lived when a child. She came from Durham, she said - that was all."

"You had a letter from her after the Baron came and took her away?"

"Yes, from London. She said that she had been to several plays and concerts, but did not care for life in town. There was too much bustle and noise and study of clothes."

"And what other letters did you receive from her?"

"Three or four, I think. They were all from places abroad. One was from Vienna, one was from Milan, and one from some place with an unpronounceable name in Hungary. The last - "

"Yes, the last?" I gasped eagerly, interrupting her.

"Well, the last I received only a fortnight ago. If you will wait a moment I will go and get it. It was so strange that I haven't destroyed it." And she went out, and I heard by the frou-frou of her skirts that she was ascending the stairs.

After five minutes of breathless anxiety she rejoined me, and handing me the letter to read, said:

"It is not in her handwriting - I wonder why?"

The paper was of foreign make, with blue lines ruled in squares. Written in a hand that was evidently foreign, for the mistakes in the orthography were many, was the following curious communication:

"My Dear Lydia:

"Perhaps you may never get this letter - the last I shall ever be able to send you. Indeed, I run great risks in sending it. Ah! you do not know the awful disaster that has happened to me, all the terrors and the tortures I endure. But no one can assist me, and I am now looking forward to the time when it will all be over. Do you recollect our old peaceful days in the garden at Chichester? I think of them always, always, and compare that sweet peace of the past with my own terrible sufferings of to-day. Ah, how I wish I might see you once again; how that I might feel your hand upon my brow, and hear your words of hope and encouragement! But happiness is now debarred from me, and I am only sinking to the grave under this slow torture of body and of soul.

"This will pass through many hands before it reaches the post. If, however, it ever does get despatched and you receive it, will you do me one last favor - a favor to an unfortunate girl who is friendless and helpless, and who will no longer trouble the world? It is this: Take this letter to London, and call upon Mr. Martin Woodroffe at 98 Cork Street, Piccadilly. Show him my letter, and tell him from me that through it all I have kept my promise, and that the secret is still safe. He will understand - and also know why I cannot write this with my own hand. If he is abroad, keep it until he returns.

"It is all I ask of you, Lydia, and I know that if this reaches you, you will not refuse me. You have been my only friend and confidante, but I now bid you farewell, for the unknown beckons me, and from the grave I cannot write. Again farewell, and for ever.

"Your loving and affectionate friend,

"Elma."

"A very strange letter, is it not?" remarked the girl at my side.
"I can't make it out. You see there is no address, but the
postmark is Russian. She is evidently in Russia."

"In Finland," I said, examining the stamp and making out the
post town to be Abo. "But have you been to London and
executed this strange commission?"

"No. We are going up next week. I intend to call upon this
person named Woodroffe."

I made no remark. He was, I knew, abroad, but I was glad at
having obtained two very important clues: first, the address of
the mysterious yachtsman, Woodroffe, alias Hornby, and,
secondly, ascertaining that the young girl I sought was somewhere in the vicinity of the town of Abo, the Finnish port on
the Baltic.

"Poor Elma, you see, speaks in her letter of some secret, Mr.
Gregg," my companion said. "She says she wishes this Mr.
Woodroffe, whoever he is, to know that she has kept her
promise and has not divulged it. This only bears out what I
have all along suspected."

"What are your suspicions?"

"Well, from her deep, thoughtful manner, and from certain
remarks she at times made to me, I believe that Elma is in
possession of some great and terrible secret - a secret which her
uncle, Baron Oberg, is desirous of learning. I know she holds
him in deadly fear - she is in terror that she may inadvertently
betray to him the truth!"

CHAPTER IX

STRANGE DISCLOSURES ARE MADE

The strange letter of Elma Heath, combined with what Lydia Moreton had told me, aroused within me a determination to investigate the mystery. From the moment I had landed from the *Lola* on that hot, breathless night at Leghorn, mystery had crowded upon mystery until it was all bewildering.

It was now proved that the sweet-faced girl, the original of the torn photograph, held a secret, and that, by her own words, she knew that death was approaching. The incomprehensible attempt upon my life, the strange actions of Hornby and Chater - who, by the way, seemed to have entirely disappeared - the assassination of the man who by masquerading as the Italian waiter had met his death, and the murder of Olinto's wife were all problems which required solution.

Had it not been for the mystery of it all - and mystery ever arouses the human curiosity - I should have given up trying to get at the truth. Yet as a man with some leisure, and knowing by that letter of Elma Heath's that she was in sore distress, I redoubled my efforts to ascertain the reason of it all.

The mystery of the *Lola* was still a mystery along the Mediterranean. At every French and Italian port the yacht's false name and general build was written in the police-books, while at Lloyd's the name *Lola* was marked down as among the mysterious craft at sea.

WILLIAM LE QUEUX

Chater was missing, while Hornby was abroad. Perhaps they were both cruising again, with their yacht repainted and bearing a fresh name. But why? What had been their motive?

Stirred by the complete mystery which now seemed to enshroud the unfortunate girl, I set before myself the task of elucidating it. Hitherto I had remained passive rather than active, but I now realized by that curious letter that at least one woman's life was at stake - that Elma Heath was in possession of some secret.

On leaving Leghorn I had given up all hope of tracing the mysterious yachtsman, and had left the matter in the hands of the Italian police. But, without any effort on my own part, I seemed to have been drawn into a veritable network of strange incidents, all of which combined to form the most complete and remarkable enigma ever presented in life. Surely no man was ever confronted by so many mysteries at one time as I was at this moment.

Fortunately I had been careful not to show my hand to anyone, and this perhaps gave me a distinct advantage. On my journey back to London, as the train swung through Peterborough and out across the rich level lands towards Hitchin, I recollected Jack Durnford's words when I had mentioned the *Lola*. What, I wondered, did he know?

Next month, in November, he was due back in London after his three years' service on the Mediterranean station. Then we should meet in a few weeks I hoped. Would he tell me anything when he became aware of all I knew? He held some secret knowledge. Was it possible that his secret was the same as that held by the unfortunate girl in far-off, dreary Finland?

I called at the house in Cork Street indicated by Elma, and learned from the old commissionaire who acted as lift-man and porter, that Mr. Woodroffe's chambers were closed.

"'E's nearly always away, sir - abroad, I think," was all I could get out of the old soldier, who, like his class, was no doubt well paid to keep his mouth closed.

For two days I lounged about Westbourne Grove watching Ferrari's restaurant. In such a busy, bustling thoroughfare, with so many shop windows as excuses for loitering, the task was easy. I saw that Olinto came regularly at ten o'clock in the morning, worked hard all day, and left at nine o'clock at night, taking an omnibus home from Royal Oak. His exterior was calm and unconcerned, unlike that of a man whose devoted wife had disappeared.

I would have approached him and explained the ghastly truth, had it not been for the fact that the poor woman's body was missing.

Those September days were full of anxiety for me. Alone and unaided I was trying to solve one of the greatest of problems, plunged as I was in a veritable sea of mystery. I wanted to see Muriel Leithcourt, and to question her further regarding Elma Heath. Therefore again I left Euston, and, traveling through the night, took my seat at the breakfast-table at Greenlaw next morning.

Sir George, who was sitting alone - it not being my aunt's habit to appear early - welcomed me, and then in his bluff manner sniffed and exclaimed:

"Nice goings on up at Rannoch! Have you heard of them?"

"No. What?" I cried breathlessly, staring at him.

"Well, my suspicions that those Leithcourts were utter outsiders turns out to be about correct."

"Why?"

"Well, it's a very funny story, and there are a dozen different distorted versions of it," he said. "But from what I can gather the true facts are these: About seven o'clock the night before last, as Leithcourt and his house-party were dressing for dinner, a telegram arrived. Mrs. Leithcourt opened it, and at once went off into hysterics, while her husband, in a breathless hurry, slipped off his evening clothes again and got into an old blue serge suit, tossed a few things into a bag, and then went along to Muriel's room to urge her to prepare for secret flight."

"Flight!" I gasped. "What, have they gone?"

"Listen, and I'll tell you. The servants have described the whole affair down in the village, so there's no doubt about it. Leithcourt showed Muriel the telegram and urged her to fly. At first she refused, but for her father's sake was induced to prepare to accompany him. Of course, the guests were in ignorance of all this. The brougham was ordered to be ready in the stable-yard and not to go round, while Mrs. Leithcourt's maid tried to bring the lady back to her senses. Leithcourt himself, it seemed, rushed hither and thither, seizing the jewel-cases of his wife and daughter and whatever valuables he could place his hand upon, while the mother and daughter were putting on their things. As he rushed down the main staircase to the library, where his check-book and some ready cash were locked in the safe, he met a stranger who had just been admitted and shown into the room. Leithcourt closed the door and faced him. What afterwards transpired, however, is a mystery, for two hours later, after he and the two women had escaped, leaving the house-party to their own diversions, the stranger was found locked in a large cupboard and insensible. The sensation was a tremendous one. Cowan, the doctor, was called, and declared that the stranger had been drugged and was suffering from some narcotic. The servant who admitted him declared that the man had said he had an appointment with his master, and that no card was necessary. He, however, gave the name of Chater."

"Chater!" I cried, starting up. "Are you certain of that name?"

"I only know what Cowan told me," was my uncle's reply.

"But do you know him?"

"Not at all. Only I've heard that name before," I said. "I knew a man out in Italy of the same name. But where is the visitor now?"

"In the hospital at Dumfries. They took him there in preference to leaving him alone at Rannoch."

"Alone?"

"Of course. Everyone has left, now the host and hostess have slipped off without saying good-bye. Scandalous affair, isn't it? But, my boy, you'll remember that I always said I didn't like those people. There's something mysterious about them, I feel certain. That telegram gave them warning of the visit of the man Chater, depend upon it, and for some reason they're afraid of him. It would be interesting to know what transpired between the two men in the library. And these are people who've been taken up by everybody - mere adventurers, I should call them!" And old Sir George sniffed again at thought of such scandal happening in the neighborhood. "If Gilrae must let Rannoch, then why in the name of Fortune doesn't he let it to respectable folk and not to the first fellow who answers his advertisement in *The Field?* It's simply disgraceful!"

"Certainly, it is a most extraordinary story," I declared. "Leithcourt evidently wished to escape from his visitor, and that's why he drugged him."

"Why he poisoned him, you mean. Cowan says the fellow is poisoned, but that he'll probably recover. He is already conscious, I hear."

I resolved to call on the doctor, who happened to be well known to me, and obtain further particulars. Therefore at eleven o'clock I drove into Dumfries and entered his consulting-room.

He was a spare, short, fair man, a trifle bald, and when I was shown in he welcomed me warmly, speaking with his pronounced Galloway accent.

"Well, it is a very mysterious case, Mr. Gregg," he said, after I had told him the object of my visit. "The gentleman is still in the hospital, and I have to keep him very quiet. He was poisoned without a doubt, and has had a very narrow escape of his life. The police got wind of the affair, and Mackenzie called to question him. But he refused to make any statement whatever, apparently treating the affair very lightly. The police, however, are mystified as to the reason of Mr. Leithcourt's sudden flight, and are anxious to get at the bottom of the curious affair."

"Naturally. And more especially after the tragedy up in Rannoch Wood a short time ago," I said.

"That's just it," said the doctor, removing his pince-nez and rubbing them. "Mackenzie seems to suspect some connection between Leithcourt's sudden disappearance and that mysterious affair. It seems very evident that the telegram was a warning to Leithcourt of the man Chater's intention of calling, and that the last-named was shown in just at the moment when the fugitive was on the point of leaving."

"Chater." I echoed. "Do you know his Christian name?"

"Hylton Chater. He is apparently a gentleman. Curious that he will tell us nothing of the reason he called, and of the scene that occurred between them."

Knowing all that I did, I was not surprised. Leithcourt had undoubtedly taken him unawares, but knights of industry never betray each other.

My next visit was to Mackenzie, for whom I had to wait nearly an hour, as he was absent in another quarter of the town.

"Ah, Mr. Gregg!" he cried gladly, as he came in to find me seated in a chair patiently reading the newspaper. "You are the very person I wish to see. Have you heard of this strange affair at Rannoch?"

"I have," was my answer. "Has the man in the hospital made any statement yet?"

"None. He refuses point-blank," answered the detective. "But my own idea is that the affair has a very close connection with the two mysteries of the wood."

"The first mystery - that of the man - proves to be a double mystery," I said.

"How? Explain it."

"Well, the waiter Olinto Santini is alive and well in London."

"What!" he gasped, starting up. "Then he is not the person you identified him to be?"

"No. But he was masquerading as Santini - made up to resemble him, I mean, even to the mole upon his face."

"But you identified him positively?"

"When a person is dead it is very easy to mistake countenances. Death alters the countenance so very much."

"That's true," he said reflectively. "But if the man we've buried is not the Italian, then the mystery is considerably increased. Why was the real man's wife here?"

"And where has her body been concealed? That's the question."

"Again a mystery. We have made a thorough search for four days, without discovering any trace of it. Quite confidentially,

I'm wondering if this man Chater knows anything. It is curious, to say the least, that the Leithcourts should have fled so hurriedly on this man's appearance. But have you actually seen Olinto Santini?"

"Yes, and have spoken with him."

"I sent up to London asking that inquiries should be made at the restaurant in Bayswater, but up to the present I have received no report."

"I have chatted with Olinto. His wife has mysteriously disappeared, but he is in ignorance that she is dead."

"You did not tell him anything?"

"Nothing."

"Ah, you did well. There is widespread conspiracy here, depend upon it, Mr. Gregg. It will be an interesting case when we get to the bottom of it all. I only wish this fellow Chater would tell us the reason he called upon Leithcourt."

"What does he say?"

"Merely that he has no wish to prosecute, and that he has no statement to make."

"Can't you compel him to say something?" I asked.

"No, I can't. That's the infernal difficulty of it. If he don't choose to speak, then we must still remain in ignorance, although I feel confident that he knows something of the strange affair up in the wood."

And although I was silent, I shared the Scotch detective's belief.

The afternoon was chill and wet as I climbed the hill

to Greenlaw.

The sudden disappearance of the tenants of Rannoch was, I found, on everyone's tongue in Dumfries. In the smoke-room of the railway hotel three men were discussing it with many grimaces and sinister hints, and the talkative young woman behind the bar asked me my opinion of the strange goings-on up at the Castle.

As I walked on alone, with the dark line of woods crowning the hill-top before me, the scene of that double tragedy, I again calmly reviewed the situation. I longed to go to the hospital and see Hylton Chater, yet when I recollected the part he had played with Hornby on board the *Lola*, I naturally hesitated. He was allied with Hornby, apparently against Leithcourt, although the latter was Hornby's friend.

What, I wondered, had transpired in the library of that gray old castle which stood out boldly before me, dark and grim, as I plodded on through the rain? How had Leithcourt succeeded in rendering his enemy insensible and hiding him in that cupboard? Did he believe that he had killed him?

If I went boldly to Chater, then it would only be the betrayal of myself. No. I decided that the man who had smoked and chatted with me so affably on that hot, breathless night in the Mediterranean must remain in ignorance of my presence, or of my knowledge. Therefore I stayed for a week at Greenlaw with eyes and ears ever open, yet exercising care that the patient in the hospital should be unaware of my presence.

Mackenzie saw him on several occasions, but he still persisted in that tantalizing silence. The inquiry into the death of the unidentified man in Rannoch Wood had been resumed, and a verdict returned of willful murder against some person unknown, while of the second crime the public had no knowledge, for the body was not discovered.

Time after time I searched the wood alone, on the pretense of shooting pigeon, but discovered nothing. When not having sport on my uncle's property, I joined various parties in the neighborhood, not because Scotland at that time attracted me, but because I desired to watch events.

Chater, as soon as he recovered, left the hospital and went south - to London, I ascertained - leaving the police utterly in the dark and filled with suspicion of the fugitives from Rannoch.

I longed to know the whereabouts of Muriel, hoping to gain from her some information regarding their visitor who had so nearly escaped with his life. That she was aware of the object of his visit was plain from the statements of the servants, all of whom had been left without either money or orders.

One day I called at the castle, the front entrance of which I found closed. Gilrae, the owner, had come up from London, met his factor there, and discharged all the late tenant's servants, keeping on only three of his own who had been in service there for a number of years. Ann Cameron, a house-maid, was one of these, and it was she whom I met when entering by the servants' hall.

On questioning her, I found her most willing to describe how she was in the corridor outside the young mistress's room when Mr. Leithcourt dashed along in breathless haste with the telegram in his hand. She heard him cry: "Look at this! Read it, Muriel. We must go. Put on your things at once, my dear. Never mind about luggage. Every minute lost is of conse-quence. What!" he cried a moment later. "You won't go? You'll stay here - stay here and face them? Good Heavens! girl, are you mad? Don't you know what this means? It means that the secret is out - the secret is out, you hear! We must fly!"

The woman told me that she distinctly heard Miss Muriel sobbing, while her father walked up and down the room speaking rapidly in a low tone. Then he came out again and returned to his dressing-room, while Miss Muriel presumably changed from her evening-gown into a dark traveling-dress.

"Did she say anything to you?" I inquired.

"Only that they were called away suddenly, sir. But," the domestic added, "the young lady was very pale and agitated, and we all knew that something terrible had happened. Mrs. Leithcourt gave orders that nothing was to be told to the guests, who dined alone, believing that their host and hostess had gone down to the village to see an old man who was dying. That was the story we told them, sir."

"And in the meantime the Leithcourts were in the express going to Carlisle?"

"Yes, sir. They say in Dumfries that the police telegraphed after them, but they had reached Carlisle and evidently changed there, and so got away."

By the administration of a judicious tip I was allowed to go up to Miss Muriel's room, an elegantly furnished little chamber in the front of the fine old place, with a deep old-fashioned window commanding a magnificent view across the broad Nithsdale.

The room had been tidied by the maids, but allowed to remain just as she had left it. I advanced to the window, in which was set the large dressing-table with its big swing-mirror and silver-topped bottles, and on gazing out saw, to my surprise, it was the only window which gave a view of that corner of Rannoch Wood where the double tragedy had taken place. Indeed, any person standing at the spot would have a clear view of that one distant window while out of sight of all the rest. A light might be placed there at night as signal, for instance; or by day a towel might be hung from the window as though to dry and yet could be plainly seen at that distance.

Another object in the room also attracted my attention - a pair of long field-glasses. Had she used these to keep watch upon that spot?

I took them up and focused them upon the boundary of the wood, finding that I could distinguish everything quite plainly.

"That's where they found the man who was murdered," explained the servant, who still stood in the doorway.

"I know," I replied. "I was just trying the glasses." Then I put them down, and on turning saw upon the mantelshelf a small, bright-red candleshade, which I took in my hand. It was made, I found, to fit upon the electric table-lamp.

"Miss Muriel was very fond of a red light," explained the young woman; and as I held it I wondered if that light had ever been placed upon the toilet-table and the blind drawn up - whether it had ever been used as a warning of danger?

As I expressed a desire to see the young lady's boudoir, the maid Cameron took me down to the luxurious little room where, the first moment I entered, one fact struck me as peculiar. The picture of Elma Heath was no longer there. The photograph had been taken from its frame, and in its place was the portrait of a broad-browed, full-bearded man in a foreign military uniform - a picture that, being soiled and faded, had evidently been placed there to fill the empty frame.

Whose hand had secured that portrait before the Leithcourt's flight? Why, indeed, should I, for the second time, discover the unhappy girl's picture missing?

"Has the gentleman who called on the evening of Mr. Leithcourt's disappearance been back here again since he left the hospital?" I inquired as a sudden idea occurred to me.

"Yes, sir. He called here in a fly on the day he came out, and at his request I took him over the castle. He went into the library, and spent half-an-hour in pacing across it, taking measurements, and examining the big cupboard in which he was found insensible. It was a strange affair, sir," added the young woman, "wasn't it?"

"Very," I replied.

"The gentleman might have been in there now had I not gone into the library and found a lot of illustrated papers, which I always put in the cupboard to keep the place tidy, thrown out on to the floor. I went to put them back but discovered the door locked. The key I afterwards found in the grate, where Mr. Leithcourt had evidently thrown it, and on opening the door imagine the shock I had when I found the visitor lying doubled up. I, of course, thought he was dead."

"And when he returned here on his recovery, did he question you?"

"Oh, yes. He asked about the Leithcourts, and especially about Miss Muriel. I believe he's rather sweet on her, by the way he spoke. And really no better or kinder lady never breathed, I'm sure. We're all very sorry indeed for her."

"But she had nothing to do with the affair."

"Of course not. But she shares in the scandal and disgrace. You should have seen the effect of the news upon the guests when they knew that the Leithcourts had gone. It was a regular pandemonium. They ordered the best champagne out of the cellars and drank it, the men cleared all the cigar-boxes, and the women rummaged in the wardrobes until they seemed like a pack of hungry wolves. Everybody went away with their trunks full of the Leithcourt's things. They took whatever they could lay their hands on, and we, the servants, couldn't stop them. I did remonstrate with one lady who was cramming into her trunk two of Miss Muriel's best evening dresses, but she told me to mind my own business and leave the room. One man I saw go away with four of Mr. Leithcourt's guns, and there was a regular squabble in the billiard-room over a set of pearl and emerald dress-studs that somebody found in his dressing-room. Crane, the valet, says they tossed for them."

"Disgraceful!" I ejaculated. "Then as soon as the host and hostess had gone, they simply swept through the rooms and cleared them?"

"Yes, sir. They took away all that was most valuable. They'd have had the silver, only Mason had thrown it into the plate-chest, all dirty as it was, locked it up and hid the key. The plate was Mr. Gilrae's, you know, sir, and Mason was responsible."

"He acted wisely," I said, surprised at the domestic's story. "Why, the guests acted like a gang of thieves."

"They were, sir. They rushed all over the house like demons let loose, and they even stole some of our things. I lost a silver chain."

"And what did the stranger say when you told him of this?"

"He smiled. It did not seem to surprise him in the least, for after all his visit was the cause of the sudden breaking up of the party, wasn't it?"

"And did you show him over the whole house?" I inquired.

"Yes, sir," responded the servant. "Curiously enough he had with him what seemed to be a large plan of the castle, and as we went from room to room he compared it with his plan. He was here for hours, and told me he wanted to make a thorough examination of the place and didn't want to be disturbed. He also said that he might probably take the place for next season, if he liked it. I think, however, he only told me this because he thought I would be more patient while he took his measurements and made his investigations. He was here from twelve till nearly six o'clock, and went through every room, even up to the turrets."

"He came into this room, I suppose?"

"Yes, sir," she responded, with just a slight hesitation, I thought. "This was the room where he stayed the longest. There was a photograph in that frame over there," she added, indicating the frame that had held the picture of Elma Heath, "a portrait of a young lady, which he begged me to give him."

"And you gave it to him?" I cried quickly.

"Well - yes, sir. He begged so hard for it, saying that it was the portrait of a friend of his."

"And he gave you something handsome for it - eh?"

The young woman, whom I knew could not refuse half-a-sovereign, colored slightly and smiled.

"And who put that picture in its place?" I asked.

"I did, sir. I found it upstairs."

"He didn't tell you who the young lady was, I suppose?"

"No, sir. He only said that that was the only photograph that existed, and that she was dead."

"Dead!" I gasped, staring at her.

"Yes, sir. That was why he was so anxious for the picture."

Elma Heath dead! Could it be true? That sweet-pictured face haunted me as no other face had ever impressed itself upon my memory. It somehow seemed to impel me to endeavor to penetrate the mystery, and yet Hylton Chater had declared that she was dead! I recollected the remarkable letter from Abo, and her own declaration that her end was near. That letter was, she said, the last she should write to her friend. Did Hylton Chater actually possess knowledge of the girl's death? Had he all along been acquainted with her whereabouts? What the young woman told me upset all my plans. If Elma Heath were really dead, then she was beyond discovery, and the truth would be hidden forever.

"After he had put the photograph in his pocket, the gentleman made a most minute search in this room," the domestic went on. "He consulted his plan, took several measurements, and then tapped on the paneling all along this wall, as though he were searching for some hidden cupboard or hiding place. I looked at the plan, and saw a mark in red ink upon it. He was trying to discover that spot , and was greatly disappointed at not being able to do so. He was in here over an hour, and made a most careful search all around."

"And what explanation did he give?"

"He only said, 'If I find what I want, Ann, I shall make you a present of a ten-pound note.' That naturally made me anxious."

"He made no other remark about the young lady's death?" I inquired anxiously.

"No. Only he sighed, and looked steadily for a long time at the photograph. I saw his lips moving, but his words were inaudible."

"You haven't any idea of the reason why he called upon Mr. Leithcourt, I suppose?"

"From what he said, I've formed my own conclusions," was her answer.

"And what is your opinion?"

"Well, I feel certain that there is, or was, something concealed in this house that he's very anxious to obtain. He came to demand it of Mr. Leithcourt, but what happened in the library we don't know. He, however, believes that Mr. Leithcourt has not taken it away, and that, whatever it may be, it is still hidden here."

CHAPTER X

I SHOW MY HAND

On my return to London next day I made inquiry at the Admiralty and learned that the battleship *Bulwark* was lying at Palermo, therefore I telegraphed to Jack Durnford, and late the same afternoon his reply came at the Cecil: -

"Due in London twentieth. Dine with me at club that evening - Jack."

The twentieth! That meant nearly a month of inactivity. In that time I could cross to Abo, make inquiries there, and ascertain, perhaps, if Elma Heath were actually dead as Chater had declared.

Two facts struck me as remarkable: Baron Oberg was said to be Polish, while the dark-bearded proprietor of the restaurant in Westbourne Grove was also of the same nationality. Then I recollected that pretty little enameled cross that Mackenzie had found in Rannoch Wood, and it suddenly occurred to me that it might possibly be the miniature of one of the European orders of chivalry. In the club library at midnight I found a copy of Cappelletti's *Storia degli Ordini Cavallereschi*, the standard work on the subject, and on searching the illustrations I at length discovered a picture of it. It was a Russian order - the coveted Order of Saint Anne, bestowed by the Czar only upon persons who have rendered eminent services to the State and to the sovereign. One fact was now certain, namely, that the owner of that tiny cross, the small replica of the fine decoration, must be a person of high official standing.

Next day I spent in making inquiries with a view to discovering the house said to be occupied by Leithcourt. As it was not either in the Directory or the Blue Book, I concluded that he had perhaps rented it furnished, and after many inquiries and considerable difficulties I found that such was the fact. He had occupied the house of Lady Heathcote, a few doors from Grosvenor Square, for the previous season, although he had lived there but very little.

Where the fugitives were in hiding I had no idea. I longed to meet Muriel again and tell her what I had discovered, yet it was plain that the trio were concealing themselves from Hylton Chater, whom I supposed to be now back in London.

The autumn days were dull and rainy, and the streets were muddy and unpleasant, as they always are at the fall of the year. Compelled to remain inactive, I idled in the club with the recollection of that pictured face ever before me - the face of the unfortunate girl who wished her last message to be conveyed to Philip Hornby. What, I wondered, was her secret? What was really her fate?

This latter question troubled me until I could bear it no longer. I felt that it was my duty to go to Finland and endeavor to learn something regarding this Baron Oberg and his niece. Frank Hutcheson had written me declaring that the weather in Leghorn was now perfect, and expressing wonder that I did not return. I was his only English friend, and I knew how dull he was when alone. Even his Majesty's Consuls sometimes suffer from homesickness, and long for the smell of the London gutters and a glass of homely bitter ale.

But you, my reader, who have lived in a foreign land for any length of time, know well how wearisome becomes the life, however brilliant, and how sweet are the recollections of our dear gray old England with her green fields, her muddy lanes, and the bustling streets of her gray, grimy cities. You have but one "home," and England Is still your home, even though you may become the most bigoted of cosmopolitans and may have no opportunity of speaking your native tongue the whole year through.

Duty - the duty of a man who had learned strange facts and knew that a defenseless woman was a victim - called me to Finland. Therefore, with my passport properly vised and my papers all in order, I one night left Hull for Stockholm by the weekly Wilson service. Four days of rough weather in the North Sea and the Baltic brought me to the Swedish capital, whence on the following day I took the small steamer which plies three times a week around the Aland Islands, and then across the Gulf of Bothnia to Korpo, and through the intricate channels and among those low-lying islands to the gray lethargic town of Abo.

It was not the first occasion on which I had trod Russian soil, and I knew too well the annoyances of the bureaucracy. Finland, however, is perhaps the most severely governed of any of the Czar's dominions, and I had my first taste of its stern, relentless officialdom at the moment of landing on the half-deserted quay.

In the wooden passport office the uniformed official, on examining my passport, discovered that at the Russian Consulate-General they had forgotten to date the vise which had been impressed with a rubber stamp. It was signed by the Consul-General, but the date was missing, whereupon the man shook his head and handed back the document curtly, saying in Russian, which I understood fairly well, although I spoke badly -

"This is not in order. It must be returned to London and dated before you can proceed."

"But it is not my fault," I protested. "It is the fault of the clerk at the Consulate-General."

"You should have examined it before leaving. You must send it to London, and return to Stockholm by to-night's boat."

"But this is outrageous!" I cried, as he had already taken the papers of a passenger behind me and was looking at them with unconcern.

"Enough!" he exclaimed, glaring at me. "You will return to-night, or if you choose to stay you will be arrested for landing without a passport."

"I shall not go back!" I declared defiantly. "Your Consul-General vised my passport, and I claim, under international law, to be allowed to proceed without hindrance."

"The steamer leaves at six o'clock," he remarked without looking up. "If you are in Abo after that it will be at your own risk."

"I am English, recollect," I said.

"To me it does not matter what or who you are. Your passport, undated, is worthless."

"I shall complain to the Ambassador at Petersburg."

"Your Ambassador does not interest me in the least. He is not Ambassador here in Finland. There is no Czar here."

"Oh! Who is ruler in this country, pray?"

"His Excellency the Governor-General, an official who has love for neither England nor the pigs of English. So recollect that."

"Yes," I said meaningly, "I shall recollect it." And I turned and went out of the little wooden office, replacing my passport in my pocket-book.

I had already been directed to the hotel, and walked there, but as I did so I saw that I was already under the surveillance of the police, for two men in plain clothes who were lounging outside the passport-office strolled on after me, evidently to watch my movements. Truly Finland was under the iron-heel of autocracy.

After taking my rooms, I strolled about the flat, uninteresting town, wondering how best to commence my search. If I had but a photograph to show people it would give me a great advantage, but I had nothing. I had never, indeed, set eyes upon the unfortunate girl.

Six o'clock came. I heard the steam siren of the departing boat bound for Sweden, but I was determined to remain there at whatever cost, therefore I returned to the hotel, and at seven dined comfortably in company with a German who had been my fellow-passenger across from Stockholm.

At eight o'clock, however, just as we were idling over dessert, two gray-coated police officers entered and arrested me on the serious charge of landing without a passport.

I accompanied them to the police-office, where I was ushered into the presence of the big, bristly Russian who held the town of Abo in terror, the Chief of Police. The officials which Russia sends into Finland are selected for their harsh discipline and hide-bound bureaucracy, and this human machine in uniform was no exception. Had he been the Minister of the Interior himself, he could not have been more self-opinionated.

"Well?" he snapped, looking up at me as I was placed before him. "Your name is Gordon Gregg, English, from Stockholm. No passport, and decline to leave even though warned - eh?"

"I have a passport," I said firmly, producing it.

He looked at it, and pointing with his finger, said: "It has no date, and is therefore worthless."

"The fault is not mine, but that of a Russian official. If you wish it to be dated, you may send it to your Consulate-General in London."

"I shall not," he cried, glaring at me angrily. "And for your insult to the law, I shall commit you to prison for one month. Perhaps you will then learn Russian manners."

"Oh! so you will commit an Englishman to prison for a month, without trial - eh? That's very interesting! Perhaps if you attempt such a thing as that they may have something to say about it in Petersburg."

"You defy me!"

"Not in the least. I have presented my passport and demand common courtesy."

"Your passport is worthless, I tell you!" he cried. "There, that's how much it is worth to me!" And snatching it up he tore it in half and tossed the pieces of blue paper in my face.

My blood was up at this insult, yet I bit my lips and remained quite calm.

"Perhaps you will kindly tell me who you are?" I asked in as quiet a voice as I could command.

"With pleasure. I am Michael Boranski, Chief of Police of the Province of Abo-Biornebourg."

"Ah! Well, Michael Boranski, I shall trouble you to pick up my passport, stick it together again, and apologize to me."

"Apologize! Me apologize!" And the fellow laughed aloud, while the police officers on either side of me grinned from ear to ear.

"You refuse?"

"Refuse? Certainly I do!"

"Very well, then," I said, re-opening my pocket-book and taking out an open letter. "Perhaps you will kindly glance at that. It is in Russian, so you can read it."

He snatched it from me with ill-grace, but not without curiosity. And then, as he read the lines, his face changed and he went paler. Raising his head, he stood staring at me open-mouthed in amazement.

"I apologize to your Excellency!" he gasped, blanched to the lips. "I most humbly apologize. I - I did not know. You told me nothing!"

"Perhaps you will kindly mend my passport, and give it a proper vise."

In an instant he was up from his chair, and having gathered the torn paper from the floor, proceeded to paste it together. On the back he endorsed that it had been torn by accident, and then gave it the proper vise, affixing the stamps.

"I trust, Excellency," he said, bowing low as he handed it to me, "I trust that this affair will not trouble you further. I assure you I had no intention of insulting you."

"Yes, you had!" I said. "You insulted me merely because I am English. But recollect in future that the man who insults an Englishman generally pays for it, and I do not intend to let this pass. There is a higher power in Finland than even the Governor-General."

"But, Excellency," whined the fellow who only ten minutes ago had been such an insulting bully, "I shall lose my position. I have a wife and six children - my wife is delicate, and my pay here is not a large one. You will forgive, won't you, Excellency?

I have apologized - I most humbly apologize."

And he took up the letter I had given him, holding it gingerly with trembling fingers. And well he might, for the document was headed:

"MINISTER OF THE IMPERIAL HOUSEHOLD, PALACE OF PETERHOF.

"The bearer of this is one Gordon Francis Gregg, British subject, whom it is Our will and command that he shall be Our guest during his journey through our dominion. And we hereby command all Governors of Provinces and minor officials to afford him all the facilities he requires and privileges and immunities as Our guest."

The above decree was in a neat copper-plate handwriting in Russian, while beneath was the sprawling signature of the ruler of one hundred and thirty millions of people, that signature that was all-powerful from the gulf of Bothnia to the Pacific - "Nicholas."

The document was the one furnished to me a year before when, at the invitation of the Russian Government, I had gone on a mission of inquiry into the state of the prisons in order to see, on behalf of the British public, whether things were as black as some writers had painted them. It had been my intention to visit the far-off penal settlements in Northern Siberia, but having gone through some twenty prisons in European Russia, my health had failed and I had been compelled to return to Italy to recuperate. The document had therefore remained in my possession because I intended to resume my journey in the following summer. It was in order that I should be permitted to go where I liked, and to see what I liked without official hindrance, that his Majesty the Emperor had, at the instigation of the Ministry of the Interior, given me that most valuable document.

Sight of it had changed the Chief of Police from a burly bully into a whining coward, for he saw that he had torn up the passport of a guest of the Czar, and the consequence was most serious if I complained. He begged of me to pardon him, urging all manner of excuses, and humbling himself before me as well as before his two inferiors, who now regarded me with awe.

"I will atone for the insult in any way your high Excellency desires," declared the official. "I will serve your Excellency in any way he may command."

His words suggested a brilliant idea. I had this man in my power; he feared me.

"Well," I said after some reluctance, "there is a little matter in which you might be of some assistance. If you will, I will reconsider my decision of complaining to Petersburg."

"And what is that, Excellency?" he gasped eagerly.

"I desire to know the whereabouts of a young English lady named Elma Heath," I said, and I wrote down the name for him upon a piece of paper. "Age about twenty, and was at school at Chichester, in England. She is a niece of a certain Baron Oberg."

"Baron Oberg!" he repeated, looking at me rather strangely, I thought.

"Yes, as she is a foreigner she will be registered in your books. She is somewhere in your province, but where I do not know. Tell me where she is, and I will say nothing more about my passport," I added.

"Then your high Excellency wishes to see the young lady?" he said reflectively, with the paper in his hand.

"Yes."

"In that case, it being commanded by the Emperor that I shall serve your Excellency, I will have immediate inquiries made," was his answer. "When I discover her whereabouts, I will do myself the pleasure of calling at your Excellency's hotel."

And I left the fellow, very satisfied that I had turned his officiousness and hatred of the English to very good account.

On that gray, dreary northern coast the long winter was fast setting in. Poor oppressed Finland suffers under a hard climate with August frosts, an eight months' winter in the north, and five months of frost in the south. Idling in sleepy Abo, where the public buildings were so mean and meager and the houses for the most part built of wood, I saw on every hand the disastrous result of the attempted Russification of the country. The hand of the oppressor, that official sent from Petersburg to crush and to conquer, was upon the honest Finnish nation. The Russian bureaucracy was trying to destroy its weaker but more successful neighbor, and in order to do so employed the harshest and most unscrupulous officials it could import.

My fellow-traveler from Stockholm, who represented a firm of paper-makers in Hamburg, and who paid an annual visit to Abo and Helsingfors, acted as my guide around the town, while I awaited the information from the humbled Chief of Police. My German friend pointed out to me how, since Russia placed her hand upon Finland, progress had been arrested, and certainly plain evidences were on every hand. There was growing discontent everywhere, for many of the newspapers had recently been suppressed and the remainder were under a severe censorship; agriculture had already decreased, and many of the cotton-spinning and saw mills were silent and deserted. The exploitation of those gigantic forests from which millions of trunks were floated down to the sea annually had now been suspended, the great landowners were deserting the country, and there was silence and depression everywhere. Finland had been separated for economic purposes from the more civilized countries, and bound to the poverty-stricken, artificially isolated and oppressed Russia. The double-headed eagle was everywhere, and the people sat silent and brooding beneath its black shadow.

"There will be an uprising here before long," declared the German confidentially, as we were taking tea one day on the wooden balcony of the hotel where the sea and the low-lying islands stretched out before us in the pale yellow of the autumn sundown. "The people will revolt, as they did in Poland. The Finnish Government can only appeal to the Czar through the Governor-General, and one can easily imagine that their suggestions never reach the Emperor. It is said here that the harsher and more corrupt the official, the greater honor does he receive from Petersburg. But trouble is brewing for Russia," he added. "A very serious trouble - depend upon it."

I looked upon the gray dismal scene, the empty port, the silent quay, the dark line of gloomy pine forest away beyond the town, the broken coast and the wide expanse of water glittering in the northern sunset. Yes. The very silence seemed to forbode evil and mystery. Truly what I saw of Finland impressed me even more than what I had witnessed in the far-off eastern provinces of European Russia.

My object, however, was not to inquire into the internal condition of Finland, or of her resentment of her powerful conqueror. I was there to find that unfortunate girl who had written so strangely to her old school friend and whose portrait had, for some hidden reason, been destroyed.

On the morning of the third day after my arrival at Abo, while sitting on the hotel veranda reading an old copy of the Paris *Journal*, many portions of which had been "blacked out" by the censor, the Chief of Police, in his dark green uniform, entered and saluted before me.

"Your Excellency, may I be permitted to speak with you in private?"

"Certainly," I responded, rising and conducting him to my bedroom, where I closed the door, invited him to a seat, and myself sat upon the edge of the bed.

"I have made various inquiries," he said, "and I think I have found the lady your Excellency is seeking. My information, however, must be furnished to you in strictest confidence," he added, "because there are reasons why I should withhold her whereabouts from you."

"What do you mean?" I inquired. "What reasons?"

"Well - the lady is living in Finland in secret."

"Then she is alive!" I exclaimed quickly. "I thought she was dead."

"To the world she is dead," responded Michael Boranski, stroking his red beard. "For that reason the information I give you must be treated as confidential."

"Why should she be in hiding? She is guilty of no offense - is she?"

The man shrugged his shoulders, but did not reply.

"And this Baron Oberg? You tell me nothing of him," I said with dissatisfaction.

"How can I when I know nothing, Excellency?" was his response.

I felt certain that the fellow was not speaking the truth, for I had noticed his surprise when I had first uttered the mysterious nobleman's name.

"As I have already said, Excellency, I am desirous of atoning for my insult, and will serve you in every manner I can. For that reason I had sought news of the young English lady - the

Mademoiselle Heath."

"But you have all foreigners registered in your books," I said. "The search was surely not a difficult one. I know your police methods in Russia too well," I laughed.

"No, the lady was not registered," he said. "There was a reason."

"Why?"

"I have told you, Excellency. She is in hiding."

"Where?"

"I regret that much as I desire, I dare not appear to have any connection with your quest. But I will direct you. Indeed, I will give you instructions to a second person to take you to her."

"Is she in Abo?"

"No. Away in the country. If your Excellency will be down at the end of the quay to-morrow at noon you will find a carriage in waiting, and the driver will have full instructions how to take you to her and how to act. Follow his directions implicitly, for he is a man I can trust."

"To-morrow!" I cried anxiously. "Why not to-day? I am ready to go at any moment."

The Chief of Police remained thoughtful for a few moments, then said -

"Well, if I could find the man, you might go to-day. Yet it is a long way, and you would not return before to-morrow."

"The roads are safe, I suppose? I don't mind driving in the night."

The official glanced at the clock, and rising exclaimed -

"Very well, I will send for the man. If we find him, then the carriage will be at the same spot at the eastern end of the quay in two hours."

"At noon. Very well. I shall keep the appointment."

"And after seeing her, you will of course keep your promise of secrecy regarding our little misunderstanding?" he asked anxiously.

"I have already given my word," was the response; and the man bowed and left, much, I think, to the surprise of the hotel-proprietor and his staff. It was an unusual thing for such a high official as the Chief of Police to visit one of their guests in person. If he desired to interview any of them, he commanded them to attend at his office, or they were escorted there by his gray-coated agents.

The day was cold, with a biting wind from the icy north, when after a hasty luncheon I put on my overcoat and strolled along the deserted quay where I lounged at the further end, watching the approach of a great pontoon of pine logs that had apparently floated out of one of the rivers and was now being navigated to the port by four men who seemed every moment in imminent danger of being washed off the raft into the sea as the waves broke over and drenched them. They had, however, lashed themselves to their raft, I saw, and now slowly piloted the great floating platform towards the quay.

I think I must have waited half an hour, when my attention was suddenly attracted by the rattle of wheels over the stones, and turning I saw an old closed carriage drawn by three horses abreast, with bells upon the harness, approaching me rapidly. When it drew up, the driver, a burly-looking, fair-headed Finn in a huge sheepskin overcoat, motioned me to enter, urging in broken Russian -

"Quickly, Excellency! - quickly! - you must not be seen!"

And then the instant I was seated, and before I could close the door, the horses plunged forward and we were tearing at full gallop out of the town.

For five miles or so we skirted the sea along a level, well-made road through a barren wind-swept country whence the meager harvest had already been garnered. There were no villages. All around was a houseless land, rolling miles of brown and green, broken and checkered by bits of forest and clumps of dark melancholy pines. The road ran ever and anon right down to where the cold, green waves broke upon the rocky shore. In a few weeks that coast would be ice-bound and snow-covered, and then the silence of the God-forsaken country would be complete.

After five miles or so, the driver pulled up and descended to readjust his harness, whereupon I got out and asked him in the best Russian I could command:

"Where are we going?"

"To Nystad."

"How far is that?"

"Sixty-eight," was his reply.

I took him to imply kilometres, as being a Finn he would not speak of versts.

"The Chief of Police has given you directions?" I asked.

"His high Excellency has told me exactly what to do," was the man's answer, as he took out his huge wooden pipe and filled it. "You wish to see the young lady?"

"Yes," I answered, "to first see her, and I do not know whether it will be necessary for me to make myself known to her. Where is she?"

"Beyond Nystad," was his vague answer with a wave of his big fat hand in the direction of the dark pine forest that stretched before us. "We shall be there about an hour after sundown."

Then I re-entered the stuffy old conveyance that rocked and rolled as we dashed away over the uneven forest road, and sat wondering to what manner of place I was being conducted.

Elma Heath was in hiding. Why? I recollected her curious letter and remembered every word of it. She wished Hornby to know that she had never revealed her secret. What secret, I wondered?

I lit an abominable cigar, and tried to smoke, but I was too filled with anxiety, too bewildered by the maze of mystery in which I now found myself. Two hours later we pulled up before a long log-built post-house just beyond a small town in a hollow that faced the sea, and I alighted to watch the steaming horses being replaced by a trio of fresh ones. The place was Dadendal, I was informed, and the proprietor of the place, when I entered and tossed off a liqueur-glass of cognac, pointed out to me a row of granite buildings fallen much to decay as the ancient convent.

Then, resuming our journey, the short day quickly drew to a close, the sun sank yellow and watery over the towering pines through which we went mile after mile, a dense, interminable forest wherein the wolves lurked in winter, often rendering the road dangerous.

The temperature fell, and it froze again. Through the window in front I could see the big Finn driver throwing his arms across his shoulders to promote circulation, in the same manner as does the London "cabby."

When night drew on we changed horses again at a small, dirty

WILLIAM LE QUEUX

post-house in the forest, at the edge of a lake, and then pushed forward again, although it was already long past the hour at which he had said we should arrive.

Time passed slowly in the darkness, for we had no light, and the horses seemed to find their way by instinct. The rolling of the lumbering old vehicle after six hours had rendered me sleepy, I think, for I recollect closing my eyes and conjuring up that strange scene on board the *Lola*.

Indeed, I suppose I must have slept, for I was awakened by a light shining into my face and the driver shaking me by the shoulder. When I roused myself and, naturally, inquired the reason, he placed his finger mysteriously upon my lips, saying:

"Hush, your high nobility, hush! Come with me. But make no noise. If we are discovered, it means death for us - death. Come, give me your hand. Slowly. Tread softly. See, here is the boat. I will get in first. We shall not be heard upon the water. So."

And the fellow led me, half-dazed, down to the bank of a broad, dark river which I could just distinguish - he led me to an unknown bourne.

CHAPTER XI

THE CASTLE OF THE TERROR

The big Finn had, I found, tied up his horses, and in the heavy old boat he rowed me down the swollen river which ran swift and turbulent around a sudden bend and then seemed to open out to a great width. In the starlight I could distinguish that it stretched gray and level to a distance, and that the opposite bank was fringed with pines.

"Where are we going?" I asked my guide in a low voice. But he only whispered:

"Hush! Excellency! Remain patient, and you shall see the young Englishwoman."

So I sat in the boat, while he allowed it to drift with the current, steering it with the great heavy oars. The river suddenly narrowed again, with high pines on either bank, a silent, lonesome reach, perhaps indeed one of the loneliest spots in all Europe. Once the dismal howl of a wolf sounded close to where we passed, but my guide made no remark.

After nearly a mile, the stream again opened out into a broad lake where, in the distance, I saw rising sheer and high from the water, a long square building of three stories, with a tall round tower at one corner - an old medieval castle it seemed to be. From one of the small windows of the tower, as we came into view of it, a light was shining upon the water, and my guide seeing it, grunted in satisfaction. It had undoubtedly been placed there as signal.

With great caution he approached the place, keeping in the deep shadow of the bank until we came exactly opposite the flanking-tower. In the lighted window I distinctly saw a dark figure of someone appear for a moment, and then my guide struck a match and held it in his fingers until it was wholly consumed.

Almost instantly the light was extinguished, and then, after waiting five minutes or so, he pulled straight across the lake to the high, dark tower that descended into the water. The place was as grim and silent as any I had ever seen, an impregnable stronghold of the days before siege guns were invented, the fortress of some feudal prince or count who had probably held the surrounding country in thraldom.

I put my hand against the black, slimy wall to prevent the boat bumping, and then distinguished just beyond me a small wooden ledge and half-a-dozen steps which led up to a low arched door. The latter had opened noiselessly, and the dark figure of a woman stood peering forth.

My guide uttered some reassuring word in Finnish in a low half-whisper, and then slowly pushed the boat along to the ledge, saying:

"Your high nobility may disembark. There is at present no danger."

I rose, gripped a big rusty chain to steady myself, and climbed into the narrow doorway in the ponderous wall, where I found myself in the darkness beside the female who had apparently been expecting our arrival and watching our signal.

Without a word she led me through a short passage, and then, striking a match, lit a big old-fashioned lantern. As the light fell upon her features I saw they were thin and hard, with deep-set eyes and a stray wisp of silver across her wrinkled brow. Around her head was a kind of hood of the same stuff as her dress, a black, coarse woolen, while around her neck was a broad linen collar. In an instant I recognized that she was a member of some religious order, some minor order perhaps, with whose habit we, in Italy, were not acquainted.

The thin ascetic countenance was that of a woman of strong character, and her funereal habit seemed much too large for her stunted, shrunken figure.

"The sister speaks French?" I hazarded in that language, knowing that in most convents throughout Europe French is known.

"Oui, m'sieur," was her answer. "And a leetle Engleesh, too - a ve-ry leetle," she smiled.

"You know why I am here?" I said, gratified that at least one person in that lonesome country could speak my own tongue.

"Yes, I have already been told," was her answer with a strong accent, as we stood in that small, bare stone room, a semi-circular chamber in the tower, once perhaps a prison. "But are you not afraid to venture here?" she asked.

"Why?"

"Well - because no strangers are permitted here, you know. If your presence here was discovered you would not leave this place alive - so I warn you."

"I am prepared to risk that," I said, smiling; at the same time my hand instinctively sought my hip-pocket to ascertain that my weapon was safe. "I wish to see Miss Elma Heath."

The old nun nodded, fumbling with her lantern. I glanced at my watch and found that it was already two o'clock in the morning.

WILLIAM LE QUEUX

"Remember that if you are discovered here you exonerate me of all blame?" she said, raising her head and peering into my face with her keen gray eyes. "By admitting you I am betraying my trust, and that I should not have done were it not compulsory."

"Compulsory! How?"

"The order of the Chief of Police. Even here, we cannot afford to offend him."

So the fellow Boranski had really kept faith with me, and at his order the closed door of the convent had been opened.

"Of course not," I answered. "Russian officialdom is all-powerful in Finland nowadays. But where is the lady?"

"You are still prepared to risk your liberty and life?" she asked in a hoarse voice, full of grim meaning.

"I am," I said. "Lead me to her."

"And when you see her you will make no effort to speak with her? Promise me that."

"Ah, Sister!" I cried. "You are asking too great a sacrifice of me. I come here from England, nay, from Italy in search of her, to question her regarding a strange mystery and to learn the truth. Surely I may be permitted to speak with her?"

"You wish to learn the truth, sir!" remarked the woman. "I thought you were her lover - that you merely wished to see her once again."

"No, I am not her lover," I answered. "Indeed, we have never yet met. But I am in search of the truth from her own lips."

"That you will never learn," she said, in a hard, changed voice.

"Because there is a conspiracy to preserve the secret!" I cried. "But I intend to solve the mystery, and for that reason I have traveled here from England."

The woman with the lantern smiled sadly, as though amused by my impetuosity.

"You are on Russian soil now, m'sieur, not English," she remarked in her broken English. "If your object were known, you would never be spared to return to your own land. Ah!" she sighed, "you do not know the mysteries and terrors of Finland. I am a French subject, born in Tours, and brought to Helsingfors when I was fifteen. I have been in Finland forty-five years. Once we were happy here, but since the Czar appointed Baron Oberg to be Governor-General - " and she shrugged her shoulders without finishing her sentence.

"Baron Oberg - Governor-General of Finland!" I gasped.

"Certainly. Did you not know?" she said, dropping into French. "It is four years now that he has held supreme power to crush and Russify these poor Finns. Ah, m'sieur! this country, once so prosperous, is a blot upon the face of Europe. His methods are the worst and most unscrupulous of any employed by Russia. Before he came here he was the best hated man in Petersburg, and that, they say, is why the Emperor sent him to us."

"And he is uncle of this young lady, Elma Heath?"

"Uncle? Ah! I don't know that, m'sieur. I have never been told so. His niece - poor young lady! - can that be? Surely not!"

"Why not?" I asked.

But the woman gave me no reason; she only exhibited her palms and sighed. She seemed to have compassion upon the girl I sought; her heart was really softer than I had believed it to be.

WILLIAM LE QUEUX

"Where does this Baron live?" I asked, surprised that he should occupy so high a place in Russian officialdom - the representative of the Czar, with powers as great as the Emperor himself.

"At the Government Palace, in Helsingfors."

"And Elma Heath is here - in this grim fortress! Why?"

"Ah, m'sieur, how can I tell? By reason of family secrets, perhaps. They account for so much, you know."

"That is exactly my opinion," I said. "She has been brought here against her will."

"Most probably. This is not a cheerful place, as you see. We have five months of ice and snow, and for four months are practically cut off from civilization and see no new face."

"Terrible!" I gasped, glancing round at those dark stone walls that seemed to breathe an air of tragedy and mystery. The old castle had, I supposed, been turned into a convent, as many have been in Germany and Austria. Back in feudal times it no doubt had been a grand old place. "And have you been here long?" I asked.

"Seven years only. But I am leaving. Even I, used as I am to a solitary life, can stand it no longer. I feel that its cold silence and dreariness will drive me mad. In winter the place is like an ice-well."

The fact that the Baron was ruler of Finland amazed me, for I had half-expected him to be some clever adventurer. Yet as the events of the past flashed through my brain, I recollected that in Rannoch Wood had been found the miniature of the Russian Order of Saint Anne, a distinction which, in all probability, had been conferred upon him. If so, the coincidence, to say the least, was a remarkable one. I questioned my companion further regarding the Baron.

"Ah, m'sieur," she declared, "they call him 'The Strangler of the Finns,' It was he who ordered the peasants of Kasko to be flogged until four of them died - and the Czar gave him the Star of White Eagle for it - he who suppressed half the newspapers and put eighteen editors in prison for publishing a report of a meeting of the Swedes in Helsingfors; he who encourages corruption and bribery among the officials for the furtherance of Russian interests; he who has ordered Russian to be the official language, who has restricted public education, who has overtaxed and ground down the people until now the mine is laid, and Finland is ready for open revolt. The prisons are filled with the innocent; women are flogged; the poor are starving, and 'The Strangler,' as they call him, reports to the Czar that Finland is submissive and is Russianized!"

I had heard something of this abominable state of affairs from time to time from the English press, but had never taken notice of the name of the oppressor. So the uncle of Elma Heath was "The Strangler of Finland," the man who, in four years, had reduced a prosperous country to a state of ruin and revolt!

"Cannot I see her?" I asked, feeling that we had remained too long there. If my presence in that place was perilous the sooner I escaped from it the better.

"Yes, come," she said. "But silence! Walk softly," and holding up the old horn lantern to give me light, she led me out into the low stone corridor again, conducting me through a number of intricate passages, all bare and gloomy, the stones worn hollow by the feet of ages. On we crept noiselessly past a number of low arched doors studded with big nails in the style of generations ago, then turning suddenly at right angles, I saw that we were in a kind of *cul de sac,* before the door of which at the end she stopped and placed her finger upon her lips. Then, motioning me to remain there, she entered, closing the door after her, and leaving me in the pitch darkness.

I strained my ears , but could hear no sound save that of

someone moving within. No word was uttered, or if so, it was whispered so low that it did not reach me. For nearly five minutes I waited in impatience outside that closed door, until again the handle turned and my conductress beckoned me in silence within.

I stepped into a small, square chamber, the floor of which was carpeted, and where, suspended high above, was a lamp that shed but a faint light over the barely-furnished place. It seemed to me to be a kind of sitting-room, with a plain deal table and a couple of chairs, but there was no stove, and the place looked chill and comfortless. Beyond was another smaller room into which the old nun disappeared for a moment; then she came forth leading a strange wan little figure in a gray gown, a figure whose face was the most perfect and most lovely I had ever seen. Her wealth of chestnut hair fell disheveled about her shoulders, and as her hands were clasped before her she looked straight at me in surprise as she was led towards me.

She walked but feebly, and her countenance was deathly pale. Her dress, as she came beneath the lamp, was, I saw, coarse, yet clean, and her beautiful, regular features, which in her photograph had held me in such fascination, were even more sweet and more matchless than I had believed them to be. I stood before her dumbfounded in admiration.

In silence she bowed gracefully, and then looked at me with astonishment, apparently wondering what I, a perfect stranger, required of her.

"Miss Elma Heath, I presume?" I exclaimed at last. "May I introduce myself to you? My name is Gordon Gregg, English by birth, cosmopolitan by instinct. I have come here to ask you a question - a question that concerns yourself. Lydia Moreton has sent me to you."

I noticed that her great brown eyes watched my lips and not my face.

Her own lips moved, but she looked at me with an inexpressible sadness. No sound escaped her.

I stood rigid before her as one turned to stone, for in that instant, in a flash indeed, I realized the awful truth.

She was both deaf and dumb!

She raised her clasped hands to me in silence, yet with tears welling in her splendid eyes.

I saw that upon her wrists were a pair of bright steel gyves.

"What is this place?" I demanded of the woman in the religious habit, when I recovered from the shock of the poor girl's terrible affliction. "Where am I?"

"This is the Castle of Kajana - the criminal lunatic asylum of Finland," was her answer. "The prisoner, as you see, has lost both speech and hearing."

"Deaf and dumb!" I cried, looking at the beautiful original of that destroyed photograph on board the *Lola*. "But she has surely not always been so!" I exclaimed.

"No. I think not always," replied the sister quietly. "But you said you intended to question her, and did I not tell you that to learn the truth was impossible?"

"But she can write responses to my questions?" I argued.

"Alas! no," was the old woman's whispered reply. "Her mind is affected. She is, unfortunately, a hopeless lunatic."

I looked straight into those sad, wide-open, yet unflinching brown eyes utterly confounded.

Those white wrists held in steel, that pale face and blanched lips, the inertness of her movements, all told their own tragic tale. And yet that letter I had read, dictated in secret most probably because her hands were not free, was certainly not the outpourings of a madwoman. She had spoken of death, it was true, yet was it not to be supposed that she was slowly being driven to suicide? She had kept her secret, and she wished the man Hornby - the man who was to marry Muriel Leithcourt - to know.

The room in which we stood was evidently an apartment set apart for her use, for beyond was the tiny bedchamber; yet the small, high-up window was closely barred, and the cold bareness of the prison was sufficient indeed to cause anyone confined there to prefer death to captivity.

Again I spoke to her slowly and kindly, but there was no response. That she was absolutely dumb was only too apparent. Yet surely she had not always been so! I had gone in search of her because the beauty of her portrait had magnetized me, and I had now found her to be even more lovely than her picture, yet, alas! suffering from an affliction that rendered her life a tragedy. The realization of the terrible truth staggered me. Such a perfect face as hers I had never before set eyes upon, so beautiful, so clear-cut, so refined, so eminently the countenance of one well-born, and yet so ineffably sad, so full of blank unutterable despair.

She placed her clasped hands to her mouth and made signs by shaking her head that she could neither understand nor respond. I therefore took my wallet from my pocket and wrote upon a piece of paper in a large hand the words: "*I come from Lydia Moreton. My name is Gordon Gregg.*"

When her eager gaze fell upon the words she became instantly filled with excitement, and nodded quickly. Then holding her steel-clasped wrists towards me she looked wistfully at me, as though imploring me to release her from the awful bondage in that silent tomb.

Though the woman who had led me there endeavored to

prevent it, I handed her the pencil, and placed the paper on the table for her to write.

The nun tried to snatch it up, but I held her arm gently and forcibly, saying in French:

"No. I wish to see if she is really insane. You will at least allow me this satisfaction."

And while we were in altercation, Elma, with the pencil in her fingers, tried to write, but by reason of her hands being bound so closely was unable. At length, however, after several attempts, she succeeded in printing in uneven capitals the response:

"I know you. You were on the yacht. I thought they killed you."

The thin-faced old woman saw her response - a reply that was surely rational enough - and her brows contracted with displeasure.

"Why are you here?" I wrote, not allowing the sister to get sight of my question.

In response, she wrote painfully and laboriously:

"I am condemned for a crime I did not commit. Take me from here, or I shall kill myself."

"Ah!" exclaimed the old woman. "You see, poor girl, she believes herself innocent! They all do."

"But why is she here?" I demanded fiercely.

"I do not know, m'sieur. It is not my duty to inquire the history of their crimes. When they are ill I nurse them; that is all."

"And who is the commandant of this fortress?"

"Colonel Smirnoff. If he knew that I had admitted you, you would never leave this place alive. This is the Schusselburg of Finland - the place of imprisonment for those who have conspired against the State."

"The prison of political conspirators, eh?"

"Alas, m'sieur, yes! The place in which some of the poor creatures are tortured in order to obtain confessions and information with as much cruelty as in the black days of the Inquisition. These walls are thick, and their cries are not heard from the oubliettes below the lake."

I had long ago heard of the horrors of Schusselburg. Indeed who has not heard of them who has traveled in Russia? The very mention of the modern Bastille on Lake Ladoga, where no prisoner has ever been known to come forth alive, is sufficient to cause any Russian to turn pale. And I was in the Schusselburg of Finland!

I turned over the sheet of paper and wrote the question -

"Did Baron Oberg send you here?"

In response, she printed the words -

"I believe so. I was arrested in Helsingfors. Tell Lydia where I am."

"Do you know Muriel Leithcourt?" I inquired by the same means, whereupon she replied that they were at school together.

"Did you see me on board the *Lola*?" I wrote.

"Yes. But I could not warn you, although I had overheard their intentions. They took me ashore when you had gone, to Siena.

After three days I found myself deaf and dumb - I was made so."

Her allegation startled me. She had been purposely afflicted!

"Who did it?"

"A doctor, I suppose. They put me under chloroform."

"Who?"

"People who said they were my friends."

I turned to the woman in the religious habit, and cried -

"Do you see what she has written? She has been maimed by some friends who intended that the secret she holds should be kept. They feared to kill her, so they bribed a doctor to deliberately operate upon her so that she could neither speak nor hear. And now they are driving her to suicide!"

"M'sieur, I am astounded!" declared the nun. "I have always believed that she was not in her right mind, yet assuredly she seems to be as sane as I am, only willfully mutilated by some pretended friend who determined that no further word should pass her lips."

"A shameful mutilation has been committed upon this poor defenseless girl!" I cried in anger. "And I will make it my duty to discover and punish the perpetrators of it."

"Ah, m'sieur. Do not act rashly, I pray of you," the woman said seriously, placing her hand upon my arm. "Recollect you are in Finland - where the Baron Oberg is all-powerful."

"I do not fear the Baron Oberg," I exclaimed. "If necessary, I will appeal to the Czar himself. Mademoiselle is kept here for the reason that she is in possession of some secret. She must be released - I will take the responsibility."

"But you must not try to release her from here. It would mean death to you both. The Castle of Kajana tells no secrets of those who die within its walls, or of those cast headlong into its waters and forgotten."

Again I turned to Elma, who stood in anxious wonder of the subject of our conversation, and had suddenly taken the old nun's hand and kissed it affectionately, perhaps in order to show me that she trusted her.

Then upon the paper I wrote -

"Is the Baron Oberg your uncle?"

She shook her head in the negative, showing that the dreaded Governor-General of Finland had only acted a part towards her in which she had been compelled to concur.

"Who is Philip Hornby?" I inquired, writing rapidly.

"My friend - at least, I believe so."

Friend! And I had all along believed him to be an adventurer and an enemy!

"Why did he go to Leghorn?" I asked.

"For a secret purpose. There was a plot to kill you, only I managed to thwart them," were the words she printed with much labor.

"Then I owe my life to you," I wrote. "And in return I will do my utmost to rescue you from here, if you do not fear to place yourself in my hands."

And to this she replied -

"I shall be thankful, for I cannot bear this awful place longer. I believe they must torture the women here. They will torture me some day. Do your best to get me out of here and I will tell you everything. But," she wrote, "I fear you can never secure my release. I am confined here on a life sentence."

"But you are English, and if you have had no trial I can complain to our Ambassador."

"No, I am a Russian subject. I was born in Russia, and went to England when I was a girl."

That altered the case entirely. As a subject of the Czar in her own country she was amenable to that disgraceful blot upon civilization that allows a person to be consigned to prison at the will of a high official, without trial or without being afforded any opportunity of appeal. I therefore at once saw a difficulty.

Yet she promised to tell me the truth if I could but secure her release!

A flood of recollections of the amazing mystery swept through my mind. A thousand questions arose within me, all of which I desired to ask her, but there, in that noisome prison-house, it was impossible. As I stood there a woman's shrill scream of excruciating pain reached me, notwithstanding those cyclopean walls. Some unfortunate prisoner was, perhaps, being tortured and confession wrung from her lips. I shuddered at the unspeakable horrors of that grim fortress.

Could I allow this refined defenseless girl to remain an inmate of that Bastille, the terrors of which I had heard men in Russia hint at with bated breath? They had willfully maimed her and deprived her of both hearing and the power of speech, and now they intended that she should be driven mad by that silence and loneliness that must always end in insanity.

"I have decided," I said suddenly, turning to the woman who had conducted me there, and having now removed the steel bonds of the prisoner with a key she secretly carried, stood

WILLIAM LE QUEUX

with folded hands in the calm attitude of the religious.

"You will not act with rashness?" she implored in quick apprehension. "Remember, your life is at stake, as well as my own."

"Her enemies intended that I, too, should die!" I answered, looking straight into those deep mysterious brown eyes which held me as beneath a spell. "They have drawn her into their power because she had no means of defense. But I will assume the position of her friend and protector."

"How?"

"The man is awaiting me in the boat outside. I intend to take her with me."

"But, m'sieur, why that is impossible!" cried the old woman in a hoarse voice. "If you were discovered by the guards who patrol the lake both night and day they would shoot you both."

"I will risk it," I said, and without another word dashed into the tiny bed chamber and tore an old brown blanket from off the narrow truckle bed.

Then, linking my arm in that of the woman whose lovely countenance had verily become the sun of my existence, I made a sign, inviting her to accompany me.

The sister barred the door, urging me to reconsider my decision.

"Leave her alone in secret, and act as you will, appeal to the Baron, to the Czar, but do not attempt, m'sieur, to rescue a prisoner from here, for it is an impossibility. The man who brought you here from Abo will not dare to accept such responsibility."

"Come," I said to Elma, although, alas! she could not hear my voice. "Let us at least make a dash for freedom."

She recognized my intentions in a moment, and allowed herself to be conducted down the long intricate corridor, walking stealthily, and making no noise.

I had seized the old horn lantern, and as the nun held back, not daring to accompany us, we stole on alone, turning back along the stone corridor until I recognized the door of the room to which I had been first conducted. All was silent, and as we crept along on tiptoe I felt the girl's grip upon my arm, a grip that told me that she placed her faith in me as her deliverer.

I own that it was a rash and headstrong act, for even beyond the lake how could we ever hope to penetrate those inter-minable inhospitable forests, so far from any hiding-place. Yet I felt it my duty to attempt the rescue. And besides, had not her marvelous beauty enmeshed me; had I not felt by some unaccountable intuition at the first moment we had met that our lives were linked in the future? She clung to me as though fearful of discovery, as we went forward in silence along that dark, low corridor where I knew the strong door in the tower opened upon the lake. Once in the boat, and we could row back to where the horses awaited us, and then away. The woman had not arrested our progress or raised an alarm, after all. Once I had mistrusted her, but I now saw that her heart was really filled with pity for the poor girl now at my side.

Without a sound we crept forward until within a few yards from that unlocked door where the boat awaited us below, when, of a sudden, the uncertain light of the lantern fell upon something that shone and a deep voice cried out of the darkness in Russian -

"Halt! or I fire!"

And, startled, we found ourselves looking down the muzzle of a loaded carbine.

A huge sentry stood with his back to the secret exit, his dark eyes shining beneath his peaked cap, as he held his weapon to his shoulder within six feet of us.

The big, bearded fellow demanded fiercely who I was.

My heart sank within me. I had acted recklessly, and had fallen into the hands of his Excellency, the Baron Xavier Oberg, the unscrupulous Governor-General - fallen into a trap which, it seemed, had been very cleverly prepared for me.

I was a prisoner in the terrible fortress whence no single person save the guards had ever been known to emerge - the Bastille of "The Strangler of Finland!"

I saw I was lost.

The muzzle of the sentry's carbine was within two feet of my chest.

"Speak!" cried the fellow. "Who are you?"

At a glance I took in the peril of the situation, and without a second's hesitation made a dive for the man beneath his weapon. He lowered it, but it was too late, for I gripped him around the waist, rendering his gun useless. It was the work of an instant, for I knew that to close with him was my only chance.

Yet if the boat was not in waiting below that closed door? If my Finn driver was not there in readiness, then I was lost. The unfortunate girl whom I was there to rescue drew back in fright against the wall for a single second, then, seeing that I had closed with the hulking fellow, she sprang forward, and with both hands seized the gun and attempted to wrest it from him. His fingers had lost the trigger, and he was trying to regain it to fire and so raise the alarm. I saw this, and with an old trick learned at Uppingham I tripped him, so that he staggered and nearly fell.

An oath escaped him, yet in that moment Elma succeeded in twisting the gun from his sinewy hands, which I now held with a strength begotten of a knowledge of my imminent peril. My whole future, as well as hers, depended upon my success in that desperate encounter. He was huge and powerful, with a strength far exceeding my own, yet I had been reckoned a good wrestler at Uppingham, and now my knowledge of that most ancient form of combat held me in good stead.

The man shouted for help, his deep, hoarse voice sounding along the stone corridors. If heard by his comrades-in-arms, then the alarm would at once be given.

We struggled desperately, swaying to and fro, he trying to throw me, while I, at every turn, practiced upon him the tricks learned in my youth. It seemed an even match, however, for he kept his feet by sheer brute force, and his muscles seemed hard and unbending as steel.

Suddenly, however, as we were striving so vigorously and desperately, the English girl slipped past us with the carbine in her hand, and with a quick movement dragged open the heavy door that gave exit to the lake.

At that instant I unfortunately made a false move, and his hand closed upon my throat like a band of steel. I fought and struggled to loose myself, exerting every muscle, but alas! he gained the advantage. I heard a splash, and saw that Elma no longer held the sentry's weapon in her hands, having thrown it into the water.

Then at the same moment I heard a voice outside cry in a low tone: "Courage, Excellency! Courage! I will come and help you."

It was the faithful Finn, who had been awaiting me in the deep shadow, and with a few strokes pulled his boat up to the narrow rickety ledge outside the door.

"Take the lady!" I succeeded in gasping in Russian. "Never mind me," and I saw to my satisfaction that he guided Elma to step into the boat, which at that moment drifted past the little platform.

I struggled valiantly, but against such a man of brute strength I was powerless. He held my throat, causing me excruciating pain, and each moment I felt my chance of victory grow smaller. My strength was failing. While I held his arms at his sides, I could keep him secure without much effort, but now with his fingers pressing in my windpipe I could not breathe.

I was slowly being strangled.

To be vanquished meant imprisonment there, perhaps even death. Victory meant Elma's life, as well as my own. Mine was therefore a fight for life. A sudden idea flashed across my mind, and I continued to struggle, at the same time gradually forcing my enemy backward towards the door. He shouted for help, but was unheard. He cursed and swore and shouted until, with a sudden and almost superhuman effort, I tripped him, bringing his head into such violent contact with the stone lintel of the door that the sound could surely be heard a considerable distance. For a moment he was stunned, and in that brief second I released his grip from my throat and hurled him backwards beyond the door.

There was the sound of the crashing of wood as the rotten platform gave way, a loud splash, and next instant the dark waters closed over the big, bearded fellow who would have snatched Elma Heath from me, and have held me prisoner in that castle of terrors. He sank like a stone, for although I stood watching for him to rise, I could only distinguish the woodwork floating away with the current.

In a moment, however, even as I stood there in horror at my

deed of self-defense, the place suddenly resounded with shouts of alarm, and in the tower above me the great old rusty bell began to swing, ringing its brazen note across the broad expanse of waters.

The fair-bearded Finn again shot the boat across to where I stood, crying -

"Jump, Excellency! For your life, jump! The guards will be upon us!"

Behind me in the passage I saw a light and the glitter of arms. A shot rang out, and a bullet whizzed past me, but I stood unharmed. Then I jumped, and nearly upset the boat, but taking an oar I began to row for life, and as we drew away from those grim, black walls the fire belched forth from three rifles.

"Row!" I shrieked, turning to see if my fair companion had been hit.

"Keep cool, Excellency," urged the Finn. "See, right away there in the shadow. We might trick them, for the patrol-boat will be at the head of the river waiting to cut us off."

Again the guards fired upon us, but in the darkness their aim was faulty. Lights appeared in the high windows of the castle, and we could see that the greatest commotion had been caused by the escape of the prisoner. The men at the door in the tower were shouting to the patrol-boats, which were nowhere to be seen, calling them to row us down and capture us, but by plying our oars rapidly we shot straight across the lake until we got under the deep shadow of the opposite shore, and then crept gradually along in the direction we had come.

"If we meet the boats, Excellency, we must run ashore and take to the woods," explained the Finn. "It is our only chance."

Scarcely had he spoken when out in the center of the lake we

WILLIAM LE QUEUX

could just distinguish a long boat with three rowers going swiftly towards the entrance to the river, which we so desired to gain.

"Look!" cried our guide, backing water, and bringing the boat to a standstill. "They are in search of us! If we are discovered they will fire. It is their orders. No boat is allowed upon this lake."

Elma sat watching our pursuers, but still calm and silent. She seemed to intrust herself entirely to me.

The guards were rowing rapidly, the oars sounding in the rowlocks, evidently in the belief that we had made for the river. But the Finlander had apparently foreseen this, and for that reason we were lying safe from observation in the deep shadow of an overhanging tree.

A gray mist was slowly rising from the water, and the Finn, noticing it, hoped that it might favor us. In Finland in late autumn the mists are often as thick as our proverbial London fogs, only whiter, denser, and more frosty.

"If we disembark we shall be compelled to make a detour of fully four days in the forest, in order to pass the marshes," he pointed out in a low whisper. "But if we can enter the river we can go ashore anywhere and get by foot to some place where the lady can lie in hiding."

"What do you advise? We are entirely in your hands. The Chief of Police told me he could trust you."

"I think it will be best to risk it," he said in Russian after a brief pause. "We will tie up the boat, and I will go along the bank and see what the guards are doing. You will remain here, and I shall not be seen. The rushes and undergrowth are higher further along. But if there is danger while I am absent get out and go straight westward until you find the marsh, then keep along its banks due south," and drawing up the boat to the bank the shrewd, big-boned fellow disappeared into the dark undergrowth.

There were no signs yet of the break of day. Indeed, the stars were now hidden, and the great plane of water was every moment growing more indistinct as we both sat in silence. My ears were strained to catch the dipping of an oar or a voice, but beyond the lapping of the water beneath the boat there was no other sound. I took the hand of the fair-faced girl at my side and pressed it. In return she pressed mine.

It was the only means by which we could exchange confidences. She whom I had sought through all those months sat at my side, yet powerless to utter one single word.

Still holding her hands in both my own I gripped them to show her that I intended to be her champion, while she turned to me in confidence as though happy that it should be so. What, I wondered, was her history? What was the mystery surrounding her? What could be that secret which had caused her enemies to thus brutally maim and mutilate her, and afterwards send her to that grim, terrible fortress that still loomed up before us in the gloom? Surely her secret must affect some person very seriously, or such drastic means would never be employed to secure her silence.

Suddenly I heard a stealthy footstep approaching, and next moment a low voice spoke which I recognized as that of our friend, the Finn.

"There is danger, Excellency - a grave danger!" he said in a low half whisper. "Three boats are in search of us."

And scarcely had he uttered those words when there was the flash of a rifle from the haze, a loud report, and again a bullet whizzed past just behind my head. In an instant the truth became apparent, for I saw the dark shadow of a boat rapidly rowed, bearing full upon us. The shot had been fired as a signal that we had been sighted, and were pursued. Other shots rang out, mingled with the wild exultant shouts of the guards as they bore down full upon us, and then I knew that, notwithstanding our escape, we were now lost. They were too close upon us to admit of eluding them. The peril we had dreaded had fallen. The Finn's presence on the bank had evidently been detected by a boat drawn up at the shore, and he had been followed to where we had lain in what we had so foolishly believed to be a safe hiding-place. Nought else was to be done but to face the inevitable. Three times the red fire of a rifle belched angrily in our faces, and yet, by good fortune, neither of us was struck. Yet we knew too well that the intention of our pursuers was to kill us.

"Quick, Excellency! Fly! while there is yet time!" gasped the Finn, grasping my hand and half dragging me from the boat, while, I, in turn, placed Elma upon the bank.

"*Hoida!* This way! Swiftly!" cried our guide, and the three of us, heedless of the consequences, plunged forward into the impenetrable darkness, just as our fierce pursuers came alongside where we had only a moment ago been seated. They shouted wildly as they sprang to land after us, but our guide, who had been born and bred in these forests, knew well how to travel in a semi-circle, and how to conceal himself. It was a race for freedom - nay, for very life.

So dark that we could see before us hardly a foot, we were compelled to place our hands in front of us to avoid collision with the big tree trunks, while ever and anon we found ourselves entangled in the mass of dead creepers and vegetable parasites that formed the dense undergrowth. Around us on every side we heard the shouts and curses of our pursuers, while above the rest we heard an authoritative voice, evidently that of a sergeant of the guard, cry -

"Shoot the man, but spare the woman! The Colonel wants her back. Don't let her escape! We shall be well rewarded. So keep on, comrades! *Mene edemmaeski!*"

But the trembling girl beside me heard nothing, and perhaps indeed it was best that she could not hear. My only fear was that our pursuers, of whom there now seemed to be a dozen, had extended, with the intention of encircling us. They, no doubt, knew every inch of that giant forest with its numerous bogs and marshes, and if they could not discover us would no doubt drive us into one or other of the bogs, where escape was impossible.

Our gallant guide, on the other hand, seemed to utterly disregard the danger and kept on, every now and then stretching out his hand and helping along the afflicted girl we had rescued from that living tomb. Headlong we went in a straight line, until suddenly we began to feel our feet sinking into the soft ground, and then the Finlander turned to the left, at right angles, and we found ourselves in a denser undergrowth, where in the darkness our hands and faces became badly scratched.

Another gun was fired as signal, echoing through the wood, but the sound came from the opposite direction to that we were traveling; therefore we hoped that we had eluded those whose earnest desire it was to capture us for the reward. Suddenly, however, a second gun, an answering signal, was fired from straight before us, and that revealed the truth. We were actually between the two parties, and they were closing in upon us! They had already driven us to the edge of the bog. The Finlander recognized our peril as quickly as I did, and halted.

"Let us turn straight back," he urged breathlessly. "We may yet elude them."

And then we again turned off at right angles, traveling as quickly as we were able back towards the lake shore. It was an exciting chase in the darkness, for we knew not whither we were going, nor into what pitfall or ravine or treacherous marsh we might fall. Once we saw afar through the trees the light of a lantern held by a guard, and already the sweet-faced girl beside me seemed tired and terribly fatigued. But we hurried on and on, striving to make no noise, and yet the crackling of wood beneath our feet seemed to us to sound like the noise of thunder.

At last, breathless, we halted to listen. We were already in sight of the gray mist where lay the silent lake that held so many secrets. There was not a sound. The guards had gone straight on, believing they had driven us into that deadly bog wherein, if we had entered, we must have been slowly sucked down and engulfed. They were surrounding it, no doubt, feeling certain of their prey.

But we crept along the water's edge, until in the gray light we could distinguish two empty boats - that of the guards and our own. We were again at the spot where we had disembarked.

"Let us row to the head of the lake," suggested the Finn. "We may then land and escape them." And a moment later we were all three in the guards' boat, rowing with all our might under the deep shadow of the bank northward, in the opposite direction to the town of Nystad.

We kept a sharp look-out for any other boat, but saw none. The signals ashore had attracted all the guards to that spot to join in the search, and now, having doubled back and again embarked, we were every moment increasing the distance between ourselves and our pursuers. I think we must have rowed several miles, for ere we landed again, upon a low, flat and barren shore, the first gray streak of day was showing in the east.

Elma noticed it, and kept her great brown eyes fixed upon it thoughtfully. It was the dawn for her - the dawn of a new life. Our eyes met; she smiled at me, and then gazed again eastward, full of silent meaning.

Having landed, we drew the boat up and concealed it in the undergrowth so that the guards, on searching, should not know the direction we had taken, and then we went straight on northward across the low-lying lands, to where the forest showed dark against the morning gray. The mist had now somewhat cleared, but the air was keen and frosty.

This wood, we found, was of tall high pines, where walking was not difficult, a wide wilderness of trees which, hour after hour, we traversed in the vain endeavor to find the rough path which our guide told us led for a hundred miles from Alavo down to Tammerfors, the manufacturing center of the country. But to discover a path in a forest forty miles wide is a matter of considerable difficulty, and for hours we wandered on and on, but alas! always in vain.

Faint and hungry, yet we still kept courage. Fortunately we found a little spring, and all three of us drank eagerly with our hands. But of food we had nothing, save a small piece of hard rye bread which the Finn had in his pocket, the remains of his evening meal; and this we gave to Elma, who, half famished, ate it quickly. We knew quite well that it would be an easy matter to die of starvation in that great trackless forest, therefore we kept on undaunted, while the yellow autumn sun struggled through the dark pines, glinting on the straight gray trunks and reflecting a golden light in that dead unbroken silence.

How many miles we trudged I have no idea. It was a consolation to know that we now had no pursuers, yet what fate lay before us we knew not. If we could only find that forest-road we might come across some wood-cutter's hut, where we could obtain rough food of some sort, yet our guide, used as he was to those enormous woods of central Finland, was utterly out of his bearings, and no mark of civilization attracted his quick, experienced eye. The light above gradually faded, and over a sharp stone Elma stumbled and ripped her shoe.

I looked at my watch, and found that it was already five o'clock. In an hour it would be dark, the beginning of the long northern night. Elma, who was weary and footsore, asked by signs to be permitted to lay down and rest. Therefore we gathered a bed of dried leaves for her, and she lay down, and while we watched she was soon asleep. The Finn, who declared that he did not suffer from the cold, removed his coat and placed it tenderly upon her shoulders.

While there was still a ray of light I watched her white refined features as she slept, and was sorely tempted to bend and imprint a kiss upon that soft inviting cheek. Yet I had no right to do so - no right to take such an advantage.

The long cold night passed wearily, and the howling of the wolves caused me to grip my revolver, yet at daybreak we arose refreshed, and notwithstanding the terrible pangs of hunger now gnawing at our vitals, we were prepared to renew our desperate dash for liberty.

Although I had paper, I possessed no pencil with which to write, therefore I could only communicate by signs with the mysterious prisoner of Kajana, the beautiful dark-eyed girl who held me irrevocably beneath the spell of her beauty. All the little acts of homage I was able to perform she accepted with a quiet, calm dignity, while in her deep luminous eyes I read an unfathomable mystery.

The mist had not cleared, for it was soon after dawn when we again moved along, hungry, chill, and yet hopeful. At a spring we obtained some water, and then, in silent procession, pressed forward in search of the rough track of the woodcutters.

Elma's torn shoe gave her considerable trouble, and noticing her limping, I induced her to sit down while I took it off, hoping to be able to mend it, but, having unlaced it, I saw that upon her stocking was a large patch of congealed blood, where her foot itself had also been cut. I managed to beat the nails of the shoe with a stone, so that its sole should not be lost, and she readjusted it, allowing me to lace it up for her and smiling the while.

Forward we trudged, ever forward, across that enormous forest where the myriad treetrunks presented the same dismal scene everywhere, a forest untrodden save by wild, half-savage lumbermen. Throughout that dull gray day we marched onward, faint with hunger, yet suffering but little pain, for the first pangs were now past, and were succeeded by slight light-headedness. My only fear was that we should be compelled to spend another night without shelter, and what its effect might be upon the delicately-reared girl whose hand I held tenderly in mine. Surely my position was a strange one. Her terrible affliction seemed to cause her to be entirely dependent upon me.

Suddenly, just as the yellow sunlight overhead had begun to fade, the flat-faced Finn, whose name he had told me was Felix Estlander, cried joyfully -

"*Polushaite!* Look, Excellency! Ah! The road at last!"

And as we glanced before us we saw that his quick, well-trained eyes had detected away in the twilight, at some distance, a path traversing our vista among the gray-green tree-trunks. Then, hurrying along, we found ourselves upon a track, on which we turned to the right - a track, rough and deeply-rutted by the felled trunks that were dragged along it to the nearest river.

Elma made a gesture of renewed hope, and all three of us redoubled our pace, expecting every moment to come upon some log hut, the owner of which would surely give us hospitality for the night. But darkness came on quickly, and yet we still pushed forward. Poor Elma was limping, and I knew that her injured foot was paining her, even though she could tell me nothing.

At last, however, after walking for nearly four hours in the almost impenetrable forest gloom, always fearing lest we might miss the path, our hearts suddenly beat quickly by seeing before us a light shining in a window, and five minutes later

Felix was knocking at the door, and asking in Finnish the occupant to give hospitality to a lady lost in the forest.

We heard a low growl like a muttered imprecation within, and when the door opened there stood upon the threshold a tall, bearded, muscular old fellow in a dirty red shirt, with a big revolver shining in his hand. A quick glance at us satisfied him that we were not thieves, and he invited us in while Felix explained that we had landed from the lake, and our boat having drifted away we had been compelled to take to the woods. The man heard the Finn's picturesque story, and then said something to me which Felix translated into Russian.

"Your Excellency is welcome to all the poor fare he has. He gives up his bed in the room yonder to the lady, so that she may rest. He is honored by your Excellency's presence."

And while he was making this explanation the herculean wood-cutter in the red shirt stirred the red embers whereon a big pot was simmering, and sending forth an appetizing odor, and in five minutes we were all three sitting down to a stew of capercailzie, with a foaming light beer as a fitting beverage. We finished the dish with such lightning rapidity that our host boiled us a number of eggs, which, I fear, denuded his larder.

The place was a poor one of two low rooms, built of rough log-pines, with double windows for the winter and a high brick stove. Cleanliness was not exactly its characteristic, nevertheless we all passed a very comfortable hour, and received a warm welcome from the lonely old fellow who passed his life so far beyond European civilization, and whose house, he told us, was often snowed up and cut off from all the world for three or four months at a time.

After we had finished our meal, I asked the sturdy old fellow for a pencil, but the nearest thing he possessed was a stick of thick charcoal, and with that it was surely difficult to communicate with our fair companion. Therefore she rose, gave me her hand, bowed smilingly, and then passed into the inner room and closed the door.

The old wood-cutter gave us some coarse tobacco, and after smoking and chatting for an hour we threw ourselves wearily upon the wooden benches and slept soundly.

Suddenly, however, at early dawn, we were startled by a loud banging at the door, the clattering of hoofs, and authoritative shouts in Russian. The old wood-cutter sprang up, and looking through a chink in the heavy shutters turned to us with blanched face, whispering breathlessly -

"The police! What can they want of me?"

"Open!" shouted the horsemen outside. "Open in the name of his Majesty!"

Felix and I sprang up facing each other.

"We are entrapped!"

In an instant our guide Felix made a dash for the door of the inner room where Elma had retired, but next second he reappeared, gasping in Russian -

"Excellency! Why, the door is open! The lady has gone!"

"Gone!" I cried, dismayed, rushing into the little room, where I found the truckle couch empty, and the door leading outside wide open. She had actually disappeared!

The police again battered at the opposite door, threatening loudly to break it in if it were not opened at once, whereupon the old wood-cutter drew the bolt and admitted them. Two big, hulking fellows in heavy riding-coats and swords strode in, while two others remained mounted outside, holding the horses.

"Your names?" demanded one of the fellows, glancing at us as we stood together in expectation.

Our host told them his name, and asked why they wished to enter.

"We are searching for a woman who has escaped from Kajana," was the reply. "Have you seen any woman here?"

"No," responded the wood-cutter. "We never see any woman out in these woods."

The police-officer strode into the inner room, glanced around to make certain that no one was concealed there, and then returning to me asked, "Who are you?"

"That is my own affair," I answered.

The mystery of Elma's disappearance while we had slept annoyed me. She seemed to have fled from me in secret. Yet could she have received some warning that the police were in search of her? She was deaf, therefore she could not have been alarmed by the banging on the door.

"Your identity is my affair," declared the man with the fair, bristly beard, an average type of the uncouth officer of police.

"Who is your chief?" I inquired, as a sudden thought occurred to me.

"Melnikoff, at Helsingfors."

"Then this is not in the district of Abo?"

"No. But what difference does it make? Who are you?"

"Gordon Gregg, British subject," I replied.

"And you are the drosky-driver from Abo," remarked the fellow, turning to Felix. "Exactly as I thought. You are the pair who bribed the nun at Kajana, and succeeded in releasing the Englishwoman. In the name of the Czar, I arrest you!"

The old wood-cutter turned pale as death. We certainly were in grave peril, for I foresaw the danger of falling into the hands of Baron Oberg, the Strangler of Finland. Yet we had a satisfaction in knowing that, be the mystery what it might, Elma had escaped.

"And on what charge, pray, do you presume to arrest me?" I inquired as coolly as I could.

"For aiding a prisoner to escape."

"Then I wish to say, first, that you have no power to arrest me; and, secondly, that if you wish me to give you satisfaction, I am perfectly willing to do so, providing you first accompany me down to Abo."

"It is outside my district," growled the fellow, but I saw that his hesitancy was due to his uncertainty as to whom I really might be.

"I desire you to take me to the Chief of Police Boranski, who will make all the explanation necessary. Until we have an interview with him, I refuse to give any information concerning myself," I said.

"But you have a passport?"

I drew it from my pocket, saying -

"It proves, I think, that my name is what I have told you."

The fellow, standing astride, read it, and handed it back to me.

"Where is the woman?" he demanded. "Tell me."

"I don't know," was my reply.

"Perhaps you will tell me," he said, turning to the old wood-cutter with a sinister expression upon his face. "Remember, these fugitives are found in your house, and you are liable to arrest."

"I don't know - indeed I don't!" protested the old fellow, trembling beneath the officer's threat. Like all his class, he feared the police, and held them in dread.

"Ah, you don't remember, I suppose!" he smiled. "Well, perhaps your memory will be refreshed by a month or two in prison. You are also arrested."

"But, your Excellency, I - "

"Enough!" blared the bristly officer. "You have given shelter to conspirators. You know the penalty in Finland for that, surely?"

"But these gentlemen are surely not conspirators!" the poor old man protested. "His Excellency is English, and the English do not plot."

"We shall see afterwards," he laughed. And then, turning to the agent of police at his side, he gave him orders to search the log-hut carefully, an investigation in which one of the men from the outside joined. They upset everything and pried everywhere.

"You may find papers or letters," said the officer. "Search thoroughly." And in every corner they rummaged, even to taking up a number of boards in the inner room which Elma had occupied. But they found nothing.

A dozen times was the old wood-cutter questioned, but he stubbornly refused to admit that he had ever set eyes upon Elma, while I insisted on my right to return to Abo and see Boranski. I knew, of course, by what we had overheard said by the prison-guards, that the Governor-General was extremely anxious to recapture the girl with whom, I frankly admit, I had now so utterly fallen in love. And it appeared that no effort was being spared to search for us. Indeed, the whole of the police in the provinces of Abo and of Helsingfors seemed to be actively making a house-to-house search.

But what could be the truth of Elma's disappearance? Had she fled of her own accord, or had she once more fallen a victim to some ingenious and dastardly plot. That gray dress of hers might, I recollected, betray her if she dared to venture near any town, while her affliction would, of itself, be plain evidence of identification. All I hoped was that she had gone and hidden herself in the forest somewhere in the vicinity to wait until the danger of recapture had passed.

For nearly half an hour I argued with the police officer whose intention it was to take me under arrest to Helsingfors. Once there, however, I knew too well that my liberty would be probably gone for ever. Whatever was the Baron's motive in holding the poor girl a prisoner, it would also be his motive to silence me. I knew too much for his liking.

"I refuse to go to Helsingfors," I said defiantly. "I am a British subject, and demand to be taken back to the port where my passport was vised." This argument I repeated time after time, until at length I succeeded in convincing him that I really had a right to be taken to Abo, and to seek the aid of the British Vice-Consul if necessary.

For as long as possible I succeeded in delaying our departure, but at length, just as the yellow sun began to struggle through the gray clouds, we were all three compelled to depart in sorrowful procession.

What, we wondered, had really happened to Elma? It was evident that she had not fallen into the hands of the police; nevertheless, the fact that the door of the inner room was open caused them to look upon the statement of the wood-cutter with distinct suspicion and disbelief.

Our captors seemed quite well aware of all the circumstances of our escape from Kajana, and were consequently filled with chagrin that Elma, the person they so much desired to recapture, had slipped through their fingers. While the police rode, we were compelled to walk before them, and after trudging ten miles or so through the forest we came across another small posse of police, who were apparently in search of us, for they expressed delight when they saw us under arrest.

"Where is the woman?" inquired one officer of the other.

"Still at liberty," replied the man who held us as prisoners. "In hiding twenty versts back, I think."

"Ah, we shall find her before long," he said confidently. "Within twelve hours we shall have searched the whole forest. She cannot escape us."

Our captors explained who we were, and then we were pushed forward again, skirting a great wide lake called the Nasjarvi, along the wooded shore of which we walked the whole day long until, at sundown, we came to a picturesque little log-built town facing the water, called Filppula. Here we obtained a hasty meal, and afterwards took the train down to Abo, where we arrived next morning, after a very uncomfortable and sleepless journey.

At nine o'clock I stood in the big bare office of Michael Boranski, where only a few days before we had had such a heated argument. As soon as the Chief of Police entered, he recognized me under arrest, and dismissed my guards with a wave of the hand - all save the officer who had brought me there. The Finnish driver and the old wood-cutter were in another room, therefore I stood alone with the police-officer of Helsingfors and the Chief of Police at Abo. The latter listened to the officer's story of my arrest without saying a word.

"The prisoner, your Excellency, desired to be brought here to you before being taken to Helsingfors. He said you would be aware of the facts."

"And so I am," remarked Boranski, with a smile. "There is no conspiracy. You must at once release this gentleman and the other two prisoners."

"But, Excellency, the Governor-General has issued orders for the prisoner's arrest and deportation to Helsingfors."

"That may be. But I am Chief of Police in Abo, and I release him."

The officer looked at me in such blank astonishment that I could not resist smiling.

"I am well aware of the reason of this Englishman's visit to the north," added Boranski. "More need not be said. Has the lady been arrested?"

"No, your Excellency. Every effort is being made to find her. Colonel Smirnoff has already been relieved of his post as Governor of Kajana, and many of the guards are under arrest for complicity in the plot to allow the woman to escape."

"Ah, yes. I see from the despatches that a reward is offered for her recapture."

"The Governor-General is determined that she shall not escape," remarked the other.

"She is probably hidden in the forest, somewhere or other."

"Of course. They are making a thorough search over every verst of it. If she is there, she will most certainly be found."

"No doubt," remarked Boranski, leaning back in his padded chair and looking at me meaningly across the littered table. "And now I wish to speak to this Englishman privately, so please leave us. Also inform the other two prisoners that they are at liberty."

"But your Excellency does this upon his own responsibility," he said anxiously. "Remember that I brought them to you under arrest."

"And I release them entirely at my own discretion," he said. "As Chief of Police of this province, I am permitted to use my jurisdiction, and I exercise it in this matter. You are liberty to report that at Helsingfors, if you so desire, but I should suggest that you say nothing unless absolutely obliged - you understand?"

The manner in which Boranski spoke apparently decided my captor, for after a moment's hesitation he said, saluting:

"If that is really your wish, then I will obey." And he left.

"Excellency!" exclaimed the Chief of Police, rising quickly and walking towards me as soon as the door was closed, and we were alone, "you have had a very narrow escape - very. I did my best to assist you. I succeeded in bribing the water-guards at Kajana in order that you might secure the lady's release. But it seems that just at the very moment when you were about to get away one of the guards turned informer and roused the governor of the castle, with the result that you all three nearly lost your lives. The whole matter has been reported to me officially, and," he added with a grim smile, "my men are now searching everywhere for you."

"But why is Baron Oberg so extremely anxious to recapture Miss Heath?" I asked earnestly.

"I have no idea," was his reply. "The secret orders from Helsingfors to me are to arrest her at all hazards - alive or dead."

"Which means that the Baron would not regret if she was dead," I remarked, in response to which he nodded in the affirmative.

I told him of the faithful services of Felix, the Finlander, whereupon he said simply:

"I told you that you might trust him implicitly."

"But now that you have shown yourself my friend," I said, "you will assist Miss Heath to escape this man, who desires to hold her prisoner in that awful place. They are driving her mad."

"I will do my best," he answered, but shaking his head dubiously. "But you must recollect that Baron Oberg is Governor-General of Finland, with all the powers of the Czar himself."

"And if Elma Heath again falls into his unscrupulous hands, she will die," I declared.

"Ah!" he sighed, looking me straight in the face, "I fear that what you say is only too true. She evidently holds some secret which he fears she will reveal. He wishes to rearrest her in order - well - " he added in a low tone, "in order to close her lips. It would not be the first time that persons have been silenced in secret at Kajana. Many fatal accidents take place in that fortress, you know."

CHAPTER XII

"THE STRANGLER"

Where was Elma? What was the cause of her inexplicable disappearance into the gloomy forest while we had slept?

I returned to the hotel where I had stayed on my arrival, a comfortable place called the Phoenix, and lunched there alone. Both Felix, the Finn, and my host, the wood-cutter, had received their *douceurs* and left, but to the last-named I had given instructions to return home at once and report by telegraph any news of my lost one.

A thousand conflicting thoughts arose within me as I sat in that crowded *salle-a-manger* filled with a gobbling crowd of the commercial men of Abo. I had, I recognized, now to deal with the most powerful man in that country, and I suffered a distinct disadvantage by being in ignorance of the reason he held that sweet English girl a prisoner. The tragedy of the dastardly manner in which she had been willfully maimed caused my blood to boil within me. I had never believed that in this civilized twentieth century such things could be.

Michael Boranski had given his pledge to assist me, yet he had most plainly explained to me his fears. The Baron was intent upon again getting Elma into his power. Was it at his orders, I wondered, that the sweet-faced girl had been deprived of speech and hearing? Had she fallen an innocent victim to his infamous scheming?

About me men were eating strange dishes and talking in Finnish, while others were smoking and drinking their vodka; but I was in no mood for observation. My only thought was of she who was now lost to me.

Why had she disappeared without warning I was at loss to imagine, yet I could only surmise that her flight had been compulsory. Some women possess a mysterious sense of intuition, a curious and indescribable faculty of knowing when evil threatens them, that presents a strange and puzzling problem to our scientists. It is unaccountable, and yet many women possess it in a very marked degree. Was it, therefore, possible that Elma had awakened, and being warned of her peril had fled without arousing us? The suggestion was possible, but I feared improbable.

Another very curious feature in the affair was the sudden manner in which Michael Boranski had exerted his power and influence in order to render me that service. He had actually bribed the guards of Kajana; he had instructed the faithful Felix, he had provided our boat, and he had ordered the nun to open the water-gate to me. Why?

There was, I felt convinced, some hidden motive in all that sudden and marked friendliness. That he really hated the English I had seen plainly when we had first met, and I had only compelled him to serve me by presenting the order signed by the Emperor, which made me his guest within the Russian dominions. Even that document did not account for the length he had gone to secure the release of the woman I now loved in secret. The more I thought it over, the more anxious did I become. I could discern no motive for his friendliness, and, truth to tell, I always distrust those who are too friendly. What straight and decided line of action should I take? Carefully I went over all the strange events that had happened in England, and while anxious to obtain some solution of the amazing problem, yet I could not bring myself to leave Finland, and allow Elma to fall into the clutches of that high official who so persistently sought her end. No. I would go to him and face him. I was anxious to see what manner of man was "The Strangler of Finland." Therefore, that same evening I left Abo, and traveled by rail up to the junction Toijala, whence, after a wait of six hours, I resumed by slow journey to Helsingfors. I put up at Kamp's, an elegant hotel on the long esplanade overlooking the port, and found the town, with its handsome streets and spacious squares, to be a much finer place than I had believed. When I inquired of the French director of my hotel for the residence of his Excellency, the Governor-General, he regarded me with some surprise, saying:

"The Baron lives up at the Palace, m'sieur - that great building opposite the Salutong. The driver of your drosky will point it out to you."

"Is his Excellency in Helsingfors at the present moment?" I asked.

"The Baron never leaves the Palace, m'sieur," responded the man. "This is a strange country, you know," he added, with a grin. "It is said that his Excellency is in hourly fear of assassination."

"Perhaps not without cause," I remarked in a low voice, at which he elevated his shoulders and smiled.

At noon I descended from a drosky before a long, gray, massive building, over the big doorway of which was a large escutcheon bearing the Russian arms emblazoned in gold, and on entering where a sentry stood on either side, a colossal concierge in livery of bright blue and gold came forward to meet me, asking in Russian:

"Whom do you wish to see?"

"His Excellency, the Governor-General."

"Have you an appointment?"

"No."

"His Excellency sees no one without an appointment," the man told me somewhat gruffly.

"I am not here on public business, but upon a private matter," I explained. "Perhaps I may see his Excellency's secretary?"

"If you wish, but I repeat that his Excellency sees no one without a previous appointment."

I knew this quite well, for the "Strangler of Finland," fearful of assassination, was as unapproachable as the Czar himself. Following the directions of the concierge, however, I crossed a great bare courtyard, and, ascending a wide stone staircase, was confronted by a servant, who, on hearing my inquiry took me into a waiting-room, and left with my card to Colonel Luganski, whom he informed me was the Baron's private secretary.

After ten minutes or so the man returned, saying:

"The Colonel will see you if you will please step this way," and following him he conducted me into the richly furnished private apartments of the Palace, across a great hall filled with fine paintings, and then up a long thickly-carpeted passage to a small, elegant room, where a tall bald-headed man in military uniform stood awaiting me.

"Your name is M'sieur Gregg," he exclaimed in very good French, "and I understand you desire audience of his Excellency, the Governor-General. I regret, however, that he never gives audience to strangers."

"The matter upon which I desire to see his Excellency is of a purely private and confidential nature," I said, for used as I was to the ways of foreign officialdom, I spoke with the same firm courtesy as himself.

"I am very sorry, m'sieur, but I fear it will be necessary in that case for you to write to his Excellency, and mark your letter 'personal.' It will then go into the Governor-General's own hands."

"What I have to say cannot be committed to writing," was my reply. "I must see Baron Oberg upon a matter which affects him personally, and which admits of no delay."

He glanced at me quickly, and then in a low voice inquired:

"Is it in regard to a - well, a conspiracy?"

His question instantly suggested to me a ruse, and I replied in the affirmative.

"Then you can place the facts before me without the slightest hesitation," he said, going to the door and slipping the bolt into its socket. "Anything spoken into my ear is as though it were spoken into that of his Excellency himself."

"I much regret, M'sieur the Colonel, that I must see the Baron in person."

"Has the plot assassination as its object - or revolt?" he asked pointedly.

"That I will explain to the Baron only."

"But I tell you he will not see you. We have so many persons here with secret information concerning Finnish conspiracies against our Russian rule. Why, if his Excellency saw everyone who desired to see him, he would be compelled to give audience the whole twenty-four hours round."

At a glance I saw that this elegant Colonel, who seemed to take the greatest pride over his exquisitely kept person and his spotless uniform, did not intend to allow me the satisfaction of an audience of that most hated official of the Czar. The latter was in fear of the dagger, the pistol, or the bomb, and consequently hedged himself in by persons of the Colonel's type - courteous, diplomatic, but utterly unbending. After some further argument, I said at last in a firm tone:

"I wish to impress upon you the extreme importance of the information I have to impart, and can only repeat that it is a matter concerning his Excellency privately. Will you therefore do me the favor to take my name to him?"

"His Excellency refuses to be troubled with the names of strangers," was his cold reply, as he turned over my card in his hand.

"But if I write upon it the nature of my business, and enclose it in an envelope, will you then take it to him?" I suggested.

He hesitated for a short time, twisting his mustache, and then replied with great reluctance:

"Well, if you are so determined, you may write your business upon your card."

I therefore took out one, and on the back wrote in French the words which I knew must have the effect of obtaining an audience for me:

> "*To give information regarding Miss Elma Heath.*"

This I enclosed in the envelope he handed to me, when, ringing a bell, he handed it to the footman who appeared, with orders to take it to his Excellency and await a reply. The response came in a few minutes.

"His Excellency will give audience to the English m'sieur."

Then I rose and followed the footman through several wide corridors filled with palms and flowers, which formed a kind of winter-garden, until we crossed a red-carpeted ante-room, where two statuesque sentries stood on guard, and the man conducting me rapped at the great polished mahogany doors of the room beyond.

A voice responded, the door was opened, and I found myself in a high, beautifully-painted room, with long windows hung with pastel-blue silk with heavy gilt fringe, a pastel-blue carpet, and upon the opposite wall a great canopy of rich purple velvet bearing the double-headed eagle embroidered in gold. The apartment was splendidly decorated, and in the center of the parquet floor, with his back to the light, was the thin, wiry figure of an elderly man in a funereal frock-coat, in the lapel of which showed the red and yellow ribbon of the Order of Saint Anne. His hands were behind his back, and he stood purposely in such a position that when I entered I could not at first see his face against the strong, gray light behind.

But when the footman had bowed and retired and we were alone, he turned slightly, and I then saw that his bony face, with high cheek-bones, slight gray side-whiskers, hard mouth and black eyes set closely together, was one that bore the mark of evil upon it - the keen, sinister countenance of one who could act without any compunction and without regret. Truly one would not be surprised at any cruel, dastardly action of a man with such a face - the face of an oppressor.

"Well?" he snapped in French in a high-pitched voice. "You want to see me concerning that mad English girl? What picturesque lies do you intend to tell me concerning her?"

"I have no intention of telling any untruths concerning her," was my quick response, as I faced him unflinchingly. "She has told me sufficient to - "

"She has told you something! Ah! I guessed as much. I expected this!" And I saw that his thin, crafty face went pale, while his eyes glanced evilly upon me. He believed that she had revealed to me her secret. He placed his hand upon the back of a chair wherein was concealed an electric button, and next instant a little stout man in shabby black appeared as though by magic through a secret door hidden in the dark paneling of the audience chamber - the man who was his personal guard against the plots for his assassination.

His Excellency spoke, and the words he uttered staggered me. I stood aghast.

"Seize that man!" he cried, pointing to me. "He is armed! He has just threatened to kill me! He is the man against whom we were recently warned - the Englishman!"

"Ah!" I cried, standing before the thin-faced official of the Czar, the unscrupulous man who had crushed Finland beneath the iron heel of Russia, and who, by his lying allegation, now held me in his power. "I see your object, Baron Oberg! You intend to arrest me as a conspirator!"

"Search the fellow. He has a revolver there in his hip-pocket," declared the Governor-General, and in an instant the short, ferret-eyed little man had run his hands down me and felt my weapon.

I drew it forth and handed it to him, saying:

"You are quite welcome to it if you fear that I am here with any sinister motive."

"He obtained admission by a clever ruse," the Baron explained to the police agent. "And then he threatened me."

"It's untrue," I protested hotly. "I have merely called to see you regarding the young English lady, Elma Heath - the unfortunate lady whom you consigned to the fortress of Kajana."

"The mad woman, you mean!" he laughed.

"She is not mad," I cried, "but as sane as you yourself. It is you who intended that the horrors of the castle should drive her insane, and thus your secret should be kept!"

"What do you suggest?" he demanded, stepping a few paces towards me.

"I mean, Xavier Oberg, that you would kill Elma Heath if you dared to do so," I answered plainly, as I faced him unflinchingly.

"You see?" he laughed, turning to the stout man at my side. "The fellow is insane. He does not know what he is talking about. Ah, my dear Malkoff, I've had a narrow escape! He came here intending to shoot me."

"I did not," I protested. "I am here to demand satisfaction on behalf of Miss Heath."

"Oh! - well, if the lady cares to come here herself, I will give her the satisfaction she desires," was his crafty reply.

"The lady has escaped you, and it is therefore hardly likely she will willingly return to Helsingfors," I said.

"It was you who succeeded, by throwing the guard into the water, in abducting her from the castle," he remarked. "But," he added sneeringly, with a sinister smile, "I presume your gallantry was prompted by affection - eh?"

"That is my own affair."

"A deaf and dumb woman is surely not a very cheerful companion!"

"And who caused her that affliction?" I cried hotly. "When she was at Chichester she possessed speech and hearing as other girls. Indeed, she was not afflicted when on board the *Lola* in Leghorn harbor only a few months ago. Perhaps you recollect the narrow escape the yacht had on the Meloria sands?"

His eyes met mine, and I saw by his drawn face and narrow brows that my words were causing him the utmost consternation. My object was to make him believe that I knew more than I really did - to hold him in fear, in fact.

"Perhaps the man whom some know as Hornby, or Woodroffe, could tell an interesting story," I went on. "He will, no doubt, when he meets Elma Heath, and finds the terrible affliction of which she has been the victim."

His thin, bony countenance was bloodless, his mouth twitched and his gray brows contracted quickly.

"I haven't the least idea what you mean, my dear sir," he stammered. "All that you say is entirely enigmatical to me. What have I to do with this mad Englishwoman's affairs?"

"Send out this man," I said, pointing to the detective Malkoff, who had appeared from behind the paneling of the audience-chamber. "Send him out, and I will tell you."

But the representative of the Czar, always as much in dread of assassination as his imperial master, refused. I saw that what I had said had upset him, and that he was not at all clear as to how much or how little of the true facts I knew.

The connection between the little miniature cross of the Order of St. Anne and that red and yellow ribbon in his button-hole struck me forcibly at that moment, and I said:

"I have no desire to make any statements before a second person. I came here to see you privately, and in private will I speak. I have certain information that will, I feel confident, be of the utmost interest to you - concerning another woman, Armida Santini."

His lips were pressed together, and I noticed how he started when I uttered the name of that woman whom I had found dead in Rannoch Wood, and whose body had so

WILLIAM LE QUEUX

mysteriously disappeared.

"And what on earth can the woman concern me?" he asked, with a brave attempt to remain cool, still speaking in French.

"Only that you knew her," was my brief reply. Then, with my eyes still fixed upon his, I asked: "Will you not now request this gentleman to retire?"

He hesitated a moment, and then with a wave of his hand dismissed the man he had summoned to his aid. A moment later the "Strangler's" personal protector had disappeared through that secret door in the paneling by which he had entered.

"Well?" asked the Baron, turning quickly to me again, his dark, evil eyes trying to fathom my intentions.

"Well?" I asked. "And what, pray, can you profit by denouncing me as an assassin? Remember, Baron, that your secret is mine," I said in a clear voice full of meaning.

"And your intention is blackmail - eh?" he snapped, walking to the window and back again. "How much do you want?"

"My intention is nothing of the kind. My object is to avenge the outrageous injury to Elma Heath."

"Of course. That is only natural, m'sieur, if you have fallen in love with her," he said. "But are not your intentions somewhat ill-advised considering her position as a criminal lunatic?"

"She is neither," I protested quickly.

"Very well. You know better than myself," he laughed. "The offense for which she was condemned to confinement in a fortress was the attempted assassination of Madame Vakuroff, wife of the General commanding the Uleaborg Military Division."

"Assassination!" I cried. "Have you actually sent her to prison as a murderess?"

"I have not. The Criminal Court of Abo did so," he said dryly. "The offense has since been proved to have been the outcome of a political conspiracy, and the Minister of the Interior in Petersburg last week signed an order for the prisoner's transportation to the island of Saghalien."

"Ah!" I remarked with set teeth. "Because you fear lest she shall write down your secret."

"You are insulting! You evidently do not know what you are saying," he exclaimed resentfully.

"I know what I am saying quite well. You have requested her removal to Saghalien in order that the truth shall be never known. But Baron Oberg," I added with mock politeness, "you may do as you will, you may send Elma Heath to her grave, you may hold me prisoner if you dare, but there are still witnesses of your crime that will rise against you."

In an instant he went ghastly pale, and I knew that my blind shot had struck its mark. The man before me was guilty of some crime, but what it was only Elma herself could tell. That he had had her arrested for an attempted political assassination only showed how ingeniously and craftily the heartless ruler of that ruined country had laid his plans. He feared Elma, and therefore had conspired to have her sent out to that dismal penal island in the far-off Pacific.

"You do not fear arrest, m'sieur?" he asked, as though with some surprise.

"Not in the least - at least, not arrest by you. You may be the representative of the Emperor in Finland, but even here there is justice for the innocent."

A sinister smile played around the thin, gray lips of the man whose very name was hated through the great empire of the Czar, and was synonymous of oppression, injustice, and heartless tyranny.

"All I can repeat," he said, "is that if you bring the young Englishwoman here I shall be quite prepared to hear her appeal." And he laughed harshly.

"You ask that because you know it is impossible," I said, whereat he again laughed in my face - a laugh which made me wonder whether Elma had not already fallen into his hands. The uncertainty of her fate held me in terrible suspense.

"I merely wish to impress upon you the fact that I have not the slightest interest whatsoever in the person in question," he said coldly. "You seem to have formed some romantic attachment towards this young woman who attempted to poison Madame Vakuroff, and to have succeeded in rescuing her from Kajana. You afterwards disregard the fact that you are liable to a long term of imprisonment yourself, and actually have the audacity to seek audience of me and make all sorts of hints and suggestions that I have held the woman a prisoner for my own ends!"

"Not only do I repeat that, Baron Oberg," I said quickly. "But I also allege that it was at your instigation that in Siena an operation was performed upon the unfortunate girl which deprived her of speech and hearing."

"At my instigation?"

"Yes, at yours!"

He laughed again, but uneasily, a forced laugh, and leaned against the edge of the big writing-table near the window.

"Well, what next?" he inquired, pretending to be interested in my allegations. "What do you want of me?"

"I desire you to give the Mademoiselle Heath her complete freedom," I said.

"Is that all?"

"All - for the present."

"But her future is not in my hands. The Minister in Petersburg has decreed her removal to Saghalien as a person dangerous to the State."

"Which means that she will be ill-treated - knouted to death, perhaps."

"We do not use the knout in the Russian prisons nowadays," he said briefly. "His Majesty has decreed its abolition."

"But you adopt torture in Kajana and Schusselburg instead."

"My time is too limited to discuss our penal system, m'sieur," he exclaimed impatiently, while I could well see that he was anxious to escape before I made any further charges against him. I had already shown him that Elma had spoken, and he feared that she had told the truth. While this would embitter him against her and cause him to seek to silence her at all hazards, it was of course in my own interests that he should fear any revelations that I might make.

"You have posed in England as the uncle of Elma Heath, and yet you here hold her prisoner. For what reason?" I demanded.

"She is held prisoner by the State - for conspiracy against Russian rule - not by herself personally."

"Who enticed her here? Why you, yourself. Who conspired to throw the guilt of this attempted murder of the general's wife upon her? You - you, the man whom they call 'The Strangler of Finland'! But I will avenge the cruel and abominable affliction you have placed upon her. Her secret - your secret,

Baron Oberg - shall be published to the world. You are her enemy - and therefore mine!"

"Very well," he growled between his teeth, advancing towards me threateningly, his fists clenched in his rage. "Recollect, m'sieur, that you have insulted me. Recollect that I am Governor-General of Finland."

"If you were Czar himself, I should not hesitate to denounce you as the tyrant and mutilator of a poor defenseless woman."

"And to whom, pray, will you tell this romantic story of yours?" he laughed hoarsely. "To your prison walls below the lake at Kajana? Yes, M'sieur Gregg, you will go there, and once within the fortress you shall never again see the light of day. You threaten me - the Governor-General of Finland!" he laughed in a strange, high-pitched key as he threw himself into a chair and scribbled something rapidly upon paper, appending his signature in his small crabbed handwriting.

"I do not threaten," I said in open defiance, "I shall act."

"And so shall I," he said with an evil grin upon his bony face as he blotted what he had written and took it up, adding: "In the darkness and silence of your living tomb, you can tell whatever strange stories you like concerning me. They are used to idiots where you are going," he added grimly.

"Oh! And where am I going?"

"Back to Kanaja. This order consigns you to confinement there as a dangerous political conspirator, as one who has threatened me - it consigns you to the cells below the lake - for life!"

I laughed aloud, and my hand sought my wallet wherein was that all-powerful document - the order of the Emperor which gave me, as an imperial guest, immunity from arrest. I would produce it as my trump-card.

Next second, however, I held my breath, and I think I must have turned pale. My pocket was empty! My wallet had been stolen! Entirely and helplessly I had fallen into the hands of the tyrant of the Czar.

His own personal interest would be to consign me to a living tomb in that grim fortress of Kajana, the horrors of which were unspeakable. I had seen enough during my inspection of the Russian prisons as a journalist to know that there, in strangled Finland, I should not be treated with the same consideration or humanity as in Petersburg or Warsaw. The Governor-General consigned me to Kajana as a "political," which was synonymous with a sentence of death in those damp, dark *oubliettes* beneath the water-dungeons every whit as awful as those of the Paris Bastile.

We faced each other, and I looked straight into his gray, bony face, and answered in a tone of defiance:

"You are Governor-General, it is true, but you will, I think, reflect before you consign me, an Englishman, to prison without trial. I know full well that the English are hated by Russia, yet I assure you that in London we entertain no love for your nation or its methods."

"Yes," he laughed, "you are quite right. Russia has no use for an effete ally such as England is."

"Effete or powerful, my country is still able to present an ultimatum when diplomacy requires it," I said. "Therefore I have no fear. Send me to prison, and I tell you that the responsibility rests upon yourself." And folding my arms I kept my eyes intently upon his, so that he should not see that I wavered.

"As for the responsibility, I certainly do not fear that, m'sieur," he said.

"But the exposure that will result - are you prepared to face that?" I asked. "Perhaps you are not aware that others beside myself - one other, indeed, who is a diplomatist - is aware of my journey here? If I do not return, your Ministry of Foreign Affairs in Petersburg will be pressed for a reason."

"Which they will not give."

"Then if they do not, the truth will be out," I said laughing harshly, for I saw how determined he had become to hold me prisoner. "Come, call up your myrmidon and send me to Kajana. It will be the first step towards your own downfall."

"We shall see," he growled.

"Ah! you surely do not think that I, after ten years' service in the British diplomatic service, would dare to come to Finland upon this quest - would dare to face the rotten and corrupt officialdom which Russia has placed within this country - without first taking some adequate precaution? No, Baron. Therefore I defy you, and I leave Helsingfors to-night."

"You will not. You are under arrest."

I laughed heartily and snapped my fingers, saying:

"Before you give me over to your police, first telegraph to your Minister of Finance, Monsieur de Witte, and inquire of him who and what I am."

"I don't understand you."

"You have merely to send my name and description to the Minister and ask for a reply," I said. "He will give you instructions - or, if you so desire, ask his Majesty yourself."

"And why, pray, does his Majesty concern himself about you?" he asked, at once puzzled.

"You will learn later, after I am confined in Kajana and your secret is known in Petersburg."

"What do you mean?"

"I mean," I said, "I mean that I have taken all the necessary steps to be forearmed against you. The day I am incarcerated by your order, the whole truth will be known. I shall not be the sufferer - but you will."

My words, purposely enigmatical, misled him. He saw the drift of my argument, and being of course unaware of how much I knew, he was still in fear of me. My only uncertainty was of the actual fate of poor Elma. My wallet had been stolen - with a purpose, without a doubt - for the thief had deprived me of that most important of all documents, the open sesame to every closed door, the ukase of the Czar.

"You defy me!" he said hoarsely, turning back to the window with the written order for my imprisonment as a political still in his hand. "But we shall see."

"You rule Finland," I said in a hard tone, "but you have no power over Gordon Gregg."

"I have power, and intend to exert it."

"For your own ruin," I remarked with a self-confident smile. "You may give your torturers orders to kill me - orders that a fatal accident shall occur within the fortress - but I tell you frankly that my death will neither erase nor conceal your own offenses. There are others, away in England, who are aware of them, and who will, in order to avenge my death, speak the truth. Remember that although Elma Heath has been deprived of both hearing and of speech, she can still write down the true facts in black and white. The Czar may be your patron, and you his favorite, but his Majesty has no tolerance of officials who are guilty of what you are guilty of. You talk of arresting me!" I added with a smile. "Why, you ought rather to go on your knees and beg my silence."

He went white with rage at my cutting sarcasm. He literally boiled over, for he saw that I was quite cool and had no fear of him or of the terrible punishment to which he intended to consign me. Besides which, he was filled with wonder regarding the exact amount of information which Elma had imparted to me.

"There are certain persons," I went on, "to whom it would be of intense interest to know the true reason why the steam-yacht *Lola* put into Leghorn; why I was entertained on board her; why the safe in the British Consulate was rifled, and why the unfortunate girl, kept a prisoner on board, was taken on shore just before the hurried sailing of the vessel. And there are other mysteries which the English police are trying to solve, namely, the reason Armida Santini and a man disguised as her husband died in Scotland at the hand of an assassin. But surely I need say no more. It is surely sufficient to convince you that if the truth were spoken, the revelations would be distinctly awkward."

"For whom?" he asked, opening his eyes.

"For you. Come, Baron," I said, "can we not yet speak frankly?"

But he was silent for a moment, a fact which was in itself proof that my pointed argument had caused him to reconsider his intention of sending me under escort back to that castle of terror.

If my journey there was in order to meet my love, I would not have cared. It was the ignorance of her whereabouts or of her fate that held me in such deep, all-consuming anxiety. Each hour that passed increased my fond and tender affection for her. And yet what irony of circumstance! She had been cruelly snatched from me at the very moment that freedom had been ours.

I think it was well that I assumed that air of defiance with the man who had ground Finland beneath his heel. He was unused to it. No one dared to go against his will, or to utter taunt or threat to him. He was paramount, with all the powers of an emperor - the power, indeed, of life and death. Therefore he was not in the habit of being either thwarted or criticised, and I could see that my words had aroused within him a boiling tumult of resentment and of rage. I told him nothing of the loss of my wallet or of the precious document that it had contained. My defiance was merely upon principle.

"Arrest me if you like. Denounce me by means of any lie that arises to your lips, but remember that the truth is known beyond the confines of the Russian Empire, and for that reason traces will be sought of me and full explanation demanded. I have taken precaution, Xavier Oberg," I added, "therefore do your worst. I repeat again that I defy you!"

He paced the big room, his thin claw-like hands still clenched, his yellow teeth grinding, his dark, deep-set eyes fixed straight before him. If he had dared, he would have struck me down at his feet. But he did not dare. I saw too plainly that even though my wallet was gone I still held the trump-card - that he feared me.

The mention I had made of the Minister of Finance, however, seemed to cause him considerable hesitation. That high official had the ear of the Emperor, and if I were a friend there might be inquiries. As I stood before him leaning against a small buhl table, I watched all the complex workings of his mind, and tried to read the mysterious motive which had caused him to consign poor Elma to Kajana.

He was a proud bully, possessing neither pity nor remorse, an average specimen of the high Russian official, a hide-bound bureaucrat, a slave to etiquette and possessing a veneer of polish. But beneath it all I saw that he was a coward in deadly fear of assassination - a coward who dreaded lest some secret should be revealed. That concealed door in the paneling with the armed guard lurking behind was sufficiently plain evidence that he was not the fearless Governor-General that was popularly supposed. He, "The Strangler of Finland," had crushed the gallant nation into submission, ruining their commerce, sapping the country by impressing its youth into the Russian army, forbidding the use of the Finnish language, and taxing the people until the factories had been compelled to close down while the peasantry starved. And now, on the verge of revolt, there had arisen a band of patriots who resented ruin, and who had already warned his Majesty by letter that if Baron Oberg were not removed from his post he would die.

These and other thoughts ran through my mind in the silence that followed our heated argument, for I saw well that he was in actual fear of me. I had led him to believe that I knew everything, and that his future was in my hands, while he, on his part, was anxious to hold me prisoner, and yet dared not do so.

My wallet had probably been stolen by some lurking police-spy, for Russian agents abound everywhere in Finland, reporting conspiracies that do not exist and denouncing the innocent as "politicals."

The Baron had halted, and was looking through one of the great windows down upon the courtyard below where the sentries were pacing. The palace was for him a gilded prison, for he dared not go out for a drive in one or other of the parks or for a blow on the water across to Hogholmen or Dagero, being compelled to remain there for months without showing himself publicly. People in Abo had told me that when he did go out into the streets of Helsingfors it was at night, and he usually disguised himself in the uniform of a private soldier of the guard, thus escaping recognition by those who, driven to desperation by injustice, sought his life.

A long silence had fallen between us, and it now occurred to me to take advantage of his hesitation. Therefore I said in a firm voice, in French -

"I think, Baron, our interview is at an end, is it not? Therefore I wish you good-day."

He turned upon me suddenly with an evil flash in his dark eyes, and a snarling imprecation in Russian upon his lips. His hand still held the order committing me to the fortress.

"But before I leave you will destroy that document. It may fall into other hands, you know," and I walked towards him with quick determination.

"I shall do nothing of the kind!" he snapped.

Without further word I snatched the paper from his thin white fingers and tore it up before his face. His countenance went livid. I do not think I have ever seen a man's face assume such an expression of fiendish vindictiveness. It was as though at that instant hell had been let loose within his heart.

But I turned upon my heel and went out, passing the sentries in the ante-room, along the flower-filled corridors and across the courtyard to the main entrance where the gorgeous concierge saluted me as I stepped forth into the square.

I had escaped by means of my own diplomacy and firmness. The Czar's representative - the man who ruled that country - feared me, and for that reason did not hold me prisoner. Yet when I recalled that evil look of revenge on my departure, I could not help certain feelings of grave apprehension arising within me.

Returning to my hotel, I smoked a cigar in my room and pondered. Where was Elma? was the chief question which arose within my mind. By remaining in Helsingfors I could achieve nothing further, now that I had made the acquaintance of the oppressor, whereas if I returned to Abo I might perchance be able to obtain some clue to my love's where-abouts. I call her my love because I both pitied and loved the poor afflicted girl who was so helpless and defenseless.

Therefore I took the midnight train back to Abo, arriving at the hotel next morning. After an hour's rest I set out anxiously in search of Felix, the drosky-driver. I found him in his log-built house in the Ludno quarter, and when he asked me in I saw, from his face, that he had news to impart.

"Well?" I inquired. "And what of the lady? Has she been found?"

"Ah! your Excellency. It is a pity you were not here yesterday," he said with a sigh.

"Why? Tell me quickly. What has happened?"

"I have been assisting the police as spy, Excellency, as I often do, and I have seen her."

"Seen her! Where?" I cried in quick anxiety.

"Here, in Abo. She arrived yesterday morning from Tammer-fors accompanied by an Englishman. She had changed her dress, and was all in black. They lunched together at the Restaurant du Nord opposite the landing stage, and an hour later left by steamer for Petersburg."

"An Englishman!" I cried. "Did you not inform the Chief of Police, Boranski?"

"Yes, your Excellency. But he said that their passports being in order it was better to allow the lady to proceed. To delay her might mean her rearrest in Finland," he added.

"Then their passports were vised here on embarking?" I exclaimed. "What was the name upon that of the Englishman?"

"I have it here written down, Excellency. I cannot pronounce your difficult English names." And he produced a scrap of dirty paper whereon was written in a Russian hand the name -

"Martin Woodroffe."

CHAPTER XIII

A DOUBLE GAME AND ITS CONSEQUENCES

I went to the railway station, and from the time-table gathered that if I left Abo by rail at noon I could be in Petersburg an hour before noon on the morrow, or about four hours before the arrival of the steamer by which the silent girl and her companion were passengers. This I decided upon doing, but before leaving I paid a visit to my friend, Boranski, who, to my surprise and delight, handed me my wallet with the Czar's letter intact, saying that it had been found upon a German thief who had been arrested at the harbor on the previous night. The fellow had, no doubt, stolen it from my pocket believing I carried my paper money in the flap.

"The affair of the English lady is a most extraordinary one," remarked the Chief of Police, toying with his pen as he sat at his big table. "She seems to have met this Englishman up at Tammerfors, or at some place further north, yet it is curious that her passport should be in order even though she fled so precipitately from Kajana. There is a mystery connected with her disappearance from the wood-cutter's hut that I confess I cannot fathom."

"Neither can I," I said. "I know the man who is with her, and cannot help fearing that he is her bitterest enemy - that he is acting in concert with the Baron."

"Then why is he taking her to the capital - beyond the

jurisdiction of the Governor-General?"

"I am going straight to Petersburg to ascertain," I said. "I have only come to thank you for your kindness in this matter. Truth to tell, I have been somewhat surprised that you should have interested yourself on my behalf," I added, looking straight at the uniformed official.

"It was not on yours, but on hers," he answered, somewhat enigmatically. "I know something of the affair, but it was my duty as a man to help the poor girl to escape from that terrible place. She has, I know, been unjustly condemned for the attempted assassination of the wife of a General - condemned with a purpose, of course. Such a thing is not unusual in Finland."

"Abominable!" I cried. "Oberg is a veritable fiend."

But the man only shrugged his shoulders, saying -

"The orders of his Excellency the Governor-General have to be obeyed, whatever they are. We often regret, but we dare not refuse to carry them out."

"Russian rule is a disgrace to our modern civilization," I declared hotly. "I have every sympathy with those who are fighting for freedom."

"Ah, you are not alone in that," he sighed, speaking in a low whisper, and glancing around. "His Majesty would order reforms and ameliorate the condition of his people, if only it were possible. But he, like his officials, are powerless. Here we speak of the great uprising with bated breath, but we, alas! know that it must come one day - very soon - and Finland will be the first to endeavor to break her bonds - and the Baron Oberg the first to fall."

For nearly an hour I sat with him, surprised to find how, although his exterior was so harsh and uncouth, yet his heart really bled for the poor starving people he was so constantly forced to oppress.

"I have ruined this town of Abo," he declared, quite frankly. "To my own knowledge five hundred innocent persons have gone to prison, and another two hundred have been exiled to Siberia. Yet what I have done is only at direct orders from Helsingfors - orders that are stern, pitiless and unjust. Men have been torn from their families and sent to the mines, women have been arrested for no offense and shipped off to Saghalien, and mere children have been cast into prison on charges of political conspiracy with their elders - in order to Russify the province! Only," he added anxiously, "I trust you will never repeat what I tell you. You have asked me why I assisted the English Mademoiselle to escape from Kajana, and I have explained the reason."

We ate a hearty meal in company at the *Sampalinna*, a restaurant built like a Swiss chalet, and at noon I entered the train on the first stage of my slow, tedious journey through the great silent forests and along the shores of the lakes of Southern Finland, by way of Tavestehus and Viborg, to Petersburg.

I was alone in the compartment, and sat moodily watching the panorama of wood and river as we slowly wound up the tortuous ascents and descended the steep gradients. I had not even a newspaper with which to while away the time, only my own apprehensive thoughts of whither my helpless love was being conducted.

Surely to no man was there ever presented such a complicated problem as that which I was now trying so vigorously to solve. I loved Elma Heath. The more I reflected, the deeper did her sweet countenance and tender grace impress themselves upon my heart. I loved her, therefore I was striving to overtake her.

The steamer, I learned, would call at Hango and Helsingfors. Would they, I wonder, disembark at either of those places?

Was the man whom I had known as Hornby, the owner of the *Lola*, taking her to place her again in the fiendish hands of Xavier Oberg? The very thought of it caused me to hold my breath.

Daylight came at last, cold and gray, over those dreary interminable marshes where game, especially snipe, seemed abundant, and at a small station at the head of a lake called Davidstadt I took my morning glass of tea; then we resumed our journey down to Viborg, where a short, thick-set Russian of the commercial class, but something of a dandy, entered my compartment, and we left express for Petersburg.

We had passed by a small station called Galitsina, near which were many villas occupied in summer by families from Petersburg, and were traveling through the dense gloomy pine-woods, when my fellow-traveler, having asked permission to smoke, commenced to chat affably. He seemed a pleasant fellow, and told me that he was a wool merchant, and that he had been having a pleasant vacation trout fishing in the Vuoski above the falls of the Imatra, where the pools between the rapids abound with fish.

He had told me that on account of the shore being so full of weeds and the clearness of the water, fishing from the banks was almost an impossibility, and how they had to accustom themselves to troll from a boat so small as to only accommodate the rower and the fisherman.

Then he remarked suddenly -

"You are English, I presume - possibly from Helsingfors?"

"No," I answered. "From Abo. I crossed from Stockholm, and am going to Petersburg."

"And I also. I live in Petersburg," he added. "We may perhaps meet one day. Do you know the capital?"

I explained that I had visited it once before, and had done the usual round of sight-seeing. His manner was brisk and to the point, as became a man of business, but when we stopped at Bele-Ostrof, on the opposite side of the small winding river that separates Finland from Russia proper, the Customs officer who came to examine our baggage exchanged a curious meaning look with him.

My fellow-traveler believed that I had not observed, yet, keenly on the alert as I now was, I was shrewd to detect the least sign or look, and I at once resolved to tell the fellow nothing further of my own affairs. He was, no doubt, a spy of "The Strangler's," who had followed me all the way from Abo, and had only entered my carriage for the final stage of the journey.

This revelation caused me some uneasiness, for even though I was able to evade the man on arrival in Petersburg, he could no doubt quickly obtain news of my whereabouts from the police to whom my passport must be sent. I pretended to doze, and lay back with my eyes half-closed watching him. When he found me disinclined to talk further, he took up the paper he had bought and became engrossed in it, while I, on my part, endeavored to form some plan by which to mislead and escape his vigilance.

The fellow meant mischief - that I knew. If Elma was flying in secret and he watched me, he would know that she was in Petersburg. At all hazards, for my love's sake as well as for mine, I saw that I must escape him. The ingeniousness and cleverness of Oberg's spies was proverbial throughout Finland, therefore he might not be alone, or in any case, on arrival in Petersburg would obtain assistance in keeping observation upon me. I knew that the Baron desired my death, and that therefore I could not be too wary of pitfalls. That fatal chair so cunningly prepared for me in Lambeth was still vividly within my memory.

As we passed Lanskaya, and ran through the outer suburbs of Petersburg, my fellow-traveler became inquisitive as to where I was going, but I was somewhat unresponsive, and busied myself with my bag until we entered the great echoing terminus whence I could see the Neva gleaming in the pale sunlight and the city beyond. The fellow made no attempt to follow me - he was too clever a secret agent for that. He merely wished me "*sdravstvuite*" raised his hat politely and disappeared.

A porter carried my bag out of the station, and I drove across the bridge to the large hotel where I had stopped before, the Europe, on the corner of the Nevski Prospect and the Michael Street. There I engaged a front room looking down into the broad Nevski, had a wash, and then watched at the window for the appearance of the spy. I had already a good four hours before the steamer from Abo was due, and I intended to satisfy myself whether or not I was being followed.

Within twenty minutes the fellow lounged along on the opposite side of the road, just as I had expected. He had changed his clothes, and presented such a different appearance that at first sight I failed to recognize him. He knew that I had driven there, and intended to follow me if I came forth. My position was one of extreme difficulty, for if I went down to the quay he would most certainly follow me.

Having watched his movements for ten minutes or so I descended to the big *salle-a-manger* and there ate my luncheon, chatting to the French waiter the while. I sat purposely in an alcove, so as to be away from the other people lunching there, and in order that I might be able to talk with the waiter without being overheard.

Just as I had finished my meal, and he was handing me my bill, I bent towards him and asked -

"Do you want to earn twenty roubles?"

"Well, m'sieur," he answered, looking at me with some surprise. "They would be acceptable. I am a married man."

"Well, I want to escape from this place without being observed. There is a disagreeable little matter regarding a lady, and I fear a fracas with a man who is awaiting me outside in the Nevski." Then, seeing that he hesitated, I assured him that I had committed no crime, and that I should return for my baggage that evening.

"You could pass through the kitchen and out by the servants' entrance," he said, after a moment's reflection. "If m'sieur so desires, I will conduct him out. The exit is in a back street which leads on to the Catherine Canal."

"Excellent!" I said. "Let us go. Of course you will say nothing?"

"Not a word, m'sieur," and he gathered up the notes plus twenty roubles with which I paid my bill, and taking my hat I followed him to the end of the *salle-a-manger* behind a high wooden screen, across the huge kitchen, and then through a long stone corridor at the end of which sat a gruff old doorkeeper. My guide spoke a word to him, and then the door opened and I found myself in a narrow back slum with the canal beyond.

My first visit was to a clothier's, where I purchased and put on a new light overcoat and then to a hatter's for a hat of different shape to that I was wearing. I carried the hat back to a quiet alley which I had noticed, and quickly exchanged the one I was wearing for it, leaving my old hat in a corner. Then I entered a *cafe* in order to while away the hours until the vessel from Finland was due.

At four o'clock I was out upon the quay, straining my eyes seaward for any sign of smoke, but could see nothing. The sun was sinking, and the broad expanse of water westward danced like liquid gold. The light died out slowly, the cold gray of evening crept on. A chill wind sprang up and swept the quay, causing me to shiver. I asked of a dock laborer whether the steamer was usually late, whereupon he told me that it was often five or six hours behind time, depending upon the delay at Helsingfors.

Twilight deepened into night, and the rain fell heavily, yet I still paced the wet flags in patience, my eyes ever seaward for the light of the vessel which I hoped bore my love. My presence there aroused some speculation among the loungers, I think; nevertheless, I waited in deepest anxiety whether, after all, Elma and Hornby had not disembarked at Helsingfors.

Soon after ten o'clock a light shone afar off, and the movement of the police and porters on the quay told me that it was the vessel. Then after a further anxious quarter of an hour it came, amid great shouting and mutual imprecations, slowly alongside the quay, and the passengers at last began to disembark in the pelting rain.

One after another they walked up the gangway, filing into the passport-office and on into the Custom House, people of all sorts and all grades - Swedes, Germans, Finns, and Russians - until suddenly I caught sight of two figures - one a man in a big tweed traveling-coat and a golf-cap, and the other the slight figure of a woman in a long dark cloak and a woolen tam-o'-shanter. The electric rays fell upon them as they came up the wet gangway together, and there once again I saw the sweet face of the silent woman whom I had grown to love with such fervent desperation. The man behind her was the same who had entertained me on board the *Lola* - the man who was said to be the lover of the fugitive Muriel Leithcourt.

Without betraying my presence I watched them pass through the passport-office and Custom House, and then, overhearing the address which Martin Woodroffe gave the *isvoshtchik*, I stood aside, wet to the skin, and saw them drive away.

At eleven o'clock on the following day I found myself installed in the Hotel de Paris, a comfortable hostelry in the Little Morskaya, having succeeded in evading the vigilance of the spy who had so cleverly followed me from Abo, and in getting my suit-case round from the Hotel Europe.

I was beneath the same roof as Elma, although she was in ignorance of my presence. Anxious to communicate with her without Woodroffe's knowledge, I was now awaiting my opportunity. He had, it appeared, taken for her a pleasant front room with sitting-room adjoining on the first floor, while he himself occupied a room on the third floor. The apartments he had engaged for her were the most expensive in the hotel, and as far as I could gather from the French waiter whom I judiciously tipped, he appeared to treat her with every consideration and kindness.

"Ah, poor young lady!" the man exclaimed as he stood in my room answering my questions, "What an affliction! She writes down all her orders - for she can utter no word."

"Has the Englishman received any visitors?" I asked.

"One man - a Russian - an official of police, I think."

"If he receives anyone else, let me know," I said. "And I want you to give Mademoiselle a letter from me in secret."

"Bien, m'sieur."

I turned to the little writing-table and scribbled a few hasty lines to my love, announcing my presence, and asking her to grant me an interview in secret as soon as Woodroffe was absent. I also warned her of the search for her instigated by the Baron, and urged her to send me a line in reply.

The note was delivered into her hand, but although I waited in suspense nearly all day she sent no reply. While Woodroffe was in the hotel I dared not show myself lest he should recognize me, therefore I was compelled to sham indisposition and to eat my meals alone in my room.

Both the means by which she had met Martin Woodroffe and the motive were equally an enigma. By that letter she had written to her schoolfellow it was apparent that she had some secret of his, for had she not wished to send him a message of reassurance that she had divulged nothing? This would seem that they were close friends; yet, on the other hand, something seemed to tell me that he was acting falsely, and was really an ally of the Baron's.

Why had he brought her to Petersburg? If he had desired to rescue her he would have taken her in the opposite direction - to Stockholm, where she would be free - whereas he took her, an escaped prisoner, into the very midst of peril. It was true that her passport was in order, yet I remembered that an order had been issued for her transportation to Saghalien, and now once arrested she must be lost to me for ever. This thought filled me with fierce anxiety. She was in Petersburg, that city where police spies swarm, and where every fresh arrival is noted and his antecedents inquired into. No attempt had been made to disguise who she was, therefore before long the police would undoubtedly come and arrest her as the escaped criminal from Kajana.

For several hours I sat at my window watching the life and movement down in the street below, my mind full of wonder and dark forebodings. Was Martin Woodroffe playing her false?

Just after half-past six o'clock the waiter entered, and handing me a note on a salver, said -

"Mademoiselle has, I believe, only this moment been able to write in secret."

I tore it open and read as follows: -

DEAR FRIEND. - *I am so surprised. I thought you were still in Abo. Woodroffe has an appointment at eight o'clock on the other side of the city, therefore come to me at 8.15. I must see you, and at once. I am in peril.* - ELMA HEATH.

My love was in peril! It was just as I had feared. I thanked

Providence that I had been sent to help her and extricate her from that awful fate to which "The Strangler of Finland" had consigned her.

At the hour she named, after the waiter had come to me and announced the Englishman's departure, I descended to her sitting-room and entered without rapping, for if I had rapped she could not, alas! have heard.

The apartment was spacious and comfortable, thickly carpeted, with heavy furniture and gilding. Before the long window were drawn curtains of dark green plush, and on one side was the high stove of white porcelain with shining brass bands, while from her low lounge-chair a slim wan figure sprang up quickly and came forward to greet me, holding out both her hands and smiling happily.

I took her hands in mine and held them tightly in silence for some moments, as I looked earnestly into those wonderfully brilliant eyes of hers. She turned away laughing, a slight flush rising to her cheeks in her confusion. Then she led me to a chair, and motioned me to be seated.

Ours was a silent meeting, but her gestures and the expression of her eyes were surely more eloquent than mere words. I knew well what pleasure that re-encounter caused her - equal pleasure with that it gave to me.

Until that moment I had never really loved. I had admired and flirted with women. What man has not? Indeed, I had admired Muriel Leithcourt. But never until now had I experienced in my heart the real flame of true burning affection. The sweetness of her expression, the tender caress of those soft, tapering hands, the deep mysterious look in those magnificent eyes, and the incomparable grace of all her movements, combined to render her the most perfect woman I had ever met - perfect in all, alas! save speech and hearing, of which, with such dastard wantonness, she had been deprived.

She touched her red lips with the tip of her forefinger, opened her hands, and shrugged her shoulders with a sad gesture of regret. Then turning quickly to some paper on the little table at her side she wrote something with a gold pencil and handed to me. It read -

"Surely Providence has sent you here! Mr. Woodroffe must have followed you from England. He is my enemy. You must take me from here and hide me. They intend to send me into exile. Have you ever been in Petersburg before? Do you know anyone here?"

Then when I had read, she handed me her pencil and below I wrote -

"I will do my best, dear friend. I have been once in Petersburg. But is it not best that we should escape at once from Russia?"

"Impossible at present," she wrote. "We should both be arrested at the frontier. It would be best to go into hiding here in Petersburg. I believed Woodroffe to be my friend, but I have found only this day that he is my enemy. He knew that I was in Kajana, and was in Abo when he learned of my escape. He went with two other men in search of us, and discovered us that night when we sought shelter at the wood-cutter's hut. Without making his presence known he waited outside until you were asleep, and then he came and looked in at my window. At first I was alarmed, but quickly I saw that he was a friend. He told me that the police were in the vicinity and intended to raid the hut, therefore I fled with him, first down to Tammerfors and then to Abo, and on here. At that time I did not see the dastardly trap he had laid in order to get me out of the Baron's clutches and wring from me my secret. If I confess, he intends to give me up to the police, who will send me to the mines."

"Does your secret concern him?" I asked in writing.

"Yes ," she wrote in response. "It would be equally in his

interests as well as those of Baron Oberg if I were sent to Saghalien and my identity effaced. I am a Russian subject, as I have already told you, therefore with a Ministerial order against me I am in deadliest peril."

"Trust in me," I scribbled quickly. "I will act upon any suggestion you make. Have you any female friend in whom you could trust to hide you until this danger is past?"

"There is one friend - a true friend. Will you take a note to her?" she wrote, to which I instantly nodded in the affirmative.

Then rising, she obtained some ink and pen and wrote a letter, the contents of which she did not show me before she sealed it. I sat watching her beautiful head bent beneath the shaded lamplight, catching her profile and noticing how eminently handsome it was, superb and unblemished in her youthful womanhood.

I watched her write the superscription upon the envelope: "Madame Olga Stassulevitch, modiste, Scredni Prospect, 231, Vasili Ostroff." I knew that the district was on the opposite side of the city, close to the Little Neva.

"Take a drosky at once, see her, and await a reply. In the meantime, I will prepare to be ready when you return," she wrote. "If Olga is not at home, ask to see the Red Priest - in Russian, '*Krasny-pastor.*' Return quickly, as I fear Woodroffe may come back. If so, I am lost."

I assured her I would not lose a single instant, and five minutes later I was tearing down the Morskaya in a drosky along the canal and across the Nicholas Bridge to the address upon the envelope.

The house was, I found, somewhat smaller than its neighbors, but not let out in flats as the others. Upon the door was a large brass plate bearing the name, "Olga Stassulevitch: modes." I pressed the electric button, and in answer a tall, clean-shaven

Russian servant opened the door.

"Madame is not at home," was his brief reply to my inquiry.

"Then I will see the Red Priest," I said in a lower tone. "I come from Elma Heath." Thereupon, without further word, the man admitted me into the long, dark hall and closed the door with an apology that the gas was not lighted. But striking a match he led me up the broad staircase and into a small, cosy, well-furnished room on the second floor, evidently the sitting-room of some studious person, judging from the books and critical reviews lying about.

For a few minutes I waited there, until the door reopened, and there entered a man of medium height, with a shock of long snow-white hair and almost patriarchal beard, whose dark eyes that age had dimmed flashed out at me with a look of curious inquiry, and whose movements were those of a person not quite at his ease.

"I have called on behalf of Mademoiselle Elma Heath, to give this letter to Madame Stassulevitch, or if she is absent to place it in the hands of the Red Priest," I explained in my best Russian.

"Very well, sir," the old man responded in quite good English. "I am the person you seek," and taking the letter he opened it and read it through.

I saw by the expression on his furrowed face that its contents caused him the utmost consternation. His countenance, already pale, blanched to the lips, while in his eyes there shot a fire of quick apprehension. The thin, almost transparent hand holding the letter trembled visibly.

"You know Mademoiselle - eh?" he asked in a hoarse, strained voice as he turned to me. "You will help her to escape?"

"I will risk my own life in order to save hers," I declared.

"And your devotion to her is prompted by what?" he inquired suspiciously.

I was silent for a moment. Then I confessed the truth.

"My affection."

"Ah!" he sighed deeply. "Poor young lady! She, who has enemies on every hand, sadly needs a friend. But can we trust you - have you no fear?"

"Of what?"

"Of being implicated in the coming revolution in Russia? Remember I am the Red Priest. Have you never heard of me? My name is Otto Kampf."

Otto Kampf!

I stood before him open-mouthed. Who in Russia had not heard of that mysterious unknown person who had directed a hundred conspiracies against the Imperial Autocrat, and yet the identity of whom the police had always failed to discover. It was believed that Kampf had once been professor of chemistry at Moscow University, and that he had invented that most terrible and destructive explosive used by the revolutionists. The ingredients of the powerful compound and the mode of firing it was the secret of the Nihilists alone - and Otto Kampf, the mysterious leader, whose personality was unknown even to the conspirators themselves, directed those constant attempts which held the Emperor and his Government in such hourly terror.

Rewards without number had been offered by the Ministry of the Interior for the betrayal and arrest of the unseen man whose power in Russia, permeating every class, was greater than that of the Emperor himself - at whose word one day the people would rise in a body and destroy their oppressors.

The Emperor, the Ministers, the police, and the bureaucrats knew this, yet they were powerless - they knew that the mysterious professor who had disappeared from Moscow fifteen years before and had never since been seen was only waiting his opportunity to strike a blow that would stagger and crush the Empire from end to end - yet of his whereabouts they were in utter ignorance.

"You are surprised," the old man laughed, noticing my amazement. "Well, you are not one of us, yet I need not impress upon you the absolute necessity, for Mademoiselle's sake, to preserve the secret of my existence. It is because you are not a member of 'The Will of the People,' that you have never heard of 'The Red Priest' - red because I wrote my ultimatum to the Czar in the blood of one of his victims knouted in the fortress of Peter and Paul, and priest because I preach the gospel of freedom and justice."

"I shall say nothing," I said, gazing at the strangely striking figure before me - the unknown man who directed the great upheaval that was to revolutionize Russia. "My only desire is to save Mademoiselle Heath."

"And you are prepared to do so at risk of your own liberty - your own life? Ah! you said you love her. Would not this be a test of your affection?"

"I am prepared for any test, as long as she escapes the trap which her enemies have set for her. I succeeded in saving her from Kajana, and I intend to save her now."

"Was it you who actually entered Kajana and snatched her from that tomb!" he exclaimed, and he took my hand enthusiastically, adding - "I have no further need to doubt you." And turning to the table he wrote an address upon a slip of paper, saying, "Take Mademoiselle there. She will find a safe place of concealment. But go quickly, for every moment places you both in more deadly peril. Hide yourself there also."

I thanked him and left at once, but as I stepped out of the house and re-entered the drosky I saw close by, lurking in the shadow, the spy of "The Strangler of Finland," who had traveled with me from Abo.

Our eyes met, and he recognized me, notwithstanding my light overcoat and new hat.

Then, with heart-sinking, the ghastly truth flashed upon me. All had been in vain. Elma was lost to me.

CHAPTER XIV

HER HIGHNESS IS INQUISITIVE

Instantly the danger was apparent, and instead of driving back to the hotel, I called out to the man to take me to the Moscow railway station, in order to put the spy off the scent. I knew he would follow me, but as he was on foot, with no drosky in sight, I should be able to reach the station before he could, and there elude him.

Over the stones we rattled, leaving the lurking agent standing in the deep shadow, but on turning back I saw him dash across the road to a by-street, where, in all probability, he had a conveyance in waiting.

Then, after we had crossed the Neva, I countermanded my order to the man, saying -

"Don't go right up to the station. Turn into the Liteinoi Prospect to the left, and put me down there. Drive quickly, and I'll pay double fare."

He whipped his horses, and we turned into that maze of dark, ill-lit, narrow streets that lies between the Vosnesenski and the Nevski, turning and winding until we emerged at last into the main thoroughfare again, and then at last we turned into the street I had indicated - a wide road of handsome buildings where I knew I was certain to be able to instantly get another drosky. I flung the man his money, alighted, and two minutes later was driving on towards the Alexander Bridge, traveling in a circle back to the hotel. Time after time I glanced behind, but saw nothing of the Baron's spy, who had evidently gone to the station with all speed, expecting that I was leaving the capital.

I found Elma in her room, ready dressed to go out, wearing a long traveling-cloak, and in her hand was a small dressing-case. She was pale and full of anxiety until I showed her the slip of paper which Otto Kampf had given me with the address written upon it, and then together we hurried forth.

The house to which we drove was, we discovered, a large one facing the Fontanka Canal, one of the best quarters of the town, and on descending I asked the liveried *dvornick* for Madame Zurloff, the name which the "Red Priest" had written.

"You mean the Princess Zurloff," remarked the man through his red beard. "Whom shall I say desires to see her?"

"Take that," I said, handing to him the piece of paper which, beside the address, bore a curious cipher-mark like three triangles joined.

He closed the door, leaving us in the wide carpeted hall, the statuary in which showed us that it was a richly-furnished place, and when a few minutes later he returned, he conducted us upstairs to a fine gilded salon, where an elderly gray-haired lady in black stood gravely to receive us.

"Allow me to present Mademoiselle Elma Heath, Princess," I said, speaking in French and bowing, and afterwards telling her my own name.

Our hostess welcomed my love in a graceful speech, but I said -

"Mademoiselle unfortunately suffers a terrible affliction. She is deaf and dumb."

"Ah, how very, very sad!" she exclaimed sympathetically. "Poor girl! poor girl!" and she placed her hand tenderly upon Elma's shoulder and looked into her eyes. Then, turning to me, she said: "So the Red Priest has sent you both to me! You are in danger of arrest, I suppose - you wish me to conceal you here?"

"I would only ask sanctuary for Mademoiselle," was my reply. "For myself, I have no fear. I am English, and therefore not a member of the Party."

"The Mademoiselle fears arrest?"

"There is an order signed for her banishment to Saghalein," I said. "She was imprisoned at Kajana, the fortress away in Finland, but I succeeded in liberating her."

"She has actually been in Kajana!" gasped the Princess. "Ah! we have all heard sufficient of the horrors of that place. And you liberated her! Why, she is the only person who has ever escaped from that living tomb to which Oberg sends his victims."

"I believe so, Princess."

"And may I take it, m'sieur, that the reason you risked your life for her is because you love her? Pardon me for suggesting this."

"You have guessed correctly," I answered. Then, knowing that Elma could not hear, I added: "I love her, but we are not lovers. I have not told her of my affection. Hers is a long and strange story, and she will perhaps tell you something of it in writing."

"Well," exclaimed the gray-haired lady smiling, leading my love across the luxurious room, the atmosphere of which was filled with the scent of flowers, and taking off her cloak with her own hands, "you are safe here, my poor child. If spies have not followed you, then you shall remain my guest as long as you desire."

"I am sure it is very good of you, Princess," I said gratefully. "Miss Heath is the victim of a vile and dastardly conspiracy. When I tell you that she has been afflicted as she is by her enemies - that an operation was performed upon her in Italy while she was unconscious - you will readily see in what deadly peril she is."

"What!" she cried. "Have her enemies actually done this? Horrible!"

"She will perhaps tell you of the strange romance that surrounds her - a mystery which I have not yet been able to fathom. She is a Russian subject, although she has been educated in England. Baron Oberg himself is, I believe, her worst and most bitter enemy."

"Ah! the Strangler!" she exclaimed with a quick flash in her dark eyes. "But his end is near. The Movement is active in Helsingfors. At any moment now we may strike our blow for freedom."

She was an enthusiastic revolutionist, I could see, unsuspected, however, by the police on account of her high position in Petersburg society. It was she who, as I afterwards discovered, had furnished the large sums of money to Kampf for the continuation of the revolutionary propaganda, and indeed secretly devoted the greater part of her revenues from her vast estates in Samara and Kazan to the Nihilist cause. Her husband, himself an enthusiast of freedom, although of the high nobility, had been killed by a fall from his horse six years before, and since that time she had retired from society and lived there quietly, making the revolutionary movement her sole occupation. The authorities believed that her retirement was due to the painful loss she had sustained, and had no suspicion that it was her money that enabled the mysterious "Red Priest" to slowly but surely complete the plot for the general uprising.

She compelled me to remove my coat, and tea was served by a Tartar footman, whose family she explained had been serfs of the Zurloffs for three centuries, and then Elma exchanged confidences with her by means of paper and pencil.

"Who is this man Martin Woodroffe, of whom she speaks?" asked the Princess presently, turning to me.

"I have met him twice - only twice," I replied, "and under strange circumstances." Then, continuing, I told her something concerning the incidents of the yacht *Lola*.

"He may be in love with her, and desires to force her into marriage," she suggested, expressing amazement at the curious narrative I had related.

"I think not, for several reasons. One is because I know she holds some secret concerning him, and another because he is engaged to an English girl named Muriel Leithcourt."

"Leithcourt? Leithcourt?" repeated the Princess, knitting her brows with a puzzled air. "Do you happen to know her father's name?"

"Philip Leithcourt."

"And has he actually been living in Scotland?"

"Yes," I answered in quick anxiety. "He rented a shoot called Rannoch, near Dumfries. A mysterious incident occurred on his estate - a double murder, or murder and suicide; which is not quite clear - but shortly afterwards there appeared one evening at the house a man named Chater, Hylton Chater, and the whole family at once fled and disappeared."

Princess Zurloff sat with her lips pressed close together, looking straight at the silent girl before her. Elma had removed her hat and cloak, and now sat in a deep easy chair of yellow silk, with the lamplight shining on her chestnut hair, settled and calm as though already thoroughly at home. I smiled to myself as I thought of the chagrin of Woodroffe when he returned to find his victim missing.

"Your Highness evidently knows the Leithcourts," I hazarded, after a brief silence.

"I have heard of them," was her unsatisfactory reply. "I go to England sometimes. When the Prince was alive, we were often at Claridge's for the season. The Prince was for five years military *attache* at the Embassy under de Staal, you know. What I know of the Leithcourts is not to their credit. But you tell me that there was a mysterious incident before their flight. Explain it to me."

At that moment the long white doors of the handsome salon were thrown open by the faithful Tartar servitor, and there entered a man whose hair fell over the collar of his heavy overcoat, but whom, in an instant, I recognized as Otto Kampf.

Both Elma and I sprang to our feet, while advancing to the Princess he bent and gallantly kissed the hand she held forth to him. Then he shook hands with Elma, and acknowledging my own greetings, took off his coat and threw it upon a chair with the air of an accustomed visitor.

"I come, Princess, in order to explain to you," he said. "Mademoiselle fears rearrest, and the only house in Petersburg that the police never suspect is this. Therefore I send her to you, knowing that with your generosity you will help her in her distress."

"It is all arranged," was her Highness's response. "She will remain here, poor girl, until it is safe for her to get out of Russia." Then, after some further conversation, and after my well-beloved had made signs of heartfelt gratitude to the man known from end to end of the Russian empire as "The Red Priest," the Princess turned to me, saying:

"I would much like to know what occurred before the Leithcourts left Scotland."

"The Leithcourts!" exclaimed Kampf in utter surprise. "Do you know the Leithcourts - and the English officer Durnford?"

I looked into his eyes in abject amazement. What connection could Jack Durnford, of the Marines, have with the adventurer Philip Leithcourt? I, however, recollected Jack's word, when I had described the visit of the *Lola* to Leghorn, and further I recollected that very shortly he would be back in London from his term of Mediterranean service.

"Well," I said after a pause, "I happen to know Captain Durnford very well, but I had no idea that he was friendly with Leithcourt."

The Red Priest smiled, stroking his white beard.

"Explain to her Highness what she desires to know, and I will tell you."

My eyes met Elma's, and I saw how intensely eager and interested she was, watching the movement of my lips and trying to make out what words I uttered.

"Well," I said, "a mysterious tragedy occurred on the edge of a wood near the house rented by Leithcourt - a tragedy which has puzzled the police to this day. An Italian named Santini and his wife were found murdered."

"Santini!" gasped Kampf, starting up. "But surely he is not dead?"

"No. That's the curious part of the affair. The man who was killed was a man disguised to represent the Italian, while the woman was actually the waiter's wife herself. I happen to know the man Santini well, for both he and his wife were for some years in my employ."

The Princess and the director of the Russian revolutionary movement exchanged quick glances. It was as though her Highness implored Kampf to reveal to me the truth, while he, on his part, was averse to doing so.

"And upon whom does suspicion rest?" asked her Highness.

"As far as I can make out, the police have no clue whatever, except one. At the spot was found a tiny miniature cross of one of the Russian orders of chivalry - the Cross of Saint Anne."

"There is no suspicion upon Leithcourt?" she asked with some undue anxiety I thought.

"No."

"Did he entertain any guests at the shooting-box?"

"A good many."

"No foreigners among them?"

"I never met any. They seemed all people from London - a smart set for the most part."

"Then why did the Leithcourts disappear so suddenly?"

"Because of the appearance of the man Chater," I replied. "It is evident that they feared him, for they took every precaution against being followed. In fact, they fled leaving a big party of friends in the house. The man Woodroffe, now at the Hotel de Paris, is a friend of Leithcourt as well as of Chater."

"He was not a guest of Leithcourt when this man representing Santini was assassinated ? " asked Kampf, again stroking his beard.

"No. As soon as Woodroffe recognized me as a visitor he left - for Hamburg."

"He was afraid to face you because of the ransacking of the British Consul's safe at Leghorn," remarked the Princess, who, at the same moment, took Elma's hand tenderly in her own and looked at her. Then, turning to me, she said: "What you have told us to-night, Mr. Gregg, throws a new light upon certain incidents that had hitherto puzzled us. The mystery of it all is a great and inscrutable one - the mystery of this poor unfortunate girl, greatest of all. But both of us will endeavor to help you to elucidate it; we will help poor Elma to crush her enemies - these cowardly villains who had maimed her."

"Ah, Princess!" I cried. "If you will only help and protect her, you will be doing an act of mercy to a defenseless woman. I love her - I admit it. I have done my utmost: I have striven to solve the dark mystery, but up to the present I have been unsuccessful, and have only remained, even till to-day, the victim of circumstance."

"Let her stay with me," the kindly woman answered, smiling tenderly upon my love. "She will be safe here, and in the meantime we will endeavor to discover the real and actual truth."

And in response I took the Princess's hand and pressed it fervently. Although that striking, white-headed man and the rather stiff, formal woman in black were the leaders of the great and all-powerful movement in Russia known through the civilized world as "The Terror," yet they were nevertheless our friends. They had pledged themselves to help us thwart our enemies.

I scribbled a few hasty words upon paper and handed it to Elma. And for answer she smiled contentedly, looking into my eyes with an expression of trust, devotion and love.

CHAPTER XV

JUST OFF THE STRAND

A week had gone by. The Nord Express had brought me posthaste across Europe from Petersburg to Calais, and I was again in London. I had left Elma in the care of the Princess Zurloff, whom I knew would conceal her from the horde of police-agents now in search of her.

The mystery had so increased until now it had become absolutely bewildering. The more I had tried to probe it, the more inexplicable had I found it. My brain was awhirl as I sat in the *wagon-lit* rushing across those wide, never-ending plains that lie between the Russian capital and Berlin and the green valleys between the Rhine-lands and the sea. The maze of mystery rendered me utterly incapable of grasping one solid tangible fact, so closely interwoven was each incident of the strange life-drama in which, through mere chance, I was now playing a leading part. I was aware of one fact only, that I loved Elma with all my soul, even though I knew not whom she really was - or her strange life story. Her sweet face, with those soft, brown eyes, so tender and intense, stood out ever before me, sleeping or waking. Each moment as the express rushed south increased the distance between us, yet was I not on my way back to England with a clear and distinct purpose? I snatched at any clue, however small, with desperate eagerness, as a drowning man clutches at a straw.

The spy from Abo had seen me on the railway platform on my

departure from Petersburg. He had overheard me buy a ticket for London, and previous to stepping into the train I had smiled at him in glad triumph. My journey was too long a one for him to follow, and I knew that I had at last outwitted him. He had expected to see Elma with me, no doubt, and his disappointment was plainly marked. But of Woodroffe I had neither seen nor heard anything.

* * * * *

It was a cold but dry November night in London, and I sat dining with Jack Durnford at a small table in the big, well-lit room of the Junior United Service Club. Easy-going and merry as of old, my friend was bubbling over with good spirits, delighted to be back again in town after three years sailing up and down the Mediterranean, from Gib. To Smyrna, maneuvering always, yet with never a chance of a fight. His well-shaven face bore the mark of the southern suns, and the backs of his hands were tanned by the heat and the sea. He was, indeed, as smart an officer as any at the Junior, for the Marines are proverbial for their neatness, and his men on board the *Bulwark* had received many a pleasing compliment from the Admiral.

"Glad to be back!" he exclaimed, as he helped himself to a "peg." "I should rather think so, old chap. You know how awfully wearying the life becomes out there. Lots going on down at Palermo, Malta, Monte Carlo, or over at Algiers, and yet we can never get a chance of it. We're always in sight of the gay places, and never land. I don't blame the youngsters for getting off from Leghorn for two days over here in town when they can. Three years is a bigger slice out of a fellow's life than anyone would suppose. But, by the way, I saw Hutcheson the other day. We put into Spezia, and he came out to see the Admiral - got despatches for him, I think. He seems as gay as ever. He lunched at mess, and said how sorry he was you'd deserted Leghorn."

"I haven't exactly deserted it," I said. "But I really don't love it like he does."

"No. A year or two of the Mediterranean blue is quite sufficient to last any fellow his lifetime. I shouldn't live in Leghorn if I had my choice. I'd prefer somewhere up in the mountains, beyond Pisa, or outside Florence, where you can have a good time in winter."

Then a silence fell between us, and I sat eating on until the end of the meal, wondering how to broach the question I so desired to put to him.

"I shall try if I can get on recruiting service at home for a bit," he said presently. "There's an appointment up in Glasgow vacant, and I shall try for it. It'll be better, at any rate, than China or the Pacific."

I was just about to turn the conversation to the visit of the mysterious *Lola* to Leghorn, when two men he knew entered the dining-room, and, recognizing him, came across to give him a welcome home. One of the newcomers was Major Bartlett, whom I at once recollected as having been a guest of Leithcourt's up at Rannoch, and the other a younger man whom Durnford introduced to me as Captain Hanbury.

"Oh, Major!" I cried, rising and grasping his hand. "I haven't seen you since Scotland, and the extraordinary ending to your house-party."

"No," he laughed. "It was an amazing affair, wasn't it? After the Leithcourts left it was like pandemonium let loose; the guests collared everything they could lay their hands upon! It's a wonder to me the disgraceful affair didn't get into the papers."

"But where's Leithcourt now?" I asked anxiously.

"Haven't the ghost of an idea," replied the Major, standing astride with his hands in his pockets. "Young Paget of ours told me the other day that he saw Muriel driving in the Terminus Road at Eastbourne, but she didn't notice him. They were a queerish lot, those Leithcourts," he added.

"Hulloa! What are you saying about the Leithcourts, Charley?" exclaimed Durnford, turning quickly from Hanbury. "I know some people of that name - Philip Leithcourt, who has a daughter named Muriel."

"Well, they sound much the same. But if you know them, my dear old chap, I really don't envy you your friends," declared the Major with a laugh.

"Why not?"

"Well, Gregg will tell you," he said. "He knows, perhaps, more than I do. But," he added, "they may not, of course, be the same people."

"I first met them yachting over at Algiers," Jack said. "And then again at Malta, where they seemed to have quite a lot of friends. They had a steam-yacht, the *Iris*, and were often up and down the Mediterranean."

"Must be the same people," declared the Major. "Leithcourt spoke once or twice of his yacht, but we all put it down as a non-existent vessel, because he was always drawing the long bow about his adventures."

"And how did you first come to know him?" I asked of the Major eagerly.

"Oh, I don't know. Somebody brought him to mess, and we struck up an acquaintance across the table. He seemed a good chap, and when he asked me to shoot I accepted. On arrival up at Rannoch, however, one thing struck me as jolly strange, and that was that among the people I was asked to meet was one of the very worst blacklegs about town. He called himself Martin Woodroffe up there - although I'd known him at the old

Corinthian Club as Dick Archer. He was believed then to be one of a clever gang of international thieves."

"When I first met him he gave me the name of Hornby," I said. "It was in Leghorn, where he was on board a yacht called the *Lola*, of which he represented himself as owner."

"He left Rannoch very suddenly," remarked Bartlett. "We understood that he was engaged to marry Muriel. If so, I'm sorry for her, poor girl."

"What!" cried Durnford, starting up. "That man to marry Muriel Leithcourt?"

"Yes," I said. "Why?"

But his countenance had turned pale, and he gave no answer to my question.

"If these same Leithcourts are really friends of yours, Durnford, old fellow, I'm sorry I've said anything against them," the Major exclaimed in an apologetic tone. "Only the end of my visit was so abrupt and so extraordinary, and the company such a mixed one, that - well, to tell you the truth, the people are a mysterious lot altogether."

"Perhaps our Leithcourts are not the same as those Jack knows," I remarked, in order to escape from a rather difficult situation; whereupon Durnford, as though eager to conceal his surprise, said with a forced laugh, "Oh! probably not," and reseated himself at table. Then the Major quickly changed the topic of conversation, and afterwards he and his friend passed along to their table and sat down to eat.

I could not help noticing that Jack Durnford was upset at what he had learnt, yet I hesitated just then to put any question to him. I resolved to approach the subject later, so as to allow him time to question me if he wished to do so.

After smoking an hour we went across to the Empire, where we spent the evening in the grand circle, meeting many men we knew and having a rather pleasant time among old acquaintances. If a man who had lived the club life of London returns from abroad, he can always run across someone he knows in the circle of the Empire about ten o'clock at night. Jack was, however, not his old self that he had been before dinner. His brow was now heavy and thoughtful, and he appeared deeply immersed in some intricate problem, for his eyes were fixed vacantly when opportunity was afforded him to think, and he appeared to desire to avoid his friends rather than to greet them.

After the theater I induced him to come round to the Cecil, and in the wicker chair in the big portico before the entrance we sat to smoke our final cigars. It is a favorite spot of mine when in London, for at afternoon, when the string band plays and the Americans and other cosmopolitans drink tea, there is a continual coming and going, a little panorama of life that to a student of men like myself is intensely interesting. And at night it is just as amusing to sit there in the shadow and watch the people returning from the theaters or dances and to speculate as to whom and what they are. At that one little corner of London just off the Strand you see more variety of men and women than perhaps at any other spot. All grades pass before you, from the pushful American commercial man interested in a patent medicine, to the proud Indian Rajah with his turbaned suite; from the variety actress to the daughter of a peer, or the wife of a millionaire pork-butcher doing Europe.

"You've been a bit down in the mouth to-night, Jack," I said presently, after we had been watching the cabs coming up, depositing the home-coming revelers from the Savoy or the Carlton.

"Yes," he sighed. "And surely I have enough to cause me - after what I've heard from Bartlett."

"What! Did the facts he told us convey any bad news to you?" I inquired with pretended ignorance.

"Yes," he said hoarsely, after a brief pause. Then he added: "Bartlett said you could tell me what happened up in Scotland, where Leithcourt had shooting. Tell me everything," he added with the air of a man in whom all hope is dead.

"Well," I began, "the Leithcourts took Rannoch Castle, close to my uncle's place, near Dumfries. I got to know them, of course, and often shot with his party. One day, however, I was amazed to notice in one of the rooms the photograph of a lady, the exact counterpart of that picture which, I recollect, I told you when in Leghorn I had found torn up on board the *Lola*. You recollect what I narrated about my strange adventure, don't you?"

"I remember every word," was his answer. "Go on. What did you do?"

"Nothing. I held my tongue. But when I discovered that the fellow who called himself Woodroffe - the man who had represented himself as the owner of the *Lola*, and who, no doubt, had had a hand in breaking open Hutcheson's safe in the Consulate - was engaged to Muriel, I became full of suspicion."

"Well?"

"Woodroffe, after meeting me, disappeared - went to Hamburg, they said, on business. Then other things occurred. A man and woman were found murdered up in the wood about a mile and a half from the castle. The man was made up to represent my man Olinto - I believe you've seen him in Leghorn?"

"What! They've killed Olinto?" he gasped, starting from his chair.

"No. The fellow was made up very much like him. But his wife Armida was killed."

"They killed the woman, and believed they had also killed her husband, eh?" he said bitterly through his teeth, and I saw that his strong hands grasped the arms of his chair firmly. "And Martin Woodroffe is engaged to Muriel Leithcourt. Are you certain of this?"

"Yes; quite certain."

"And is there no suspicion as to who is the assassin of the woman Santini and this mysterious man who posed as her husband?"

"None whatever."

For some time Jack Durnford smoked in silence, and I could just distinguish his white, hard face in the faint light, for it was now late, and the big electric lamps had been turned out and we were in semi-darkness.

"That fellow shall never marry Muriel," he declared in a fierce, hoarse voice. "What you have just told me reveals the truth. Did you meet Chater?"

"He appeared suddenly at Rannoch, and the Leithcourts fled precipitately and have not since been heard of."

"Ah, no wonder!" he remarked with a dry laugh. "No wonder! But look here, Gordon, I'm not going to stand by and let that scoundrel Woodroffe marry Muriel."

"You love her, perhaps?" I hazarded.

"Yes, I do love her," he admitted. "And, by heaven!" he cried, "I will tell the truth and crush the whole of their ingenious plot. Have you met Elma Heath?" he asked.

"Yes," I said in quick anxiety.

"Then listen," he said in a low, earnest voice. "Listen, and I'll tell you something.

"There is a greater mystery surrounding that yacht, the *Lola*, than you have ever imagined, my dear old chap," declared Jack Durnford, looking me straight in the face. "When you told me about it on the quarter-deck that day outside Leghorn, I was half a mind to tell you what I knew. Only one fact prevented me - my disinclination to reveal my own secrets. I loved Muriel Leithcourt, yet, afloat as I was, I could never see her - I could not obtain from her own lips the explanation I desired. Yet I would not prejudge her - no, and I won't now!" he added with a fierce resolution.

"I love her," he went on, "and she reciprocates my love. Ours is a secret engagement made in Malta two years ago, and yet you tell me that she has pledged herself to that fellow Woodroffe - the man known here in London as Dick Archer. I can't believe it - I really can't, old fellow. She could never write to me as she has done, urging patience and secrecy until my return."

"Unless, of course, she desired to gain time," I suggested.

But my friend was silent; his brows were deep knit.

"Woodroffe is at the present moment in Petersburg," I said. "I've just come back from there."

"In St. Petersburg!" he gasped, surprised. "Then he is with that villainous official, Baron Oberg, the Governor-General of Finland."

"No; Oberg is living shut up in his palace at Helsingfors, fearing to go out lest he shall be assassinated," was my answer.

"And Elma? What has become of her?"

"She is in hiding in Petersburg, awaiting such time as I can get her safely out of Russia," and then, continuing, I explained how she had been maimed and rendered deaf and dumb.

"What!" he cried fiercely. "Have they actually done that to the poor girl? Then they feared that she should reveal the nature of their plot, for she had seen and heard."

"Seen and heard what?"

"Be patient; we will elucidate this mystery, and the motive of this terrible infliction upon her. Muriel wrote to me saying that poor Elma, her friend, had disappeared, and she feared that some evil had also happened to her. So Oberg had sent her to his fortress - his own private Bastille - the place to which, on pretended charges of conspiracy against Russia, he sends those who thwart him to a living tomb."

"I have seen him, and I have defied him," I said.

"You have! Man alive! be careful. He's not a fellow who sticks at trifles," said Jack warningly.

"I don't fear," I replied. "Elma's enemies are also mine."

"Then I take it, old fellow, that notwithstanding her affliction, you are actually in love with her?"

"I intend to rescue, and to marry her," I answered quite frankly.

"But first we must tear aside this veil of mystery and ascertain all the facts concerning her," he said. "At present I only know one or two very vague details. The baron is certainly not her uncle, as he represents himself to be, but it seems certain that she is the daughter of Anglo-Russian parents, and was born in Russia and brought to England when a child."

"But from whom do you expect I can obtain the true facts

concerning her, and the reason of the baron's desire to keep her silent?"

"Ah!" he said, twisting his mustache thoughtfully. "That's just the question. For a solution of the problem we must first fathom the motive of the Leithcourts and the reason they fled in fear before that fellow Chater. That Muriel is innocent of any complicity in their plot, whatever it may be, I feel convinced. She may be the victim of that blackleg Woodroffe, who, as Bartlett has told you, is one of the most expert swindlers in London, and who has already done two terms of penal servitude."

"But what was the motive in breaking open the Consul's safe, if not to obtain the Foreign Office or Admiralty ciphers? Perhaps they wanted to steal them and sell them to a foreign government?"

"No; that was not their object. I've thought over it many, many times since you told me, and I feel convinced that Woodroffe is too shrewd a fellow not to have known that no Consul goes away on leave and allows his ciphers to remain behind. When he leaves his post he always deposits those precious books either at the Foreign Office here or with his Consul-General, or with a Consul at another port. They'd surely ascertain all that before they made the raid, you bet. The affair was a risky one, and Dick Archer is known as a man of many precautions."

"But he is on extremely friendly terms with Elma. It was he who succeeded in finding her in Finland, and taking her beyond Oberg's sphere of influence to Petersburg."

"Then it is certainly only an affected friendship, with some sinister motive underlying it."

"She wrote a letter from her island prison to an old school-fellow named Lydia Moreton, asking her to see Woodroffe at his rooms in Cork Street, and tell him that through all she was suffering she had kept her promise to him, and that the secret was still safe."

"Exactly. And now the fellow fears that as you are so actively searching out the truth, she may yield to your demands and explain. He therefore intends to silence her."

"What! to kill her, you mean?" I gasped, in quick apprehension.

"Well, he might do so, in order to save himself, you see," Jack replied, adding: "He certainly would have no compunction if he thought that it would not be brought home to him. Only he, no doubt, fears you, because you have found her, and are in love with her."

I admitted the force of his argument, but recollected that my dear one was safe in concealment, and that the Princess was our friend, even though I, as an Englishman, had no sympathy with the doctrine of the bomb and the knife.

I tried to get from him all that he knew concerning Elma, but he seemed, for some curious reason, disinclined to tell. All I could gather was that Leithcourt was in league with Chater and Woodroffe, and that Muriel had acted as an entirely innocent agent. What the conspiracy was, or what was its motive, I could not discern. I was as far off the solution of the problem as ever.

"We must first find Muriel," he declared, when I pressed him to tell me everything he knew. "There are facts you have told me which negative my own theories, and only from her can we obtain the real truth."

"But surely you know where she is? She writes to you," I said.

"The last letter, which I received at Gib. ten days ago, was from the Hotel Bristol, at Botzen, in the Tyrol, yet Bartlett says she has been seen down at Eastbourne."

"But you have an address where you always write to her, I suppose?"

"Yes, a secret one. I have written and made an appointment, but she has not kept it. She has been prevented, of course. She may be with her parents, and unable to come to London."

"You did not know that they had fled, and were in hiding?"

"Of course not. What I've heard to-night is news to me - amazing news."

"And does it not convey to you the truth?"

"It does - a ghastly truth concerning Elma Heath," he answered in a low voice, as though speaking to himself.

"Tell me. What? I'm dying, Jack, to know everything concerning her. Who is that fellow Oberg?"

"Her enemy. She, by mere accident, learned his secret and Woodroffe's, and they now both live in deadly fear of her."

"And for that reason she was taken to Siena, where some villainous Italian doctor was bribed to render her deaf and dumb."

He nodded in the affirmative.

"But Chater?"

"I know very little concerning him. He may have conspired with them, or he may be innocent. It seems as though he were antagonistic to their schemes, if Leithcourt and his family really fled from him."

"And yet he was on board the *Lola*. Indeed, he may have helped to commit the burglary at the Consulate," I said.

"Quite likely," he answered. "But our first object must be to rediscover Muriel. Paget says she is in Eastbourne. If she is there, we shall easily find her. They publish visitors' lists in the papers, don't they, like they do at Hastings?" Then he added: "Visitors' lists are most annoying when you find your name printed in them when you are supposed officially to be somewhere else. I was had once like that by the Bournemouth papers, when I was supposed to be on duty over at Queenstown. I narrowly escaped a terrible wigging."

"Shall we go to Eastbourne?" I suggested eagerly. "I'll go there with you in the morning."

"Or would it not be best to send an urgent wire to the address where I always write? She would then reply here, no doubt. If she's in Eastbourne, there may be reasons why she cannot come up to town. If her people are in hiding, of course she won't come. But she'll make an appointment with me, no doubt."

"Very well. Send a wire," I said. "And make it urgent. It will then be forwarded. But as regards Olinto? Would you like to see him? He might tell you more than he has told me."

"No; by no means. He must not know that I have returned to London," declared my friend quickly. "You had better not see him - you understand."

"Then his interests are - well, not exactly our own?"

"No."

"But why don't you tell me more about Elma?" I urged, for I was eager to learn all he knew. "Come, do tell me!" I implored.

"I've told you practically everything, my dear old fellow," was his response. "The revelation of the true facts of the affair can be made only by Muriel. I tell you, we must find her."

"Yes, we must - at all hazards," I said. "Let's go across to the telegraph office opposite Charing Cross. It's open always." And we rose and walked out along the Strand, now nearly deserted, and despatched an urgent message to Muriel at an address in Hurlingham Road, Fulham.

Afterwards we stood outside on the curb, still talking, I loth to part from him, when there passed by in the shadow two men in dark overcoats, who crossed the road behind us to the front of Charing Cross station, and then continued on towards Trafalgar Square.

As the light of the street lamp fell upon them, I thought I recognized the face of one as that of a person I had seen before, yet I was not at all certain, and my failure to remember whom the passer-by resembled prevented me from saying anything further to Jack than:

"A fellow I know has just gone by, I think."

"We seem to be meeting hosts of friends to-night," he laughed. "After all, old chap, it does one good to come back to our dear, dirty old town again. We abuse it when we are here, and talk of the life in Paris, and Vienna, and Brussels, but when we are away there is no place on earth so dear to us, for it is 'home.' But there!" he laughed, "I'm actually growing romantic. Ah! if we could only find Muriel! But we must to-morrow. Ta-ta! I shall go around to the club and sleep, for I haven't fixed on any diggings yet. Come in at ten to-morrow, and we will decide upon some plan. One thing is plainly certain; Elma must at once be got out of Russia. She's in deadly peril of her life there."

"Yes," I said. "And you will help me?"

"With all my heart, old fellow," answered my friend, warmly grasping my hand, and then we parted, he strolling along towards the National Gallery on his way back to the "Junior," while I returned to the *Cecil* alone.

CHAPTER XVI

MARKED MEN

"Captain Durnford?" I inquired of the hall-porter of the club next morning.

"Not here, sir."

"But he slept here last night," I remarked. "I have an appointment with him."

The man consulted the big book before him, and answered:

"Captain Durnford went out at 9:27 last night, sir, but has not returned."

Strange, I thought, but although I waited in the club nearly an hour, he did not put in an appearance. I called again at noon, and he had not come in, and again at two o'clock, but he had not even then made his appearance. Then I began to be anxious. I returned to the hotel, resolved to wait for a few hours longer. He might have altered his mind and gone to Eastbourne in search of Muriel; yet, had he done so, he would surely have telegraphed to me.

About four o'clock, as I was passing through the big hall of the hotel, I heard a voice behind me utter a greeting in Italian, and turning in surprise, found Olinto, dressed in his best suit of black, standing hat in hand.

In an instant I recollected what Jack had told me, and regarded him with some suspicion.

"Signor Commendatore," he said in a low voice, as though fearing to be overheard, "may I be permitted to speak in private with you?"

"Certainly," I said, and I took him in the lift up to my room.

"I have come to warn you, signore," he said, when I had given him a seat. "Your enemies mean harm to you."

"And who are they, pray?" I asked, biting my lips. "The same, I suppose, who prepared that ingenious trap in Lambeth?"

"I am not here to reveal to you who they are, signore, only to warn you to have a care of yourself," was the Italian's reply.

"Look here, Olinto!" I exclaimed determinedly, "I've had enough of this confounded mystery. Tell me the truth regarding the assassination of your poor wife up in Scotland."

"Ah, signore!" he answered sadly in a changed voice, "I do not know. It was a plot. Someone represented me - but he was killed also. They believed they had struck me down," he added, with a bitter laugh. "Poor Armida's body was found concealed behind a rock on the opposite side of the wood. I saw it - ah!" he cried shuddering.

"Then you are ignorant of the identity of your wife's assassin?"

"Entirely."

"Tell me one thing," I said. "Did Armida possess any trinket in the form of a little enameled cross - like a miniature cross of cavaliere?"

"Yes; I gave it to her. I found it on the floor at the Mansion House, where I was engaged as odd waiter for a banquet. I know I ought to have given it up to the Lord Mayor's servants, but it was such a pretty little thing that I was tempted to keep it. It probably had fallen from the coat of one of the diplomatists dining there."

I was silent. The faint suspicion that Oberg had been at that spot was now entirely removed. The only clue I had was satisfactorily accounted for.

"Why do you ask, Signor Commendatore?" he added.

"Because the cross was found at the spot, and was believed to have been dropped by the assassin," I said.

The police had, it seemed, succeeded in discovering the unfortunate woman after all, and had found that she was his wife.

"You know a man named Leithcourt?" I asked a few moments later. "Now, tell the truth. In this affair, Olinto, our interests are mutual, are they not?"

He nodded, after a moment's hesitation.

"And you know also a man named Archer - who is sometimes known as Hornby, or Woodroffe - as well as a friend of his called Chater."

"Si, signore," he said. "I have met them all - to my regret."

"And have you ever met a Russian - a certain Baron Oberg - and his niece, Elma Heath?"

"His niece? She isn't his niece."

"Then who is she?" I demanded.

"How do I know? I have seen her once or twice. But she's dead, isn't she? She knew the secret of those men, and they intended to kill her. I tried to prevent them taking her away on the yacht, and I would have gone to the police - only I dare not."

"Why?"

"Well, because my own hands were not quite clean," he answered after a pause, his eyes fixed upon mine the while. "I knew they intended to silence her, but I was powerless to save her, poor young lady. They took her on board Leithcourt's yacht, the *Iris*, and they sailed for the Mediterranean, I believe."

"Then the name and appearance of the yacht was altered on the voyage, and it became the *Lola*," I said.

"No doubt," he smiled. "The *Iris* was a steamer of many names, and had, I believe, been painted nearly all the colors of the rainbow at various times. It was a mysterious vessel, but she exists no more. They scuttled her somewhere up in the Baltic, I've heard."

"And who is this Oberg?" I inquired, urging him to reveal to me all he knew concerning him.

"He stands in great fear of the poor young lady, I believe, for it was at his instigation that Leithcourt and his friends took her on that fatal yachting cruise."

"And what was your connection with them?"

"Well, I was Leithcourt's servant," was his reply. "I was steward on the *Iris* for a year, until I suppose they thought that I began to see too much, and then I was placed in a position ashore."

"And what did you see?"

"More than I care to tell, signore. If they were arrested I should be arrested, too, you see."

"But I mean to solve this mystery, Olinto," I said fiercely, for I was in no trifling mood. "I'll fathom it if it costs me my life."

"If the signore solves it himself, then I cannot be charged with revealing the truth," was the man's diplomatic reply. "But I fear that they are far too wary."

"Armida has lost her life. Surely that is sufficient incentive for you to bring them all to justice?"

"Of course. But if the law falls upon them, it will also fall upon me."

I explained the terrible affliction to which my love had been subjected by those heartless brutes, whereupon he cried enthusiastically:

"Then she is not dead! She can tell us everything!"

"But cannot you tell us?"

"No; not all. The secret she knows has never been revealed. They feared she might be incautious, and for that reason Oberg made the villainous suggestion of the yachting trip. She was to be drowned - accidentally, of course."

"She is in St. Petersburg now. I left her a week ago."

"In Russia! Ah, signore, for her sake, don't allow the young lady to remain there. The Baron is all-powerful. He does what he wishes in Russia, and the more merciless he is to the people he governs, the greater rewards he receives from the Czar. I have never been in Russia, but surely it must be a strange country, signore!"

"Well," I said, sitting upon the edge of the bed and looking at him. "Are you prepared to denounce them if I bring the

Signorina Heath here, to England?"

"But what is the use, if we have no clear proof?" was his evasive reply. I could see plainly that he feared being himself implicated in some extraordinary plot, the exact nature of which he so steadfastly refused to reveal to me.

We talked on for fully half an hour, and from his conversation I gathered that he was well acquainted with Elma.

"Ah, signore, she was such a pleasant and kind-hearted young lady. I always felt very sorry for her. She was in deadly fear of them."

"Because they were thieves?" I hazarded.

"Ah, worse!"

"But why did they induce you to entice me to that house in Lambeth? Why did they so evidently desire that I should be killed?"

"By accident," he interrupted, correcting me. "Always by accident," and he smiled grimly.

"Surely you know their secret motive?" I remarked.

"At the time I did not," he declared. "I acted on their instructions, being compelled to, for they hold my future in their hands. Therefore I could not disobey. You knew too much, therefore you were marked down for death - just as you are now."

"And who is it who is now seeking my life?" I inquired gravely. "I only returned from Russia yesterday."

"Your movements are well known," answered the young Italian. "You cannot be too careful. Woodroffe has been in Russia with you, has he not?"

I replied in the affirmative, whereupon he said:

"I thought so, but was not quite sure."

"And Chater?" I inquired; "where is he?"

"In London."

"And the Leithcourts?"

He shrugged his shoulders with a gesture of ignorance, adding: "The Signorina Muriel returned to London from Eastbourne this morning."

"Where can I find her?" I inquired eagerly. "It is of the utmost importance that I should see her."

"She is with a relation, a cousin, I think, at Bassett Road, Notting Hill. The house is called 'Holmwood.'"

"You have seen her?"

"No. I heard she had returned."

"And her father is still in hiding from Chater?"

"He is still in hiding, but Chater is his best friend."

"That is curious," I remarked, recollecting the hurried departure from Rannoch. "They've made it up, I suppose?"

"They never quarreled, to my knowledge."

"Then why did Leithcourt leave Scotland so hurriedly on Chater's arrival? You know all about the affair, of course?"

He nodded, saying with a grim smile, "Yes; I know. The party up there must have been a very interesting one. If the police could have made a raid on the place they would have found among the guests certain persons long 'wanted.' But the arrival of Chater and the flight of Leithcourt had an ulterior object. Chater had never been Leithcourt's enemy."

"But I can't understand that," I said. "Why should Leithcourt have attacked Chater, rendered him unconscious, and shut him up in the cupboard in the library?"

"Was it Leithcourt who did that?" he asked dubiously. "I think not. It was another of the guests who was Chater's bitterest enemy. But Philip Leithcourt took advantage of the fracas in order to make believe that he had fled because of Chater's arrival. Ah!" he added, "you haven't any idea of their ruses. They are amazing!"

"So it seems," I said, nevertheless only half convinced that the Italian was telling me the truth. If it was really, as he had said, that the arrival of Chater and the flight was merely a "blind," then the mystery was again deepened.

"Then who was the man who attacked Chater?" I asked.

"Only Chater himself knows. It was one of the guests, that is quite evident."

"And you say that the flight had been prearranged?" I remarked.

"Yes, with a distinct motive," he said; then, after a pause, he added, with a strange, earnest look in his dark eyes, "Pardon me, Signor Commendatore, if I presume to suggest something, will you not?"

"Certainly. What do you suggest?"

"That you should remain here, in this hotel, and not venture out."

"For fear of something unfortunate happening to me!" I

laughed. "I'm really not afraid, Olinto," I added. "You know I carry this," and I drew out my revolver from my hip-pocket.

"I know, signore," he said anxiously. "But you might not be afforded opportunity for using it. When they lay a trap they bait it well."

"I know. They're a set of the most ingenious scoundrels in London, it is very evident. Yet I don't fear them in the least," I declared. "I must rescue the Signorina Heath."

"But, signore, have a care for yourself," cried the Italian, laying his hand upon my arm. "You are a marked man. Ah! do I not know," he exclaimed breathlessly. "If you go out you may run right into - well, the fatal accident."

"Never fear, Olinto," I said reassuringly. "I shall keep my eyes well open. Here, in London, one's life is safer than anywhere else in the world, perhaps - certainly safer than in some places I could name in your own country, eh?" at which he grinned.

The next moment he grew serious again, and said:

"I only warn the signore that if he goes out it is at his own peril."

"Then let it be so," I laughed, feeling self-confident that no one could lead me into any trap. I was neither a foreigner nor a country cousin. I knew London too well. He was silent and shook his head; then, after telling me that he was still at the same restaurant in Westbourne Grove, he took his departure, warning me once more not to go forth.

Half an hour later, disregarding his words, I strode out into the Strand, and again walked round to the "Junior." The short wintry day had ended, the gas-lamps were lit, and the darkness of night was gradually creeping on.

Jack had not been to the club, and I began now to grow

thoroughly uneasy. He had parted from me at the corner of the Strand with only a five minutes' walk before him, and yet he had apparently disappeared. My first impulse was to drive to Notting Hill to inquire of Muriel if she had news of him, but somehow the Italian's warning words made me wonder if he had met with foul play.

I suddenly recollected those two men who had passed by as we had talked, and how that the features of one had seemed strangely familiar. Therefore I took a cab to the police-station down at Whitehall, and made inquiry of the inspector on duty in the big bare office with its flaring gas-jets in wire globes. He heard me to the end, then turning back the book of "occurrences" before him, glanced through the ruled entries.

"I should think this is the gentleman, sir," he said. And he read to me the entry as follows:

"P.C. 462A reports that at 2.07 a.m., while on duty outside the National Gallery, he heard a revolver shot, followed by a man's cry. He ran to the corner of Suffolk Street, where he found a gentleman lying upon the pavement suffering from a serious shot-wound in the chest and quite unconscious. He obtained the assistance of P.C.'s 218A and 343A, and the gentleman, who was not identified, was taken to the Charing Cross Hospital, where the house-surgeon expressed a doubt whether he could live. Neither P.C.'s recollect having noticed any suspicious-looking person in the vicinity.

"JOHN PERCIVAL, *Inspector.*"

I waited for no more, but rushed round to the hospital in the cab, and was, five minutes later, taken along the ward, where I identified poor Jack lying in bed, white-faced and unconscious.

"The doctor was here a quarter of an hour ago," whispered the sister. "And he fears he is sinking."

"He has uttered no words?" I asked anxiously. "Made no statement?"

"None. He has never regained consciousness, and I fear, sir, he never will. It is a case of deliberate murder, the police told me early this morning."

I clenched my fists and swore a fierce revenge for that dastardly act. And as I stood beside the narrow bed, I realized that what Olinto had said regarding my own peril was the actual truth. I was a marked man. Was I never to penetrate that inscrutable and ever-increasing mystery?

CHAPTER XVII

THE TRUTH ABOUT THE "LOLA"

Throughout the long night I called many times at the hospital, but the reply was always the same. Jack had not regained consciousness, and the doctor regarded his case as hopeless.

In the morning I drove in hot haste to Bassett Road, Notting Hill, and at the address Olinto had given me found Muriel. When she entered the room with folding doors into which I had been shown, I saw that she was pale and apprehensive, for we had not met since her flight, and she was, no doubt, at a loss for an explanation. But I did not press her for one. I merely told her that the Italian Santini had given me her address and that I came as bearer of unfortunate news.

"What is it?" she gasped quickly.

"It concerns Captain Durnford," I replied. "He has been injured in the street, and is in Charing Cross Hospital."

"Ah!" she cried. "I see. You do not explain the truth. By your face I can tell there is something more. He's dead! Tell me the worst."

"No, Miss Leithcourt," I said gravely, "not dead, but the doctors fear that he may not recover. His wound is dangerous. He has been shot by some unknown person."

"Shot!" she echoed, bursting into tears. "Then they have followed him, after all! They have deceived me, and now, as they intend to take him from me, I will myself protect him. You, Mr. Gregg, have been in peril of your life, that I know, but Jack's enemies are yours, and they shall not go unpunished. May I see him?"

"I fear not, but we will ask at the hospital." And after the exchange of some further explanations, we took a hansom back to Charing Cross.

At first the sister refused to allow Muriel to see the patient, but she implored so earnestly that at last she consented, and the distressed girl in the black coat and hat crept on tiptoe to the bedside.

"He was conscious for a quarter of an hour or so," whispered the nurse who sat there, "He asked after some lady named Muriel."

The girl at my side burst into low sobbing.

"Tell him," she said, "that Muriel is here - that she has seen him, and is waiting for him to recover."

We were not allowed to linger there, and on leaving the hospital I took her back again to Notting Hill, promising to keep her well informed of Jack's condition. He had returned to consciousness, therefore there was now a faint hope for his recovery.

Day succeeded day, and although I was not allowed to visit my friend, I was told that he was very slowly progressing. I idled at the Hotel Cecil longing daily for news of Elma. Only once did a letter come from her, a brief, well-written note from which it appeared that she was quite well and happy, although she longed to be able to go out. The Princess was very kind indeed to her, and, she added, was making secret arrangements for her escape across the Russian frontier into Germany.

WILLIAM LE QUEUX

I knew what that meant. Use was to be made of certain Russian officials who were secretly allied with the Revolutionists in order to secure her safe conduct beyond the power of that order of exile of the tyrant de Plehve. I wrote to her under cover to the Princess, but there had been no time yet for a reply.

I saw Muriel many times, but never once did she refer to Rannoch or their sudden departure. Her only thought was of the man she loved.

"I always believed that you were engaged to Mr. Woodroffe," I said one day, when I called to tell her of Jack's latest bulletin.

"It is true that he asked me to marry him," she responded. "But there were reasons why I did not accept."

"Reasons connected with his past, eh?"

She smiled, and then said:

"Ah, Mr. Gregg, it is all a strange and very tragic story. I must see Jack. When do you think they will allow me to go to him?"

I explained that the doctor feared to cause the patient any undue excitement, but that in two or three days there was hope of her being allowed to visit him. Several times the police made inquiry of me, but I could tell them nothing. I could not for the life of me recollect where I had before seen the face of that man who had passed in the darkness.

One afternoon, ten days after the attempt upon Jack, I was allowed to sit by his bedside and question him.

"Ah, Gordon, old fellow!" he said faintly, "I've had a narrow escape - by Jove! After I left you I walked quickly on towards the club, when, all of a sudden, two scoundrels sprang out of Suffolk Street, and one of them fired a revolver full at me. Then I knew no more."

"But who were the men? Did you recognize them?"

"No, not at all. That's the worst of it."

"But Muriel knows who they were!" I said.

"Ah, yes! Bring her here, won't you?" the poor fellow implored, "I'm dying to see her once again."

Then I told him how she had looked upon him while unconscious, and how I had taken the daily bulletin to her. For an hour I talked with him, urging him to get well soon, so that we could unite in probing the mystery, and bringing to justice those responsible for the dastardly act.

"Muriel knows, and if she loves you she will no doubt assist us," I said.

"Oh, she does love me, Gordon, I know that," said the prostrate man, smiling contentedly, and when I left I promised to bring her there on the morrow.

This I did, but having conducted her to the bed at the end of the ward I discreetly withdrew. What she said to him I am not, of course, aware. All I know is that an hour later when I returned I found them the happiest pair possible to conceive, and I clearly saw that Jack's trust in her was not ill-placed.

But of Elma? No further word had come from her, and I began to grow uneasy. The days went on. I wrote twice, but no reply was forthcoming. At last I could bear the suspense no longer, and began to contemplate returning to Russia.

Jack, when at last discharged from the hospital, came across to the Cecil and lived with me in preference to the "Junior." He was very weak at first, and I looked after him, while every day Muriel came and ate with us, brightening our lives by her smart and merry chatter. She knew that I loved Elma and was also aware of the exciting events in Russia, Jack having told her of them during their long drives in hansoms when he went out with her to take the air.

One day I received a brief note from the Princess in Petersburg, urging me to remain patient and saying Elma was quite safe and well. There were reasons, however, why she was unable to write, she added. What were they, I wondered? Yet I could only wait until I received word to travel back to Russia and fetch her home. The Princess had promised to arrange everything.

December came, and we still remained on at the hotel. Once Olinto had written me repeating his warning, but I did not heed it. I somehow distrusted the fellow.

Jack, now thoroughly recovered, called almost daily at Bassett Road, and would often bring Muriel to the Cecil to tea or to luncheon. Often I inquired the whereabouts of her father and of Hylton Chater, but she declared herself in entire ignorance, and believed they were abroad.

One afternoon, shortly before Christmas, as we were idling in the American bar of the hotel, my friend told me that Muriel had invited us to tea at her cousin's that afternoon, and accordingly we went there in company.

The drawing-room into which we were ushered was familiar to me as the apartment wherein I had told Muriel of the attempt upon her lover's life.

As we sat together Muriel, a smart figure in a pale blue gown, poured tea for us and chatted more merrily, I thought, than ever before. She seemed quick and nervous and yet full of happiness, as she should indeed have been, for Jack Durnford was one of the best fellows in the world, and his restoration to health little short of miraculous.

"Gordon," he said to me with a sudden seriousness when tea had ended and we had placed down our cups. "I want to tell you something – something I've been longing always to tell you, and now I have got dear Muriel's consent. I want to tell you about her father and his friends."

"And about Elma, too?" I said in quick eagerness. "Yes, tell me everything."

"No, not everything, for I don't know it myself. But what I know I will explain as briefly as I can, and leave you to form your own conclusions. It is," he went on, "a strange - most amazing story. When I myself became first cognizant of the mystery I was on board the flagship the *Renown*, under Admiral Sir John Fisher. We were lying in Malta when there arrived the English yacht *Iris*, owned by Mr. Philip Leithcourt, and among those on board cruising for pleasure were Mr. Martin Woodroffe, Mr. Hylton Chater, and the owner's wife and daughter Muriel.

"Muriel and I met first at a tennis-party, and afterwards frequently at various houses in Malta, for anyone who goes there and entertains is soon entertained in return. A mutual attachment sprang up between Muriel and myself," he said, placing his hand tenderly upon hers and smiling, "and we often met in secret and took long walks, until quite suddenly Leithcourt said that it was necessary to sail for Smyrna to pick up some friends who had been traveling in Palestine. The night they sailed a great consternation was caused on the island by the news that the safe in the Admiral Superintendent's office had been opened by expert safe-breakers, and certain most important secret documents stolen."

"Well?" I asked, much interested.

"Again, two months later, when the villa of the Prince of Montevachi, at Palmero, was broken into and the whole of the famous jewels of the Princess stolen, it was a very strange fact that the *Iris* was at the moment in that port. But it was not until the third occasion, when the yacht was at Villefranche, and our squadron being at Toulon I got four days' leave to go along the Riviera, that my suspicions were aroused, for at the very hour when I was dining at the London House at Nice with Muriel and a schoolfellow of hers, Elma Heath - who was spending the winter there with a lady who was Baron Oberg's cousin - that a great robbery was committed in one of the big hotels up at Cimiez, the wife of an American millionaire losing jewels valued at thirty thousand pounds. Then the robberies, coincident with the visit of the yacht, aroused my strong suspicion. I remarked the nature of those documents stolen from Malta, and recognized that they could only be of service to a foreign government. Then came the Leghorn incident of which you told me. The yacht's name had been changed to the *Lola*, and she had been repainted. I made searching inquiry, and found that on the evening she was purposely run aground in order to strike up a friendship at the Consulate, a Russian gunboat was lying in the vicinity. The Consul's safe was rifled, and the scheme certainly was to transfer anything obtained from it to the Russian gunboat."

"But what was in the safe?" I asked.

"Fortunately nothing. But you see they knew that our squadron was due in Leghorn, and that some extremely important despatches were on the way to the Admiral - secret orders based upon the decision of the British Cabinet as to the vexed question of Russian ships passing the Dardanelles - they expected that they would be lodged in the safe until the arrival of the squadron, as they always are. They were, however, bitterly disappointed because the despatches had not arrived."

"And then?"

"Well, the only Russian who appeared to have any connection with them was Baron Oberg, the Governor-General of Finland, whose habit it was to spend part of the winter in the Mediterranean. From Elma Heath's conversation at dinner that evening at Nice I gathered that she and her uncle had been guests on the *Iris* on several occasions, although I must say that Muriel was extremely reticent regarding all that concerned the yacht."

"Of course," she said quickly. "Now that I have told you the truth, Jack, don't you think it was only natural?"

"Most certainly, dear," he answered, still holding her hand. "Yours was not a secret that you could very well tell to me until you could thoroughly trust me, especially as your father had been implicated in the theft of those documents from Malta. The truth is," he said, turning to me, "Philip Leithcourt has all along been the catspaw of Baron Oberg. A few years ago he was a well-known money-lender in the city, and in that capacity met the Baron, who, being in disgrace, required a loan. He was also in the habit of having certain shady transactions with that daring gang of continental thieves of whom Dick Archer and Hylton Chater were leaders. For this reason he purchased a yacht for their use, so that they might not only use it for the purpose of storing the stolen goods, but for the purpose of sailing from place to place under the guise of wealthy Englishmen traveling for pleasure. Upon that vessel, indeed, was stored thousands and thousands of pounds' worth of jewels and objects of value, the proceeds of many great robberies in England, France and Belgium. Sometimes they traveled for the purpose of disposing of the jewels in various inland towns where the gems, having been recut, were not recognized, while at other times, Chater and Archer, assisted by Mackintosh, the captain, and Olinto Santini, the steward, sailed for a port, landed, committed a robbery, and then sailed away again, quite unsuspected, as rich Englishmen."

"And the crew?" I asked, after a pause.

"They were, of course, well paid, and were kept in ignorance of what the supposed owner and his friends did ashore."

"But Oberg's connection with it?" I asked, surprised at those revelations.

"Ah!" exclaimed Muriel. "The ingenuity of that crafty villain is fiendish. Before he got into the Czar's favor he owed my father a large sum, and then sought how to evade repayment. By means of his spies he discovered the real purpose of the cruises of the *Iris* - for I was often taken on board with a maid in order to allay any suspicion that might arise if only men were cruising. Then he not only compelled my father to cancel the debt, but he impressed the vessel and those who owned and navigated it into the secret service of Russia. A dozen times did we make attempts to obtain secret papers from Italian, French and English dockyards, but only once in the case of Malta and once at Toulon did we succeed. Ah! Mr. Gregg," she added, "you do not know all the anxiety I suffered, how at every hour we were in danger of betrayal or capture, and of the hundred narrow escapes we have had of Custom House officers rummaging the yacht for contraband. You will no doubt recollect the sensation caused by the theft of the jewels of the Princess Wilhelmine of Schaumbourg-Lippe from the lady's-maid in the rapide between Cannes and Les Arcs, the robbery from the Marseilles branch of the Credit Lyonnais, and the great haul of plate from the chateau of Bardon, the Paris millionaire, close to Arcachon."

"Yes," I said, for they were all robberies of which I had read in the newspapers a couple of years before.

"Well," she said, "they were all committed by Archer or Woodroffe and his gang - with accomplices ashore, of course - and never once did it seem that any suspicion fell upon us. While the police were frantically searching hither and thither, we used to weigh anchor and calmly steam away with our booty on board. We had with us an old Dutch lapidary, and one of the cabins was fitted as a workshop, where he altered the appearance of the stones, and prepared them ready for sale, while the gold was melted in a crucible and put ashore to be sent to agents in Hamburg."

"But that night in Leghorn?" I said. "What happened to poor Elma?"

"I do not know," was Muriel's reply. "We were both on board together, and standing at the crack of the door watched you sitting at dinner that evening. Elma told me that she believed that there was a plot against your life, but why she would not tell me. She evidently knew of the proposed rifling of the safe at the Consulate. Oberg himself was also on board, locked in his own cabin. Elma must have overheard some conversation between the Baron and one of the others, for she was in great fear the whole time lest they might injure you. Yet it seemed, after all, as though their idea was the same as always, to worm themselves into your confidence. The instant, however, you went ashore, Chater, Woodroffe - whom you called Hornby - and Mackintosh, the captain - who, by the way, was an old ticket-of-leave man - went ashore, and, of course, broke into the Consulate. Then, as soon as they returned, Elma came to my cabin, awoke me, and said that the Baron was taking her ashore, and that they were to travel overland back to London. She was ready dressed to go, therefore I kissed her, and promising to meet her soon, we parted. That was the last I saw of her. What happened to her afterwards only she alone can tell us."

"But she is not the Baron's niece?" I said.

"No. There is some mystery," declared Muriel. "She holds some secret which he fears she may divulge. But of what nature, I am in ignorance."

"Then you say that your father has never taken any active part in the robberies?" I remarked.

"No. He commenced by lending money, and amassed a considerable fortune. Then avarice seized him, as it does so many men, and coming into contact with Archer and his friends, he saw that the idea of the yacht was a safe and profitable one. Therefore he purchased the vessel, and ran it at the disposition of the thieves, and subsequently under compulsion in the secret service of Russia, as I have already described to you. The profits were colossal. In one year my father's share was eighty thousand pounds."

"And where is your father now?" I asked.

"Ah!" she exclaimed sadly, her face pale and haggard.

"I have heard that the vessel was scuttled somewhere in the Baltic."

"That is true. Oberg's purpose having been served, he demanded half the property on board, or he would give notice to the Russian naval authorities that the pirate yacht was afloat. He attempted to blackmail my father, as he had already done so many times, but his scheme was frustrated. My father, because of his inhuman treatment of poor Elma, defied him, when it appears that Oberg, who was in Helsingfors, telegraphed to the admiral of the Russian fleet in the Baltic. The crew from the *Iris* were at once landed at Riga, and only Mackintosh and my father put to sea again. Ah! my father was desperate, for he knew the merciless character of that man whose victim he had been for so long. They watched a Russian cruiser bearing down upon them, when, just as it drew near, they got off in a boat and blew up the yacht, which sank in three minutes with its ill-obtained wealth on board."

"And your father?"

She was silent, and I saw tears standing in her eyes.

"There was a tragedy," Jack explained in a low, hoarse voice. "He and the captain did not, unfortunately, get sufficiently far from the yacht when they blew her up, and they went down with her."

And I looked in silence at Muriel, who stood with her head bent and her white face covered with her hands.

Almost at the same moment there was a low tap at the door, and the servant-maid announced:

"Mr. Santini, miss."

"Ah!" exclaimed Jack quickly, as Olinto entered the room. "Then you had my note! We have asked you here to reveal to us this dastardly plot which seemed to have been formed against Mr. Gregg and myself. As you know, I've had a narrow escape."

"I know, signore. And the Signor Commendatore is also threatened."

"By whom?"

"By those who killed my poor wife, and who intended also to silence me," was his answer.

"The same who compelled you take me to that house where the fatal chair was prepared, eh?"

"It was Archer, who, fearing that you came to London in search of them, devised that devilish contrivance," he said in his broken English. Then continuing, he went on fiercely: "Now that I have discovered why my poor Armida was killed, I will tell the truth, and not spare them. Since you left Scotland, signore, I have been up in Dumfries, and have discovered several facts which prove that for some reason known only to himself, Leithcourt, while at Rannoch, wrote to both Armida and myself separately, making an appointment to see us at the same time at that spot on the edge of the wood, as he had some secret commission to entrust to us. The letter addressed to me apparently fell into someone else's hands - probably one of the secret agents of Baron Oberg, who were always watching Leithcourt's doings, and he, anxious to learn what was intended, made himself up to look like me, and kept the appointment in my place. Armida, having received the letter unknown to me, went up to Scotland, and was also there at the appointed time. What actually transpired can only be surmised, yet it seems that Leithcourt was in the habit of going up to that spot and loitering there in the evening in order to meet Chater in secret, as the latter was in hiding in a small hotel in Dumfries. Therefore those who formed the plot must have endeavored to throw suspicion upon Leithcourt. It is plain, however, as both myself and Armida knew the gang, it was to their interest to get rid of us, because the suspicions of the police had at last become aroused. Poor Armida was therefore deliberately enticed there to her death, while the inquisitive man whom the assassin took to be myself was also struck down."

"By whom?"

"Not by Chater, for he was in London on that night."

"Then by Woodroffe?" Durnford said.

"Without a doubt. It was all most cleverly thought out. It was to his advantage alone to close our lips, because in that same fatal chair in Lambeth old Jacob Moser, the Jew bullion-broker of Hatton Garden, met his death - a most dastardly crime, with which none of his friends were associated, and of which we alone held knowledge. He therefore wrote to us as though from Leithcourt, calling us up to Rannoch, in order to strike the blows in the darkness," he added in his peculiar Italian manner. "Besides, he feared we would tell the signore the truth."

"You have not told the police?"

"I dare not, signore. Surely the less the police know about this matter the better, otherwise the Signorina Leithcourt must suffer for her father's avarice and evil-doing."

"Yes," cried Jack anxiously. "That's right, Olinto. The police must know nothing. The reprisals we must make ourselves. But who was it who shot me in Suffolk Street?"

"The same man, Martin Woodroffe."

"Then the assassin is back from Russia?"

"He followed closely behind the Signor Commendatore. Markoff, a clever secret agent of Baron Oberg's, came with him."

Then for the first time I recollected that the man I had recognized in the Strand was a fellow I had seen lounging in the ante-room of the palace of the Governor-General of Finland. The pair, fearing that I should reveal what I knew, were undoubtedly in London to take my life in secret. Now that Leithcourt was dead, Woodroffe had united forces with Oberg, and intended to silence me because they feared that Elma, besides escaping them, had also revealed her secret.

"I trust that the Signorina Leithcourt has explained the story of the yacht and its crew," Olinto remarked. "And has also shown you how I was implicated. You will therefore discern the reason why I have hitherto feared to give you any explanation."

"Yes," I said, "Miss Leithcourt has told me a great deal, but not everything. I cannot yet gather for what reason she and her father fled from Rannoch."

"Then I will tell you," said Muriel quickly. "My father suspected Woodroffe of being the assassin in Rannoch Wood, for he knew that he had broken away from the original compact, and had now allied himself with Oberg. Yet it was also my father's object to appear in fear of them, because he was only awaiting an opportunity to lay plans for poor Elma's rescue from Finland. Therefore one evening Woodroffe called, and my father encountered him in the avenue, and admitted him with his own latchkey by one of the side doors of the castle, afterwards taking him up to the study. He knew that he had come to try and make terms for Oberg, therefore he saw that he must fly at once to Newcastle, where the *Iris* was lying, get on board, and sail away.

"With some excuse he left him in the study, and then warned

my mother and myself to prepare to leave. But while we were packing, it appeared that Chater, who had followed, was shown into the study by the butler, or rather he entered there himself, being well acquainted with the house. Thus the two men, now bitter enemies, met. A fierce quarrel must have ensued, and Chater was poisoned and concealed, Woodroffe, of course, believing he had killed him. My father entered the study again, and seeing only Woodroffe there, did not know what had occurred. Some words probably arose, when my father again turned and left. Then we fled to Carlisle and on to Newcastle, and next morning were on board the yacht out in the North Sea, afterwards landing at Rotterdam. Those," she added, "are briefly the facts, as my poor father related them to me."

"And what of poor Elma - and of her secret? When, I wonder, shall I see her?" I cried in despair.

"You will see her now, signore," answered Olinto. "A servant of the Princess Zurloff brought her to London this afternoon, and I have just conveyed her from the station. She is in the next room, in ignorance, however, that you are here."

And without another word I fled forward joyfully, and threw open the folding-doors which separated me from my silent love.

Silent, yes! But she could, nevertheless, tell her story - surely the strangest that any woman has ever lived to tell.

CHAPTER XVIII

CONTAINS ELMA'S STORY

Before me stood my love, a slim, tragic, rather wan figure in a heavy dark traveling-coat and felt toque, her sweet lips parted and a look of bewildered amazement upon her countenance as I burst in so suddenly upon her.

In silence I grasped her tiny black-gloved hand, and then, also in silence, raised it passionately to my eager lips. Her soft, dark eyes - those eyes that spoke although she was mute - met mine, and in them was a look that I had never seen there before - a look which as plainly as any words told me that my wild fevered passion was reciprocated.

She gazed beyond into the room where the others had assembled, and then looked at me inquiringly, whereupon I led her forward to where they were, and Muriel fell upon her and kissed her with tears streaming from her eyes.

"I prepared this surprise for you, Mr. Gregg," Muriel said, laughing through her tears of joy. "Olinto learnt that she was on her way to London, and I sent him to meet her. The Princess has managed magnificently, has she not?"

"Yes. Thank God she is free!" I exclaimed. "But we must induce her to tell us everything."

Muriel was already helping my love out of her heavy Russian

coat, a costly garment lined with sable, and when, after greeting Jack and Olinto, she was comfortably seated, I took some notepaper from the little writing-table by the window and scribbled in pencil the words:

"I need not write how delighted I am that you are safe - that the Almighty has heard my prayers for you. Jack and Muriel have told me all about Leithcourt and his scoundrelly associates. I know, too, dear - for I may call you that, may I not? - how terribly you must have suffered in silence through it all. Leithcourt is dead. He sank the yacht with all the stolen property on board, but by accident was himself engulfed."

Bending and watching intently as I wrote, she drew back in horror and surprise at the words. Then I added: "We are all four determined that the guilty shall not go unpunished, and that the affliction placed upon you shall be adequately avenged. You are my own love - I am bold enough to call you so. Some strong but mysterious bond of affinity between us caused me to seek you out, and your pictured face seemed to call me to your side although I was unaware of your peril. I was sent to you by the unseen power to extricate you from the hands of your enemies. Therefore tell us everything - all that you know - without fear, for now that we are united no harm can assail us."

She took the pencil, and holding it in her white fingers sat staring first at us, and then looking hesitatingly at the white paper before her. Her position, amid a hundred conflicting emotions, was one of extreme difficulty. It seemed as though even now she was loth to reveal to us the absolute truth.

Muriel, standing behind her chair, tenderly stroked back the wealth of chestnut hair from her white brow. Her complexion was perfect, even though her face was pale and jaded, and her eyes heavy, consequent upon her long, weary journey from the now frozen North.

Presently, when by signs both Jack and Olinto had urged her

to write, she bent suddenly, and her pencil began to run swiftly over the paper.

All of us stood exchanging glances in silence, neither looking over her, but each determined to wait in patience until the end. Once started, however, she did not pause. Sheet after sheet she covered. The silence for a long time was complete, broken only by the rapid running of the pencil over the rough surface of the paper. She had apparently become seized by a sudden determination to explain everything, now that she saw we were in real, dead earnest.

I watched her sweet face bent so intently, and as the firelight fell across it found it incomparable. Yes; she was afflicted by loss of speech, it was true, yet she was surely inexpressibly sweet and womanly, peerless above all others.

With a deep-drawn sigh she at last finished, and, her head still bowed in an attitude of humiliation, it seemed, she handed what she had written to me.

In breathless eagerness I read as follows:

"Is it true, dear love - for I call you so in return - that you were impelled towards me by the mysterious hand that directs all things? You came in search of me, and you risked your life for mine at Kajana, therefore you have a right to know the truth. You, as my champion, and the Princess as my friend, have contrived to effect my freedom. Were it not for you, I should ere this have been on my way to Saghalien, to the tomb to which Oberg had so ingeniously contrived to consign me. Ah! You do not know - you never can know - all that I have suffered ever since I was a girl."

Here the statement broke off, and recommenced as follows:

"In order that you should understand the truth, I had better begin at the beginning. My father was an English merchant in Petersburg, and my mother, Vera Bessanoff, who, before her marriage with my father, was celebrated at Court for her beauty, and was one of the maids-of-honor to the Czarina. She was the only daughter of Count Paul Bessanoff, ex-Governor of Kharkoff, and before marrying my father she had, with her mother, been a well-known figure in society. Immediately after her marriage her father died, leaving her in possession of an ample fortune, which, with my father's own wealth, placed them among the richest and most influential in Petersburg.

"Among my father's most intimate friends was Baron Xavier Oberg - who, at that time, held a very subordinate position in the Ministry of the Interior - and from my earliest recollections I can remember him coming frequently to our house and being invited to the brilliant entertainments which my mother gave. When I was thirteen, however, my father died of a chill contracted while boar-hunting on his estate in Kiev, and within a few months a further disaster happened to us. One night, while I was sitting alone reading aloud to my mother, two strangers were announced, and on being shown in they arrested my dear mother on a charge of complicity in a revolutionary plot against the Czar which had been discovered at Peterhof. I stood defiant and indignant, for my mother was certainly no Nihilist, yet they said that the bomb had been introduced into the palace by the Countess Anna Shiproff, one of the ladies-in-waiting, who was an intimate friend of my mother's and often used to visit her. They alleged that the conspiracy had been hatched in our house, color being lent to that theory by the fact that a year before a well-known Russian with whom my father had had many business dealings had been proved to be the author of the plot by which the Czar's train was blown up near Lividia. They tore my mother away from me and placed her in that gray prison-van, the sight of which in the streets of Petersburg strikes terror into the heart of every Russian, for a person once in that rumbling vehicle is, as you know, lost for ever to the world. I watched her from the window being placed in that fatal conveyance, and then I think I must have fainted, for I recollect nothing more until I found myself upon the floor, with the gray dawn spreading, and all the horrible truth came back to me. My mother was gone from me for ever!

"In sheer desperation I went to the Ministry of the Interior and sought an interview with the Baron, who, when I told him of the disaster, appeared greatly concerned, and went at once to the Police Department to make inquiry. Next day, however, he came to me with the news that the charge against my mother had been proved by a statement of the woman Shiproff herself, and that she had already started on her long journey to Siberia - she had been exiled to one of those dreaded Arctic settlements beyond Yakutsk, a place where it is almost eternal winter, and where the conditions of life are such that half the convicts are insane. The Baron, however, declared that, as my father's friend, it was his duty to act as guardian to me, and that as my father had been English I ought to be put to an English school. Therefore, with his self-assumed title of uncle, he took me to Chichester. For years I remained there, until one day he came suddenly and fetched me away, taking me over to Helsingfors - for the Czar had now appointed him Governor-General to Finland. There, for the first time, he introduced me to his son Michael, a pimply-faced lieutenant of cavalry, and said in a most decisive manner that I must marry him. I naturally refused to marry a man of whom I knew so little, whereupon, finding me obdurate, he quickly altered his tactics and became kindness itself, saying that as I was young he would allow me a year in which to make up my mind.

"A week later, while living in the palace at Helsingfors, I overheard a conversation between the Governor-General and his son, which revealed to me a staggering truth that I had never suspected. It was Oberg himself who had denounced my mother to the Minister of the Interior, and had made those cruel, baseless charges against her! Then I discerned the reason. She being exiled, her fortune, as well as that of my father, came to me. The reason they were scheming for Michael to marry me was in order to obtain control of my money. I saw at once how helpless I was in the hands of that unscrupulous pair, and I recognized, too, sufficient of the Baron's methods as 'The Strangler of Finland,' to show me what kind of character he was beneath that calm, eminently respectable black-coated exterior. After deliberately sending my poor mother to Siberia, he had assumed the role of my guardian in order that he might, when I came of age, obtain control of my inheritance, the idea no doubt being that I should marry Michael, and then, after the necessary legal formalities, I should, on a trumped-up charge of conspiracy, share the same fate as my mother had done."

"The infernal scoundrel!" I ejaculated, when I read her words, while from Jack, who had been looking over my shoulder, escaped a fierce and forcible vow of vengeance.

"The Baron took me with him to Petersburg when he went on official business, and we remained there nearly a month," the narrative went on. "While there I received a secret message from 'The Red Priest,' the unseen and unknown power of Nihilism, who has for so many years baffled the police. I went to see him, and he revealed to me how Oberg had contrived to have my mother banished upon a false charge. He warned me against the man who had pretended to be my father's friend, and also told me that he had known my father intimately, and that if I got into any further difficulty I was to communicate with him and he would assist me. Oberg took me back to Helsingfors a few months later, and in summer we went to England. He was a marvelously clever diplomatist. His tactics he could change at will. When I was at school he was rough and brutal in his manner towards me, as he was to all; but now he seemed to be endeavoring to inspire my confidence by treating me with kindly regard and pleasant affability.

"In London, at Claridge's, we met my old schoolfellow Muriel and her father - a friend of Oberg's - and in response to their invitation went for a cruise on their yacht, the *Iris*, from Southampton. Our party was a very pleasant one, and included Woodroffe and Chater, while our cruise across the Bay of Biscay and along the Portuguese coast proved most delightful. One night, while we were lying outside Lisbon, Woodroffe and Chater, together with Olinto, went ashore, and when they returned in the early hours of the morning they awoke me by crossing the deck above my head. Then I heard someone outside my cabin-door working as though with a screwdriver, unscrewing a screw from the woodwork. This aroused my interest, and next day I made a minute examination of the paneling, where, in one part, I found two small brass screws that had evidently been recently removed. Therefore I succeeded in getting hold of a screwdriver from the carpenter's shop, and next night, when everyone was asleep, I crept out and unscrewed the panel, when to my surprise I saw that the secret cavity behind was filled with beautiful jewelry, diamond collars, tiaras, necklets, fine pearls, emeralds and turquoises, all *thrown* in indiscriminately.

"I replaced the panel and kept careful watch. At Marseilles, where we called, more jewelry and a heavy bagful of plate was brought aboard and secreted behind another panel. Then I knew that the men were thieves.

"But surely," continued the strange story my mute love had written, "I need not describe all that occurred upon that eventful voyage, except to tell you of one very curious incident which occurred. I had spoken confidentially with Muriel regarding my suspicions of the men who were our fellow-guests, and when in secret I showed her several places on board the yacht where valuables were secreted, she also became convinced that the men were expert thieves to whom her father, for some unexplained reason, rendered assistance and asylum. She told me that since she had left school she had been on quite a number of cruises, and that the same party always accompanied her father. She had, however, never suspected the truth until I pointed it out to her. Well, one hot summer's night we were lying off Naples, and as it was a grand festa ashore and there was to be a gala performance at the theater, Leithcourt took a box and the whole party were rowed ashore. The crew were also given shore-leave for the evening, but as the great heat had upset me I declined to accompany the theater-party, and remained on board with one sailor named Wilson to constitute the watch. We had anchored about half a mile from land, and earlier in the evening the Baron had gone ashore to send telegrams to Russia, and had not returned.

"About ten o'clock I went below to try and sleep, but I had a slight attack of fever, and was unable. Therefore I redressed and sat with the light still out, gazing across the starlit bay. Presently from my port-hole I saw a shore-boat approaching, and recognized in it the Baron with a well-dressed stranger. They both came on board, and the boatman, having been paid, pulled back to the shore. Then the Baron and his friend - a dark, middle-aged, full-bearded man, evidently a person of refinement - went below to the saloon, and after a few moments called to the man Wilson who was on the watch, and gave him a glass of whisky and water, which he took up on deck to drink at his leisure.

"The unusual character of my fellow-guests on board that craft was such that my suspicion was constantly on the alert, therefore curiosity tempted me to creep along and peep in at the crack of the door standing ajar. A closer view revealed the fact that the stranger was a high Russian official to whom I had once been introduced at the Government Palace at Helsing-fors, the Privy-Councillor and Senator Paul Polovstoff. They were smoking together, and were discussing in Russian the means by which he, Polovstoff, had arranged to obtain plans of some new British fortifications at Gibraltar. From what he said, it seemed that some Russian woman, married to an Englishman, a captain in the garrison, had been impressed into the secret service against her will, but that she had, in order to save herself, promised to obtain the photographs and plans that were required. I heard the Englishman's name, and I resolved to take some steps to inform him in secret of the intentions of the Russian agent.

"Presently the two men took fresh cigars, ascended on deck, and cast themselves in the long cane chairs amidships. Still all curiosity to hear further details on the ingenious piece of espionage against my own nation, I took off my shoes and crept up to a spot where I could crouch concealed and overhear their conversation, for the Italian night was calm and still. They talked mainly about affairs in Finland, and with some of Oberg's expressions of opinion Polovstoff ventured to differ. This aroused the Baron's anger, and I knew from the cold sarcasm of his remarks, and the peculiarly hard tone of his voice, that he was more incensed than he outwardly showed himself to be. He rose and stood with his back to the bulwarks facing his friend, who still sat leaning back in his deck-chair insisting upon his own views. He was quite calm, and not in the least perturbed by the evil glint in the Baron's eye. Perhaps he did not know him so well as I did. He did not know what that look meant. Suddenly, while the Privy-Councillor lay back in his chair pulling thoughtfully at his cigar, there was a bright, blood-red flash, a dull report, and a man's short agonized cry. Startled, I leaned around the corner of the deck-house, when, to my abject horror, I saw under the electric rays the Czar's Privy-Councillor lying sideways in his chair with part of his face blown away. Then the hideous truth in an instant became apparent. The cigar which Oberg had pressed upon him down in the saloon had exploded, and the small missile concealed inside the diabolical contrivance had passed upwards into his brain. For a moment I stood utterly stupefied, yet as I looked I saw the Baron, in a paroxysm of rage, shake his fist in the dead man's face, and cry with a fearful imprecation: 'You hound! You have plotted to replace me in the Czar's favor. You intended to become Governor-General of Finland! You knew certain facts which you intended to put before his Majesty, knowing that the revelations would result in my disgrace and downfall. But, you infernal cur, you did not know that those who attempt to thwart Xavier Oberg either die by accident or go for life to Kajana or the mines!' And he spurned the body with his foot and laughed to himself as he gloated over his dastardly crime.

"I watched his rage, unable to utter a single word. I saw him, after he had searched the dead man's pockets, raise the inert body with its awful featureless face and drag it to the bulwarks. Then I rushed forward and faced him.

"In an instant he sprang at me, and I screamed. But no aid came. The man Wilson was sleeping soundly in the bows, for the whisky he had given him had been doctored," went on the narrative. "Upon his face was a fierce, murderous look such as I had never seen before. 'You!' he screamed, his dark eyes starting from their sockets as he realized that I had been a witness of his cowardly crime. 'You have spied upon me, girl!' he hissed, 'and you shall die also!' I sank upon my knees imploring him to spare me, but he only laughed at my entreaty. 'See!' he cried, 'as you saw how he enjoyed his cigar, you may as well see this!' And with an effort he raised the dead body in his arms, poised it for a moment on the vessel's side, and then, with a hoarse laugh of triumph, heaved it into the sea. There was a splash, and then we were alone. 'And you!' he cried in a fierce voice - 'you who have spied upon me - you will follow! The water there will close your chattering mouth!' I shrieked, begged, and implored, but his trembling hands were upon my throat. First he dragged me to my feet, then he threw me upon my knees, and at last, with that grim brutality which characterizes him, he directed me to go and get a mop and bucket from the forecastle and remove the dark red stains from the chair and deck. This he actually forced me to do, gloating over my horror as I removed for him the traces of his cowardly crime. Then, with his hand upon my shoulder, he said, 'Girl! Recollect that you keep to-night's work secret. If not, you shall die a death more painful than that dog has died - one in which you shall experience all the tortures of the damned. Recollect, not a single word - or death! Now, go to your cabin, and never pry into my affairs again.'

"I went back to my cabin as I was bid, and sat speechless in abject horror. The fiendish actions of the man who was my guardian frightened me. And yet I was utterly helpless. What could I do? Who in holy Russia would hear me? Oberg was a power in the Empire; the Czar himself trusted him. If I spoke, who would believe me; who would heed the words of a defenseless girl whom he would at once declare to be hysterical? Thus I waited alone in the darkness, watching the lights of the port gleaming across the placid waters until nearly one o'clock, when the gay party returned, and the Baron greeted them merrily as though nothing had happened. But my heart was frozen within me by the recollection of the awful crime that had been committed."

*   *   *   *   *

"Why! Now I remember!" cried Muriel, amazed. "I remember that night quite well, how white you were when you came to my cabin and asked to be allowed to sleep in my spare berth. You would tell me nothing, and only said you were ill. None of us had any idea that such a terrible tragedy had been enacted. But of course the Baron had arranged it all, for it was at his instigation, I recollect, that the crew had been given shore-leave. Mackintosh suggested that only half the crew should go, but he declared that if Wilson alone were left it would be sufficient."

"I, too, recollect the affair quite well," Jack declared, tugging at his mustache, utterly amazed at my love's strange story. It was a plain statement of hard, astounding facts, and she now stood clinging to me, looking eagerly into my eyes, reading every thought that passed through my mind. "A great sensation was caused when the body was discovered. The squadron was lying off Naples about a week after the *Iris* had left, and while we were there the body was washed up near Sorrento. At first but little notice was taken of it, but by the marks on the dead man's linen it was discovered that he was Polovstoff, one of the highest Russian officials who had, it was said, been warned on several occasions by the Nihilists. It was, therefore, concluded that his death had been due to Nihilist vengeance."

Elma pointed to the paper, and made a sign that I was to read on. This I did, and the statement ran as follows:

"The real reason why the Baron spared my life was because, if I died, my fortune would pass to a distant cousin living at Durham. Yet his manner towards me was now most polite and pleasant - a change that I felt boded no good. He intended to

WILLIAM LE QUEUX

obtain my money by marrying me to his son Michael, whose evil reputation as a gambler was well known in Petersburg. We traveled back to Finland in the autumn, and in the winter he took me to stay with his sister in Nice. Yet almost daily he referred to that tragedy at Naples, and threatened me with death if ever I uttered a single word, or even admitted that I had ever seen the man who was his rival and his victim."

"Last June," commenced another paragraph, "we were in Helsingfors, when one day the Baron called me suddenly and told me to prepare for a journey. We were to cross to Stockholm and thence to Hull, where the *Iris* was awaiting us, for Mr. Leithcourt and Muriel had invited us for a summer cruise to the Greek Islands. We boarded the yacht much against my will, yet I was powerless, and dare not allege the facts that I had already established concerning our fellow-guests. Muriel and I, it seems, were taken merely in order to blind the shore-guards and Customs officials as to the real nature of the vessel, which when safely out of the Channel, was repainted and renamed the *Lola*, until her exterior presented quite a different appearance from the *Iris*.

"The port of Leghorn was our first place of call, and for some reason we ran purposely upon a sandbank and were towed off by Italian torpedo-boats. Next evening you came on board and dined, Muriel and myself having strict orders not to show ourselves. We, however, watched you, and I saw you pick up my photograph which I had that day torn up. Then immediately after you had left, Woodroffe, Chater and Mackintosh went ashore and were away a couple of hours in the middle of the night. Just before they returned the Baron rapped at the door of my cabin saying that he must go ashore, and telling me to dress and accompany him. He would never allow me the luxury of a maid, fearing, I suppose, that she might learn too much. In obedience I rose and dressed, and when I went forth he told me to get my traveling-cloak and dressing-bag, adding that he was compelled to go north, as to continue the cruise would occupy too much time. He was due back at his official duties, he said. As soon as I had finished packing, the three men returned to the vessel, all of them looking dark-faced and disappointed. Woodroffe whispered some words to the Baron, after which I went to Muriel's cabin and wished her good-bye, and we went ashore, taking the train first to Colle Salvetti, thence to Pisa, and afterwards to the beautiful old city of Siena, which I had so longed to see. One of my teeth gave me pain, and the Baron, after a couple of days at the Hotel de Sienne, took me to a queer-looking little old Italian - a dentist who, he said, enjoyed an excellent reputation. I was quick to notice that the two men had met before, and as I sat in the chair and gas was given to me I saw them exchange meaning glances. In a few moments I became insensible, but when I awoke an hour later I was astounded to feel a curious soreness in my ears. My tongue, too, seemed paralyzed, and in a few moments the awful truth dawned upon me. I had been rendered deaf and dumb!

"The Baron pretended to be greatly concerned about me," it went on, "but I quickly realized that I had been the victim of a foul and dastardly plot, and that he had conceived it, fearing lest I might speak the truth concerning the Privy-Councillor Polovstoff, for of exposure he lived in constant fear. To encompass my end would be against his own interests, as he would lose my fortune, so he had silenced me lest I should reveal the terrible truth concerning both him and his associates. He was not rich, and I have reason to believe that from time to time he gave information as to persons who possessed valuable jewels, and thus shared in the plunder obtained by those on the yacht.

"From Italy we traveled on to Berlin, thence to Petersburg, and back to dreary Helsingfors, journeying as quickly as we could, yet never allowing me opportunity of being with strangers. Both my ears and tongue were very painful, but I said nothing. He was surely a fiend in a black coat, and my only thought now was how to escape him. From the moment when that so-called dentist had ruined my hearing and deprived me of power of speech, he kept me aloof from everyone. The fear that I should reveal everything had apparently grown to haunt him, and he had conceived that terrible mode of silencing my lips. But the true depth of his villainy was not yet apparent until I was back in Finland.

"On the night of our arrival he called in his son, who had traveled with us from Petersburg, and in writing again demanded that I should marry him. I wrote my reply - a firm refusal. He struck the table angrily with his fist and wrote saying that I should either marry his son or die. Then next day, while walking alone out beyond the town of Helsingfors, as I often used to do, I was arrested upon the false charge of an attempt upon the life of Madame Vakuroff and transported, without trial, to the terrible fortress of Kajana, some of the horrors of which you have yourself experienced. The charge against me was necessary before I could be incarcerated there, but once within, it was the scheme of the Governor-General to obtain my consent to the marriage by threats and by the constant terrors of the place. He even went so far as to obtain a ministerial order for my banishment to Saghalien and brought it to me to Kajana, declaring that if in one month I did not consent he should allow me to be sent to exile. While I was in Kajana he knew that his secret was safe, therefore by every means in his power he urged me to consent to the odious union.

"All the rest is known to you - how Providence directed you to me as my deliverer, and how Woodroffe followed you in secret, and pretending to be my friend took me with him to Petersburg. He had learnt of my fortune from the Baron, and intended to marry me himself. But now that all is over it appears to me like some terrible dream. I never believed that so much iniquity existed in the world, or that men could fight a defenseless woman with such double-dealing and cruel ingenuity. Ah! The tortures I endured in Kajana are beyond human conception. Yet surely Oberg and Woodroffe will obtain their well-merited deserts - if not in this world, then in the world to come. Are we not taught by Holy Writ to forgive our enemies? Therefore, let us forgive."

There my silent love's strange story ended. A bald, straight-forward narrative that held us all for some moments absolutely speechless - one of the strangest and most startling stories ever revealed.

She watched every expression of my countenance, and then, when I had finished reading and placed my arm tenderly about her slim waist, she raised her beautiful face to mine to receive the passionate kiss I imprinted upon those soft, full lips.

"This, of course, makes everything plain," exclaimed Jack. "Polovstoff was a very liberal-minded and upright official who was greatly in the favor of the Czar, and a serious rival to Oberg, whose drastic and merciless methods in Finland were not exactly approved by the Emperor. The Baron was well aware of this, and by ingeniously enticing him on board the *Iris* he succeeded by handing that small bomb concealed in a cigar - a Nihilist contrivance that had probably been seized by his police in Finland - in freeing himself from the rival who was destined to occupy his post."

"Yes," I said with a sigh. "The mystery is cleared up, it is true, yet my poor Elma is still the victim." And I kissed my love passionately again and again upon the lips.

CONCLUSION

Nearly two years have now gone by.

There have been changes in holy Russia - many great and amazing changes consequent upon war and its disasters. Russia is no longer the great power that she once was supposed to be. Many events that have startled the world have occurred since that day when I first enfolded my silent love within my arms. One of them is known to you all.

You read in the newspapers, without a doubt, how the Baron Xavier Oberg, the persecutor of Finland, the enemy of education, the relentless foe of the defenseless, the man who ordered women to be knouted to death in Kajana, the heartless official whom the Finns called "The Strangler," was blown to pieces by a bomb thrown beneath his carriage as he drove to the railway station at Helsingfors on his way to have audience with the Emperor.

The secret truth was that the "Red Priest" decreed that Oberg should die, and the plot was swiftly put into execution, and although five hundred arrests were made the police are unaware to this day of the identity of the person who directed it, or of who threw the fatal missile. From pillar to post the revolutionists have been hunted by the bloodhounds of police, yet the "Red Priest" still lives on quietly in Petersburg, and the Princess Zurloff, still unsuspected, devotes the greater part of her enormous income to the cause of freedom.

Of Jack and Muriel I need only say they were married about three months after Elma's return from Russia, and at the present time they are living on the outskirts of Glasgow, where Jack has secured the shore appointment which he so long coveted.

By some means - exactly how is not quite certain - the police discovered that Dick Archer, alias Woodroffe, alias Hornby, was concerned in the clever robbery of a dressing-bag, containing the Dowager Lady Lancashire's jewels, from her footman on Euston platform, and after a long search they found him hiding at an hotel in Liverpool. When, however, they went to arrest him, he laughed in the faces of the detectives, placed something swiftly in his mouth and swallowed it before they could prevent him - then ten minutes later he fell dead. He knew what terrible revelations must be made if we gave evidence against him, and he therefore preferred death by his own hand to that following a judicial sentence.

Chater, although one of the most expert jewel thieves in Europe, had never been actually guilty of any graver offense, and when we heard that he was in San Francisco, where he had opened a small bar and was trying to live honestly, we resolved to allow him to remain there. Indeed, Jack wrote to him about nine months ago warning him never to set foot on English soil again on pain of arrest.

Olinto Santini has recently opened a small restaurant in Western Road, Brighton, and is, I believe, doing very well.

And ourselves! Well, what can I really tell you? Mere words fail to tell you of the completeness of our happiness. It is idyllic - that is all I can say.

My proposal of marriage was made to Elma a very few days after she wrote down her startling and romantic story, and a year ago at a little village church in Hertfordshire we became man and wife, there being present at our wedding Madame

Heath, my bride's mother, to whom, by my exertions in official quarters in Petersburg, the Czar's clemency was extended, and she was released from that far-off Arctic prison to which she had been sent with such cruel injustice.

Two of the greatest London specialists have continually treated my dear wife, and under them she has already recovered her speech - so far, indeed, that she can now whisper in a low, soft voice. But they tell me they are hopeful that ere long her voice will become stronger, and speech practically restored. Already, too, she can begin to hear.

After all the storms and perils of the past, our lives are now indeed full of a calm, sweet peace. In our own comfortable little house, with its trellised porch covered with roses and honeysuckle, that faces the blue Channel at St. Margaret's Bay, beyond Dover, we lead a life of mutual trust and boundless love. We are supremely content - the happiest pair in all the world, we think.

Often as we sit together at evening, gazing out upon the great ships passing darkly away into the mysterious afterglow, our hands clasp mutually in a silence more eloquent than words, and as we gaze into each other's eyes there occurs to us the Divine injunction: "WHOM GOD HATH JOINED, LET NO MAN PUT ASUNDER."

Choose from Thousands of 1stWorldLibrary Classics By

Adolphus WilliamWard
Aesop
Agatha Christie
Alexander Aaronsohn
Alexander Kielland
Alexandre Dumas
Alfred Gatty
Alfred Ollivant
Alice Duer Miller
Alice Turner Curtis
Alice Dunbar
Ambrose Bierce
Amelia E. Barr
Andrew Lang
Andrew McFarland Davis
Anna Sewell
Annie Besant
Annie Hamilton Donnell
Annie Payson Call
Anton Chekhov
Arnold Bennett
Arthur Conan Doyle
Arthur Ransome
Atticus
B. M. Bower
Basil King
Bayard Taylor
Ben Macomber
Booth Tarkington
Bram Stoker
C. Collodi
C. E. Orr
C. M. Ingleby
Carolyn Wells
Catherine Parr Traill
Charles A. Eastman
Charles Dickens
Charles Dudley Warner
Charles Farrar Browne
Charles Ives
Charles Kingsley
Charles Lathrop Pack
Charles Whibley
Charles Willing Beale
Charlotte M. Braeme
Charlotte M.Yonge
Clair W. Hayes
Clarence Day Jr.
Clarence E. Mulford

Clemence Housman
Confucius
Cornelis DeWitt Wilcox
Cyril Burleigh
D. H. Lawrence
Daniel Defoe
David Garnett
Don Carlos Janes
Donald Keyhole
Dorothy Kilner
Dougan Clark
E. Nesbit
E.P.Roe
E. Phillips Oppenheim
Edgar Allan Poe
Edgar Rice Burroughs
Edith Wharton
Edward J. O'Biren
John Cournos
Edwin L. Arnold
Eleanor Atkins
Elizabeth Cleghorn
Gaskell
Elizabeth Von Arnim
Ellem Key
Emily Dickinson
Erasmus W. Jones
Ernie Howard Pie
Ethel Turner
Ethel Watts Mumford
Eugenie Foa
Eugene Wood
Evelyn Everett-Green
Everard Cotes
F. J. Cross
Federick Austin Ogg
Ferdinand Ossendowski
Francis Bacon
Francis Darwin
Frances Hodgson Burnett
Frank Gee Patchin
Frank Harris
Frank Jewett Mather
Frank L. Packard
Frederick Trevor Hill
Frederick Winslow Taylor
Friedrich Kerst
Friedrich Nietzsche
Fyodor Dostoyevsky

Gabrielle E. Jackson
Garrett P. Serviss
Gaston Leroux
George Ade
Geroge Bernard Shaw
George Ebers
George Eliot
George MacDonald
George Orwell
George Tucker
George W. Cable
George Wharton James
Gertrude Atherton
Grace E. King
Grant Allen
Guillermo A. Sherwell
Gulielma Zollinger
Gustav Flaubert
H. A. Cody
H. B. Irving
H. G. Wells
H. H. Munro
H. Irving Hancock
H. Rider Haggard
H. W. C. Davis
Hamilton Wright Mabie
Hans Christian Andersen
Harold Avery
Harold McGrath
Harriet Beecher Stowe
Harry Houidini
Helent Hunt Jackson
Helen Nicolay
Hendy David Thoreau
Henrik Ibsen
Henry Adams
Henry Ford
Henry Frost
Henry James
Henry Jones Ford
Henry Seton Merriman
Henry Wadsworth
Longfellow
Henry W Longfellow
Herbert A. Giles
Herbert N. Casson
Herman Hesse
Homer
Honore De Balzac

Horace Walpole	Laurence Housman	Robert Lansing
Horatio Alger, Jr.	Leo Tolstoy	Robert Michael Ballantyne
Howard Pyle	Leonid Andreyev	Robert W. Chambers
Howard R. Garis	Lewis Carroll	Rosa Nouchette Carey
Hugh Lofting	Lilian Bell	Ross Kay
Hugh Walpole	Lloyd Osbourne	Rudyard Kipling
Humphry Ward	Louis Tracy	Samuel B. Allison
Ian Maclaren	Louisa May Alcott	Samuel Hopkins Adams
Israel Abrahams	Lucy Fitch Perkins	Sarah Bernhardt
J.G.Austin	Lucy Maud Montgomery	Selma Lagerlof
J. Henri Fabre	Lydia Miller Middleton	Sherwood Anderson
J. M. Barrie	Lyndon Orr	Sigmund Freud
J. Macdonald Oxley	M. H. Adams	Standish O'Grady
J. S. Knowles	Margaret E. Sangster	Stanley Weyman
J. Storer Clouston	Margaret Vandercook	Stella Benson
Jack London	Maria Edgeworth	Stephen Crane
Jacob Abbott	Maria Thompson Daviess	Stewart Edward White
James Allen	Mariano Azuela	Stijn Streuvels
James Lane Allen	Marion Polk Angellotti	Swami Abhedananda
James Andrews	Mark Overton	Swami Parmananda
James Baldwin	Mark Twain	T. S. Ackland
James DeMille	Mary Austin	The Princess Der Ling
James Joyce	Mary Cole	Thomas A. Janvier
James Oliver Curwood	Mary Rowlandson	Thomas A Kempis
James Oppenheim	Mary Wollstonecraft	Thomas Anderton
James Otis	Shelley	Thomas Bailey Aldrich
Jane Austen	Max Beerbohm	Thomas Bulfinch
Jens Peter Jacobsen	Myra Kelly	Thomas De Quincey
Jerome K. Jerome	Nathaniel Hawthrone	Thomas H. Huxley
John Burroughs	O. F. Walton	Thomas Hardy
John F. Kennedy	Oscar Wilde	Thomas More
John Gay	Owen Johnson	Thornton W. Burgess
John Glasworthy	P.G.Wodehouse	U. S. Grant
John Habberton	Paul and Mable Thorn	Valentine Williams
John Joy Bell	Paul G. Tomlinson	Victor Appleton
John Milton	Paul Severing	Virginia Woolf
John Philip Sousa	Peter B. Kyne	Walter Scott
Jonathan Swift	Plato	Washington Irving
Joseph Carey	R. Derby Holmes	Wilbur Lawton
Joseph Conrad	R. L. Stevenson	Wilkie Collins
Joseph Jacobs	Rabindranath Tagore	Willa Cather
Julian Hawthrone	Rahul Alvares	Willard F. Baker
Julies Vernes	Ralph Waldo Emmerson	William Makepeace
Justin Huntly McCarthy	Rene Descartes	Thackeray
Kakuzo Okakura	Rex E. Beach	William W. Walter
Kenneth Grahame	Richard Harding Davis	Winston Churchill
Kate Langley Bosher	Richard Jefferies	Yei Theodora Ozaki
L. A. Abbot	Robert Barr	Young E. Allison
L. T. Meade	Robert Frost	Zane Grey
L. Frank Baum	Robert Gordon Anderson	
Laura Lee Hope	Robert L. Drake	

www.ingramcontent.com/pod-product-compliance
Lightning Source LLC
Chambersburg PA
CBHW021306250626
47155CB00002B/403